Resounding Praise for *New York Times* Bestselling Author

DENNIS LEHANE and

PRAYERS FOR RAIN

"With plot twists, mistaken identities, and vivid visual descriptions, *Prayers for Rain* is difficult to put down."
Austin American-Statesman

"Fine characterizations and edgy dialogue.... Packed with punchy action sequences, uneasy stretches where the reader squirms in anticipation of impending disaster, and plenty of dark humor. Dennis Lehane has all the tools of a future Grand Master—the dialogue of Parker, the plotting of Block, the psychological suspense of Rendell—and in *Prayers for Rain* he shows them off to fine effect."
Houston Chronicle

"*Prayers for Rain* ... has all the elements a good mystery needs: a strong cast of characters and sense of place, gripping suspense, fluid dialogue, and meticulous plotting.... The book is a page-turner ... like riding a killer roller coaster: Just when you think you can breathe a sigh of relief, there's another loop-the-loop ahead.... Lehane's dialogue is fast and funny.... He's a gifted storyteller."
Boston Globe

"Boy, does he know how to write."
ELMORE LEONARD

"Lehane shows a gift for stringing out scenes and creating tension—sexual, homicidal, you name it—that makes a reader eager to find out what comes next.... But don't race ahead and cheat yourself out of the local pleasures."
People (Beach Read of the Week)

"Gripping and fast-paced ... which is, of course, what successful storytelling is all about."
St. Petersburg Times

Also by Dennis Lehane

DENNIS LEHANE

PRAYERS FOR RAIN

wm

WILLIAM MORROW
An Imprint of HarperCollinsPublishers

PRAYERS FOR RAIN. Copyright © 1999 by Dennis Lehane. All rights reserved. Printed in the United States of America. No part of this book may be used or reproduced in any manner whatsoever without written permission except in the case of brief quotations embodied in critical articles and reviews. For information, address HarperCollins Publishers, 195 Broadway, New York, NY 10007.

HarperCollins books may be purchased for educational, business, or sales promotional use. For information, please e-mail the Special Markets Department at SPsales@harpercollins.com.

First William Morrow hardcover printing: June 1999
First HarperTorch paperback printing: May 2000
First Harper premium paperback printing: August 2010

FIRST WILLIAM MORROW PAPERBACK EDITION PUBLISHED 2013.

Library of Congress Cataloging-in-Publication Data has been applied for.

ISBN 978-0-06-222405-7

18 19 PC/LSC 10 9 8 7 6 5

For my friends
John Dempsey, Chris Mullen, and Susan Hayes,
who let me steal some
of their best lines
and don't sue.

And
Andre,
who is deeply missed.

ACKNOWLEDGMENTS

Thanks to Dr. Keith Ablow, for answering my questions about psychiatry; Tom Corcoran, for setting me straight on the '68 Shelby; Chris and Julie Gleason, for helping out with English lit. questions I'm embarrassed I had to ask; Detective Michael Lawn of the Watertown Police Department, for explaining accident-scene procedures; Dr. Laura Need, for providing the heart condition; Emily Sperling of the Cape Cod Cranberry Growers' Association; Paul and Maureen Welch, for leading me to Plymouth; and MM, for clarifying U.S. Postal Service procedures.

Thanks also to Jessica Baumgardner, Eleanor Cox, Michael Murphy, Sharyn Rosenblum, and my brother Gerry for propping me up during the New York trips.

And finally, as always, my deepest gratitude to Claire Wachtel, Ann Rittenberg, and Sheila for reading the drafts, pulling no punches, and keeping me honest.

I heard the old, old men say,
"All that's beautiful drifts away
Like the waters."

—W. B. YEATS

PRAYERS FOR RAIN

In the dream, I have a son. He's about five, but he speaks with the voice and intelligence of a fifteen-year-old. He sits in the seat beside me, buckled tightly, his legs just barely reaching the edge of the car seat. It's a big car, old, with a steering wheel as large as the rim of a bicycle tire, and we drive it through a late December morning the color of dull chrome. We are somewhere rural, south of Massachusetts but north of the Mason-Dixon Line—Delaware, maybe, or southern New Jersey—and red-and-white-checkered silos peek up in the distance from furrowed harvest fields frosted the pale gray of newspaper with last week's snow. There is nothing around us but the fields and the distant silos, a windmill frozen stiff and silent, miles of black telephone wire glistening with ice. No other cars, no people. Just my son and myself and the hard slate road carved through fields of frozen wheat.

My son says, "Patrick."

"Yeah?"

"It's a good day."

I look out at the still gray morning, the sheer quiet. Beyond the farthest silo, a wisp of dusky smoke rises

1

from a chimney. Though I can't see the structure, I can imagine the warmth of the house. I can smell food roasting in an oven and see exposed cherry beams over a kitchen constructed of honey-colored wood. An apron hangs from the handle of the oven door. I feel how good it is to be inside on a hushed December morning.

I look at my son. I say, "Yeah, it is."

My son says, "We'll drive all day. We'll drive all night. We'll drive forever."

I say, "Sure."

My son looks out his window. He says, "Dad."

"Yeah."

"We'll never stop driving."

I turn my head and he is looking up at me with my own eyes.

I say, "Okay. We'll never stop driving."

He puts his hand on mine. "If we stop driving, we run out of air."

"Yeah."

"If we run out of air, we die."

"We do."

"I don't want to die, Dad."

I run my hand over his smooth hair. "I don't either."

"So we'll never stop driving."

"No, buddy." I smile at him. I can smell his skin, his hair, a newborn's scent in a five-year-old's body. "We'll never stop driving."

"Good."

He settles back in his seat, then falls asleep with his cheek pressed to the back of my hand.

Ahead of me, the slate road stretches through the dusty white fields, and my hand on the wheel is light and sure. The road is straight and flat and lies ahead of me for a thousand miles. *The old snow rustles as the wind picks it off the fields and swirls small tempests of it in the cracks of tar in front of my grille.*

I will never stop driving. I will never get out of the car. I will not run out of gas. I will not get hungry. It's warm here. I have my son. He's safe. I'm safe. I will never stop driving. I will not tire. I will never stop.

The road lies open and endless before me.

My son turns his head away from my hand and says, "Where's Mom?"

"I don't know," I say.

"But it's okay?" He looks up at me.

"It's okay," I say. "It's fine. Go back to sleep."

My son goes back to sleep. I keep driving.

And both of us vanish when I wake.

1

The first time I met Karen Nichols, she struck me as the kind of woman who ironed her socks.

She was blond and petite and stepped out of a kelly-green 1998 VW Bug as Bubba and I crossed the avenue toward St. Bartholomew's Church with our morning coffee in hand. It was February, but winter had forgotten to show up that year. Except for one snowstorm and a few days in the subzeros, it had been damn near balmy. Today it was in the high forties, and it was only ten in the morning. Say all you want about global warming, but as long as it saves me from shoveling the walk, I'm for it.

Karen Nichols placed a hand over her eyebrows, even though the morning sun wasn't all that strong, and smiled uncertainly at me.

"Mr. Kenzie?"

I gave her my eats-his-veggies-loves-his-mom smile and proffered my hand. "Miss Nichols?"

She laughed for some reason. "Karen, yes. I'm early."

Her hand slid into mine and felt so smooth and uncallused it could have been gloved. "Call me Patrick. That's Mr. Rogowski."

Bubba grunted and slugged his coffee.

Karen Nichols's hand dropped from mine and she jerked back slightly, as if afraid she'd have to extend her hand to Bubba. Afraid if she did, she might not get it back.

She wore a brown suede jacket that fell to midthigh over a charcoal cable-knit crewneck, crisp blue jeans, and bright white Reeboks. None of her apparel looked as if a wrinkle, stain, or wisp of dust had been within a country mile of it.

She placed delicate fingers on her smooth neck. "A couple of real PIs. Wow." Her soft blue eyes crinkled with her button nose and she laughed again.

"I'm the PI," I said. "He's just slumming."

Bubba grunted again and kicked me in the ass.

"Down, boy," I said. "Heel."

Bubba sipped some coffee.

Karen Nichols looked as if she'd made a mistake coming here. I decided then not to lead her up to my belfry office. If people were uncertain about hiring me, taking them to the belfry usually wasn't good PR.

School was out because it was Saturday, and the air was moist and without a chill, so Karen Nichols, Bubba, and I walked to a bench in the schoolyard. I sat down. Karen Nichols used an immaculate white handkerchief to dust the surface, then she sat down. Bubba frowned at the lack of space on the bench, frowned at me, then sat on the ground in front of us, crossed his legs, peered up expectantly.

"Good doggie," I said.

Bubba gave me a look that said I'd pay for that as soon as we were away from polite company.

"Miss Nichols," I said, "how did you hear about me?"

She tore her gaze away from Bubba and looked into my eyes for a moment in utter confusion. Her blond hair was cut as short as a small boy's and reminded me of pictures I've seen of women in Berlin in the 1920s. It was sculpted tight against the skull with gel, and even though it wouldn't be moving on its own unless she stepped into the wake of a jet engine, she'd clipped it over her left ear, just below the part, with a small black barrette that had a june bug painted on it.

Her wide blue eyes cleared and she made that short, nervous laugh again. "My boyfriend."

"And his name is . . ." I said, guessing Tad or Ty or Hunter.

"David Wetterau."

So much for my psychic abilities.

"I'm afraid I've never heard of him."

"He met someone who used to work with you. A woman?"

Bubba raised his head, glared at me. Bubba blamed me for Angie ending our partnership, for Angie moving out of the neighborhood, buying a Honda, dressing in Anne Klein suits, and generally not hanging out with us anymore.

"Angela Gennaro?" I asked Karen Nichols.

She smiled. "Yes. That's her name."

Bubba grunted again. Pretty soon he'd start howling at the moon.

"And why do you need a private detective, Miss Nichols?"

"Karen." She turned on the bench toward me, tucked an imaginary strand of hair behind her ear.

"Karen. Why do you need a detective?"

A sad, crumpled smile bent her pursed lips and she looked down at her knees for a moment. "There's a guy at the gym I go to?"

I nodded.

She swallowed. I guess she'd been hoping I'd figure it all out from that one sentence. I was certain she was about to tell me something unpleasant and even more certain that she had, at best, only a very passing acquaintance with things unpleasant.

"He's been hitting on me, following me to the parking lot. At first it was just, you know, annoying?" She raised her head, searched my eyes for understanding. "Then it got uglier. He began calling me at home. I went out of my way to avoid him at the gym, but a couple of times I saw him parked out in front of the house. David finally got fed up and went to talk to him. He denied it all and then he threatened David." She blinked, twisted the fingers of her left hand in the fist she'd made of her right. "David's not physically . . . formidable? Is that the right word?"

I nodded.

"So, Cody—that's his name, Cody Falk—he laughed at David and called me the same night."

Cody. I hated him already on general principle.

"He called and told me how much he knew I wanted it, how I'd probably never had a good, a good—"

"Fuck," Bubba said.

She jerked a little, glanced at him, and then quickly back to me. "Yeah. A good, well . . . in my life. And he knew I secretly wanted him to give me one. I left this note on his car. I know it was stupid, but I . . . well, I left it."

She reached into her purse, extracted a wrinkled piece of purple notepaper. In perfect Palmer script, she'd written:

> *Mr. Falk,*
> *Please leave me alone.*
> *Karen Nichols*

"The next time I went to the gym," she said, "I came back to my car, and he'd put it back on my windshield in the same place I'd left it on his. If you turn it over, Mr. Kenzie, you'll see what he wrote." She pointed at the paper in my hand.

I turned it over. On the reverse side, Cody Falk had written a single word:

> *No.*

I was really starting to dislike this prick.

"Then yesterday?" Her eyes filled and she swallowed several times and a thick tremor pulsed in the center of her soft, white throat.

I placed a hand on hers and she curled her fingers into it.

"What did he do?" I said.

She sucked a breath into her mouth and I heard it rattle wetly against the back of her throat. "He vandalized my car."

Bubba and I both did a double take, looked out at the gleaming green VW Bug parked by the schoolyard gate. It looked as if it had just been driven off the lot, still probably had that new-car smell inside.

"That car?" I said.

"What?" She followed my gaze. "Oh, no, no. That's David's car."

"A guy?" Bubba said. "A *guy* drives that car?"

I shook my head at him.

Bubba scowled, then looked down at his combat boots and pulled them up on his knees.

Karen shook her head as if to clear it. "I drive a Corolla. I wanted the Camry, but we couldn't afford it. David's starting a new business, we both have student loans we're still paying off, so I got the Corolla. And now it's ruined. He poured acid all over it. He punctured the radiator. The mechanic said he poured syrup into the engine."

"Did you tell the police?"

She nodded, her small body trembling. "There's no proof it was him. He told the police he was at a movie that night and people saw him going in and leaving. He . . ." Her face caved in on itself and reddened. "They can't touch him, and the insurance company won't cover the damages."

Bubba raised his head, cocked it at me.

"Why not?" I said.

"Because they never got my last payment. And I . . . I sent it. I sent it out over three weeks ago. They said they sent a notice, but I never got it. And, and . . ." She lowered her head and tears fell to her knees.

She had a stuffed animal collection, I was pretty

sure. Her totaled Corolla had either a smiley face or a Jesus fish affixed to the bumper. She read John Grisham novels, listened to soft rock, loved going to bridal showers, and had never seen a Spike Lee movie.

She had never expected anything like this to happen in her life.

"Karen," I said softly, "what's the name of your insurance company?"

She raised her head, wiped her tears with the back of her hand. "State Mutual."

"And the post office branch you sent the check through?"

"Well, I live in Newton Upper Falls," she said, "but I'm not sure. My boyfriend?" She looked down at her spotless white sneakers, as if abashed. "He lives in Back Bay and I'm over there a lot."

She said it as if it were a sin, and I found myself wondering where they grew people like her, and if there was a seed, and how I could get my hands on it if I ever had a daughter.

"Have you ever been late on a payment before?"

She shook her head. "Never."

"How long have you been insured there?"

"Since I graduated college. Seven years."

"Where's Cody Falk live?"

She patted her eyes with the heels of her hands to make sure the tears were dry. She wore no makeup, so nothing had run. She was as blandly beautiful as any woman in a Noxzema ad.

"I don't know. But he's at the gym every night at seven."

"What gym?"

"The Mount Auburn Club in Watertown." She bit down on her lower lip, then tried for that Ivory Snow smile of hers. "I feel so ridiculous."

"Miss Nichols," I said, "you're not supposed to deal with people like Cody Falk. Do you understand that? No one is. He's just a bad person and you didn't do anything to cause this. He did."

"Yeah?" She managed to get a full smile out, but fear and confusion still swam in her eyes.

"Yeah. He's the bad guy. He likes making people afraid."

"He does." She nodded. "You see it in his eyes. The more uncomfortable he made me feel in the parking lot one night, the more he seemed to enjoy it."

Bubba chuckled. "You wanna talk uncomfortable? Just wait till we visit Cody."

Karen Nichols looked at Bubba and for just a moment she seemed to pity Cody Falk.

In my office, I placed a call to my attorney, Cheswick Hartman.

Karen Nichols had driven off in her boyfriend's VW. I'd instructed her to drive straight to her insurance company and drop off a replacement check. When she said they wouldn't honor the claim, I assured her they would by the time she got there. She wondered aloud if she could pay my fee and I told her if she could afford one day, she'd be fine, because that's all this would take.

"One day?"

"One day," I said.

"But what about Cody?"

"You'll never hear from Cody again." I closed her car door, and she drove off, giving me a little wave as she reached the first traffic light.

"Look up 'cute' in the dictionary," I said to Bubba as we sat in my office. "See if Karen Nichols's picture is beside the definition."

Bubba looked at the small stack of books on my windowsill. "How do I tell which one's the dictionary?"

Cheswick came on the line and I told him about Karen Nichols's trouble with her insurance claim.

"No missed payments?"

"Never."

"No problem. You said it's a Corolla?"

"Uh-huh."

"What's that, a twenty-five-thousand-dollar car?"

"More like fourteen."

Cheswick chuckled. "Cars really go that cheap?" Cheswick owned a Bentley, a Mercedes V10, and two Range Rovers that I knew of. When he wanted to be one with the common folk, he drove a Lexus.

"They'll pay the claim," he said.

"They said they wouldn't," I said, just to get a rise out of him.

"And go up against me? I hang up the phone without satisfaction, they'll know they're already fifty thousand in the hole. They'll pay," he repeated.

When I hung up, Bubba said, "What'd he say?"

"He said they'll pay."

He nodded. "So will Cody, dude. So will Cody."

* * *

Bubba went back to his warehouse for a while to clear up some business, and I called Devin Amronklin, a homicide cop who's one of the few cops left in this city who will talk to me anymore.

"Homicide."

"Say it like you mean it, baby."

"Hey-hey. If it ain't *numero uno* persona non grata with the Boston Police Department. Been pulled over recently?"

"Nope."

"Don't. You'd be amazed what some guys here want to find in your trunk."

I closed my eyes for a moment. Being at the top of the police department's shit list was not where I'd planned to be at this point in my life.

"You can't be too popular," I said. "You're the one who put the cuffs on a fellow cop."

"Nobody's ever liked me," Devin said, "but most of them are scared of me, so that's just as good. You, on the other hand, are a renowned cream puff."

"Renowned, huh?"

"What's up?"

"I need a check on a Cody Falk. Priors, anything to do with stalking."

"And I get what for this?"

"Permanent friendship?"

"One of my nieces," he said, "wants the entire Beanie Babies collection for her birthday."

"And you don't want to go into a toy store."

"And I'm still paying serious child support for a kid who won't talk to me."

"So you want me to purchase said Beanie Babies, as well."

"Ten should do."

"Ten?" I said. "You've gotta be—"

"Falk with an 'F'?"

"As in flimflam," I said and hung up.

Devin called back in an hour and told me to bring the Beanie Babies by his apartment the next night.

"Cody Falk, age thirty-three. No convictions."

"However . . ."

"However," Devin said, "arrested once for violating a restraining order against one Bronwyn Blythe. Charges dropped. Arrested for assault of Sara Little. Charges dropped when Miss Little refused to testify and moved out of state. Named as a suspect in the rape of one Anne Bernstein, brought in for questioning. Charges never filed because Miss Bernstein refused to swear out a complaint, submit to a rape examination, or identify her attacker."

"Nice guy," I said.

"Sounds like a peach, yeah."

"That's it?"

"Except that he has a juvenile record, but it's been sealed."

"Of course."

"He bothering somebody again?"

"Maybe," I said carefully.

"Wear gloves," Devin said and hung up.

2

Cody Falk drove a pearl-gray Audi Quattro, and at nine-thirty that night, we watched him exit the Mount Auburn Club, his hair freshly combed and still wet, the butt of a tennis racket sticking out of his gym bag. He wore a soft black leather jacket over a cream linen vest, a white shirt buttoned at the throat, and faded jeans. He was very tan. He moved like he expected things to get out of his way.

"I really hate this guy," I said to Bubba. "And I don't even know him."

"Hate's cool," Bubba said. "Don't cost nothing."

Cody's Audi beeped twice as he used the remote attached to his key chain to disengage the alarm and pop the trunk.

"If you'd just let me," Bubba said, "he would have blown up about now."

Bubba had wanted to strap some C-4 to the engine block and wire the charge to the Audi's alarm transmitter. C-4. Take out half of Watertown, blow the Mount Auburn Club to somewhere over Rhode Island. Bubba couldn't see why this wasn't a good idea.

"You don't kill a guy for trashing a woman's car."

"Yeah?" Bubba said. "Where's that written?"

I have to admit he had me there.

"Plus," Bubba said, "you know, he gets the chance he'll rape her."

I nodded.

"I hate rape-os," Bubba said.

"Me, too."

"It'd be cool if he never did it again."

I turned in my seat. "We're not killing him."

Bubba shrugged.

Cody Falk closed his trunk and stood by it a moment, his strong chin tilted up as he looked at the tennis courts fronting the parking lot. He looked like he was posing for something, a portrait maybe, and with his rich, dark hair and chiseled features, his carefully sculpted torso and soft, expensive clothes, he could have easily passed for a model. He seemed aware that he was being watched, but not by us; he seemed the kind of guy who always thought he was being watched, with either admiration or envy. It was Cody Falk's world, we were just living in it.

Cody pulled out of the parking lot and took a right, and we followed him through Watertown and around the edge of Cambridge. He took a left on Concord Street and headed into Belmont, one of the tonier of our tony suburbs.

"How come you park in a driveway and drive on a parkway?" Bubba yawned into his fist, looked out the window.

"I have no idea."

"You said that the last time I asked you."

"And?"

"And I just wish someone would give me a good answer. It pisses me off."

We left the main road and followed Cody Falk into a smoke-brown neighborhood of tall oaks and chocolate Tudors, the fallen sun having left a haze of deep bronze in its wake that gave the late winter streets an autumn glow, an air of rarefied ease, inherited wealth, stained-glass private libraries full of dark teak and delicate tapestries.

"Glad we took the Porsche," Bubba said.

"You don't think the Crown Vic would have fit in?"

My Porsche is a '63 Roadster. I bought the shell and little else ten years ago and spent the next five purchasing parts and restoring it. I don't love it, per se, but I have to admit that when I'm behind the wheel, I do feel like the coolest guy in Boston. Maybe the world. Angie used to say that's because I still have a lot of growing up to do. Angie was probably right, but then, until very recently, she drove a station wagon.

Cody Falk pulled into a small driveway beside a large stucco colonial and I cut my headlights and pulled in behind him as the garage door rolled up with a whir. Even with his windows closed, I could hear the bass thumping from his car speakers, and we rolled right up the driveway behind him without his hearing a thing. I cut the engine just before we would have followed him into the garage. He got out of the Audi and we left the Porsche as the garage door began to close. He popped his trunk, and Bubba and I stepped under the door and in there with him.

He jumped back when he saw me, and shoved his hands out in front of him as if warding off a horde. Then his eyes began to narrow. I'm not a particularly big guy and Cody looked fit and tall and well muscled. His fear of a stranger in his garage was already giving way to calculation as he sized me up, saw I had no weapon.

Then Bubba shut the trunk that had blocked him from Cody's view, and Cody gasped. Bubba has that effect on people. He has the face of a deranged two-year-old—as if the features softened and stopped maturing around the same time his brain and conscience did—and it sits atop a body that reminds me of a steel boxcar with limbs.

"Who the hell—"

Bubba had taken Cody's tennis racket from his bag, and he twirled it lightly in his hand. "How come you park in driveways, but drive on parkways?" he asked Cody.

I looked at Bubba and rolled my eyes.

"What? How the fuck do I know?"

Bubba shrugged. Then he smashed the tennis racket down onto the Audi's trunk, drove a gouge in the center that was about nine inches long.

"Cody," I said as the garage door slammed closed behind me, "you don't say a word unless I ask you a direct question. We clear?"

He stared at me.

"That was a direct question, Cody."

"Uh, yeah, we're clear." Cody glanced at Bubba, seemed to shrink into himself.

Bubba removed the tennis racket cover and dropped it on the floor.

"Please don't hit the car again," Cody said.

Bubba held up a comforting hand. He nodded. Then he sliced a pretty fluid backhand through the air and connected with the Audi's rear window. The glass made a loud popping noise before it dropped all over Cody's backseat.

"Jesus!"

"What did I say about talking, Cody?"

"But he just smashed my—"

Bubba flung the tennis racket like a tomahawk and it hit Cody Falk in the center of the forehead, knocked him back into the garage wall. He crumpled to the floor and blood streamed from the gash over his right eyebrow and he looked like he was going to cry.

I picked him up by his hair and slammed his back into the driver's door.

"What do you do for a living, Cody?"

"I . . . What?"

"What do you do?"

"I'm a restaurateur."

"A what?" Bubba said.

I looked back over my shoulder at him. "He owns restaurants."

"Oh."

"Which ones?" I asked Cody.

"The Boatyard in Nahant. I own the Flagstaff downtown, and part of Tremont Street Grill, the Fours in Brookline. I . . . I—"

"Sshh," I said. "Anyone in the house?"

"What?" He looked around wildly. "No. No. I'm single."

I pulled Cody to his feet. "Cody, you like to harass

women. Maybe even rape them sometimes, knock them around when they don't play ball?"

Cody's eyes darkened as a thick drop of blood began its descent down the bridge of his nose. "No, I don't. Who—"

I backhanded the wound on his forehead and he yelped.

"Quiet, Cody. Quiet. If you ever bother a woman again—any woman—we'll burn down your restaurants and put you in a wheelchair for life. Do you understand?"

Something about women brought out the stupid in Cody. Maybe it was the telling him he couldn't have them in the manner he'd come to enjoy. Whatever the case, he shook his head. He tightened his jaw. A predatory amusement crept into his eyes as if he believed he'd found my Achilles' heel: a concern for the "weaker" sex.

Cody said, "Well. Yes, well. I don't think I can do that."

I stepped aside as Bubba came around the car, pulled a .22 from his trench coat, screwed on the silencer, pointed it at the center of Cody Falk's face and pulled the trigger.

The hammer dropped on an empty chamber, but Cody didn't seem to realize that at first. He closed his eyes and screamed, "No!" and fell on his ass.

We stood over him as he opened his eyes. He touched his nose with his fingers, surprised to realize it was still there.

"What happened?" I asked Bubba.

"Dunno. I loaded it."

"Try again."

"Sure."

Cody's hands shot out in front of him. "Wait!"

Bubba pointed the muzzle at Cody's chest and pulled the trigger again.

Another dry click.

Cody flopped on the floor, his eyes screwed shut again, his face contorted into a puttylike mask of horror. Tears sprouted from under his lids and the sharp smell of urine rose from a burgeoning stain along his left pant leg.

"Damn," Bubba said. He raised the gun to his face, scowled at it, and pointed down again just as Cody opened one eye.

Cody clamped the eye closed as Bubba pulled the trigger a third time, hit another empty chamber.

"You buy that thing at a yard sale?" I asked.

"Shut up. It'll work." Bubba flicked his wrist and the cylinder snapped open. One golden eye of a slug stared up at us, disrupting an otherwise unbroken circle of small black holes. "See? There's one in there."

"One," I said.

"One'll do."

Cody suddenly vaulted up off the floor toward us.

I raised my foot, stepped on his chest, and knocked him back down.

Bubba flicked the cylinder closed and pointed the gun. He dry-fired once and Cody screamed. He dry-fired a second time, and Cody made this weird laughing-crying sound.

He placed his hands over his eyes and said, "No, no, no, no, no, no, no, no," then did that laughing-crying thing again.

"Sixth time's the charm," Bubba said.

Cody looked up at the suppressor muzzle and ground the back of his head into the floor. His mouth was wide open, as if he were screaming, but all that came out was a soft, high-pitched "Na, na, na."

I squatted down by him, yanked his right ear up to my mouth.

"I hate people who victimize women, Cody. Fucking hate 'em. I always find myself thinking, What if that woman was my sister? My mother? You see?"

Cody tried to twist his ear from my grip, but I held on tight. His eyes rolled back into his head and his cheeks puffed in and out.

"Look at me."

Cody wrenched his eyes back to focus and looked up into my face.

"If the insurance doesn't pay for her car, Cody, we're coming back with the bill."

The panic in his eyes ebbed as clarity replaced it. "I never touched that bitch's car."

"Bubba."

Bubba took aim at Cody's head.

"No! Listen, listen, listen. I . . . I . . . Karen Nichols, right?"

I held up a hand to Bubba.

"Okay, I, whatever you call it, I stalked her a bit. Just a game. Just a game. But not her car. I never—"

I brought my fist down on his stomach. The air blew out of his lungs and his mouth repeatedly chomped open and shut trying to get some oxygen.

"Okay, Cody. It's a game. And this is the last inning. Understand this: I hear a woman—any woman—is being stalked in this city? Gets raped in this city? Has a bad fucking *hair day* in this city, Cody, and I'm just going to assume it's you who did it. And we'll come back."

"And paralyze your dumb fucking ass," Bubba said.

A burst of air exploded from Cody Falk's lungs as he got them working again.

"Say you understand, Cody."

"I understand," Cody managed.

I looked at Bubba. He shrugged. I nodded.

Bubba unscrewed the silencer from the .22. He placed the gun in one pocket of his trench coat, the suppressor in the other. He walked over to the wall and picked up the tennis racket. He walked back and stood over Cody Falk.

I said, "You need to know how serious we are, Cody."

"I know! I know!" Shrieking now.

"You think he knows?" I asked Bubba.

"I think he knows," Bubba said.

A guttural sigh of relief escaped Cody's lips and he looked up into Bubba's face with a gratitude that was almost embarrassing to witness.

Bubba smiled and smashed the tennis racket down into Cody Falk's groin.

Cody sat up like the base of his spine was on fire. The world's loudest hiccup burst from his mouth, and he wrapped his arms around his stomach and puked in his own lap.

Bubba said, "You can never be too sure, though, can ya?" and tossed the tennis racket over the hood of the car.

I watched Cody struggle with the bolts of pain shooting up his body, seizing his intestines, his chest cavity, his lungs. Sweat poured down his face like a summer shower.

Bubba opened the small wooden door that led out of the garage.

Cody eventually turned his head toward mine and the grimace on his face reminded me of a skeleton's smile.

I watched his eyes to see if the fear would turn to rage, if the vulnerability would be replaced by that casual superiority of the born predator. I waited to see that look Karen Nichols had seen in the parking lot, the same one I'd glimpsed just before Bubba pulled the .22's trigger that first time.

I waited some more.

The pain began to subside and the grimace re-laxed on Cody Falk's face; the skin loosened up by his hairline, and his breathing returned to a semiregular rhythm. But the fear stayed. It was dug in deep, and I knew it would be several nights before he slept more than an hour or two, a month at least before he could shut the garage door behind him while he was still inside. For a long, long time, he would, at least once a day, look over his shoulder for Bubba and me. Cody Falk, I was almost certain, would spend the rest of his life in a state of fear.

I reached into my coat pocket and pulled out the note Karen Nichols had left on his car. I crumpled it into a ball.

"Cody," I whispered.

His eyes snapped to attention.

"Next time, the lights will just go out." I tilted his chin up with my fingers. "You understand? You'll never hear us or see us."

I shoved the balled-up note into his mouth. His eyes widened and he tried not to gag. I slapped the underside of his chin and his mouth closed.

I stood up, walked to the door, kept my back to him.

"And you'll die, Cody. You'll die."

3

It would be six months before I gave any serious thought to Karen Nichols again.

A week after we dealt with Cody Falk, I received a check in the mail from her, a smiley face drawn within the "o" in her name, yellow ducklings embossed along the borders of the check, a card enclosed that said, "Thanks! You're the absolute best!"

Given what would happen, I'd like to say I never heard from her again until that morning six months later when I heard the news on the radio, but the truth is she called once several weeks after I'd received her check.

She reached my answering machine. I came in an hour later to grab a pair of sunglasses, heard the message. The office was closed that week because I was taking off to Bermuda with Vanessa Moore, a defense attorney who had no more interest in a serious relationship than I did. She liked beaches, though, and she liked daiquiris and sloe gin fizzes and nooners followed by late afternoon massages. She looked mouthwatering in a business suit, coronary-inducing in a bikini, and she was the only person I knew at the time who was at least as shallow as I was. So, for a month or two, we were a good match.

I found my sunglasses in a lower desk drawer as Karen Nichols's voice played through a tinny speaker. It took me a minute to recognize it, not because I'd forgotten how she sounded, but because this didn't sound like her voice. It sounded hoarse and weary and ragged.

"Hey, Mr. Kenzie. This is Karen. You, ahm, helped me out a month ago, maybe six weeks? Yeah, so, ahm, look, give me a call. I, ah, I'd like to run something by you." There was a pause. "Okay, so, yeah, just give me a call." And she left her number.

Vanessa beeped the horn out on the avenue.

Our plane left in an hour, and traffic would be a bitch, and Vanessa could do this thing with her hips and calf muscles that was probably outlawed in most of Western civilization.

I reached for the replay button and Vanessa beeped again, louder and longer, and my finger jumped and hit the erase button instead. I know what Freud would have made of the mistake, and he'd probably be right. But I had Karen Nichols's number somewhere, and I'd be back in a week, and I'd remember to call her. Clients had to understand that I had a life, too.

So I went to my life, let Karen Nichols go to hers, and, of course, forgot to call her back.

Months later, when I heard about her on the radio, I was driving back from Maine with Tony Traverna, a bail jumper who was usually considered by those who knew him as both the best safecracker in Boston and the dumbest man in the universe.

Tony T, the jokes went, couldn't outwit a can of soup. Put Tony T in a room full of horse shit and twenty-four hours later he'd still be looking for the horse. Tony T thought manual labor was the president of Mexico, and had once wondered aloud what night they broadcast *Saturday Night Live*.

Whenever Tony had jumped bail before, he'd gone to Maine. He'd driven, even though he didn't have a driver's license. Tony'd never had a license because he'd failed the written part of the exam. Nine times. He could drive, though, and the savant part of him ensured that man had yet to invent a lock he couldn't crack. So he'd boost a car and drive three hours to his late father's fishing cabin in Maine. Along the way, he'd pick up a few cases of Heineken and several bottles of Bacardi, because in addition to having the world's smallest brain, Tony T seemed determined to have the world's hardest liver, and then he'd hunker down in the cabin and watch cartoons on Nickelodeon until someone came to get him.

Tony Traverna had made some serious cash over the years, and even when you took into consideration all the money he'd burned on the booze and the hookers he paid to dress up like Indian squaws and call him "Trigger," you had to figure he had plenty stashed away somewhere. Enough, anyway, for a plane ticket. But instead of jumping bail and flying off to Florida or Alaska or someplace he'd be harder to find, Tony always drove to Maine. Maybe, as someone once said, he was afraid to fly. Or maybe, as someone else suggested, he didn't know what planes were.

Tony T's bond was held by Mo Bags, an ex-cop and practicing hard-ass who would have gone after Tony himself with Mace and stun guns, brass knuckles and nunchucks, if it weren't for a recent flare-up of gout that bit into Mo's right hip like fire ants every time he drove a car for more than twenty miles. Besides, Tony and I had a history. Mo knew I'd find him, no problem, and Tony wouldn't bolt on me. This time Tony's bail had been put up by his girlfriend, Jill Dermott. Jill was the latest in a long line of women who looked at Tony and felt swept off their feet by a need to mother the man. It had been this way most of Tony's life, or at least the portion I was familiar with. Tony walked into a bar (and he was always walking into a bar) and took a seat and started talking to the bartender or the person on the seat beside him, and half an hour later, most of the unmarried women in the bar (and a few of the married ones) were huddled on the seats around Tony, buying him drinks, listening to the slow, light cadence of his voice and deciding that all this boy needed to fix him up was nurture, love, and maybe some night classes.

Tony had a soft voice and one of those small but open faces that induce trust. Mournful almond eyes loomed above a crooked nose and an even more crooked smile, a permanent turn of the lips that seemed to say Tony had been there, too, my friend, and, really, what could you do about it except buy a round and share your story with new and old friends alike?

With that face, if Tony had chosen to be a con man, he'd have done all right. But Tony, ultimately, wasn't smart enough to run a con, and maybe he was just too nice. Tony liked people. They seemed to confuse him the way just about everything did, but he genuinely liked them, too. Unfortunately, he also liked safes. Liked them a lot. Maybe just a hair more than people. He had an ear that could hear a feather settle on the surface of the moon and fingers so nimble he could solve a Rubik's Cube one-handed without glancing at it. In his twenty-eight years on the planet, Tony had cracked so many safes that anytime an all-night burn job left a gutted shell in place of a bank vault, cops drove over to Tony's Southie apartment even before they stopped at Dunkin' Donuts, and judges cut search-and-seizure warrants in the time it takes most of us to write a check.

Tony's real problem, though, at least in the legal sense, wasn't the safes, and it wasn't the stupidity (though it didn't help); it was the drink. All but two of Tony's jail terms had come from DUIs, and his latest was no different—driving north in the southbound lane of Northern Avenue at three in the morning, resisting arrest (he'd kept driving), malicious destruction of property (he'd crashed), and fleeing the scene of an accident (he'd climbed a telephone pole because he had a theory the cops might not notice him twenty feet above the wrecked car on a dark night).

When I entered the fishing cabin, Tony looked up from the living room floor with a face that said, What took you so long? He sighed and used the remote to flick off *Rugrats*, then stood unsteadily and slapped his thighs to get the blood flowing through them again.

"Hey, Patrick. Mo send you?"

I nodded.

Tony looked around for his shoes, found them under a throw pillow on the floor. "Beer?"

I looked around the cabin. In the day and a half he'd been here, Tony had managed to fill every windowsill with empty Heineken bottles. The green glass captured the sun glinting off the lake and then refracted it into the room in tiny beams so that the entire cabin glowed the emerald of a tavern on St. Patrick's Day.

"No, thanks, Tony. I'm trying to cut back on beer for breakfast."

"Religious thing?"

"Something like that."

He crossed one leg over the other and pulled the ankle up to his waist, hopped around on the other foot as he tried to get a shoe on. "You gonna cuff me?"

"You going to bolt?"

He got the shoe on somehow, then stumbled as he dropped the foot to the floor. "Nah, man. You know that."

I nodded. "So no cuffs, then."

He gave me a grateful smile, then raised the other foot off the floor and started hopping around again as he tried to put on the second shoe. Tony got the shoe over his foot, then stumbled back into the couch and fell on his ass, short of breath from all that hopping. Tony's shoes didn't have laces, just Velcro flaps.

Word was that—oh, never mind. You can guess. Tony strapped the Velcro flaps together and stood.

I let him gather up a change of clothes, his Game Boy, and some comic books for the ride. At the door, he stopped and looked hopefully at the fridge.

"Mind if I grab a roadie?"

I couldn't see what harm a beer on the ride could do to a guy heading off to jail. "Sure."

Tony opened the fridge and pulled out an entire twelve-pack.

"You know," he said as we left the cabin, "in case we hit traffic or something."

We did hit some traffic, as it turned out—small squalls of it outside Lewiston, then Portland, the beach communities of Kennebunkport and Ogunquit. The soft summer morning was turning into a white sear of a day, the trees and roads and other cars glinting pale, hard, and angry under a high sun.

Tony sat in the back of the black '91 Cherokee I'd picked up when the engine of my Crown Victoria seized up that spring. The Cherokee was great for the rare bounty hunt because it had come with a steel gate between the seats and the stow bed in back. Tony sat on the other side of the gate, his back against the vinyl seat cover over the spare tire. He stretched out his legs like a cat settling into a sun-baked windowsill and cracked open his third beer of the early afternoon, then burped up the vapor of the second.

"Excuse yourself, man."

Tony caught my eyes in the rearview. "Excuse me. Didn't realize you were such a stickler for, ahm—"

"Common courtesy?"

"That, yeah."

"I let you think it's okay to burp in my ride, Tony, then you'll think it's okay to take a leak."

"Nah, man. Wish I'd brought a big cup or something, though."

"We'll stop at the next exit."

"You're all right, Patrick."

"Oh, yeah, I'm swell."

We actually made several stops in Maine and one in New Hampshire. This will happen when you allow an alcoholic bail jumper into your car with a twelve-pack, but, in truth, I didn't mind all that much. I enjoyed Tony's company in the same way you'd enjoy an afternoon with a twelve-year-old nephew who was a little slow on the uptake but irrevocably good-natured.

Somewhere during the New Hampshire leg of our trip, Tony's Game Boy stopped blipping and beeping, and I looked in the rearview to see that he'd passed out back there, snoring softly, his lips flapping gently as one foot wagged back and forth like a dog's tail.

We'd just passed into Massachusetts and I'd pressed the seek button on my car radio and tried to get lucky and pick up WFNX while I was still a good distance from their weak antenna when Karen Nichols's name floated out of a tangle of static and air hiss. The digital call numbers raced by on the radio's LED screen, paused for just a moment on a thin signal at 99.6:

". . . now identified as Karen Nichols of Newton, apparently jumped from—"

The tuner left the station and jumped to 100.7.

I swerved the car slightly as I reached for the manual tune button and brought it back to 99.6.

Tony woke up in the back and said, "What?"

"Sssh." I held up a finger.

". . . police department sources say. How Miss Nichols gained entrance to the observation deck of the Custom House is not yet known. Turning to weather, meteorologist Gil Hutton says to expect more heat . . ."

Tony rubbed his eyes. "Crazy shit, huh?"

"You know about this?"

He yawned. "Saw it on the news this morning. Chick took a buck-naked header off the Custom House, forgot that gravity kills, man. You know? Gravity kills."

"Shut up, Tony."

He recoiled as if I'd swatted him, turned away from me, and scrounged through the twelve-pack for another beer.

There could be another Karen Nichols in Newton. Probably several. It was a mundane, pedestrian American name. As boring and common as Mike Smith or Ann Adams.

But something cold and spreading through my stomach told me that the Karen Nichols who'd jumped from the Custom House observation deck was the same one I'd met six months ago. The one who ironed her socks and had a stuffed animal collection.

That Karen Nichols didn't seem like a woman who'd jump nude from a building. But, still, I knew. I knew.

"Tony?"

He looked up at me with the injured eyes of a hamster in the rain. "Yeah?"

"Sorry I snapped at you."

"Yeah, okay." He took a sip from his beer, continued to watch me warily.

"The woman who jumped," I said, not even sure why I was explaining myself to a guy like Tony, "I may have known her."

"Oh, shit, man. I'm sorry. Fucking people sometimes, you know?"

I looked at the highway, tinted a metallic blue under the harsh sun. Even with the air-conditioning running at max, I could feel the heat needle the skin at the nape of my neck.

Tony's eyes were wet and the smile that rolled up his cheeks was too big, too wide. "It calls to you sometimes, man. You know?"

"The booze?"

He shook his head. "Like with your friend who jumped?" He got up on his knees, pressed his nose to the grate between us. "It's, like, I went out on this guy's boat once, right? I can't *swim*, but I go out on a *boat*. We get stuck in this storm, swear to God, and the boat's, like, tipping all the way to the left, then all the way to the right, the fucking waves look like big-ass roads curling up at us on all sides. And, okay, I'm scared shitless, 'cause I fall in, I'm done. But I'm also, I dunno how to say it, I feel kinda *content*, okay? I feel like, 'Good. My questions'll be answered. No more wondering how and when and why I'm gonna die. I am gonna die. Right now. And that's kinda a relief.' You ever feel that way?"

I glanced over my shoulder at his face pressed against the small squares of steel, the flesh of his cheeks spilling over to my side of the gate and filling the squares like soft, white chestnuts.

"Once," I said.

"Yeah?" His eyes widened and he leaned back from the gate a bit. "When?"

"Guy had a shotgun pointed at my face. I was pretty sure he was going to pull the trigger."

"And for just a second"—Tony held his thumb and forefinger a hairsbreadth apart—"just one second, you thought, This could be cool. Right?"

I smiled at him in the rearview. "Maybe, something like that. I don't know anymore."

He sat back on his haunches. "That's how I felt on that boat. Maybe your friend, maybe she felt that way last night. Like, 'Wow, I've never flown. Let's give this a try.' You know what I'm trying to say?"

"Not really, no." I looked in the rearview. "Tony, why did you go on that boat?"

He rubbed his chin. "'Cause I couldn't swim." He shrugged.

Close to the end of our trip, and the road seemed endless before me, the weight of the final thirty miles hanging behind my eyes like a steel pendulum.

"Come on," I said. "Really."

Tony tilted his chin up, and his face grew pinched with thought.

"It's the not knowing," he said. And then he burped.

"What is?"

"Why I went on the boat, I guess. The not knowing—all the not knowing in this fucking life, you know? It gets to you. Makes you crazy. You just want to know."

"Even if you can't fly?"

Tony smiled. "*Because* you can't fly."

He patted the gate between us with his palm. He burped again, then excused himself. He curled up on the floor and sang the theme song to *The Flint-stones* very softly.

By the time we reached Boston, he was snoring again.

4

When I walked through his front door with Tony Traverna, Mo Bags looked up from his meatball and Italian sausage sub and said, "Hey, fucko! How ya doing?"

I was pretty sure he was talking to Tony, but with Mo sometimes you couldn't tell.

He dropped the sub, wiped his greasy fingers and mouth on a napkin, then came around his desk as I dropped Tony in a chair.

Tony said, "Hey, Mo."

"Don't 'Hey Mo' me, scumbag. Give me your wrist."

"Mo," I said, "come on."

"What?" Mo snapped a cuff around Tony's left wrist, then attached the other end to the chair arm.

"How's the gout?" Tony seemed genuinely concerned.

"Better'n you, mutt. Better'n you."

"Good to hear." Tony belched.

Mo narrowed his eyes at me. "He drunk?"

"I don't know." I spied a copy of the *Trib* on Mo's leather couch. "Tony, you drunk?"

"Nah, man. Hey, Mo, you got a bathroom I can use?"

"This guy's drunk," Mo said.

I lifted the sports page off the pile of newspaper, found the front page underneath. Karen Nichols had made it above the fold: WOMAN JUMPS FROM CUSTOM HOUSE. Beside the article was a full color photo of the Custom House at night.

"Guy is fucking drunk," Mo said. "Kenzie?"

Tony belched again, then began singing "Raindrops Keep Fallin' on My Head."

"Okay. He's drunk," I said. "Where's my money?"

"You let him drink?" Mo wheezed like a chunk of meatball had lodged in his esophagus.

I picked up the newspaper, read the lead. "Mo."

Tony heard the tone of my voice and stopped singing.

Mo was too fired up to notice, though. "I dunno here, Kenzie. I don't fucking know about guys like you. You're gonna give me a bad rep."

"You already have a bad rep," I said. "Pay me."

The article began: "An apparently distraught Newton woman jumped to her death late last night from the observatory deck of one of the city's most cherished monuments."

Mo asked Tony, "You believe this fucking guy?"

"Sure."

"Shut up, fucko. No one's talking to you."

"I need a bathroom."

"What'd I say?" Mo breathed loudly through his

nostrils, paced behind Tony, and lightly rapped the back of his head with his knuckles.

"Tony," I said, "it's just past this couch, through that door."

Mo laughed. "What, he's going to take the chair with him?"

Tony unlocked the cuff around his wrist with a sudden snap and walked into the bathroom.

Mo said, "Hey!"

Tony looked back at him. "I gotta *go*, man."

"Identified as Karen Nichols," the article continued, "the woman left behind her wallet and clothes on the observatory deck before leaping to her death . . ."

A half-pound hunk of ham hit my shoulder and I turned to see Mo pulling back his clenched fist.

"The fuck you doing, Kenzie?"

I went back to reading the paper. "My money, Mo."

"You dating this mug? You fucking buy him beers, maybe get him in the mood for love?"

The observatory deck of the Custom House is twenty-six stories up. Dropping, you'd probably glimpse the top of Beacon Hill, Government Center, skyscrapers in the financial district, and finally Faneuil Hall and Quincy Marketplace. All in a second or two—a mélange of brick and glass and yellow light before you hit cobblestone. Part of you would bounce, the other part wouldn't.

"You hearing me, Kenzie?" Mo went to punch me again.

I slipped the punch, dropped the paper, and closed my right hand around his throat. I backed him into his desk and pushed him onto his back.

Tony stepped out of the bathroom and said, "Like, shit. Wow."

"Which drawer?" I asked Mo.

His eyes bulged in a frantic question.

"Which drawer is my money in, Mo?"

I eased my grip on his throat.

"Middle drawer."

"It better not be a check."

"No, no. Cash."

I let him go and he lay there wheezing as I went around the desk, opened the drawer, and found my money wrapped in a rubber band.

Tony sat back in the chair and recuffed his own wrist.

Mo sat up and his bulk dropped his feet to the floor. He rubbed his throat, gacked like a cat spitting up a hair ball.

I came back around the desk and picked the newspaper up off the floor.

Mo's tiny eyes darkened into bitterness.

I straightened the pages of the paper, folded it neatly, and tucked it under my arm.

"Mo," I said, "you have a pimp's piece in the holster on your left ankle, and a lead sap in your back pocket."

Mo's eyes hardened some more.

"Reach for either of them, I'll show you exactly how bad my mood is today."

Mo coughed. He dropped his eyes from mine. He rasped, "Your name is shit now in this business."

"Gosh," I said. "More's the pity, huh?"

Mo said, "You'll see. You'll see. Without Gennaro,

I hear you need every penny you can get. You'll be begging me for work come winter. Begging."

I looked down at Tony. "You be okay?"

He gave me a thumbs-up.

"At Nashua Street," I told him, "there's a guard named Bill Kuzmich. Tell him you're a friend of mine, he'll watch out for you."

"Cool," Tony said. "Think he'd bring me a keg every now and then?"

"Oh, sure, Tony. That'll happen."

I read the paper sitting in my car outside Mo Bags Bail Bonds on Ocean Street in Chinatown. There wasn't much in the article I hadn't heard off the radio, but there was a picture of Karen Nichols taken from her driver's license.

It was the same Karen Nichols who'd hired me six months before. In the picture she looked as bright and innocent as she had the day I met her, smiling into the camera as if the photographer had just told her what a pretty dress she had on, and what nice shoes, too.

She'd entered the Custom House during the afternoon, taken a tour of the observation deck, even talked to someone in the Realtor's office about the new time-sharing opportunities available since the state had decided to pick up some extra cash by selling a historical landmark to the Marriott Corporation. The Realtor, Mary Hughes, recalled her as being vague about her employment, easily distracted.

At five, when they closed the observation deck to anyone but time-sharers with codes for the keyless entry system, Karen had hidden somewhere on the deck, and then at nine, she'd jumped.

For four hours, she'd sat up there, twenty-six stories above blue cement, and considered whether she'd go through with it or not. I wondered if she'd huddled in a corner, or walked around, or looked out at the city, up at the sky, around at the lights. How much of her life and its pivots and dips and hard, sudden L-turns had replayed in her head? At what moment had it all crystallized to the point where she'd hoisted her legs over that four-foot balcony wall and stepped into black space?

I placed the paper on the passenger seat, closed my eyes for a bit.

Behind my lids, she fell. She was pale and thin against a night sky and she dropped, with the off-white limestone of the Custom House rushing behind her like a waterfall.

I opened my eyes, watched a pair of med students from Tufts puff cigarettes desperately as they hurried along Ocean in their white lab coats.

I looked up at the MO BAGS BAIL BONDS sign, and wondered where my Johnny Tough Guy act had come from. My entire life, I'd done a good job staying away from macho histrionics. I was pretty secure that I could handle myself in a violent confrontation, and that was enough, because I was just as certain, having grown up where I did, that there were always people crazier and tougher and meaner and faster than I was. And they were only too happy to prove it. So many guys I'd known from childhood had died or been jailed or, in one case, met with quadriplegia because they'd needed to show the world how bad-ass they were. But the world, in my experience, is like Vegas: You may walk away a winner once or twice, but if you go to the table too often, roll the dice too much, the world will swat you into place and take your wallet, your future, or both.

Karen Nichols's death bugged me, that was part of it. But more than simply that, I think, was the dawning realization over the last year that I'd lost my taste for my profession. I was tired of skip-tracing and shutterbugging insurance frauds and men playing house with bony trophy mistresses and women playing more than match point with their Argentinian tennis instructors. I was tired, I think, of people—their predictable vices, their predictable needs and wants and dormant desires. The pathetic silliness of the whole damn species. And without Angie to roll her eyes along with my own, to add sardonic running commentary to the whole tattered pageant, it just wasn't fun anymore.

Karen Nichols's hopeful, homecoming-queen smile stared up from the passenger seat, all white teeth and good health and beatific ignorance.

She'd come to me for help. I'd thought I'd provided it, and maybe I had. But during the six months that followed, she'd unraveled so completely from the person I'd met that it might as well have been a stranger in the body that dropped from the Custom House last night.

And, yes, the worst of it—she'd called me. Six weeks after I'd dealt with Cody Falk. Four months before she died. Somewhere in the middle of all that fatal unraveling.

And I hadn't returned the call.

I'd been busy.

She'd been drowning, and I'd been busy.

I glanced down at her face again, resisted the urge to turn away from the hope in her eyes.

"Okay," I said aloud. "Okay, Karen. I'll see what I can turn up. I'll see what I can do."

A Chinese woman passing in front of the Jeep caught me talking to myself. She stared at me. I waved. She shook her head and walked away.

She was still shaking her head as I started the Jeep and pulled out of my parking spot.

Crazy, she seemed to be thinking. The whole damn planet of us. We're all so crazy.

5

What we presume about strangers when we first meet them is often correct. The guy sitting beside you at a bar, for example, who wears a blue shirt, has fingernails caked with dirt, and smells of motor oil, you can safely presume is a mechanic. To assume more is trickier, yet it's something we all do every day. Our mechanic, we'd probably guess, drinks Budweiser. Watches football. Likes movies in which lots of shit blows up. Lives in an apartment that smells like his clothes.

There's a good chance these assumptions are on the mark.

And just as good a chance that they're not.

When I met Karen Nichols, I assumed she'd grown up in the suburbs, came from comfortably middle-class parents, spent her formative years sheltered from dissension and mess and people who weren't white. I further assumed (all in an instant, the span of a handshake) that her father was a doctor or the owner of a modest, successful business, a small chain of golf shops, perhaps. Her mother was a homemaker until the kids went to school, and then she worked part-time at a book-store or maybe for an attorney.

The truth was that when Karen Nichols was six years old, her father, a marine lieutenant stationed at Fort Devens, was shot by another lieutenant in the kitchen of Karen's home. The shooter's name was Reginald Crowe, Uncle Reggie to Karen, even though he hadn't been a blood relation. He'd been her father's best friend and next-door neighbor and he shot her father twice in the chest with a .45 as the two sat having Saturday afternoon beers.

Karen, who had been next door playing with the Crowe children, heard the shots and came rushing into her home to find Uncle Reggie standing over her father. Uncle Reggie, seeing Karen, promptly put the gun to his own heart and fired.

There was a picture of the two corpses that some enterprising *Trib* reporter had found in Fort De-vens's files and published in his paper two days after Karen leapt to her death.

The headline above the page 3 story read: SINS OF SUICIDE-WOMAN'S PAST HAUNT PRES-ENT, and the story reenergized water-cooler con-versation around the city for at least half an hour.

I never would have guessed Karen, at six, had been such a close witness to horror. The house in the suburbs came a few years later, when her mother was remarried to a cardiologist who lived in Weston. Karen Nichols, from that point, grew up untouched and unchallenged.

And while I was pretty sure that the only reason Karen's death received any news play whatsoever stemmed more from the building from which she chose to jump than any curiosity regarding her need to do so, I also think that she became, for a moment, a morbid reminder of the ways in which the world or the fates could mangle your dreams. Because in the six months since I'd seen her last, Karen Nichols's life had been on a slide steeper than a fall from the Eiger.

A month after I'd solved her Cody Falk problem, her boyfriend, David Wetterau, had tripped while jaywalking during rush hour on Congress Street. The trip hadn't been much—a fall to both knees that tore a hole in one pant leg—but while he was down, a Cadillac, swerving to miss him, had clipped his forehead with the corner of its rear fender. Wetterau had been comatose ever since.

Over the next five months, Karen Nichols slipped ever downward, losing her job, her car, and finally her apartment. Not even the police could ascertain where she'd lived her final two months. Psychiatrists popped up on the news shows to explain that David Wetterau's accident coupled with her father's tragic death had snapped something in Karen's psyche, cut her loose from conventional cares and thought processes in a way that ultimately contributed to her death.

I was raised Catholic, so I'm well versed in the story of Job, but Karen's string of bad luck in the months before her death bothered me. I know luck, both good and bad, runs in streaks. I know bad streaks often run a long, long time, with one tragedy perpetuating the next, until all of them, major and minor, seem to be going off like a string of firecrackers on the Fourth of July. I know that sometimes bad shit simply happens to good people. And yet, if it started with Cody Falk, I decided, then maybe it hadn't stopped on his end. Yes, we'd scared him witless, but people are stupid, particularly predators. Maybe he'd gotten over his fear and decided to come at Karen from her flank, instead of head-on, destroy her fragile world for siccing Bubba and me on him.

Cody, I determined, would need a second visit.

First, though, I wanted to talk to the cops investigating Karen's death, see if they'd tell me anything that could help keep me from dropping in on Cody halfcocked.

"Detectives Thomas and Stapleton," Devin told me. "I'll reach out, tell 'em to talk to you. Give it a few days, though."

"I'd love to make contact quicker."

"And I'd love to take a shower with Cameron Diaz. Neither's going to happen, though."

So, I waited. And waited. I eventually left a few messages and bit back on my urge to drive over to Cody Falk's and beat answers out of him before I knew the proper questions to ask.

In the middle of all the waiting, I got restless and copied down Karen Nichols's last known address from her file, noted from the newspaper accounts that she'd been employed in the Catering Department of the Four Seasons Hotel, and left the office.

Karen Nichols's former roommate was named Dara Goldklang. While we spoke in the living room she'd shared with Karen for two years, Dara ran a treadmill facing the windows as if she were in the final lap of a track meet. She wore a white sports bra and black spandex shorts and kept looking back over her shoulder at me.

"Until David was hurt," she said, "Karen was barely here. Always over at David's. Pretty much just picked up her mail here, did some laundry, took it to David's for another week. She was moony over that guy. Lived for him."

"What was she like? I only met her once."

"Karen was sweet," she said, then followed that almost immediately with: "Does my butt look big to you?"

"No."

"You didn't look." She puffed her cheeks as she ran. "Come on. Look. My boyfriend says it's getting big."

I turned my head. Her ass was the size of a crab apple. If her boyfriend thought it was big, I wondered on which twelve-year-old he'd seen a smaller one.

"Your boyfriend's wrong." I sat back in some kind of red leather beanbag thing supported by a glass bowl and base. It may have been the ugliest piece of furniture I'd ever seen. It was definitely the ugliest I'd ever sat in.

"He says I need to tone up my calves."

I glanced at the muscles in the backs of her calves. They looked like flat stones bulging under the skin.

"And get a boob job," she puffed. She turned back toward me so I could glimpse the orbs under her sports bra. They were about the size, shape, and firmness of two regulation baseballs.

"What's your boyfriend do?" I asked. "Physical training?"

She laughed, and her tongue fell over her lower lip. "Puh-lease. He's a trader on State Street. *His* body is for shit, like he's got a little Buddha under his abs, stringy arms, ass starting to sag."

"But yet he wants you to be perfect?"

She nodded.

"Seems hypocritical," I said.

She held up her hands. "Yeah, well, I make twenty-two-five as a restaurant manager, and he drives a Ferrari. How shallow of me, right?" She shrugged. "I like the furniture in his condo. I like eating at Cafe Louis and Aujourd'hui. I like this watch he bought me."

She held up her wrist so I could see it. Stainless steel and sporty, and maybe ran a grand or more, all so you could be perfectly accessorized while you worked up a sweat.

"Very nice," I said.

"What do you drive?"

"An Escort," I lied.

"See?" She wagged a finger over her shoulder at me. "You're cute and all, but your clothes, that car?" She shook her head. "Ah, no. Couldn't sleep with a guy like you."

"Wasn't aware I'd asked."

She swiveled her head back in my direction, stared at me as fresh dots of perspiration broke out on her forehead. Then she laughed.

I laughed back.

What a hoot it was in there for thirty seconds or so.

"So, Dara," I said, "why'd Karen lose her place in this apartment?"

She turned away, stared back out the window. "Well, it was sad, right? Karen, like I said, was sweet. She was also kinda, well, naive if you know what I mean. She had no practical reality touchstones."

"Practical reality touchstones," I said slowly.

She nodded. "That's what my therapist calls them—you know, the things we all have that ground us, and not just people but tenants and—"

"Tenets?" I asked.

"Huh?"

"Tenets," I said. "Tenants are people who live in your building. Tenets are principles, articles of faith."

"Right. That's what I said. Tenets and principles and, you know, the little sayings and ideals and philosophies we hold on to to get us through the day. Karen didn't have any of those. She just had David. He was her life."

"So, when he got hurt . . ."

She nodded. "Hey, don't get me wrong, I understand how traumatic it was for her." Her back had picked up a sheen of perspiration that made her skin glow in the afternoon sun. "I was filled with sympathy. I cried for her. But after a *month*, it's like, Life Goes On."

"That would be a tenet?"

She looked over her shoulder to see if I was fucking with her. I kept my gaze even and empathetic.

She nodded. "But Karen, she just kept sleeping all day, walking around in yesterday's clothes. Sometimes, you could smell her. She just, well, she just fell apart. You know? And it was sad, broke my heart, but again, like, Get Over It."

Tenet number two, I figured.

"Okay? I even tried to hook her up."

"On dates?" I asked.

"Yeah." She laughed. "I mean, okay, David was great. But *David* is a *vegetable*. I mean, hel-lo! Knock all you want, nobody's home anymore. There are other fish in the sea. This ain't *Romeo and Juliet*. Life is real. Life is hard. So, I'm going, Karen, you got to get out there and see some guys. A good lay maybe would have, I dunno, cleared her head."

She looked back over her shoulder at me as she pressed a button on the treadmill console several times and the rubber belt below her feet gradually slowed to the pace of geriatric mall-walker. Her strides became longer, slower, and looser.

"Was I wrong?" she asked the window.

I let the question pass unanswered. "So, Karen's depressed, she's sleeping all day. Did she miss work?"

Dara Goldklang nodded. "That's why she got shit-canned. Blew off too many shifts. When she did go in, she looked wrung-out wet, if you know what I'm saying—split ends, no makeup, runs in her stockings."

"Heavens to Murgatroid," I said.

"Look, I told her. I did."

The treadmill wound down to a full stop, and Dara Goldklang stepped off, wiped her face and throat with a towel, drank some water from a plastic bottle. She lowered the bottle, lips still pursed, and locked eyes with me.

Maybe she was trying to get past my clothes and the car she thought I drove. Maybe she was looking to slum, clear her head via the method to which she seemed accustomed.

I said, "So she lost her job, and the money started to run out."

She tilted her head back and opened her mouth, poured some water in without her lips ever touching the bottle. She swallowed a few times, then lowered her chin, dabbed her lips with a corner of the towel.

"She was out of money before that. There was something screwy with David's medical insurance."

"What kind of screwy?"

She shrugged. "Karen was trying to pay some of his medical bills. They were huge. It wiped her out. And I said, you know, a couple of months not paying rent is all right. I don't *like* it, but I understand. But the third month, I said, you know, she had to go if she couldn't come up with it. I mean, we were friends and all—good friends—but this is life."

"Life," I said. "Sure."

Her eyes widened to coasters as she nodded at me. "The thing is, life, right? I mean, it's a train. It just keeps moving, and you have to run ahead of it, okay. You stop to catch your breath too long? It runs you over. So, sooner or later, you have to stop being so other-centered and Look Out for Number One."

"Good tenet," I said.

She smiled. She walked over to the ugly chair and lowered her hand toward me. "Need help getting up?"

"No, I'm fine. Chair's not that bad."

She laughed and her tongue fell over her lower lip again, like Jordan's when he'd drive for a layup.

"I wasn't talking about the chair."

I stood and she stepped back. "I know you weren't, Dara."

She put a hand at the small of her back, leaned into it as she took another sip of water. "And the problem," she said in a singsong, "lies, ah, where, exactly?"

"I got standards," I said as I walked to the door.

"About strangers?"

"About humans," I said, and let myself out.

6

The inside of Pickup on South Street, David Wetterau's fledgling film equipment supply company, was a warehouse littered with 16-millimeter cameras, 35-millimeter cameras, lenses, lights, light filters, tripods, dollies, and dolly tracks. Small tables were bolted to the floor and spaced out twenty feet apart along the east wall, where young guys worked on checking in equipment, while along the west wall, a young guy and a young woman rolled a mammoth, crane-shaped dolly along tracks, the woman sitting up top, working a wheel that rose from the center like one you'd find in a truck driver's cab.

The employees or student interns, both male and female, were a collection of baggy shorts, wrinkled T-shirts, canvas sneakers or battered Doc Martens with no socks, and at least one earring each glinting from heads that were either submerged under mountains of hair or had none at all. I liked them right off, probably because they reminded me of the kids I'd hung out with in college. Low-key dudes and dudettes with the fever of artistic ambition in their pupils, motor mouths when they got drunk, and an encyclopedic knowledge of the city's best used-record stores, used-book stores, used-clothing stores—just about any purveyor of secondhand goods.

Pickup on South Street had been founded by David Wetterau and Ray Dupuis. Ray Dupuis was one of the guys with shaved heads, and the only thing that separated him from the others was that he seemed a few years older and his wrinkled T-shirt was silk. He propped his Chuck Taylors up on a scarred desk that had been hastily placed in the middle of all the chaos, leaned back in a ratty leather office chair, and spread his arms at the lunacy around him.

"My kingdom." He gave me a wry smile.

"Lotta work?"

He fingered the fleshy, dark pockets under his eyes. "Uh, yeah."

Two guys came bounding through the warehouse. They ran side by side, pacing themselves, even though they seemed to be running at top speed. The one on the left had what looked like a combination of a camera and metal detector strapped to his chest and a heavy belt around his waist with bulging pockets that reminded me of a soldier's ammo and supply belt.

"Get a little ahead of me, a little ahead of me," the cameraman said.

The kid on the outside did.

"Now! Stop and turn! Stop and turn!"

The other kid put the brakes on, then spun and started running back the other way, and the cameraman whipped in place and tracked him.

Then he stopped. He threw up his hands and screamed, "Aaron! You call that racking?"

A collection of rags with a spillage of dark hair and a dripping Fu Manchu looked up from a boxy remote in his hands. "I'm racking, Eric. I'm racking. It's the lights, dude."

"Bullshit!" Eric screamed. "The lights are fine."

Ray Dupuis smiled and turned his head away from Eric, who looked like his head was about to explode with rage.

"Steadicam guys," Dupuis said. "They're like kickers in the NFL. Very specialized talent, very sensitive personalities."

"That thing strapped to his chest is a Steadicam?" I said.

He nodded.

"I always thought it was on wheels."

"Nope."

"So the opening shot of *Full Metal Jacket*," I said, "that's one guy moving around those barracks with a camera strapped to his chest?"

"Sure. Same with that shot in *GoodFellas*. You think they could have rolled a machine down those steps?"

"I never thought of it that way."

He nodded at the kid holding the boxy remote. "And that's the focus puller over there. He's trying to rack focus by remote."

I looked back at the young guys as they prepped to try the shot again, fine-tune whatever needed fine-tuning.

I couldn't think of anything else to say but, "Cool."

"So you're a cinephile, Mr. Kenzie?"

I nodded. "Mostly the older ones, to be honest."

He raised his eyebrows. "So you know where our name comes from?"

"Of course," I said. "Sam Fuller, 1953. Awful movie, great title."

He smiled. "That's just what David said." He pointed at Eric as Eric rushed by again. "That's what David was supposed to pick up the day he was hurt."

"The Steadicam?"

He nodded. "That's why I don't get it."

"Get what?"

"The accident. He wasn't supposed to be there."

"On the corner of Congress and Purchase?"

"Yeah."

"Where was he supposed to be?"

"Natick."

"Natick," I said. "Birthplace of Doug Flutie and girls with big hair?"

He nodded. "And the Natick Mall, of course."

"Of course. But Natick's about twenty miles away."

"Yup. And that's where the Steadicam was." He gestured with his head at it. "That piece of equipment makes most of the stuff we have here—all of which costs a goddamn fortune—look cheap. The guy in Natick was fire-saling it. Rock bottom. David *raced* out of here. But he never arrived. Next thing, he's back downtown on that corner." He pointed out the window in the direction of the financial district a few blocks north.

"You tell the police this?"

He nodded. "They got back to me a few days later, said they had absolutely no doubt it was an accident. I spoke at length to a detective, and I came away pretty convinced they were right. David tripped in broad daylight in front of something like forty witnesses. So I guess I don't question that what happened to him was an accident, I'd just like to know what the hell made him turn back from Natick before he arrived and come back into the city. I told the detective this, and he said his job was to determine whether it was an accident, and on that score, he was satisfied. Everything else was 'irrelevant.' His word."

"You?"

He rubbed his smooth head. "David wasn't irrelevant. David was just a terrific guy. I'm not saying he was perfect. He had flaws, okay, but—"

"Such as?"

"Well, he had no head for the nuts-and-bolts of hard business, and he was a pretty serious flirt when Karen wasn't around."

"Did he fool around on her?" I asked.

"No." He shook his head emphatically. "No, it was more like he enjoyed knowing he still had it. He liked the attention of pretty women, knowing they dug his action. Yeah, it was childish, and down the road maybe all that playing with fire would have gotten him burned, but he truly loved Karen, and he was determined to stay faithful to her."

"With his body, if not his mind," I said.

"Exactly." He smiled, then sighed. "Look, I bankrolled this company with Daddy's money, okay? I signed off on the loans. Without my name, no way it would have got off the ground. And I have a passion for it, and I'm not dumb, but David, he had talent. He was the face of this company, and the soul. People did business with us because David went out and made the contacts. David reached out to the independent film companies, the industrials, the commercials guys. It was David who convinced Warner Brothers that they should get their Panther dolly through us when they were shooting that Costner movie here last year, and once they liked the dolly they came back to us for replacement thirty-fives, replacement lights, filters, booms." He chuckled. "You name it, they were always breaking something. Then they began to transfer their raw stock on our Rank when theirs went down, and cut their second-unit stuff on our Avids. And it was David who pulled that money in. Not me. David had charm and pizzazz, but more than that, you believed him. His word was his bond, and he never fucked anyone on a deal. David would have made this company. Without him?" He looked around the room, gave all that youth and energy and equipment a small shrug and a sad smile. "We'll probably go under within eighteen months."

"Who profits if you do?"

He thought about it for a bit, drummed his palms on his bare knees. "A few rival companies, I suppose, but not in any huge way. We weren't taking all that much business, so I'm not sure we'll leave all that much business to scoop up if we go under."

"You got the Warner Brothers gig."

"True. But Eight Millimeter got the Branagh film Fox Searchlight did here, and Martini Shot landed the Mamet film. I mean, we all had our slices of pie, and none were too big or too little. I can tell you that nobody's going to make millions or even hundreds of thousands because David's no longer on the scene."

He placed his hands behind his head and looked up at the steel rafters and exposed heating pipes. "It would have been nice, though. As David used to say, we might not have gotten rich, but we might have gotten comfy."

"What about the insurance?"

He used his hands to push his head back toward me, looked into my eyes with his elbows framing his face. "What about it?"

"I heard Karen Nichols was going broke trying to pay David's medical bills."

"And that led you to believe . . . ?"

"That he wasn't insured."

Ray Dupuis studied me, his eyelids hooded, his body very still. I waited, but after a minute of his staring, I held out my hands.

"Look, Ray, I'm not after anyone in this place. You had to do some creative financing to keep afloat? Fine. Or you—"

"It was David," he said quietly.

"What?"

He dropped his heels off the desk and his hands fell from behind his head.

"David sent a—" His face screwed up as if he were chewing tabs of acid, and he looked away for a minute. When he spoke again, his voice was almost a whisper. "You learn not to trust. Particularly in this business where everyone's charming, everyone's your friend, everyone loves you until you give them the bill. David, I swear to Christ, I had always believed was different. I trusted him."

"But?"

" 'But.' " He snorted at the word, looked back up at

the rafters with a defeated grin. "About six weeks before he was hurt, David canceled the insurance policy. Not on the equipment, just on the employees, himself included. The quarterly payment was due, and instead of paying it, he canceled. I'm sure he was rolling the dice—you know, borrowing from Peter to pay Paul, planning to move the money someplace else, maybe into the Steadicam."

"Was money that tight?"

"Oh, yeah. My personal finances are tight, and Daddy's locked the vault for a while. We have a lot of outstanding bills sitting on our clients' desks, and once they're paid, we'll be okay, but the last few months have been lean. So, sure, I can see why David did it. I just don't understand why he didn't tell me, and why the money he saved never left the company bank account."

"It's still there?"

He nodded. "It was when he got hurt. I paid the insurance with it, bottomed out the rest of the account putting twenty percent down on the Steadicam, taking out a loan for the rest."

"But you're sure it was David who contacted the insurance agency?"

For a few minutes, he seemed unsure whether he should kick me out of the office or come all the way clean. In the end, he chose the latter, and I was glad, because I doubt I could have lived with the indignity of having my ass chucked to the street by a group of guys who'd collectively seen *Star Wars* more times than they'd had sex.

He glanced around to make sure no one in the warehouse was paying attention to us, and then he used a small key to unlock a lower desk drawer. After rifling through it for a few moments, he withdrew a single sheet of paper and handed it across the desk to me.

It was a copy of a letter from Wetterau sent to their insurance company. It expressly stated that Wetterau, Chief Financial Officer of Pickup on South Street, wished to cancel the HMO coverage of all employees, including himself. At the bottom, he'd signed it.

Ray Dupuis said, "The insurance company sent that to me when I filed a claim on David's behalf. They refused to pay a dime. I came up with what I could, Karen came up with what she could before she stopped coming up with anything at all, and the bill keeps growing. David had no family, so ultimately, I guess, the state will pay for it, but Karen and I were both afraid he'd end up warehoused in some shitty facility, so we tried to get him first-class care for a while, but it was just too much for two people ultimately."

"Did you know Karen well?"

He nodded several times. "Sure."

"What'd you think of her?"

"She's the girl the hero gets at the end of the movie. You know the one? Not the hot, sexy babe who ultimately turns out to be trouble, but the good girl. The one who'd never write you a Dear John if you were off at war. The one who's always there, you just have to be smart enough to see it. Barbara Bel Geddes in *Vertigo*, if only Jimmy Stewart had been smart enough to see past her glasses."

"Yeah."

"It was kinda surreal."

"How so?"

"Well, they don't make women like Karen except in the movies."

"Are you saying it was an act?"

"No. I was just never sure when I was with Karen if she knew who she was. If she'd worked so hard at becoming an ideal that she lost the person inside of her."

"And once David was hurt?"

He shrugged. "She held on for a while, and then she cracked, man. I mean, it was horrible to see. She'd come in here, and I'd want to ask for her license to make sure I was dealing with the same person. She was drunk mostly, high. She was a fucking mess. It was like—what happens to you when you live your whole life like a movie, and the movie ends?"

I didn't say anything.

"It's like those child actors," he said. "They play a part as long as they can, but they're fighting a battle against hormonal evolution and they can't win. One day they wake up, they're no longer kids, they're no longer movie stars, there're no parts out there for them, and they drown."

"So, Karen?"

His eyes filled for a moment and he blew air out through his mouth in a loud push. "Oh, Christ, she broke my heart. All our hearts. She lived for David. Anyone who saw them for two seconds knew that. And when David was hurt, she died. It just took her body four months to follow."

We sat in silence for a bit, and then I handed him back the letter to the insurance company. He held it lightly in his hands and stared down at it. Eventually he smiled bitterly.

"No 'P,'" he said, and shook his head.

"What's that?"

He turned the letter in his hands so I could see it. "David's middle name was Phillip. When we started this company, all of a sudden he signed his name with a big 'P' in the middle. Only on company documents and company checks, never anything else. I used to say the 'P' was for 'pretentious,' rag his ass a little bit about it."

I looked at the signature. "But there's no 'P' there."

He nodded, then dropped the letter in the drawer. "I guess he wasn't feeling particularly pretentious that day."

"Ray."

"Yeah?"

"Could I have a copy of that and something you have with his signature that *does* have the 'P'?"

He shrugged. "Sure." He found a memo David had written and signed with a wide, looping "P."

I followed him to a grimy Xerox machine, and he placed the letter under the lid.

"What're you thinking?" he asked me.

"I'm not sure yet."

He pulled the copy out of the tray and handed it to me. "It's just a 'P,' Mr. Kenzie." He made a copy of the memo, gave it to me.

I nodded. "You got something with your signature on it?"

"Of course." He led me back to the desk, handed me a memo he'd written and signed.

"You know what the trick to forgery is?" I said as I took the memo and turned it upside down.

"Good handwriting?"

I shook my head. "Gestalt."

"Gestalt."

"You see the signature as a shape, not a collection of singular letters."

Carefully, under his overturned signature, I used a pen to copy the shape I saw above the pen point. When I finished, I turned it around, showed it to him.

He looked at it, opened his mouth, and raised his eyebrows. "That's not bad. Wow."

"And that's my first try, Ray. Think what I could do with practice."

7

I called Devin again, woke him up.

"Any luck with Ms. Diaz?"

"None. Chicks, man, you know?"

"I can't get Detectives Thomas or Stapleton to return my calls."

"Stapleton was one of Doyle's golden boys, that's why."

"Ah."

"You could see Hoffa having coffee in a diner, and Stapleton wouldn't take your call."

"Thomas?"

"She's less predictable. And she's working solo today."

"Lucky me."

"Yeah, well, you Micks. What can I say? Hang on. Let me find out where she is."

I waited two or three minutes, and then he came back on the line. "You owe me, or do I even have to mention that?"

"It's a given," I said.

"It's always a given." Devin sighed. "Detective Thomas is working a death-by-stupidity in Back

Bay. Go to the alley between Newbury and Comm Ave."

"Cross blocks?"

"Dartmouth and Exeter. Don't fuck with her. She's hard-core, man. Eat you, spit you out, and never even break her stride."

Detective Joella Thomas stepped out of the alley at the Dartmouth Street end and crab-walked under some crime scene tape, stripping off a pair of latex gloves as she went. As she slid out from under the other side of the yellow tape, she straightened from her crouch and snapped one glove clear of her fingertips, shook the white talc off her ebony skin. She called to a guy sitting on the bumper of the forensics van.

"Larry, he's yours now."

Larry didn't even look up from his sports page. "He still dead?"

"Getting more so." Joella pulled off the other glove, noticed me standing beside her, but kept her gaze on Larry.

"He tell you anything?" Larry turned a page of the paper.

Joella Thomas rolled a Life Saver from side to side in her mouth and nodded. "Said the 'afterlife'?"

"Yeah?"

"Ain't nothing but a house party."

"Good news. I'll tell the wife." Larry closed his paper, tossed it into the van behind him. "Fucking Sox, Detective, you know what I'm saying?"

Joella Thomas shrugged. "I'm a hockey fan."

"Fucking Bruins, then, too." Larry turned his back to us and foraged in the forensics van.

Joella Thomas started to turn away, then seemed to remember my presence. She rolled her head back slowly in my direction, looked at me through the dusky gold lenses of her rimless sunglasses. "What?"

"Detective Thomas?" I proffered my hand.

She gave the fingers a quick squeeze and squared her shoulders so that she was facing me.

"Patrick Kenzie. Devin Amronklin may have mentioned me."

She cocked her head and I heard the Life Saver rattle against a back tooth. "Couldn't come by the station, Mr. Kenzie?"

"I thought I'd speed things up."

She placed her hands in the pockets of her suit jacket, leaned back on her heels. "Don't like being in a police station since you brought down a cop, that it, Mr. Kenzie?"

"The cells do seem that much closer."

"Uh-huh." She stepped back as Larry and two other forensics cops walked between us.

"Detective," I said, "I'm real sorry an investigation of mine led to the arrest of a fellow—"

"Blah, blah, blah." Joella Thomas waved a long hand in front of my face. "Don't care about him, Mr. Kenzie. He was old school, old boy network." She turned toward the curb. "I look old school to you?"

"Anything but."

Joella Thomas was a slim six feet tall. She wore an olive double-breasted suit over a black T-shirt. Her gold shield hung from black nylon cord around

her neck and matched the gold of the three hoop
earrings in her left earlobe. The right lobe was as
bare and smooth as her shaven head.

As we stood on the sidewalk, the deepening heat
and morning dew rose off the pavement in a fine
mist. It was early Sunday morning and the yuppies'
Krups coffeemakers were probably just beginning to
percolate, the dog walkers just arriving at the doors.

Joella stripped off a twist of foil on her roll of
Life Savers and removed one. "Mint?"

She extended the roll and I took one.

"Thanks."

She placed the roll back in the pocket of her suit
jacket. She looked back in the alley, then up at the
roof.

I followed her gaze. "Jumper?"

She shook her head. "Faller. Went on the roof to
shoot up during a party. Sat on the edge, spiked, and
looked up at the stars." She pantomimed someone
leaning too far back. "Must have seen a comet."

"Ouch," I said.

Joella Thomas tore off a piece of her scone and
dipped it in her oversize mug of tea before sliding it
onto her tongue. "So you want to know about Karen
Nichols."

"Yup."

She chewed, then swallowed a sip of tea. "You
worried she was pushed?"

"Was she?"

"Nope." She sat back in her chair, watched an old
man toss small pieces of bread to some pigeons outside. The old man's face was pinched and small and

his nose was hooked so that he looked a lot like the birds he fed. We were in Jorge's Cafe de Jose, a block from the crime scene. Jorge's served nine different types of scones, a variety of fifteen muffins, squares of tofu, and seemed to have cornered the market on bran.

Joella Thomas said, "It was suicide." She shrugged. "It was clean—death by gravity. No signs of struggle, no scuff marks from other shoes anywhere near the place she jumped from. Hell, it doesn't get any cleaner."

"And her suicide made sense?"

"In what way?"

"She'd been melancholy over the boyfriend's accident, et cetera?"

"One assumes."

"And that would be enough?"

"Oh, I see what you're getting at." She nodded, then shook her head. "Look, suicides? They rarely make sense. Tell you something else, most people who do it don't leave a note. Maybe ten percent. The rest, they just off themselves, leave everyone wondering."

"There must be a common thread or two."

"Between victims?" Another sip of tea, another shake of the head. "All of them, obviously, are depressed. But who isn't? Do you wake up every day thinking, Wow, it certainly is just super to be alive?"

I chuckled and shook my head.

"Didn't think so. Neither do I. How about your past?"

"Huh?"

"Your past." She waved a spoon in my direction,

then stirred her tea. "You completely settled with everything that's ever happened to you in your past, or are there some things—things you don't talk about—that bug you, make you wince when you think about them twenty years later?"

I considered the question. Once, when I was very young—six or seven—and I'd just taken several swats of my father's belt, I walked into the bedroom I shared with my sister, saw her kneeling by her dolls, and punched her in the back of the head as hard as I could. The look on her face—shock, fear, but also a sudden weary resignation—was a look that drove itself into my brain like a nail. Even now, more than twenty-five years later, her nine-year-old face jumped out at me in a Back Bay coffee shop and I felt a wave of shame so total it threatened to crumple me in its clenched fist.

And that was just one memory. The list was long, accrued over a lifetime of mistakes and bad judgment and impulse.

"I can see it in your face," Joella Thomas said. "You got pieces of your past you'll never be reconciled with."

"You?"

She nodded. "Oh, yeah." She leaned back in her chair, looked up at the ceiling fan above us, exhaled loudly. "Oh, yeah," she said again. "The thing is, we all do. We all carry our past and we all mess up our present and we all have days we don't see much point struggling on toward our future. Suicides are just people who commit. They say, 'More of *this*? The hell with that. Time to get off the bus.' And most times you never even know what straw it was that broke their back. I've seen some that, I mean, seemed to make *no* sense. A young mother in Brighton last year? All accounts, loved her husband, her kids, her dog. Had a great job. Great relationship with her parents. No money worries. So, all right, she's the bridesmaid in her best friend's wedding. After the wedding, she goes home, hangs herself in the bathroom, still wearing that ugly chiffon dress. Now, was it something about the wedding that got to her? Was she secretly in love with the groom? Or maybe the bride? Or did she remember her own wedding and all the hopes she'd had, and while watching her friends exchange vows, she was forced to face how cold and unlike her fantasy her own marriage was? Or did she suddenly just get tired of living this long-ass life?" Joella gave me a slow roll of her shoulders. "I don't know. No one does. I can tell you that not one person who knew her—not one—saw it coming."

My coffee had cooled, but I took a sip anyway.

"Mr. Kenzie," Joella Thomas said, "Karen Nichols killed herself. That's not debatable. You waste your time looking for why—what good's that going to do?"

"You never knew her," I said. "This wasn't normal."

"Nothing's normal," Joella Thomas said.

"You find out where she lived her last two months?"

She shook her head. "Some landlord will call it in when he needs to rent the apartment."

"Until then?"

"Until then, she's dead. She don't mind the delay."

I rolled my eyes.

She rolled hers back at me. She leaned forward in her chair and studied me with those ghostly irises.

"Let me ask you something."

"Sure," I said.

"With all due respect, because you seem like a good guy."

"Shoot."

"You met Karen Nichols, what, once?"

"Once, yeah."

"And you believe me when I say she killed herself, all alone, no help?"

"I do."

"So, Mr. Kenzie, why in the hell do you care what happened to her *before* she offed herself?"

I sat back in my chair. "You ever feel like you screwed up and want to make things right?"

"Sure."

"Karen Nichols," I said, "left a message on my answering machine four months ago. She asked me to call her back. I didn't."

"So?"

"So the reason I didn't wasn't good enough."

She slipped on her sunglasses, then allowed them to slide down the bridge of her nose. She peered over the tops of the rims at me. "And you think you're so cool—do I got this?—that if you'd just returned her call, she'd be alive today?"

"No. I think I owe her a little for blowing her off for a bad reason."

She stared at me, her mouth slightly open.

"You think I'm nuts."

"I think you're nuts. She was a grown woman. She—"

"Her fiancé gets hit by a car. Was that an accident?"

She nodded. "I checked. There were forty-six people around him when he tripped and they all say that's what happened—he tripped. A patrol car was parked a block away on Atlantic and Congress. It moved on the sound of impact, reached the scene roughly twelve seconds after the accident. The guy whose car hit Wetterau was a tourist, name of Steven Kearns. He was so devastated, he still sends flowers to Wetterau's hospital bed every day."

"Okay," I said. "Why'd Karen Nichols fall completely apart—lose her job, her apartment?"

"Hallmarks of depression," Joella Thomas said. "You get so locked into your own funk, you forget your responsibilities to the real world."

A pair of middle-aged women with matching Versace sunglasses pushed up on top of their heads paused near our table, trays in hand, and looked around for an open seat. One of them glanced at my near-empty cup of coffee and Joella's crumbs and sighed loudly.

"Nice sigh," Joella said. "Come from practice?"

The woman seemed not to have heard her. She looked at her friend. Her friend sighed.

"It's catching," I said.

One woman said to the other, "I find certain behaviors inappropriate, don't you?"

Joella gave me a big smile. " 'Inappropriate,' " she said. "They want to call me a coon, so they say 'inappropriate' instead. Fits their self-image." She turned her head up at the women, who looked everywhere but at us. "Don't it?"

The women sighed some more.

"Mmm," Joella said as if they'd confirmed something. "Shall we go?" She stood.

I looked at her crumbs and teacup, my coffee cup.

"Leave it," she said. "The sisters here will get it." She caught the eye of the first sigher. "Ain't that right, honey?"

The woman looked back toward the counter.

"Yeah," Joella Thomas said with a broad smile, "that's right. Girl power, Mr. Kenzie, it's a beautiful thing."

When we reached the street, the women were still standing by the table, holding their trays, waiting for valet service apparently, practicing their sighs.

We walked a bit, the morning breeze smelling of jasmine, the street beginning to fill with people juggling armloads of Sunday newspaper with white bags of coffee and muffins, cups of juice.

"Why'd she hire you in the first place?" Joella said.

"She was being stalked."

"You dealt with the stalker?"

"Uh-huh."

"You think he got the message?"

"I did at the time." I stopped and she stopped with me. "Detective, was Karen Nichols raped or assaulted in the months before she died?"

Joella Thomas searched my face for something— hints of dementia possibly, the fever of a man on a self-destructive quest.

"If she was," she said, "would you go after her stalker again?"

"No."

"Really? What would you do?"

"I'd relay my information to an officer of the law."

She smiled broadly, a stunning flash of some of the whitest teeth I've ever seen. "Uh-huh."

"Really."

She nodded to herself. "The answer is no. She wasn't raped or assaulted, to the best of my knowledge."

"Okay."

"But, Mr. Kenzie?"

"Yeah."

"And if what I'm about to tell you leaks to the press, I'll destroy you."

"Understood."

"I mean, annihilate you."

"Got it."

She stuffed her hands in her pockets, leaned her tall frame back against a lamppost. "So you don't think I'm just a chummy cop, blabs away to every PI in the city, that guy you took down on the force last year?"

I waited.

"He didn't like women cops and he sure as hell didn't like black women cops, and if you *did* stand up for yourself, he told everyone you were a lesbian. When you took him down, there was a lot of reshuffling in the department and I got transferred out of his department and into Homicide."

"Where you belonged."

"Which I *deserved*. So, let's just say what I'm about to pass on to you is a little payback. Okay?"

"Okay."

"Your dead friend was picked up twice for solicitation in Springfield."

"She was hooking?"

She nodded. "She was a prostitute, Mr. Kenzie, yeah."

8

Karen Nichols's mother and stepfather, Carrie and Christopher Dawe, lived in Weston in a sprawling colonial replica of Jefferson's Monticello. It sat on a street of similarly sprawling homes with lawns the size of Vancouver that glistened with dew from gently hissing sprinklers. I'd taken the Porsche and had it waxed and washed before I arrived, and I'd dressed in the sort of casual summer attire the kids on *90210* seemed to favor—a light cashmere vest over a spanking new white T-shirt, Ralph Lauren khakis, and tan loafers. The getup would have gotten my ass kicked in maybe three or four seconds if I'd walked down Dorchester Ave., but out here, it seemed to be de rigueur. If I'd only had the five-hundred-dollar shades and wasn't Irish, someone probably would have invited me to play golf. But that's Weston for you—it didn't get to be the priciest suburb of a pricey city without having some standards.

As I walked up the slate path that led to the Dawes' front door, they opened it wide, stood with arms slung around each other's lower backs and waved to me like Robert Young and Jane Wyatt on a nineteen-inch black-and-white.

"Mr. Kenzie?" Dr. Dawe said.

"Yes, sir. Good to meet you." I reached the doorway and received two firm handshakes.

"How was the drive?" Mrs. Dawe said. "You took the Pike, I hope?"

"Yes, ma'am. It was fine. No traffic."

"Terrific," Dr. Dawe said. "Come on in, Mr. Kenzie. Come on in."

He wore a faded T-shirt over rumpled khakis. His dark hair and trim goatee were flecked with distinguished gray and he had a giving smile. He didn't fit my image of the mercurial Mass General surgeon type with the bulging stock portfolio and a God complex. He looked more like he should be giving a poetry reading in Inman Square, sipping herbal tea and quoting Ferlinghetti.

She wore a black-and-gray-checkered oxford over black stretch pants and black sandals, and her hair was a lustrous dark cranberry. She was at least fifty, or so I assumed given what I knew about Karen Nichols, but she looked ten years younger and in her casual clothes made me think of a college girl at her first sorority sleepover, drinking wine from the bottle and sitting cross-legged on the floor.

They whisked me through a marble foyer bathed in amber light, past a white staircase that curved gracefully up and to the left like a swan craning its head, and into a cozy dual office space with exposed cherry beams on the ceiling, muted Orientals on the floor, and a sense of aged plumpness in the leather captain's chairs and matching sofa and armchairs.

The room was large, but it seemed small at first, because it was painted a dark salmon and precisely stuffed with books and CDs and a triumphantly kitschy half canoe that had been stood upright and turned into a case to hold knickknacks and paperbacks with weathered spines and a row of actual 33⅓ rpm albums, mostly from the sixties—Dylan and Joan Baez sharing space with Donovan and the Byrds; Peter, Paul & Mary; and Blind Faith. Fishing rods and hats and painstakingly detailed model schooners shared space on the walls and the shelves and desktops, and a faded farm table stood behind the couch under what I believe were original paintings by Pollock and Basquiat and a lithograph by Warhol. I had no problem with the Pollock and Basquiat, though I'd never replace the Marvin the Martian poster in my bedroom with either of them, but I sat in a position so I wouldn't have to look at the Warhol. I think Warhol is to art what Rush is to rock music, which is to say, I think he sucks.

Dr. Dawe's desk occupied the west corner, the hutch piled high with medical journals and texts, two of the model ships, microcassettes forming a pile around a microrecorder. Carrie Dawe's sat in the east corner, clean and minimalist save for a leather-bound notebook with a sterling silver pen on top and a creamy stack of typewritten paper to its right. Upon a second glance I realized both desks were handmade, constructed of Northern California redwood or Far Eastern teak, it was hard to tell in the soft, diffused light. Using the same process one used to build log cabins, the wood had been hand-carved and laid in place, then left to age and expand for a few years until the pieces melded to one another with more adherence and strength than could ever be accomplished with sheet metal and a blowtorch. Only then would it be sold. Through private auction, I'm sure. The faded farm table, upon second glance, wasn't faux rustic, it was truly rustic and French.

The room might have said cozy, but it said cozy with exquisite taste and a bottomless wallet.

I sat on one end of the sofa and Carrie Dawe took the other end, sitting cross-legged, as I'd somehow known she would, idly straightening the tassels on the summer afghan thrown over the back of the sofa as she considered me with soft green eyes.

Dr. Dawe settled into one of the captain's chairs and wheeled it over to the other side of the coffee table between us.

"So, Mr. Kenzie, my wife tells me you're a private investigator."

"Yes, sir."

"I don't think I've ever met one before." He stroked his goatee. "Honey?"

Carrie Dawe shook her head and crooked her index finger at me. "You're the first."

"Wow," I said. "Gosh."

Dr. Dawe rubbed his palms together and leaned forward. "What was your favorite case?"

I smiled. "There've been so many."

"Really? Well, come on, tell us about one."

"Actually, sir, I'd love to, but I'm slightly pressed for time and if it wouldn't trouble you both too much, I'd just like to ask some questions about Karen."

He swept his palm out over the coffee table. "Ask away, Mr. Kenzie. Ask away."

"How did you know my daughter?" Carrie Dawe asked softly.

I turned my head, met her green eyes, saw a glint of what might have been grief slide along the sheen of the pupils before vanishing.

"She hired me six months ago."

"Why was that?" she asked.

"She was being harassed by a man."

"And you made him stop?"

I nodded. "Yes, ma'am, I did."

"Well, thank you, Mr. Kenzie. I'm sure that helped Karen."

"Mrs. Dawe," I said, "did Karen have any enemies?"

She gave me a bewildered smile. "No, Mr. Kenzie. Karen was not the type of girl who made enemies. She was far too innocuous a creature for that."

Innocuous, I thought. Creature, I thought.

Carrie Dawe tilted her head in the direction of her husband and he picked up the ball.

"Mr. Kenzie, according to the police, Karen committed suicide."

"Yes."

"Is there any reason we should doubt the soundness of their conclusion?"

I shook my head. "None, sir."

"Uh-huh." He nodded to himself and seemed to drift for a minute, his eyes floating across my face and then around the room. Eventually he looked back into my eyes. He smiled and patted his knees as if he'd come to some sort of definitive decision. "I'd say some tea would be nice about now. Wouldn't you?"

There must have been an intercom system in the room, or the help waited right outside the door, because no sooner had he said it than the office door opened and a small woman entered holding a service tray with three delicate, brass Raj tea sets on top.

The woman was in her mid-thirties and dressed simply in T-shirt and shorts. Her hair was short and dull brown and rose in Astroturf spikes from her skull. Her skin was very pale and very bad, cheeks and chin sprayed with acne, neck blotchy, exposed arms dry and flaky.

She kept her eyes down and deposited the tray on the coffee table between us.

"Thank you, Siobhan," Mrs. Dawe said.

"Yes, ma'am. Will there be anything else?"

She had a brogue thicker than even my mother's had been. *Will* came out *wail*, *there* as *thur*, *else* as *ailse*. It only gets that thick in the North, in the gray cold towns where the refineries stand and the soot hovers like a cloud.

The Dawes didn't answer. They studiously removed the three parts of their respective Raj tea sets, the cream in the tin on top, the sugar below, the tea itself at the bottom, and fixed their drinks in cups so delicate I'd be afraid to sneeze in the same area code.

Siobhan waited, casting a quick furtive glance from under lowered lids in my direction as the heat rose up her pale skin.

Dr. Dawe finished preparing his tea with a long, scraping stir of the spoon around the edges of the china. He raised it to his lips, noticed I hadn't touched mine, then noticed Siobhan standing to my left.

"Siobhan," he said. "Good God, girl, you're excused." He laughed. "In fact, you look tired, kid. Why don't you take the afternoon off?"

"Yes, Doctor. Thank you."

"Thank *you*," he said. "This tea is wonderful."

She left the room with her shoulders hunched and her back bent, and once she'd closed the door behind her, Dr. Dawe said, "Great kid. Just great. Been with us pretty much since she stepped off the boat fourteen years ago. Yes . . ." he said softly. "So, Mr. Kenzie, we were wondering why you're investigating my stepdaughter's death if there's nothing to investigate?" He crinkled his nose over his teacup at me and then took a sip.

"Well, sir," I said as I lifted the cream container off the top, "I'm more interested in her life, actually, the last six months before she died."

"And why is that?" Carrie Dawe asked.

I poured some steaming tea into the cup, added a dash of sugar and some cream. Somewhere my mother rolled over in her grave—cream was for coffee, milk was for tea.

"She didn't strike me as the suicidal type," I said.

"Aren't we all?" Carrie Dawe asked.

I looked at her. "Ma'am?"

"Given the right—or should I say, the wrong—circumstances, aren't we all capable of suicide? A tragedy here, a tragedy there . . ."

Mrs. Dawe studied me over her teacup and I took

a sip from my own before I spoke. Dr. Dawe had been right, it was excellent tea, cream or no cream. Sorry, Mom.

"I'm sure we all are," I said, "but Karen's decline seemed, well, drastic."

"And you base this opinion on intimate knowledge?" Dr. Dawe said.

"Excuse me?"

He waved his cup at me. "Were you and my stepdaughter intimate?"

I gave him what I'm sure was a confused narrowing of my eyes, and he raised his eyebrows up and down gleefully.

"Come on, Mr. Kenzie, we don't speak ill of the dead around here, but we know Karen's sexual activities were, well, rampant in the months before she died."

"How do you know that?"

"She was coarse," Carrie Dawe said. "She spoke with sudden explicitness. She was drinking, using drugs. It would have been sadder if it weren't so clichéd. She even propositioned my husband once."

I looked back at Dr. Dawe and he nodded and placed his teacup back on the coffee table. "Oh, yes, Mr. Kenzie. Oh, yes. It was a veritable Tennessee Williams play every time Karen dropped by."

"I didn't see that part of her," I said. "I met her before David was hurt."

Carrie Dawe said, "And how did she strike you?"

"She struck me as kind and sweet and, yes, maybe a little too innocent for the world, but innocent just the same, Mrs. Dawe. Not the type of woman who'd jump naked off the Custom House."

Carrie Dawe pursed her lips and nodded. She looked off past me, past her husband, to a point somewhere high up on the wall. She took a sip of tea that was as loud as boots dropping through autumn leaves.

"Did he send you?" she said eventually.

"What? Who?"

She turned her head back, held me in those cool green eyes. "We're tapped out, Mr. Kenzie. Mention that, won't you?"

Very slowly, I said, "I have no idea what you're talking about."

She gave me a chuckle so light it sounded like a wind chime. "I'm sure you do."

But Dr. Dawe said, "Maybe not. Maybe not."

She looked at him and then they both looked at me and suddenly I was aware of a polite fever in their gazes that made me want to bug out of my skin, throw my skeleton through the window, go clacking like mad down the streets of Weston.

Dr. Dawe said, "If you're not here to extort, Mr. Kenzie, then why are you here?"

I turned to him and the light in his face seemed more like sickness. "I'm not sure everything that happened to your daughter in the months before she died was accidental."

He leaned forward, all grave seriousness. "Is it a 'hunch'? Something in your 'gut,' Starsky?" The manic twinkle returned to his eyes and he leaned back. "I'll give you forty-eight hours to solve the case, but if you can't, you'll be walking a beat in Roxbury come winter." He clapped his hands together. "How was that?"

"I'm just trying to find out why your daughter died."

"She died," Carrie Dawe said, "because she was weak."

"How's that, ma'am?"

She gave me a warm smile. "There's no mystery here, Mr. Kenzie. Karen was weak. A few things didn't go her way, and she cracked under the strain. My daughter, whom I gave birth to, was weak. She needed constant reassuring. She needed a psychiatrist for twenty years. She needed someone to hold her hand and tell her things would be all right. That the world worked." She held out her hands as if to say *Que sera, sera.* "Well, the world doesn't work. And Karen found that out. And it crushed her."

"Studies have shown," Christopher Dawe said with his head tilted toward his wife, "that suicide is an inherently passive-aggressive act. Have you heard that, Mr. Kenzie?"

"I have."

"That it's meant not so much to hurt the person who kills herself, but to hurt those she leaves behind." He poured some more tea into his cup. "Look at me, Mr. Kenzie."

I looked.

"I am a cerebral man. It has brought me no small measure of success." His dark eyes flashed with pride. "But, being a man of intellect, possibly I'm less attuned to the emotional needs of others. Possibly I could have been more emotionally supportive of Karen as she grew up."

His wife said, "You did a fine job, Christopher."

He waved her off. His eyes bore into my own. "I

knew Karen never got over the death of her natural father, and in hindsight, maybe I should have worked harder to assure her of my love. But we're flawed creatures, Mr. Kenzie. All of us. You, me, Karen. And life is regret. So my wife and I will, I promise you, regret often over the coming years the things we didn't do with our daughter. But that regret is not for the consumption of others. That regret is ours, sir. As this loss is ours. And whatever your odd quest is, I don't mind telling you, I find it kind of sad."

Mrs. Dawe said, "Mr. Kenzie, may I ask you a question?"

I looked back at her. "Sure."

She placed her teacup back on its saucer. "Is it necrophilia?"

"What?"

"This interest in my daughter?" She reached out and wiped her fingers along the top of the coffee table.

"Ah, no, ma'am."

"You're sure?"

"Positive."

"Then what is it, sir?"

"In all truth, ma'am, I'm not really sure."

"Please, Mr. Kenzie, you must have some idea." She smoothed the tails of her shirt against her thighs.

I felt awkward suddenly, felt the size of the room shrink around me. I felt powerless. To try to sum up my desire to right wrongs whose victim was well beyond benefiting from my efforts seemed impossible. How do you explain the pulls that dictate and often define your life in a few concise sentences?

"I'm waiting, Mr. Kenzie."

I raised a helpless arm to the absurdity of it. "She struck me as someone who played by all the rules."

"And what rules are those?" Dr. Dawe said.

"Society's, I guess. She worked the job, she opened the dual checking account with her fiancé and saved for the future. She dressed and spoke the way Madison Avenue tells us we're supposed to. She bought the Corolla when she wanted the Camry."

"You're losing me," Karen's mother said.

"She played by the rules," I said, "and she got stomped anyway. All I want to know is if any of that stomping wasn't accidental."

"Mmm-hmm," Carrie Dawe said. "Do you make much money tilting at windmills these days, Mr. Kenzie?"

I smiled. "It's a living."

She considered the tea service to her right. "She was buried in a closed casket."

"Ma'am?"

"Karen," she said. "Buried in a closed casket because what there was to look at wasn't fit for public display." She looked up at me and her eyes shone wetly in the gathering gray of the room. "Even her method of suicide, you see, was aggressive, meant to hurt us. She robbed her friends and family of the ability to view her one last time, to mourn her in the correct custom."

I had absolutely no idea what to say to that, so I kept quiet.

Carrie Dawe gave me a weary backward flutter of her hand. "When Karen lost David and then her job and finally her apartment, she came to us. For money. For a place to live. She was quite obviously doing drugs by this point. I refused—not Christopher, Mr. Kenzie, *I*—to subsidize her self-absorption and drug use. We continued to pay her psychiatrist's bills, but I determined that she should otherwise learn to stand on her own two feet. In retrospect, it may have been a mistake. But in the same circumstances, I think I would elect to follow the very same course again." She leaned forward, beckoned me to do the same. "Does that strike you as cruel?" she asked.

"Not necessarily," I said.

Dr. Dawe clapped his hands together again, the sound as loud as buckshot in the still room.

"Well, this has just been great! Can't think of the last time I had so much fun." He stood, held out his hand. "But, all good things must come to an end. Mr. Kenzie, we thank you for regaling us, and hope it won't be too many seasons before you and your minstrels return this way again."

He opened the door and stood by it.

His wife stayed where she was. She poured herself some more tea. She was stirring the sugar in when she said, "Do take care, Mr. Kenzie."

"Goodbye, Mrs. Dawe."

"Goodbye, Mr. Kenzie," she said in a lazy singsong as she poured her cream.

Dr. Dawe led me into the foyer and I noticed the photographs for the first time. They were on the far wall, and would have been to my left as I'd entered, but because I'd been blocked on either side by the Dawes and moving so quickly, blinded by their niceness and pep, I hadn't seen them.

There were at least twenty of them, and all were of a small dark-haired girl. Some were baby pictures, some were of the child as she grew. A younger Dr. and Mrs. Dawe were in most of them, holding the child, kissing the child, laughing with the child. In none of the pictures did the child appear to be older than four.

Karen was in some of the pictures, very young and with braces, but always smiling, her blond hair and perfect skin and aura of pristine, upper-middle-class perfection seeming to carry, in hindsight, a kind of piercing desperation. There was a tall, slim young man in several of the photos as well. His hair was thinning and the hairline itself rose rapidly in a succession of photos as the child grew, so it was hard to guess the man's age except to place him somewhere in his twenties. The doctor's brother, I assumed. They had the same squeezed-heart shape to their faces and bright, displaced gaze, always searching, rarely remaining still, so that the young man in the photos gave one the sense that the camera had consistently captured his image as he was about to look away from it.

I peered up at them. "You have another daughter, Doctor?"

He stepped up beside me and placed a light hand under my elbow. "Will you need directions back to the Pike, Mr. Kenzie?"

"How old is she now?" I asked.

"That's a terrific cashmere," Dr. Dawe said. "Neiman's?"

He turned me to the door.

"Saks," I said. "Who's the young guy? Brother? Son?"

"Saks," he repeated with a pleased nod. "I should have known."

"Who's blackmailing you, Doctor?"

His gleeful eyes danced. "Drive carefully, Mr. Kenzie. Lotta nuts on the road."

Lotta fucking nuts in this house, I thought, as he gently pushed me out the door.

9

Dr. Christopher Dawe stood in his doorway and watched me walk to my car, which was parked behind a forest-green Jaguar at the base of his driveway. I don't know what he expected to accomplish by this; maybe he was afraid if he didn't play sentinel, I'd dash back into the house, raid the bathroom for those little perfumed balls of soap. I climbed in the Porsche and felt paper crackle under me as I sat behind the wheel. I reached under my butt, pulled a piece of paper off the seat, and placed it on the passenger seat as I backed out into the street. I pulled past the house as Dr. Dawe shut the front door, drove up a block to a stop sign, and looked at the note on the seat beside me:

They lie.
Weston High School ASAP.

The handwriting was cramped, scratchy, and feminine. I drove another block and pulled my Eastern Massachusetts map book from under the passenger seat, flipped through it until I found the page devoted to Weston. The high school was half a grid from where I sat, roughly eight blocks east and two north.

I drove over there through the sun-dappled streets and found Siobhan waiting under a tree by the far corner of the tennis courts that fronted the parking lot. She kept her head down as she hurried over to the car and climbed in the passenger seat.

"Take a left out of the lot," she said, "and drive fast, yeah?"

I did. "Where we going?"

"Just away. This town has eyes, Mr. Kenzie."

So we left Weston, Siobhan keeping her small head down and chewing the flesh around her fingernails. She would glance up occasionally to tell me to take a right here, a left there, and then lower her head again. When I'd start to ask her questions, she'd shake her head as if somehow we could be overheard in a convertible traveling forty miles an hour down half-empty roads. A few more quick directives from her, and we pulled into a parking lot behind Saint Regina's College. Regina's was an all-female, private Catholic college, where the middle class and pious tucked away their daughters in hopes they'd somehow forget about sex. It had the opposite effect, of course; when I'd been in college we'd made several Friday night pilgrimages out here and came home mauled and a bit dazed by the ferocity of good Catholic girls and their pent-up appetites.

Siobhan stepped out of the car as soon as I pulled into a space, and I killed the engine and followed her along a path that led around to the front of the main dorm quad. We walked for a bit in silence, passed through the still and empty campus like survivors of a neutron bomb; the grass and trees were parched and yellowing. The wide chocolate buildings and low limestone walls seemed stricken somehow, as if without voices to bounce off their facades, they grew weak, threatened to melt in the heat.

"They are evil people."

"The Dawes?"

She nodded. "He thinks he's a god, he does."

"Don't most doctors?"

She smiled. "I guess so, yeah."

We reached a small stone bridge that overlooked a tiny pond gone silver in the heat. Siobhan chose a spot at the midway point to place her elbows. I joined her and we looked down into the water, our reflections staring back up at us from the metallic surface.

"Evil," Siobhan said. "He enjoys torture—mental torture. He enjoys showing people how intelligent he is and how dumb they are."

"And with Karen?"

She leaned her small upper body over the rail of the bridge. She stared at her reflection below, as if uncertain how it got there and who it belonged to. "Ah," she said as if the word were an expletive and shook her head. "He treated her like a pet. He called her his 'dim little bulb.'" She pursed her lips and exhaled heavily. "His sweet dim little bulb."

"Did you know Karen well?"

She shrugged. "Since I came there thirteen years ago, sure. She was a nice person until near the end."

"And then?"

"Then," she said flatly, her eyes on a gaggle of mallards as they waddled down the slope on the far side of the river. "Then she was a touch insane, I'd think. Ah, she wanted to die, Mr. Kenzie. So, so much."

"Wanted to die or wanted to be saved?"

She turned her head toward me. "Aren't they the same thing? Wishing to be saved? In *this* world, yeah? It's . . ." Her small face grew bitter and gray and she shook her head several times.

"It's what?" I said.

She looked at me like I was a child who'd asked why fire burns or seasons change.

"Well, it's like praying for rain, isn't it, Mr. Kenzie?" She raised her hands to the clear, white sky. "Praying for rain in the middle of a desert."

We left the bridge and wandered out across a wide soccer field and then through a small stand of trees and small slopes that led to a collection of dorm quads. Siobhan tilted her head up at the tall buildings.

"I always wondered what it would be like to go to university."

"You didn't go back home?"

She shook her head. "No money. And I wasn't the brightest in the bunch, if you know what I mean."

"Tell me about the Dawes," I said. "You said they were evil. Not sorta nasty, but evil."

She nodded and sat on a limestone bench, pulled a crumpled pack of cigarettes from her shirt pocket, offered me one. When I shook my head, she extracted a bent cigarette from the pack, straightened it between her fingers, and lit it. She pulled a stray piece of tobacco off the tip of her tongue before she spoke.

"The Dawes had a Christmas party one year," she said. "There was a storm that night, so the party was sparsely attended, and there was far more food served than eaten. Mrs. Dawe had once caught me taking leftovers after a party, and she made it very clear that leftovers were for the poor, yeah, and I was to dispose of all food following a party. So, after this particular party, I did. At three that morning, Dr. Dawe entered my bedroom holding the husk of the turkey. He threw the turkey on the bed. He raged at me for throwing away food. He screamed that he had grown up poor and what I'd thrown out would have fed his family for a week." She took another hit off her cigarette, pulled another piece of tobacco off her tongue. "He made me eat it."

"What?"

She nodded. "He sat on the edge of the bed and he fed it to me, piece by piece, until dawn."

"That's—"

"Against the law, I'm sure. Have you ever tried to get a job as domestic help, Mr. Kenzie?"

I held her gaze. "You're an illegal, aren't you, Siobhan?"

She stared into my eyes with that flat, sullen gaze of hers, a look that said if she'd ever had expectations, they'd been dispelled on her travels, a long time ago.

"I think you should limit your questions to things that concern you, Mr. Kenzie."

I held up a hand and nodded.

"So you ate food that had been thrown in the trash."

"Oh, he washed it," she said with sarcasm that died wetly in her throat. "He was quite clear about that. He washed it before he came up, and then he fed it to me." She smiled brightly through her hard, acne-stained skin. "That's your good doctor, Mr. Kenzie."

"This abuse," I said eventually, "did it ever cross the line into anything more than psychological?"

"Ah, no," she said, "not with me. I don't think with Karen, either. He looks down on women, Mr. Kenzie. I doubt he thinks we're worthy of his touch." She thought about it some more, then shook her head emphatically. "No, I spent a lot of time with Karen near the end. We'd drink a lot, to tell you the truth. I think she would have told me that. She was no fan of her stepfather."

"Tell me about her."

She crossed one leg over the other, puffed her cigarette. "She was a wreck, Mr. Kenzie. She begged them to take her back for just a few weeks, you know. Begged. On her knees in front of her mother. And her mother said, Oh, we couldn't possibly, dear. You have to learn to—what was the word?—self-rely. That was it. You must learn to self-rely, dear. Karen cried something awful at her feet, and her mother had me bring tea. So Karen would meet me for drinks, yeah, and then she'd go boff strangers."

"Do you know where she was staying?"

"A motel," she said, and the word sounded forlorn. "I don't know the name. She said it was in the . . . sticks was what she called it."

I nodded.

"That's all she told me. The sticks, a motel. I think . . ." She looked down at her knee, flicked her cigarette away from the bench.

"What?"

"She suddenly had money the last two months. Cash. I didn't ask where she got it, but . . ."

"You suspected . . ."

"Prostitution," she said. "She suddenly became profane regarding sex. It wasn't like her."

"That's what I don't get," I said. "Six months ago, she was a whole different person. She was—"

"All sweetness and purity, yeah?"

I nodded.

"You wouldn't believe she had a dirty thought in her body."

"Exactly."

"That was always her way, yeah. She dealt with it—all that fucking madness in that fucking house—by becoming that thing. I don't think it was natural, though, you know. I think it was who she wished she could have been."

"What about that shrine of photographs in the foyer?" I asked. "There's a young guy in them, looks like he could be the doctor's little brother, and then that little girl."

She sighed. "Naomi. The only child they had to-gether."

"She die?"

Siobhan nodded. "A long time ago. She'd be four-teen, I think, possibly fifteen by now. She died just before her fourth birthday."

"How?"

"There's a small pond behind the house. It was winter, and she chased a ball out onto the frozen surface." She shrugged. "She fell through."

"Who was watching her?"

"Wesley."

I could see the small child on the white frozen surface for a moment, reaching for the ball, and then . . .

A small shudder corkscrewed in my bones.

"Wesley," I said. "He's Dr. Dawe's little brother?"

She shook her head. "Son. Dr. Dawe was a widower when he met Carrie, a widower with one child. She was a widow with one child. They wed, had their own together, and she died."

"And Wesley . . ."

"He had nothing to do with Naomi's death," she said with a hint of anger in her voice. "But he was blamed, because he was supposed to be watching. He took his eye off her for a moment, yeah, and she dashed onto the pond. Dr. Dawe blamed his son because he couldn't blame God, could he?"

"Do you know how I could get in touch with Wesley?"

She lit another bent cigarette, shook her head. "He left the family long ago. The doctor won't allow his name to be spoken in the house."

"Was Karen in touch with him?"

Another shake of the head. "He'd been gone, oh, ten years, I believe. I don't think anyone knew what became of him." She took a small hit off her cigarette. "So what are you going to do next?"

I shrugged. "I don't know. Hey, Siobhan, the Dawes said Karen saw a psychiatrist. You know the shrink's name?"

She started to shake her head.

"Come on," I said. "You must have heard it over the years."

Her mouth parted slightly, but then she shook her head again. "I'm sorry, but I really can't recall it."

I stood from the bench. "Okay. I'll find out somehow."

Siobhan looked into my eyes for a long time, the smoke from her cigarette rising up between us. She was so sober, so stripped of levity, I wondered if the laughs she'd had in her life were separated by months or years.

"What are you after here, then, Mr. Kenzie?"

"A reason why she died," I said.

"She died because she came from a fucking horror show of a family. She died because David was hurt. She died because she couldn't handle it."

I gave her a small, helpless smile. "That's what I keep hearing."

"So why, if I might ask, isn't that good enough for you?"

"It might have to be, eventually." I shrugged. "I'm just playing out the hand, Siobhan. I'm just trying to find that one concrete thing that makes me say, 'Okay. I understand now. Maybe I'd do the same thing given those circumstances.'"

"Ah," she said, "you're such a Catholic. Always looking for reasons."

I chuckled. "Lapsed, Siobhan. Permanently lapsed."

She rolled her eyes at that, leaned back, and smoked for a bit without saying a word.

The sun drifted behind some greasy white clouds,

and Siobhan said, "You're looking for a reason, yeah? Start with the man who raped her."

"Excuse me?"

"She was raped, Mr. Kenzie. Six weeks before she died."

"She told you this?"

Siobhan nodded.

"She give you a name?"

She shook her head. "She said only that she'd been promised he wouldn't bother her, and then he did."

"Cody fucking Falk," I whispered.

"Who's that?"

"A ghost," I said. "He just doesn't know it yet."

10

Cody Falk rose at six-thirty the next morning and stood on his back porch with a bath towel around his waist and sipped his morning coffee. Once again, he seemed to be posing for envisioned admirers, his strong chin tilted up slightly, coffee cup held sturdily aloft, his eyes slightly dewy through my binoculars. He looked out at his backyard as if surveying his fiefdom. In his head, I was pretty sure, a voice-over for a Calvin Klein commercial played.

He raised a fist to stifle a yawn, as if the commercial had begun to bore him, and then he sauntered back inside, closed the sliding glass doors behind him, and threw the lock.

I left my spot and drove around the block. I parked two houses down from Cody's and walked up to his front door. Three hours ago, I'd found his backup keys tucked away in a magnetic Hide-a-Key caddy attached to the underside of his drainpipe, and I used them to let myself in.

The house smelled of those potpourri leaves people buy at Crate & Barrel, and it looked like

Cody had ordered the rest of the house from the same catalogue. It was rustic, Santa Fe mission chic right down the line. A cherry-wood dining set sat just off to my left. The seat-cushion prints were faux Native American and matched the rug underneath. An oak chest and hutch with Aztec moldings served as Cody's liquor cabinet, and it was fully stocked, most of the bottles only a third full. The walls had been painted dark gold. It looked like the kind of room an interior decorator would try to sell you on. Step out of Boston and into Austin, Cody, you'll feel so much better about yourself.

I heard the shower turn on upstairs, and I left the dining room.

In the kitchen, four high-backed bar stools surrounded a butcher-block table in the center of the floor. The blond oak cabinets were half full, mostly goblets and martini glasses, a few canned vegetables, some Middle Eastern rice mixes. Judging by the stack of takeout menus to gourmet supermarkets and restaurants, I determined Cody didn't cook in much. The sink held two plates, rinsed clean of food, a coffee cup, three glasses.

I opened the fridge. Four bottles of Tremont Ale, a carton of half-and-half, and a container of pork fried rice. No condiments. No milk or baking soda or produce. No sense that there'd ever been anything in there but the beer, the half-and-half, and last night's Chinese.

I went back through the dining room and entrance foyer and I could smell the leather in the living room before I entered. Again, a southwestern motif—dark oak chairs with hard straight backs supporting cranberry leather. A coffee table on stubby legs. Everything smelled well-oiled and new. A stack of magazines and glossy circulars on the coffee table seemed typical of the owner—*GQ, Men's Health, Details*, for Christ's sake, and catalogues to Brookstone, Sharper Image, Pottery Barn. The hardwood floors gleamed.

You could photograph the lower half of the house and put it in a magazine. Everything matched, yet nothing gave any discernible clues to the owner himself. The gleaming hardwood floors only accentuated the warm, dark coldness of the place. These were rooms meant to be looked at, not enjoyed.

Upstairs, the shower shut off.

I left the living room and climbed the stairs quickly, tugging gloves over my hands as I went. At the top, I removed the lead sap from my back pocket, listened outside the bathroom door as Cody Falk exited the shower stall and began to dry himself. The plan, such as it was, was simple: Karen Nichols had been raped; Cody Falk was a rapist; make sure Cody Falk never raped again.

I lowered myself to one knee and looked through the peephole into the bathroom. Cody was bent at the waist, drying his ankles, the top of his head pointed directly at the door. He was roughly three feet away.

When I kicked the door in, it hit Cody Falk in the head and he stumbled back and then fell on his ass. He looked up at me, and I hit him with the sap about a quarter of a second before I realized the man on the floor wasn't Cody Falk.

He was blond, and large, a bit overly defined in

the arms and chest. He flopped back on the Italian marble and arched his back and then wheezed like fresh tuna tossed to a loading dock.

There were two doors leading into the bathroom—the one I'd come through and one to my left. Cody Falk stood in the one to my left. He was fully clothed and held a lug wrench in his hand, and he smiled when he swung it at my head.

I took a step back, and the guy on the floor wrapped his arms around my ankle. Cody's swing missed my left eye socket by a whisper, but it tagged my ear, and a holy city's worth of cathedral bells rang in my head all at once.

The guy on the floor was strong. Even in his weakened condition, he yanked back hard on my leg. I stomped on his head and punched Cody in the mouth.

It wasn't much of a punch. I was off balance, and my ear was buzzing, and I never was much of a boxer in the first place. Still, it caught Cody off guard, lit up something surprised and self-pitying in his eyes. Most important, it backed him up.

The guy on the floor screamed when I stomped his head a second time. I pulled my leg from his grasp, and took a step toward Cody. Cody touched his lips and raised the wrench again.

The guy on the floor managed to snag my pant leg and twist it, and I stumbled.

Cody gasped in surprise as the stumble served up my head like a tethered balloon.

With the second hit, everything in the room turned a squishy gray, and my shoulder spun into the wall.

The guy on the floor got up on his knees and rammed his head into the small of my back, and Cody beamed as he raised the wrench over his head.

I don't remember the third hit.

What exactly should we do here, Leonard?"

"Just what I've been saying, Mr. Falk. Call the police."

"Ah, Leonard, it's a bit more complicated than that."

I opened my eyes and saw double. Two Cody Falks—one solid, the other transparent and ghostly—paced the kitchen. He drummed his fingers on the countertops and kept licking at the cut on his swollen upper lip.

I was on the floor, back against a wall, feet against the base of the butcher-block counter. My arms were tied at the wrist behind me. I felt around back there with my fingers. Twine of some sort. Not necessarily the best thing to tie someone up with, but it still did the trick.

Cody and Leonard weren't looking at me. Cody paced back and forth along the counter by the sink. Leonard sat up on a bar stool, a towel filled with ice pressed to the back of his head. A few red pimples lined the side of his neck, and his large jaw jutted out of his small face like Lincoln's on Rushmore. A steroid case, I guessed, sculpting his muscles and fighting 'roid rage until his joints turned necrotic. All to impress chicks he'd be too impotent to fuck when game time finally rolled around.

"Guy broke into your home, Mr. Falk. Assaulted both of us."

"Mmm," Cody touched his upper lip gingerly. He glanced down at me, his two heads moving quickly, and my stomach eddied.

I met his eyes as he gave me a broad smile and matching wave of his hand. "Welcome back, Mr. Kenzie."

I smacked my lips together against the taste of cotton balls dipped in battery acid. He knew my name, which meant he probably had my wallet. Not good.

Cody squatted down by me, and the transparent Cody jelled a bit more with the solid Cody, so now it was like looking at one and a half Codys instead of two.

"How you feeling?"

I gave him a grimace.

"Not so good, huh? You going to puke?"

I bit down on some bile in my chest. "Trying not to."

He tilted his head toward the butcher block. "Leonard puked. He also has a nasty bruise on his lower spine from hitting the floor. He's kinda pissed off, Patrick."

Leonard scowled at me.

"What's Leonard's capacity here?"

"He's a bodyguard." Cody slapped my cheek, not too hard, but not too gently, either. "After you and your friend came to visit that time, I thought I might need some protection."

"And the WWF was having a yard sale?" I asked.

Leonard leaned over the counter and the muscles in his forearm flexed. "Keep talking, bitch. Just—"

Cody waved him off. "So where is your friend,

Pat? The big dumb one who likes to hit people with tennis rackets."

I tried to tilt my head in the direction of the front of the house, but it hurt too much and the nausea kicked in double-time.

"Out on the street, Cody."

Cody shook his head. "No, no. We took a walk while you slept this off. There's no one out there."

"You sure?"

A wisp of doubt flickered in his eyes, then vanished. "He'd have come crashing through here by now, I think."

"When he does, Cody, what are you going to do?"

Cody pulled a .38 from his waistband, waved it in my face. "Shoot him, of course."

"Sure," I said, "make him mad."

Cody chuckled, then shoved the gun barrel up against my left nostril. "Ever since you humiliated me, Pat, I've dreamed of something like this. Gives me a hard-on, to tell you the truth. What do you think of that?"

"I think your erogenous zones need rewiring."

He pulled back on the hammer with his thumb, dug harder into my nostril.

"So, you going to kill me now, Cody?"

He shrugged. "I gotta be honest, I thought I'd killed you up in the bathroom. I've never knocked someone out before. I've never even tried."

"Beginner's luck, then. Kudos."

He smiled, slapped my face again. I blinked, and when I opened my eyes, both Codys had returned, the transparent one just to the right of the real one.

"Mr. Falk," Leonard said.

"Hmm?" He peered at something on the side of my head.

"This is bad news. Either call the police, or we take him someplace and do him."

Cody nodded, then leaned in to take a closer look at the side of my head. "You're bleeding pretty bad."

"From the temple?"

He shook his head. "More the ear."

I noticed a distant, high-pitched hum in there for the first time. "Inner or outer?"

"Both."

"Well, you did take a few good swings."

He seemed pleased. "Thanks. I wanted to make sure I did it right."

He took the gun barrel out of my nostril and sat back on the floor in front of me, kept the .38 pointed at the center of my face.

As I watched, the idea grew in his brain, and an icy realization billowed in his eyes and sucked the heat out of the room.

I knew what he was going to say before he said it.

"What if we really did kill him?" Cody asked Leonard.

Leonard's eyes widened and he put the towel filled with ice down on the counter in front of him.

"Well . . ."

"You'd expect a bonus, of course," Cody said.

"Mr. Falk, sure, yeah, but we'd need to really think this through."

"How so?" Cody winked at me from the other side of the gun hammer. "We have his wallet and keys.

That's his Porsche parked in front of the Lowen-
steins'. We pull the car into the garage, dump him
in the trunk, and then drive him somewhere." He
leaned forward, grazed the gun barrel across my lips.
"And shoot—no, stab him to death."

Leonard's wide eyes met my own.

"You know, Leonard," I said, "you 'do' me. Just
like in the movies."

Cody reached out and slapped me again. It was
starting to get annoying.

"Killing someone," Leonard managed, "is not
something you just decide to do, Mr. Falk."

"Why's that?"

"It, ahm . . . well—"

"It's not easy," I said to Cody. "There's always
things you forget."

"Such as?" Cody seemed only mildly curious.

"Such as who knows I'm here. Who would figure
out I was here, in either case. Who would come looking for you."

Cody laughed. "And, lemme see if I remember
this—'burn down my restaurants and paralyze my
dumb fucking ass'? Is that right?"

"For starters."

Cody gave it some thought. He leaned his head
against the butcher block and his lids fell to half-mast
and he watched me with a burgeoning excitement.
He seemed giddy, like a twelve-year-old at his first
peep show.

"I really like this idea," he said.

"Great, Cody." I gave him an emphatic nod. "I'm
happy for you."

He opened his eyes wide and leaned in close to me. I could smell the bitter mixture of coffee and toothpaste on his breath.

"I can already hear you screaming." A slim tongue flicked up to the cut on his lip. "You're on your back and it's arched and I stab you in the chest." He sliced a clenched fist through the air. "And I pull the knife back out and I stab you a second time." His eyes glistened. "And then a third. A fourth. You're screaming your head off and the blood's popping up in spurts from your chest, and I just keep stabbing." He sliced the air several more times, his mouth broadening into a rictus grin.

"No way . . ." Leonard said, and then his throat dried up. He swallowed several times. "Mr. Falk? No way, if we're going to do this, we can get him out of here until nightfall. That's, like, a long time away."

Cody kept his eyes on me, studying me the way you'd study an ant trying to carry away your napkin at a picnic. "We move him out through the garage, put him in the trunk of his car."

"And then what?" Leonard said. His eyes flashed my way, then back to Cody. "We drive him around all day? In a '63 Porsche? Sir? We can't do him in the daylight. It won't work."

Cody got a look on his face like it was Christmas Eve and he'd just been told he couldn't open his presents until morning. He turned his head and looked back at Leonard. "Are you going gutless, Leonard?"

"No, Mr. Falk. Just trying to help here."

Cody looked at the clock on the wall above my

head. He looked out at his backyard. He looked at me. Then he slammed his palm on the floor several times and screamed, "Fuck me! Fuck me! Fuck me!"

He dropped to his knees and kicked out the cabinet door below the butcher block.

He reared forward like an animal, the tendons stretched on his neck, and screwed his face up into mine until the tips of our noses touched.

"You," he said, "are going to die. You understand, prick?"

I didn't say anything.

Cody butted his forehead into mine. "I asked if you understood."

I gave him a flat and bloodless glare.

He butted his forehead into mine a second time.

I bit down against the sharp stabs of pain filling the front of my skull and still said nothing.

Cody slapped my face and then scrambled to his feet. "What if we kill him right here? Right now?"

Leonard held out his huge hands. "Evidence, Mr. Falk. Evidence. Let's say one person knew or even suspects he was coming here and then he turns up dead. A forensics team, right? They'll find pieces of him in places you never thought they'd go. Cracks in the running boards you didn't even know existed will have chunks of his skull in it."

Cody leaned against the butcher block. He ran his palm over his mouth several times and breathed heavily through his nostrils.

Eventually, he said, "So we keep him here till dark. That's your advice."

Leonard nodded. "Yeah, sir."

"And then take him where?"

Leonard shrugged. "I know a dump in Medford will do the trick."

"A dump?" Cody said. "Like someone's shitty apartment? Or an honest-to-God dump?"

"An honest-to-God dump."

Cody gave it a lot of thought. He circled the butcher block a few times. He ran some water in the sink, but instead of running his hand through it and wiping his face, he just leaned over and sniffed it for a while. He stretched until the muscles in his lower back cracked. He looked at me several times and chewed his inner cheek.

"All right," he said eventually. "I can live with this." He smiled at Leonard. "But it's cool, isn't it?"

"What's that, sir?"

He clapped his hands together hard, then clenched them into fists and raised them over his head. "This! Leonard, we have a chance to do something monumental. Monufucking-mental!"

"Yes, sir. In the meantime?" Leonard leaned into the butcher-block counter and looked as if a semi had settled across his shoulder blades.

Cody waved his hand. "In the meantime, I don't fucking care. He can watch pornos with us in the living room. I'll cook eggs and spoon-feed him. Fatten the calf and all that."

Leonard looked like he didn't have a clue what Cody was babbling about, but he nodded and said, "Yes, sir. Good idea."

Cody dropped to his knees in front of me. "You like eggs, Pat?"

I met his smiling eyes. "Did you rape her?"

He cocked his head to the left, stared off into space for a bit. "Who?"

"You know who, Cody."

"What do you think?"

"I think you're the most logical suspect or I wouldn't be here."

"She wrote me letters," he said.

"What?"

He nodded. "You didn't know that part. She'd write me letters asking me why I wasn't getting her signals. Wasn't I man enough?"

"Bullshit."

He giggled and slapped his thigh. "No, no. That's the great part."

"Letters," I said. "Why would Karen Nichols write letters to you, Cody?"

"Because she wanted it, Pat. She was dying for it. She was as cock hungry as they all are."

I shook my head.

"Don't believe me? Ha! Hang on, I'll get them."

He stood up and handed the gun to Leonard.

Leonard said, "What am I supposed to—?"

"Shoot him if he moves."

"He's tied up."

"I pay your freight, Leonard. Don't fucking back-talk me."

Cody walked out of the kitchen and then his footsteps charged up the stairs.

Leonard placed the gun on the counter and sighed.

"Leonard," I said.

"Don't talk to me, bitch."

"He's warming to this idea. He's not going to—"

"I said—"

"—chill out by noon, if that's what you're hoping."

"—shut your fucking hole."

"Killing someone, he's thinking, how ballsy. A new *experience*."

"Shut *up*." Leonard placed the heels of his hands over his eyes.

"And when he does, Leonard, I mean come on, you think he's smart enough not to get caught?"

"Lotta people don't."

"Sure," I said, "but this is strictly A ball around here. He'll fuck up. Take a kill trophy home with him, tell a friend or a stranger in a bar. And then what, Leonard? You think he's going to stand tall when the DA shows up?"

"I'm telling you to shut the—"

"He'll roll like a bowling ball on a ski slope, Leonard. Give you up like he's buttering toast."

Leonard picked up the gun, pointed it at me. "Shut up or I'll do you myself. Right now."

"Okay," I said. "Just one thing, Leonard. Just—"

"Stop saying my name!" He lowered the gun, put his hands to his eyes again.

"—one more thing, and I'm not shitting around here. I got some ugly, ugly friends. I mean, pray the cops get to you first."

He raised his head, pulled his hands from his eyes. "You think I'm scared of your friends?"

"I think you're starting to be. And that's smart, Leonard. You ever done time?"

He shook his head.

"Bullshit. My guess is you've even run with a crew or two. Strictly North Shore, I'm guessing."

He said, "Fuck off. You think your shit talk can

scare me? I got a black belt, motherfucker. I'm a seventh degree—"

"You could be the bastard love child of Bruce Lee and Jackie Chan, Leonard, and Bubba Rogowski and his crew will eat you up like rats on a bag of ground beef."

Leonard picked up the gun again when he heard Bubba's name. He didn't point it. He just gripped it.

Upstairs, Cody's footsteps hammered the floor as he ran back and forth in the bedroom.

Leonard blew air out his rubbery lips. "Bubba Rogowski," he whispered, then cleared his throat. "Nope. Never heard of him."

"Sure, Leonard," I said. "Sure."

Leonard looked at the gun in his hand. Then looked into my face.

"Really, I—"

"'Member the Billyclub Morton hit, Leonard? Come on. He was a North Shore guy."

Leonard nodded, and his left cheekbone developed a small tic.

I said, "You heard who did Billyclub, didn't you? I mean, it's one of his more notorious hits. I hear Billyclub's skull looked like a tomato blown apart by dynamite. Heard they had to ID through dentals. Heard—"

Leonard said, "Okay, okay. Okay? Fuck."

A drawer was wrenched off its runners upstairs, and Cody screamed, "Eureka!"

I resisted the urge to toss a panicky look over my shoulder or up at the ceiling. I kept my voice calm and soft.

I said, "Leave, Leonard. Take the gun with you and walk away. Do it now and do it fast."

"I—"

"Leonard," I hissed. "Either the cops or Bubba Rogowski. Someone's going to nail you on this. You know it. Cody's strictly Toys 'R' Us in this department. No more fucking around, you piece of shit. You're either in this to the wall or you're walking now."

Leonard said, "I don't want to kill you, man. I just—"

"Then, go," I said softly. "No more time. Now or never."

Leonard stood. He placed a sweaty palm on the butcher block and took several deep breaths.

I straightened my back against the wall and pushed up, felt my head swim and a momentary numbness find my nose and mouth as I reached my full height.

"Take the gun," I said. "Go."

Leonard looked at me, his face a mask of stupidity and fear and confusion.

I nodded.

He ran a hand over his mouth.

I held his eyes.

And then Leonard nodded.

I resisted the urge to chuck a sigh of relief the size of a mountain out of my lungs.

He walked past me and let himself out the glass door that led to the back deck. He didn't look back. Once he reached the deck, he picked up speed, lowered his head, and cut through the yard, let himself out the side gate.

One down, I thought, shaking my head and puffing air into my cheeks to try and clear my vision.

I heard Cody's footsteps approach the staircase.

One to go.

11

I did several quick squats to return blood to my legs and sucked up as much of the oxygen in the room as I could.

Cody's feet hit the top of the staircase and he started to descend.

I inched my way along the wall toward the corner of the kitchen.

When Cody came down the bottom of the stairs, he shouted, "Eureka!" again. He bounded around the corner and tripped over my foot, and a sheaf of brightly colored paper flew from his hands as he toppled into a bar stool and slammed his right hip and shoulder hard off the floor.

I doubt I've ever kicked anything as hard as I kicked Cody. I kicked his ribs and his groin, his stomach, his spine, and his head. I stomped on the backs of his knees, his shoulders, and both ankles. One of the ankles made a hard cracking sound as it snapped, and Cody ground his face into the floor and screamed.

"Where do you keep your knives?" I said.

"My ankle! My fucking ankle, you—"

I drove my heel down along the side of his head, and he screamed again.

"Where, Cody? Or I do the ankle again." I thought of that gun in my face, that look in his eyes when he decided to take my life, and I gave him another kick to the ribs.

"Top drawer. The butcher block."

I went around the butcher block and turned my back to the drawer as I pulled it open. I cut my fingers on the first knife blade, worked my way up to the handle, and pulled it out.

Cody rose to his knees.

I came back around the butcher block and stood over him as I worked the knife up between my wrists.

"Stay down, Cody."

Cody turned on his side and pulled his knee up to his chest. He reached down and touched his ankle, hissed through his teeth, and rolled over on his back.

I worked the blade up and down against the twine, felt it slice through, felt my wrists begin to spread apart. I kept slicing and watched Cody roll around at my feet.

The strands around my wrist suddenly separated and my wrists pulled free of one another.

I placed the knife on the counter and shook my hands in small circles for a full minute to get the circulation back.

I looked down at Cody on the floor as he held his ankle aloft, gripped his knee, and moaned, and I felt an exhaustion that had become all too common lately—a bitterness with what I did and what I'd become that had taken residence in my bone marrow like errant T cells.

I'd had hopes, it seemed, of becoming someone else at some point during my younger life. Hadn't I? What kind of life was this—dealing with the Leonards and Cody Falks, breaking into homes and committing felonious assault, snapping the anklebones of human beings, however putrid those human beings might be?

Cody's breath was coming in harsh sucking hisses as the shock wore off and the pain took hold.

I stepped over him and picked up the brightly colored sheets of paper he'd dropped on his way in. There were ten of them, all addressed to Cody, all written in a girlish scrawl.

All were signed Karen Nichols.

Cody,

At the club, you seem to love your body as much as I do. I watch you with those weights and the sweat beads on your skin and I think of running my tongue up the inside of your thighs. I wonder when you're going to make good on your promises. That night in the parking lot, didn't you see it in my eyes? Haven't you ever been teased, Cody? Some women don't want to be courted, they want to be taken. They want to be ground down and held down. They want you to shove yourself in, Cody, not slide. Don't be gentle, asshole. You want it? Come take it.

    Are you up for that, Cody?
    Or is it all just talk?

Waiting,
Karen Nichols

The rest were more of the same—taunting, pleading, daring Cody to force himself on her.

Among the pages, I also found the note Karen had left on Cody's car, the one I'd balled up and stuffed in his mouth. Cody had smoothed it out, kept it as a souvenir.

Cody looked up at me. There was blood in his mouth, and a broken tooth or two rattled when he spoke.

"See? She asked for it. Literally."

I folded nine of the pages, put them in my jacket. I kept the tenth and the note I'd shoved in Cody's mouth in my hand. I nodded.

"When did you and Karen finally have, ah, sex?"

"Last month. She sent me her new address. It's in one of those letters."

I cleared my throat. "The sex, Cody, was it good?"

He rolled his eyes back into his head for a moment. "It was mean. A good mean. The best mean I've had in a while."

I wanted to get my gun from my glove box and just unload it into him. I wanted to see parts of him rip free of his bones.

I leaned back against the wall for a moment, closed my eyes. "Did she protest? Did she fight you?"

"Of course," he said. "That was the game. She kept it up until I left. Even cried. She was a twisted sister, totally into the game. Just how I like it."

I opened my eyes, but kept them on the far counter and fridge. I couldn't look at Cody for a moment or two. I couldn't.

"You held on to this note she left on your car, Cody." I dangled it by my leg.

Out of the corner of my eye, I saw him smile
through the blood and move his head on the floor in
an approximation of a nod.

"Of course. That was the beginning of the game.
First contact."

"You notice anything different between the note
and these letters?"

Now I looked directly at him. I forced myself to.

He said, "Nope. Should I have?"

I squatted by him and he turned his head to look
up into my face.

"Yeah, Cody, you should have."

"Why's that?"

I held the letter in my left hand, the note in my
right, and placed them in front of his eyes.

"Because the handwriting doesn't match, Cody.
It's not even close."

He tried to roll away from me, his eyes bulging
with horror. He flinched violently as if I'd already
hit him.

When I stood, he rolled again, flattened himself
below the sink.

I stayed where I was, watched him try to burrow
into the wood cabinet. Then I took the butcher
knife and walked into the living room. I found a
lamp with a long cord, and I cut the cord, came back
into the kitchen, and tied Cody's hands behind his
back with it.

He said, "What're you going to do?"

I said nothing. I yanked his arms back and tied off
the end of the cord to the steel leg of his refrigerator.
It was a small leg, and thin, but stronger than four
Codys even after a day of rape and workout.

"Where's my wallet, car keys, stuff like that?"

He tilted his head up at the cabinet above the oven, and I opened it, found all my personal belongings in there.

As I stuffed them in my pockets, Cody said, "You're going to torture me."

I shook my head. "I'm done hurting you, Cody."

He pressed the back of his head into the refrigerator and closed his eyes.

"But I am going to make a phone call."

Cody opened one eye.

"See, I know this guy . . ."

Cody turned his head, looked up at me.

"Well, I'll tell you about him when I get back."

"What?" Cody said. "No, tell me. What guy?"

I left him there and let myself out the sliding glass doors onto his porch. I left the yard through the tall wooden gate, then through Cody's side yard and reached the front of the house. I picked up the morning *Trib* off the front steps, stood for a moment, and listened to the neighborhood around me. It was still. No one about. While my luck was holding, I decided to make the best of it. I walked to my Porsche, hopped inside, and drove up Cody's driveway, stopping at the garage. Here, I was covered from prying eyes by Cody's house to my right and the long line of thick oaks and poplars that formed the edge of Cody's property line to my left.

I let myself into the garage through the door Bubba and I had left through last time, and used my cellular as I stood in the cool dark by Cody's Audi.

"McGuire's," a man's voice said.

"This Big Rich?"

"This is Big Rich." The voice was wary now.

"Hey, Big Rich, it's Patrick Kenzie. I'm looking for Sully."

"Oh, hey, Patrick! What's going on?"

"Same old."

"I hear that, brother. Yeah, hang on, Sully's in back."

I waited a moment and then Martin Sullivan picked up the line in the back room of McGuire's tavern.

"Sully."

"What's up, Sul?"

"Patrick. What's shaking?"

"I got a live one for you."

His voice darkened. "No shit? No doubts?"

"None whatsoever."

"And someone's tried to reason with him?"

"Uh-huh. Conversion seems out of the question."

"Well, it's rare," Sully said. "That disease is like Ebola, man."

"Yeah."

"He waiting?"

"Yeah. He's not going anywhere."

"I got a pen."

I gave him the address.

"Look, Sul, there are some extenuating circumstances here. Barely, but they exist."

"So?"

"So don't make the damage permanent, just severe."

"All right."

"Thanks, man."

"No sweat. You be there?"

"I'll be long gone," I said.

"Thanks for the tip, brother. I owe you."

"You don't owe anybody anything, man."

"Peace." He hung up.

I found a roll of electrical tape on a shelf and then let myself back into the house through the other door in the garage, came out into a rec room, empty except for a Stair-Master in the center, a few curling bars on the floor. I walked through that and opened another door onto the kitchen, took two steps, and was standing over Cody Falk again.

"What guy?" he said immediately. "You said you knew a guy. Who are you talking about?"

I said, "Cody, this is very important."

"What guy?"

"Shut up about the guy. I'll get to him. Cody, listen to me."

He looked up at me, all sweet and harmless and willing to please suddenly, the fear treading water like mad behind his eyes.

"I need an honest answer, and I don't care what it is. I won't blame you on this one. I just need to know. Did you or did you not vandalize Karen Nichols's car?"

The same confusion I'd seen in his face that night I'd come here with Bubba filled it again.

"No," he said firmly. "I . . . I mean, that's not my style. Why would I fuck up a perfectly good car?"

I nodded. He was telling the truth.

And some small alarm bell had gone off in my head that night in the garage with Bubba, but I'd been too angry at Cody's stalking and rape history to listen to it.

"You really didn't, did you?"

He shook his head. "No." He glanced at his ankle. "Could I have some ice?"

"Don't you want to hear about this guy?"

He swallowed and his Adam's apple bobbed. "Who is he?"

"He's a nice guy mostly. Regular dude, works a job, has a life. But a decade ago two sick fucks broke into his house and raped his wife and daughter when he wasn't home. They never caught the guys. His wife recovered as best women can after encounters with assholes like you, but his daughter, Cody? She just locked herself up in her brain and floated away. She's in an institution now, ten years later. She doesn't talk. She just stares out into space. Twenty-three years old now, and she looks forty." I lowered myself to my haunches in front of Cody. "So, this guy? Ever since, he hears about a rapist, he gathers this, I dunno, posse, I guess you'd call it, and they ... Well, you ever hear the story about that guy a few years back in the D Street projects—they found him bleeding from every orifice with his own dick cut off and stuck in his mouth?"

Cody ground the back of his head into the fridge and gagged.

"So you're familiar with that story," I said. "That's not urban legend, that's fact, Cody. That was my buddy and his crew."

Cody's voice was a whisper. "Please."

"Please?" I raised my eyebrows. "That's good. Try that with this guy and his friends."

"Please," he said again. "Don't."

"Keep working at it, Cody," I said. "You almost got the hang of it."

"No," Cody moaned.

I pulled a foot of electrical tape from the roll, snapped it off in my teeth. "See, I figure with Karen, maybe half of it was a mistake. You did get those notes and you are dumb, so . . ." I shrugged.

"Please," he said. "Please, please, please."

"But there have been a lot of other women, haven't there, Cody? Ones who never *asked* for it. Ones who never pressed charges."

Cody tried to drop his eyes before I could see the truth there.

"Wait," he whispered. "I have money."

"Spend it on a therapist. After my buddy and his friends get through with you, you're going to need one."

I slapped the electrical tape over his mouth and his eyes bulged.

He screamed and the sound was muffled and helpless behind the tape.

"Bon voyage, Cody." I walked to the glass doors. "Bon voyage."

12

The priest who presided over the noon mass at Saint Dominick of the Sacred Heart Church acted like he had tickets for the Sox game at one. Father McKendrick strode up the front aisle at the stroke of twelve with two altar boys who had to jog to keep pace. He riffled through the greeting, penitential rite, and opening prayer like his Bible was afire. He zipped through Paul's Letter to the Romans as if Paul drank too much coffee. By the time he slammed through the Gospel According to Luke and waved the parishioners to sit, it was seven past noon and most of the people in the pews looked wiped.

He gripped the lectern in both hands, stared down into the pews with a coldness bordering on disdain. "Paul wrote: 'We must wake from darkness and clothe ourselves in the armor of light.' What does that mean, you think—to wake from darkness, to wear armor of light?"

In the days when I went with any regularity, I'd always liked this part of the mass least. The priest would attempt to explain deeply symbolic language penned almost two thousand years ago and then apply his explanation to the Berlin Wall, the Vietnam War, *Roe v. Wade*, the Bruins' Stanley Cup chances. He'd wear you out with his grasping.

"Well, it means what it says," Father McKendrick said as if he were talking to a room full of first-graders who'd ridden in on the short bus. "It means get out of bed. Leave the darkness of your venal desires, your petty bickerings, your hating of your neighbors and distrust of your spouse and allowing your children to be raised and corrupted by TV. Get outside, Paul says, out in the fresh air! Into the light! God is the moon and the stars and He is most definitely the sun. Feel the sun's warmth. Pass that warmth on. Do good things. Give extra to the collection boxes today. Feel the Lord working in you. Donate the clothes you *like* to a shelter. Feel the Lord. He is the armor of light. Get out and do what's right." He thumped the lectern for emphasis. "Do what's *light*. Do you see?"

I looked around the pews. Several people nodded. No one looked like he had the first clue as to what Father McKendrick was talking about.

"Well then," he said. "Good. All rise."

We stood back up. I glanced at my watch. Two minutes flat. The fastest sermon I'd ever witnessed. Father McKendrick definitely had Red Sox tickets.

The parishioners looked dazed, but happy. The only thing good Catholics love more than God is a short service. Keep your organ music, your choir, keep your incense and processionals. Give us a priest with one eye on the Bible and the other on the clock, and we'll pack the place like it's a turkey raffle the week before Thanksgiving.

As the ushers worked backward through the pews with wicker donation baskets, Father McKendrick ripped through the offering of the gifts and the blessing of the host with a look on his face that told the two eleven-year-olds assisting him that this wasn't JV, this was varsity, so step up your game, boys, and make it snappy.

Roughly three and a half minutes later, just after bolting through the Our Father, the Reverend McKendrick had us offer the sign of peace. He didn't look too happy about it, but there were rules, I guess. I shook the hands of the husband and wife beside me, as well of those of the three old men in the pew behind me and the two old women in the pew ahead.

I managed to catch Angie's eye as I did. She was up front, nine rows from the altar, and as she turned to shake the hand of the pudgy teenage boy behind her, she saw me. Something maybe a little surprised, a little happy, and a little hurt passed over her face, and then she dipped her chin slightly in recognition. I hadn't seen her in six months, but I manfully resisted the urge to wave and let out a loud whoop. We were in church, after all, where loud displays of affection are frowned on. Further, we were in Father McKendrick's church, and I had the feeling that if I whooped, he'd send me to hell.

Another seven minutes, and we were out of there. If it was all up to McKendrick, we would have hit the street in four, but several older parishioners slowed the line during Holy Communion and Father McKendrick watched them struggle to approach him on their walkers with a face that said, God might have all day, but I don't.

On the sidewalk outside the church, I watched Angie exit and stop at the top of the stairs to speak to an older gentleman in a seersucker suit. She shook his trembling hand with both of hers, stooped as he said something to her, smiled broadly when he finished. I caught the pudgy thirteen-year-old craning his head out from behind his mother's arm to peer at Angie's cleavage while she was stooped over the man in the seersucker. The kid felt my eyes on him and turned to look at me, his face blooming red with good old-fashioned Catholic guilt around a minefield of acne. I shook a stern finger at him, and the kid blessed himself hurriedly and looked down at his shoes. Next Saturday, he'd be in the confessional, owning up to feelings of lust. At his age, probably a thousand counts of it.

That'll be six hundred Hail Marys, my son.

Yes, Faddah.

You'll go blind, son.

Yes, Faddah.

Angie worked her way down through the crowd milling on the stone steps. She used the backs of her fingers to move the bangs out of her eyes, though she could have solved the problem simply by raising her head. She kept it down, though, as she approached me, fearful perhaps that I'd see something in her face that would either make my day or break my heart.

She'd cut her hair. Cut it short. All those abundant tangles of rich cocoa, streaked with auburn during late spring and summer, rope-thick tresses that had flowed to her lower back and splayed completely across her pillow and onto mine, that could take an hour to brush if she were dressing up for the night—were gone, replaced by a chin-skimming bob that dropped in sweeps over her cheekbones and ended hard at the nape of her neck.

Bubba would weep if he knew. Well, maybe not weep. Shoot someone. Her hairdresser, for starters.

"Don't say a word about the hair," she said when she raised her head.

"What hair?"

"Thank you."

"No, I meant it—what hair?"

Her caramel eyes were dark pools. "Why are you here?"

"I heard the sermons rocked."

She shifted her weight from her right foot to the left. "Ha."

"I can't drop by?" I said. "See an old pal?"

Her lips tightened. "We agreed after the last drop-by that the phone would do. Didn't we?"

Her eyes filled with hurt and embarrassment and damaged pride.

The last time was winter. We'd met for coffee. Had lunch. Moved on to drinks. Like pals do. Then we were suddenly on the living room rug in her new apartment, voices hoarse, clothes back in the dining room. It had been angry, mournful, violent, exhilarating, empty sex. And after, back in the dining room, picking up our clothes and feeling the room's winter chill suck the heat from our flesh, Angie had said, "I'm with someone."

"Someone?" I found my thermal sweatshirt under a chair, pulled it over my head.

"Someone else. We can't do this. This ride has to end."

"Come back to me, then. The hell with Someone."

Naked from the waist up and pissed off about it, she looked at me, her fingers untangling the straps of the bra she'd found on the dining room table. As a guy, I had the better deal—I could dress quicker; find my boxers, jeans, and sweatshirt, and I was good to go.

Angie, untangling that bra, looked abandoned.

"We don't work, Patrick."

"Sure, we do."

On went the bra with a hard sense of finality as she snapped the straps together in back and searched the chair seats for her sweater.

"No, we don't. We want to, but we don't. All the little things? We're fine. But the crucial things? We're a mess."

"And you and Someone?" I said, and stepped into my shoes. "You're all hunky-dory across the board, are you?"

"Could be, Patrick. Could be."

I watched her pull the sweater over her head, then shrug that abundant hair out of the collar.

I picked my jacket up off the floor. "If Someone's so simpatico with you, Ange, what was what we just did in the living room?"

"A dream," she said.

I glanced across the foyer at the rug. "Nice dream."

"Maybe," she said in a monotone. "But I'm up now."

It was a late afternoon in January when I left

Angie's. The city was stripped of color. I slipped on the ice and grabbed the trunk of a black tree to steady myself. I stood with my hand on the tree for a long time. I stood and waited for something to fill me up again.

Eventually, I moved on. It was getting dark and colder and I had no gloves. I had no gloves, and the wind was picking up.

"You heard about Karen Nichols," I said as Angie and I walked under sun-mottled trees in Bay Village.

"Who hasn't?"

The afternoon was cloudy, marked by a humid breeze that caressed the skin, then sank into the pores like soap, and smelled of thick, sudden rain.

Angie glanced up at the thick mass of gauze and bandage over my ear. "What happened, by the way?"

"Someone hit me with a lug wrench. Nothing broken, just very badly bruised."

"Internal bleeding?"

"There was some." I shrugged. "They flushed it out in the emergency room."

"Bet that was fun."

"A ball."

"You get beat up a lot, Patrick."

I rolled my eyes at her, pushed the conversation away from my physical abilities or lack thereof.

"I need to know more about David Wetterau."

"Why?"

"You referred Karen Nichols to me through him. Correct?"

"Yeah."

"How'd you come to know him in the first place?"

"He was starting a small business. Sallis & Salk did his background checks for him and his partner."

Sallis & Salk was the company Angie worked for now, a monster high-tech security firm that handled everything from guarding heads of state to installing and monitoring burglar alarms. Most of their operatives were ex-cops or ex-Feds, and all of them looked really good in dark suits.

Angie stopped. "Where's your case here, Patrick?"

"There isn't one, technically."

"Technically." She shook her head.

"Ange," I said, "I have reason to believe that all the bad luck that happened to Karen in the months before she died wasn't accidental."

She leaned back against the banister of a wrought-iron railing fronting a brownstone. She ran a hand through her short hair, seemed to sag in the heat for a moment. In the old-world tradition of her parents, Angie always dressed up for church. Today she wore cream-colored, pleated linen pants, a white sleeveless silk blouse, and a blue linen blazer she'd removed as soon as we'd started walking.

Even with the hack job she'd done to her hair (and, okay, it wasn't a hack job; it was actually quite attractive, if you hadn't known her before), she still looked six or seven steps above tremendous.

She stared at me and her mouth formed a perfect oval of unasked questions.

"You're going to tell me I'm crazy," I said.

She shook her head slowly. "You're a good investigator. You wouldn't make something like this up."

"Thanks," I said softly. It was a bigger relief than

I'd expected to have at least one person not question the sanity of my investigation.

We started walking again. Bay Village is in the South End and is often derisively called Gay Village by the homophobes and family-values crowd because of the predominance of same-sex couples in the neighborhood. Angie had moved here last autumn, a few weeks after she'd left my apartment. It was about three miles from my Dorchester neighborhood, but it might as well have been on the far side of Pluto. A close-knit few blocks of bowfront chocolate brownstones and red cobblestone, Bay Village is planted firmly between Columbus Avenue and the Mass Pike. As the rest of the South End becomes ever trendier—the galleries and mochaccino houses and L.A. deco bars sprouting like ragweed, and the residents who salvaged the whole area from urban decay during the seventies and eighties getting pushed out by transplants looking to buy low now and sell high next month—Bay Village seems the last remnant of bygone days when everyone knew each other. True to its reputation, most of the people we passed were gay or lesbian couples, at least two-thirds out walking dogs, and they all waved to Angie, exchanged a few hellos and comments on the weather, a tidbit of neighborhood gossip. It occurred to me that this was far more like a true neighborhood than any I'd been in recently in the city, including my own. These people knew each other, seemed to watch out for each other. One guy even mentioned that he'd shooed off two kids he'd noticed eyeing Angie's car late last night and suggested she get a Lojack system. Maybe I was missing some greater subtlety, but this seemed the epitome of the family-values concept, and I wondered how those good Christians ensconced in the sterility and affectation of the suburbs saw themselves as poster children for the whole ideal, yet couldn't tell you the name of the family four houses over on a bet.

I told Angie everything I knew so far about Karen Nichols's final months—her steep drop into alcohol and drug abuse, the letters forged in her name and sent to Cody Falk, my certainty that Cody hadn't been the one to vandalize her car, her rape and arrest for solicitation.

"Jesus," she said when I got to the rape part, but otherwise she remained silent as we wound our way through the South End and then crossed Huntington Avenue and walked along the expanse of the Christian Science Church Headquarters with its glimmering pool and domed buildings.

When I finished, Angie said, "So why are you interested in David Wetterau?"

"That's the first strand that was pulled. That's where Karen's unraveling began."

"And you think he may have been pushed into traffic?"

I shrugged. "Normally, with forty-six witnesses, I'd doubt it, but given that on that particular day he wasn't supposed to be anywhere near that particular corner, and now with these letters someone sent to Cody, I'm pretty sure someone was going out of their way to destroy Karen Nichols."

"And *drive* her to suicide?"

"Not necessarily, though I'm not ruling it out. For

now, let's just say I think someone was determined to destroy her life in increments."

She nodded and we sat on the edge of the pool, and she idly ran her fingers through the water.

"Wetterau and Ray Dupuis set up their film equipment supply company, and Sallis & Salk ran checks on all of their employees and interns. They all came out clean."

"What about Wetterau?"

"What about him?"

"Did he check out?"

She glanced at her reflection in the glassy water. "He hired us."

"But he wasn't the money man. He drove a VW, and Karen told me they'd bought a Corolla because they couldn't swing a Camry. Did Ray Dupuis ask for a background check on his partner?"

She watched a ripple flow from her swaying fingers. "Yeah." She nodded, eyes still on the water. "Wetterau checked out, Patrick. With flying colors."

"Is there anyone at Sallis & Salk who does handwriting analysis?"

"Sure. We have at least two forgery experts. Why?"

I handed her the two samples I had of Wetterau's signature—one with the "P" and one without.

"Could you do me a favor and see if both these signatures were written by the same hand?"

She took them from me. "I guess."

She turned, pulled a knee up to her chest, propped her chin on top, and stared at me.

"What?" I said.

"Nothing. Just looking."

"See anything good?"

She turned her head back toward the church, a dismissive gesture, one that said flirting wasn't part of the menu today.

I kicked at the stone foundation of the wading pool and tried not to say what I'd been feeling these past few months. Eventually, though, I gave in.

"Ange," I said, "it's starting to wear me down."

She gave me a confused look. "Karen Nichols?"

"All of it. The job, the . . . It's not . . ."

"Fun anymore?" She gave me a small smile.

I smiled back. "Yeah. Exactly."

She lowered her eyes. "Who said life's supposed to be fun?"

"Who said it's not?"

The small smile tugged her lips again. "Yeah. Point taken. You're thinking of quitting?"

I shrugged. I was still relatively young, but that would change.

"All the broken bones getting to you?"

"All the broken lives," I said.

She lowered her knee and her fingers found the water again. "What would you do?"

I stood, stretched aches and cramps in my back that had been there since Cody Falk's house that morning. "I don't know. I'm just really . . . tired."

"And Karen Nichols?"

I looked back at her. Sitting on the ledge by the glassy pool, her skin honeyed by the summer and her dark eyes as wide and frighteningly intelligent as ever, every inch of her just broke my heart.

"I want to speak for her," I said. "I want to prove to

someone—maybe the someone who tried to destroy her life, maybe just to myself—that her life had value. That make sense?"

She looked up at me and her face was tender and open. "Yeah. Yeah, it does, Patrick." She shook her hand free of water and stood up on the pavement beside me. "I'll make you a deal."

"Shoot."

"If you can prove that David Wetterau's accident deserves a second look, I'll come in on the case. Pro bono."

"What about Sallis & Salk?"

She sighed. "I dunno. It's like I'm starting to worry that all the shit cases they've been assigning me aren't simply about paying my dues. It's . . ." She raised her hand from the water, then dropped it again. "Whatever. Look, I don't break a sweat over there. I can help you—use a vacation day here and there if I have to—and maybe it'll be—"

"Fun?"

She smiled. "Yeah."

"So I prove Wetterau's accident was fishy, and you come on the case. That's the deal?"

"I don't *come on* the case. I help you with it here and there, when I can." She stood.

"Sounds good."

I held out my hand. She shook it. The press of her palm against mine opened holes in my chest and stomach. I was starving for her. I'd melt right there if she asked.

She pulled her hand back, stuffed it in her pocket as if it were burning.

"I—"

She stepped back from whatever she saw in my face. "Don't say it."

I shrugged. "Okay. I do, though."

"Sssh." She put a finger to her lips, smiled around it, but her eyes shimmered with moisture. "Sssh," she said again.

13

The Holly Martens Inn sat fifty yards off an overgrown, yellowed grass stretch of Route 147 in Mishawauk, a blip-on-the-map sort of town not far from Springfield. A two-story cinder-block collection of units arranged in one long T, the Holly Martens ran across the length of a brown dirt field and ended at a puddle so wide and black there could have been dinosaur remains in it. The Holly Martens looked as if it had been part of an army base or air-raid shelter in the fifties, and nothing about the design seemed to beckon the weary traveler to a second stay. A swimming pool sat to my left as I pulled in toward the front office. Empty and surrounded by chain link with cyclone wire on top, it was littered with shattered green and brown beer bottles, lawn chairs caked with rust, fast-food wrappers, and a three-wheel shopping cart. A peeling sign affixed to the chain link read: NO LIFEGUARD ON DUTY SWIM AT YOUR OWN RISK. Maybe they'd drained the pool because people kept throwing their beer bottles in it. Maybe the beer bottles had been thrown in

147

because they'd drained the pool. Maybe the lifeguard had taken the water with him when he left. Maybe I had to stop wondering about things that didn't concern me.

The front office smelled like matted animal hair, wood shavings, Lysol, and newspapers spoiled by fecal pellets and dribbles of urine. That's because behind the reception desk were at least seven cages, and all of them had rodents inside. Mostly guinea pigs, a few hamsters squeaking at their hamster wheels, feet pedaling like crazy, snouts pointed up at the wheel as they wondered why they couldn't reach the top.

Just no rats, I thought. Please, no rats.

The woman behind the desk was bleached blond and very slim. Her body looked like it was all gristle, like the fatty deposits had run off with the lifeguard, taken her breasts and her ass with them. Her skin was so tan and hard it reminded me of knotted wood. She could have been anywhere between twenty-eight and thirty-eight, and there was a sense to her of a dozen lives lived and spent before she'd turned twenty-five.

She gave me a great, wide-open smile that had a touch of challenge in it. "Hey! You the guy that called?"

"Called?" I said. "About what?"

The cigarette between her lips jumped. " 'Bout the unit."

"No," I said. "I'm a private investigator."

She laughed with the cigarette gritted between her teeth. "No shit?"

"No shit."

She removed the cigarette, flicked the ash on the

floor behind her, and leaned into the counter. "Like Magnum?"

"Just like Magnum," I said, and tried to give my eyebrows that patented Tom Selleck rise and fall.

"I catch it in repeats," she said. "Boy, he was cute-cute. You know?" She arched an eyebrow at me, lowered her voice. "How come men don't wear mustaches no more?"

"Because people immediately assume they're either homosexual or redneck?" I offered.

She nodded. "There you go, there you go. Damn, it's a shame."

"No argument," I said.

"Nothing like a man with a good mustache."

"Damn straight."

"So what can I do for ya?"

I showed her the driver's-license photo of Karen Nichols I'd cut from the newspaper. "Know her?"

She gave the photo a good long look, then shook her head. "But ain't that the woman, though?"

"What woman?"

"The one jumped off that building downtown?"

I nodded. "I heard she may have stayed here for a while."

"Nah." She lowered her voice. "She looks a little too, ahm, buttoned-down for a place like this. You know?"

"What kind of people stay here?" I asked, as if I didn't know already.

"Oh, nice folks," she said. "Great folks. Salt of the earth, you know? But maybe they're a little rougher-looking than your average. A lot of bikers."

Check, I thought.

"Truckers."

Check again.

"Folks needing a place to, ahm, get their heads together, take stock."

Read: junkies and recent parolees.

"Many single women?"

Her bright eyes clouded over. "All right, honey, let's cut to the chase. What are you after here?"

Just like a hardened moll. Magnum would have been impressed.

I said, "Has any woman been staying here who hasn't paid her rent in a while? A week or more, say?"

She glanced down at the ledger below her. She leaned her elbow on the counter and the fun returned to her eyes. "Maybe."

"Maybe?" I leaned my elbow on the counter near hers.

She smiled at me, moved her elbow a little closer. "Yeah, maybe."

"Can you tell me anything about her?"

"Oh, sure," she said. She smiled. She had a great smile; you could see the child in it, before the road wear and the cigarettes and the sun poisoning. "My old man can tell you even more."

I wasn't sure if "old man" meant father or husband. These parts, it could mean either. Hell, these parts, it could mean both.

I kept my elbow where it was. Out in the sticks, living dangerously. "Such as?"

"Such as, why don't we spread some introductions around first? What's your name?"

"Patrick Kenzie," I said. "My friends call me Magnum."

"Shit." She gave me a low chuckle. "I bet they don't."

"I bet you're right."

She opened her palm and extended it. I did the same and we shook with our elbows resting on the counter like we were about to arm wrestle.

"Name's Holly," she said.

"Holly Martens?" I said. "Like the guy in the old movie?"

"Who?"

The Third Man," I said.

She shrugged. "My old man? He takes over this place, it's called Molly Martenson's Lie Down. Got a real nice neon sign on the roof, lights up sweet at night. So my old man, Warren, he's got this friend, Joe, and Joe's real good with fixing stuff. So, Joe, he knocks out the M, replaces it with an H, and then blacks out the O-N-'postrophe-S. Ain't centered, but it looks good at night all the same."

"What about the Lie Down part?"

"Wasn't on the neon sign."

"Thank the Lord."

She slapped the countertop. "That's what I said!"

"Holly!" someone called from the back. "Goddamn gerbil shit on my paperwork."

"Don't own no gerbils!" she called back.

"Well, the friggin midget pig thing, then. What I tell you about letting 'em out of their cages?"

"I raise guinea pigs," she said softly, as if it were a secret dear to her heart.

"I noticed. Hamsters, too."

She nodded. "Had some ferrets, but they died."

"Damn," I said.

"You like ferrets?"

"Not even a little bit." I smiled.

"You need to loosen up. Ferrets are fun." She clucked her tongue. "Whole damn lot of fun."

I heard a clacking and squeaking from behind her that was too heavy for the hamster wheels, and Warren rolled out into the front office in a black leather and bright chrome wheelchair.

His legs were gone below the knees, but the rest of him was massive. He wore a sleeveless black T-shirt over a chest as broad as the hull of a small boat, and thick red cords stood out angrily under the flesh over his forearms and biceps. His hair was bleached blond like Holly's, shaved tight against the temples, but swept back high off the forehead and hanging down to his shoulder blades. Jaw muscles the size of tea saucers worked up and down in his face, and his hands, clad in black leather fingerless gloves, looked capable of snapping an oak fence post like it was plywood.

He didn't look at me as he approached Holly. He said, "Honey?"

She turned her head and looked into his handsome face with such immediate and total love that it invaded the room like a fourth body.

"Baby?"

"You know where I put them pills?" Warren wheeled himself up near the desk, peered in its lower counters.

"The white ones?"

He still hadn't looked at me. "Nah. Those yellow ones, hon. The three o'clock ones."

She cocked her head as if trying to remember. Then that wonderful smile broke across her face and she clapped her hands together, and Warren smiled, too, enthralled by her.

"'Course I do, baby!" She reached under the counter and pulled out an amber bottle of pills. "Think fast."

She tossed them at him, and he snatched them from the air without glancing in their direction, his eyes on her.

He popped two in his mouth and chewed them. His eyes were still locked with hers when he said, "What you looking for, Magnum?"

"A dead woman's last effects."

He reached out and took Holly's hand. He ran his thumb over the back of it, peered at the skin as if committing each freckle to memory.

"Why?"

"She died."

"You said that." He turned her hand over so it was palm up, traced the lines with his finger. Holly ran her free hand through the hair on top of his head.

"She died," I said, "and no one gives a shit."

"Oh, but you do, huh? You're a real great guy that way, right?" Running his fingers along her wrist now.

"I'm trying."

"This woman—she small and blond and fucked up on quaaludes and Midori from seven in the morning on?"

"She was small and blond. The rest I wouldn't know about."

"C'mere, honey." He tugged Holly gently onto his lap and then stroked strands of hair off her neck. Holly chewed her lower lip and looked into his eyes and the underside of her chin quivered.

Warren turned his head so that Holly's chest was pressed against his ear and looked directly at me for the first time. Seeing his face full on, I was surprised by how young he looked. Late twenties, maybe, a child's blue eyes, cheeks as smooth as a debutante's, a surfer boy's sun-washed purity.

"You ever read what Denby wrote about *The Third Man*?" Warren asked me.

Denby was David Denby, I assumed, long the film critic for *New York* magazine. Hardly someone I expected to hear referenced by Warren, particularly after his wife had claimed to not even know what movie I'd been talking about.

"Can't say I have."

"He said no adult in the postwar world had the right to be as innocent as Holly Martens was."

His wife said, "Hey!"

He touched her nose with his fingertip. "The movie character, honey, not you."

"Oh. Okay, then."

He looked back at me. "You agree, Mr. Detective?"

I nodded. "I always thought Calloway was the only hero in that movie."

He snapped his fingers. "Trevor Howard. Me, too." He looked up at his wife, and she buried her face in his hair, smelled it. "This woman's effects—you wouldn't be looking for anything of value in it, would you?"

"You mean like jewelry?"

"Jewelry, cameras, any shit you could pawn."

"No," I said. "I'm looking for reasons why she died."

"The woman you're looking for," he said, "stayed in Fifteen B. Small, blond, called herself Karen Wetterau."

"That'd be her."

"Come on." He waved me through the small wooden gate beside the desk. "We'll take a look together."

I reached his wheelchair, and Holly turned her cheek on his head and looked up at me with sleepy eyes.

"Why you being so nice?" I asked.

Warren shrugged. "'Cause Karen Wetterau? Nobody was ever nice to her."

14

There was a barn out back, about three hundred yards from the rear of the motel, past a blighted grove of bent or broken trees and a small clearing dyed black with motor oil. Warren Martens propelled his wheelchair through decayed branches and the mulch of a few seasons' worth of unraked leaves, the litter of nip bottles and abandoned car parts, and the crumbled foundation of a building that had probably died somewhere around the time Lincoln did, as if he were riding atop a lane of fresh blacktop.

Holly had stayed back in the office in case anyone showed up here because the Ritz was full, and Warren led me out the back and down a wooden ramp toward the sagging barn where he stored the contents of abandoned units. He got ahead of me in the grove, pumping those wheels until the spokes hummed through crackling leaves. The leather back of his chair had a Harley-Davidson eagle sewn into the center and bumper stickers affixed on either side of the bird: RIDERS ARE EV-

ERYWHERE; ONE DAY AT A TIME; BIKE WEEK, LACONIA, NH; LOVE HAPPENS.

"Who's your favorite actor?" he called back over his shoulder as his thick arms pumped the wheels over crackling leaves.

"Current or old-time?"

"Current."

"Denzel," I said. "You?"

"I'd have to say Kevin Spacey."

"He is good."

"Fan of his since *Wiseguy*. 'Member that show?"

"Mel Profitt," I said, "and his incestuous sister, Susan."

"Well, all right." He tipped a hand back and I slapped it. "Okay," he said, getting excited now that he'd found a fellow cine-geek out here in the dead trees. "Favorite current actress, and you can't say Michelle Pfeiffer."

"Why not?"

"The babe factor's too prevalent. Could skew the objectivity of the poll."

"Oh," I said. "Joan Allen, then. You?"

"Sigourney. With or without automatic weapons." He glanced over at me as I caught up, walked alongside him. "Old-time actor?"

"Lancaster," I said. "No contest."

"Mitchum," he said. "No contest. Actress?"

"Ava Gardner."

"Gene Tierney," he said.

"We might not agree on specifics, Warren; but I'd say we both got impeccable taste."

"Ain't that the truth?" He chuckled, leaned his

head back, and watched the black branches roll overhead. "It's true what they say about good movies, though."

"What do they say?"

He kept his head tilted back, kept thrusting the wheelchair forward as if he knew every inch of this wasteland. "They transport you. I mean, I see a good movie? I don't *forget* I don't have legs. I *have* legs. They're Mitchum's because I'm Mitchum and those are my hands running down Jane Greer's bare arms. Good movies, man, they give you another life. A whole other future for a while."

"For two hours," I said.

"Yeah." He chuckled again, but it was more wistful. "Yeah," he repeated, even more softly, and I felt the sharp tonnage of his life roll over us for a moment—the broken motel, the blighted trees, the phantom limbs at thirty, and those hamsters climbing their hamster wheels back in the office, squeaking like mad.

"It wasn't a motorcycle accident," he said, as if answering a question he knew I wanted to ask. "Most people see me, they think I dumped my hog on a turn." He looked back over his shoulder at me and shook his head. "I was shacking up here one night when it was still Molly Martenson's Lie Down. Shacking up with a woman wasn't my wife. Holly shows up—all piss and vinegar and fuck you, motherfucker—and she throws her wedding ring at me in the room and bolts. I go chasing her. There wasn't no fence around the pool then, but it was still empty, and I slipped. I fell in the deep end." He shrugged.

"Cracked myself in half." He waved his arm at our surroundings. "Got all this in the lawsuit."

He wheeled to a stop by the barn and unlocked the padlock over the door. The barn had been red once, but the sun and neglect had turned it a sallow salmon, and it sagged hard to its left, leaning into the dark earth as if any moment it would roll onto its side and go to sleep.

I wondered how a cracked spine had led to the removal of both of Warren's lower legs, but I decided he'd tell me if he felt like it, leave me wondering if he didn't.

"Funny thing is," he said, "Holly loves me twice as much now. Maybe it's 'cause I can't go out catting around no more. Right?"

"Maybe," I said.

He smiled. "Used to think that myself. But you know what it is? What it really is?"

"No."

"Holly, she's just one of those people truly comes alive only when someone needs her. Like those midget pigs of hers. Simple bastards would die if left to their own devices." He looked up at me, then nodded to himself and opened the barn door, and I followed him inside.

Most of the barn was a flea market of three-legged coffee tables, ripped lamp shades, cracked mirrors, and TVs with picture tubes shattered by fists or feet. Rusted hot plates hung from their cords against the rear wall alongside third-rate paintings of empty fields, clowns, and flowers in vases, all the surfaces soiled by orange juice or grime or coffee.

The front third of the barn, though, was a collection of discarded suitcases and clothes, books and shoes, costume jewelry spilling from a cardboard box. To my left, Holly or Warren had used yellow rope to cordon off a section neatly stacked with a never-used blender; cups, glasses, and china still in the boxes from the store; and a pewter serving plate that bore the engraving LOU & DINA, ALWAYS-N-FOREVER, APRIL 4, 1997.

Warren saw me staring at it.

"Yeah. Newlyweds. Come here on their wedding night, unwrapped their gifts, then had this big blowout around three A.M. She takes off in the car, cans still tied to the rear bumper. He runs down the road after her, half naked. Last I ever saw of them. Holly won't let me sell the stuff. Says they'll be back. I say, 'Honey, it's been two years.' Holly says, 'They'll come back.' And that's that."

"That's that," I said, still a bit in awe of those gifts and that serving plate, the half-naked groom chasing his bride into oblivion at 3 A.M., all those cans rattling up the road.

Warren wheeled to my right. "Here's her stuff. Karen Wetterau's. Ain't much."

I walked over to a cardboard Chiquita Banana produce carton, lifted the cover off. "How long since you last saw her?"

"A week. Next I heard, she dove off the Custom House."

I looked at him. "You knew."

"Sure, I did."

"Holly?"

He shook his head. "She wasn't lying to you. She's

the kind of woman puts a positive spin on *every-thing*. If she can't, then it didn't happen. Something in her don't allow herself to make the necessary connections. But I saw the picture in the paper, and it took a couple minutes, but I put it together. She looked real different, but it was still her."

"What was she like?"

"Sad. Saddest person I come across in a long, long time. Dying from all that sad. I don't drink no more, but I'd sit with her some nights while she did. Sooner or later, she'd come on to me. One of the times I turned her down, she gets all nasty, starts insinuating that my equipment don't work. I go, 'Karen, lot of things got lost in that accident, but not that.' Hell, I'm still eighteen that way; soldier stands to attention when the breeze shifts. Anyway, I say, 'Look, no offense, but I love my wife.' And she laughs. She says, 'No one loves. No one loves.' And I'll tell you something, man, she believed it."

"No one loves," I said.

"No one loves." He nodded.

He scratched the crown of his head, looked around the barn as I picked up a framed photo from the top of the box. The glass had been shattered, and pebbles of it stuck in the frame's grooves. The photo was of Karen's father, wearing his marine best, holding his daughter's hand, both of them blinking in the glare.

"Karen," Warren said, "I think she was in a black hole. So the whole world's a black hole. She's sur-rounded by people who think love is bullshit, then love *is* bullshit."

Another photo, glass also shattered. Karen and a

good-looking, dark haired guy. David Wetterau, I assumed. Both of them tanned and dressed in pastels, standing on the deck of a cruise ship, eyes a little glassy from the daiquiris in their hands. Big smiles. All was right with the world.

"She told me she'd been engaged to a guy got hit by a car."

I nodded. Another photo of her and Wetterau, more pebbles of glass falling to my hand as I lifted it. Another set of big smiles, this one taken at a party, Happy Birthday streamers hanging behind their heads, stretched across someone's living room wall.

"You know she was hooking?" I asked as I placed the photo on the floor beside the other two.

"I figured," he said. "Guys coming over a lot, only a couple of them coming back a second time."

"You talk to her about it?" I lifted a stack of collection notices mailed to her old address in Newton, a Polaroid of her and David Wetterau.

"She denied it. Then she offered to blow me for fifty bucks." He rolled his shoulders, glanced down at the frames on the floor. "I should have kicked her out, but, man, she seemed kicked enough."

I found returned mail—all bills, all stamped with red lettering: RETURNED DUE TO LACK OF POSTAGE. I put it aside, removed two T-shirts, a pair of shorts, some white panties and socks, a stopped watch.

"You said most guys never came back. What about the ones who did?"

"There were just two of 'em. One I saw a lot—little redheaded snot about my age. He paid for the room."

"Cash?"

"Yup."

"The other guy?"

"Better-looking. Blond, maybe thirty-five. Would come by at night."

Underneath the clothes, I found a white cardboard box about six inches tall. I removed the pink ribbon on top and opened it.

Warren, looking over my shoulder, said, "Shit, huh? Holly didn't tell me about those."

Wedding invitations. Maybe two hundred, written in calligraphy on pale pink linen: DR. AND MRS. CHRISTOPHER DAWE REQUEST THE PLEASURE OF YOUR COMPANY FOR THE WEDDING OF THEIR DAUGHTER, MISS KAREN ANN NICHOLS, TO MR. DAVID WETTERAU ON SEPTEMBER 10, 1999.

"Next month," I said.

"Shit," Warren said again. "Little early to have had 'em, don't you think? She'd have had to order them eight, nine months before the wedding."

"My sister ordered them eleven months in advance. She's an Emily Post kind of girl." I shrugged. "So was Karen when I met her."

"No shit?"

"No shit, Warren."

I placed the invitations back in their box and tied the ribbon neatly back on top. Six or seven months ago, she'd sat at a table, smelling the linen, probably, running her finger over the lettering. Happy.

Underneath a crossword puzzle book, I found another set of photos. These were unframed, in a plain white envelope bearing a Boston postmark, dated May 15 of this year. There was no return address. The envelope had been mailed to Karen's Newton apartment. More photos of David Wetterau. Except the woman in the photos with him wasn't Karen Nichols. She was brunette, dressed all in black, a model's thin frame, an air of aloofness behind her black sunglasses. In the photos, she and David Wetterau sat at an outdoor café. They held hands in one. Kissed in another.

Warren looked at them as I shuffled through them. "Ah, that's not good."

I shook my head. The trees surrounding the café were stripped. I put the liaison at sometime in February, during our balmy nonwinter, not long after Bubba and I had visited Cody Falk, and right before David Wetterau got his skull crushed.

"You think she took them?" Warren asked.

"No. These shots were done by a pro—telephoto lens shot from a roof, perfect framing of the subjects." I leafed through them slowly so he could see what I meant. "Zoom close-ups of their hands entwined."

"So you think someone was hired to take those."

"Yeah."

"Someone like you?"

I nodded. "Someone like me, Warren."

Warren looked at the photos in my hand again. "But he's not *really* doing anything wrong with this girl."

"True," I said. "But, Warren, if you received photos like these of Holly and a strange guy, how would you feel?"

His face darkened and he didn't speak for a few moments. "Yeah," he admitted eventually, "you got a point."

"The question is *why* someone would give these photos to Karen."

"To screw with her head, you think?"

I shrugged. "That's definitely a possibility."

The box was almost empty. I found her passport and birth certificate next, and then a prescription bottle of Prozac. I barely glanced at it. Prozac seemed the very least she would have been entitled to after David's accident, but then I noticed the date of the prescription: 10/23/98. She'd been taking an antidepressant long before I met her.

I held the bottle in my palm, read the prescribing doctor's name: D. Bourne.

"Mind if I take this?"

Warren shook his head. "Be my guest."

I pocketed the vial. All that was left in the box was a sheet of white paper. I turned it over and lifted it out of the box.

It was a page of session notes bearing Dr. Diane Bourne's letterhead and dated April 6, 1994. The subject was Karen Nichols, and it read in part:

> . . . *Client's repressive nature is extremely prominent. She seems to live in a constant state of denial—denial of the effects of her father's death, denial of her tortured relationship with both mother and stepfather, denial of her own sexual inclinations which in this therapist's opinion are bisexual and bear incestuous overtones. Client follows classic passive-aggressive behavioral patterns and is wholly unaccepting of any attempts to gain self-awareness. Client has dangerously low self-esteem, confused*

sexual identity, and in this therapist's opinion, a
potentially lethal fantasy version of how the world
works. If further sessions do not yield progress, may
suggest voluntary committal to a qualified psychi-
atric hospital . . .

                                        D. Bourne

"What's that?" Warren wanted to know.

"It's the session notes of Karen's psychiatrist."

"Well, what the hell was she doing with it?"

I glanced down at his confused face. "That's the question of the hour, isn't it?"

With Warren's blessing, I kept the session notes and pictures of David Wetterau with the other woman, then I gathered the other photos, the clothes, the broken watch and passport and wedding invitations, and placed them back into the box. I looked in at what served as evidence of Karen Nichols's existence, and I pinched the bridge of my nose between thumb and forefinger and closed my eyes for a second.

"People can be tiring, can't they?" Warren said.

"Yeah, they can." I stood and walked to the door.

"Man, you must be tired all the time."

As he locked the barn back up outside, I said, "These two guys you said were around Karen."

"Yeah."

"Were they together?"

"Sometimes. Sometimes not."

"Anything else you can tell me about them?"

"The redheaded guy, like I said, was a snot. A weasel. Kinda guy thinks he's smarter'n everyone else. He peeled off a stack of hundreds when he checked her in like they were ones. You know? Karen's all sagging into him, and he's looking at her like she's meat, winking at me and Holly. A real piece of shit."

"Height, weight, that sort of stuff?"

"I'd say he was about five-ten, maybe five-nine. Freckles all over his face, dweeby haircut. Weighed maybe one-fifty, one-sixty. Dressed artsy—silk shirts, black jeans, shiny Docs on his feet."

"And the other guy?"

"Slick. Drove a black '68 Shelby Mustang GT-500 convertible. Like, what, four hundred of them produced?"

"Around there, yeah."

"Dressed rich-boy shabby—jeans with little rips in 'em, V-neck sweaters over white T-shirts. Two-hundred-dollar shades. Never came in the office, never heard him speak, but I got the feeling he was in charge."

"Why?"

He shrugged. "Something about him. The geek and Karen always walked behind him, moved real fast when he spoke. I dunno. I maybe saw the guy five times, always from a distance, and he made me feel nervous, somehow. Like I wasn't worthy to look upon him or something."

He wheeled his way back through the black fields, and I followed. The day grew deader and more humid around us. Instead of pointing toward the ramp at the back of the office, he led me to a picnic table, its surface covered in small splinters peeking up out of the wood like hair. Warren stopped by the table, and I sat up on top, pretty sure my jeans would protect me from the splinters.

He wouldn't look at me. He kept his head down, eyes on the divots ripped in the gnarled wood.

"I gave in once," he said.

"Gave in?"

"To Karen. She kept on talking about dark gods and dark rides and places she could take you and . . ." He looked back over his shoulder at the motel office, and the silhouette of his wife moved past a curtain. "I don't . . . I mean, what makes a man who has the best woman the world can offer—what makes him . . . ?"

"Fuck around?" I said.

He met my eyes and his were small, now, shamed. "Yeah."

"I don't know," I said gently. "You tell me."

He drummed his fingers on the armrest of his chair, looked off past me at the wasteland of broken trees and black earth. "It's the darkness, you know? The chance to disappear into, I mean, really bad places while you're doing something that feels really damn good. Sometimes, you don't want to be on top of a woman who looks at you with all this love in her eyes. You want to be on top of a woman who looks into your face and *knows* you. Knows the bad you, the nasty you." He looked at me. "And likes that you. Wants that you."

"So, you and Karen . . ."

"Fucked all night, man. Like animals. And it was good. She was crazy. No inhibitions."

"And afterward?"

He looked away again, took a deep breath, and let it out slow. "Afterward, she said, 'See?'"

"See."

He nodded. " 'See? No one loves.' "

We stayed out there by the picnic table for a while, neither of us speaking. Cicadas hummed through the scrawny treetops and raccoons clawed through the brambles on the far side of the clearing. The barn seemed to sag another inch, and Karen Nichols's voice whispered through the rural blight:

See? No one loves.

No one loves.

15

I had taken my work to a bar when Angie found me later that night. The bar was Bubba's, a place called Live Bootleg on the Dorchester-Southie line, and even though Bubba was out of the country—off to Northern Ireland, the rumor was, to pick up the arms they'd allegedly laid down over there—my drinks were still on the house.

This would have been great if I'd been in a drinking mood, but I wasn't. I nursed the same beer for an hour, and it was still half full when Shakes Dooley, the owner of record, replaced it with a fresh one.

"It's a crime," Shakes said as he drained the old beer into the sink, "to see a fine, healthy man such as yourself wasting a perfectly honest lager."

I said, "Mmm-hmm," and went back to my notes.

Sometimes I find it easier to concentrate in a small crowd. Alone, in my apartment or office, I can feel the night ticking past me, another day gone down for the count. In a bar, though, on a late Sunday afternoon, when I can hear the hollow, distant crack of bats from a Red Sox game on the TV, the solid drop of pool balls falling into pockets from the back room, the idle chatter of men and women playing keno and scratch cards as they do their best to ward off Monday and its horn honks and barking bosses and drudging responsibilities—I find the noises mingle together into a soft, constant buzzing, and my mind clears of all else but the notes laid before me between a coaster and a bowl of peanuts.

From the morass of things I'd learned about Karen Nichols, I had compiled a bare chronological outline on a fresh sheet of yellow legal paper. Once that was done, I doodled in random notes beside hard facts. Sometime during all this, the Red Sox had lost, and the crowd had thinned slightly, though it had never been much of a crowd in the first place. Tom Waits played on the jukebox, and two voices were getting heated and raw back in the poolroom.

K. Nichols
(b. 11/16/70; d. 8/4/99)

a. Father dies, 1976.
b. Mother marries Dr. Christopher Dawe, '79, moves to Weston.
c. Graduates Mount Alvernia HS, '88.
d. Graduates Johnson & Wales, Hospitality Mgmt., '92.
e. Hired, Four Seasons Hotel, Boston, Catering Dept., '92.
f. Promoted Asst. Mgr., Catering Dept., '96.
g. Engaged to D. Wetterau, '98.
h. Stalked by C. Falk. Car vandalized. First contact w/ me: February '99.

   i. D. Wetterau accident, March 15, '99. (Call Devin or Oscar again, try to see BPD report.)

   j. Car insurance cxld due to lack of payment.

   k. May, receives photos of D. Wetterau and other woman.

   l. Fired from job, May 18, '99, due to tardiness, multiple absences.

  m. Leaves apartment, May 30, '99.

   n. Moves into Holly Martens Inn, June 15, '99. (Two weeks missing. Where'd she stay?)

   o. Seen w/ Red-Haired Geek and Blond Rich Guy @ HM Inn, June–August '99.

   p. C. Falk receives nine letters signed K. Nichols, March–July, '99.

   q. Karen receives private psychiatrist's notes, date uncertain.

   r. Raped by C. Falk, July '99.

   s. Arrested for solicitation, July '99, Springfield Bus Depot.

   t. Suicide, August 4, '99.

Overview: Falsified letters sent to C. Falk suggest third-party involvement in K. Nichols's "bad luck." C. Falk *not* being vandalizer of car suggests same. Third Party could be Red-Haired Geek, Blond Rich Guy, or both. (Or neither.) Possession of psychiatrist's notes suggests possibility of Third Party being employee of psychiatrist. Further, ability by psychiatric employees to garner personal info of private citizens supplies opportunity to Third Party to infiltrate K. Nichols's life. Motive, however, seems nonexistent. Further, assumptions—

"Motive for what?" Angie said.

I put my hand over the page, looked back over my shoulder at her. "Didn't your mama ever teach you—?"

"It's rude to read over someone's shoulder, yes." She dropped her bag on the empty seat to her left and sat down beside me. "How's it coming?"

I sighed. "If only the dead could talk."

"Then they wouldn't be dead."

"Staggering," I said, "that intellect of yours."

She backhanded my shoulder and tossed her cigarettes and lighter on the bar in front of her.

"Angela!" Shakes Dooley came bounding down the bar, took her hand, and leaned over to kiss her cheek. "Well, if it ain't been too many days."

"Hey, Shakes. Don't say a word about the hair, okay?"

"What hair?" Shakes said.

"That's what I keep saying."

Angie hit me again. "Can I get a vodka straight, Shakes?"

Shakes pumped her hand vigorously before letting it go. "Finally, a real drinker!"

"Going broke on my buddy here?" Angie lit a cigarette.

"He drinks like a nun these days. People are starting to talk." Shakes poured a generous helping of chilled Finlandia into a glass and placed it before Angie.

"So," I said when Shakes left us alone, "come crawling back, eh?"

She gave me a smoky chuckle and took a sip of Finlandia. "Keep it up. It'll make torturing you later that much more pleasurable."

"Okay, I'll bite. What brings you here, Sicilian Spice?"

She rolled her eyes as she took another drink. "I got some oddities regarding David Wetterau." She held up her index finger. "Two, actually. The first was easy. That letter he wrote to the insurance company? My guy says it's a definite forgery."

I turned on my stool. "You already looked into this?"

She reached for her cigarettes, extracted one.

"On a Sunday," I said.

She lit the cigarette, her eyebrows raised.

"And turned something up," I said.

She curled her fingers and blew on them, polished an imaginary medal on her chest. "Two things."

"Okay," I said. "You're the coolest."

She placed a hand behind her ear and leaned in.

"You're aces. You're the bomb. You put the 'B' in bad-ass. You're the coolest."

"Already said that." She leaned in a little closer, hand still behind her ear.

I cleared my throat. "You are, without question or reservation, the smartest, most resourceful, perceptive private detective in the entire city of Boston."

Her mouth broke into that wide, slightly lopsided grin that can blow holes in my chest.

"Was that so difficult?" she said.

"Shoulda rolled right off my tongue. I don't know what's wrong with me."

"Just out of practice kissing ass, I guess."

I leaned back, took a lingering look at the curve of her hip, the press of flesh on her stool.

"Speaking of asses," I said, "allow me to note that yours still looks tremendous."

She waved her cigarette in my face. "Wood back in the pants, perv."

I placed my hands on the bar. "Yes'm."

"Oddity number two." Angie put a steno note-pad on the bar and flipped it open. She swiveled her stool so that our knees almost touched. "Just before five on the day he was hurt, David Wetterau calls Greg Dunne, the Steadicam guy, and begs off. Says his mother is ill."

"Was she?"

She nodded. "Of cancer. Five years ago. She died in '94."

"So he lies about—"

She held up a hand. "Not done yet." She stubbed her cigarette in the ashtray, left several chunks of coal still burning red. She hunched forward and our knees touched. "At four-forty, Wetterau received a call on his cell phone. It lasted four minutes and originated from a pay phone on High Street."

"Just around the block from the corner of Congress and Purchase."

"One block down, one over, to be exact. But that's not the most curious thing. Our contact at Cellular One told me where Wetterau was when he received the call."

"I'm breathless."

"Heading west on the Pike, just outside Natick."

"So at four-forty, he's heading to get the Steadicam."

"And at five-twenty he's in the middle of the intersection at Congress and Purchase."

"About to get his head squashed."

"Right. He parks his car in a garage on South Street, walks up Atlantic to Congress, and he's crossing Purchase when he trips."

"You talk to any cops about it?"

"Well, you know how the police feel these days about us in general and me in particular."

I nodded. "Maybe you'll think twice next time before you shoot a cop."

"Ha-ha," she said. "Luckily, Sallis & Salk has excellent relationships with the BPD."

"So you had someone from there call."

"Nah. I called Devin."

"You called Devin."

"Uh-huh. I asked him and he got back to me in about ten minutes."

"Ten minutes."

"Maybe fifteen. Anyway, I have the witness statements. All forty-six of them." She patted the soft leather bag on the chair to her left. "Ta-da!"

"'Nother drink, folks?" Shakes Dooley emptied Angie's ashtray and wiped the condensation ring from under her glass.

"Sure," Angie said.

"And for the missus?" Shakes asked me.

"Fine for now, Shakes. Thanks."

Shakes said, "What a pussy," under his breath, and walked off to get Angie another Finlandia.

"So let me get this straight," I said to Angie, "you call Devin and fifteen minutes later you have something I've been trying to get for four days."

" 'Bout the size of it."

Shakes placed her drink in front of her. "There you go, doll."

" 'Doll,' " I said when he walked away. "Who the hell says 'doll' anymore?"

"Yet he somehow makes it work," Angie said, and sipped some vodka. "Go figure."

"Man, I'm pissed at Devin."

"Why? You bug him all the time for favors. I haven't called him in almost a year."

"True."

"Plus, I'm prettier."

"Debatable."

She snorted. "Ask around, pal."

I took a sip of my beer. It was warm. Popular with Europeans, I know, but so are blood sausage and Steven Seagal.

On Shakes's next pass, I ordered a fresh one.

"Sure, I'll be taking your car keys next." He placed a frosty Beck's in front of me, shot a look at Angie, and walked away.

"I'm getting dissed way too much lately."

"Probably because you date defense attorneys who think a good wardrobe makes up for that lack-of-brains thing."

I turned on my chair. "Oh, you know her?"

"No. I've heard half the men in the twelfth ward do, though."

"Hiss," I said. "Meow."

She gave me a rueful smile as she lit another

cigarette. "Cat's got to have claws to make it a fight. What I hear, all she's got is a nice briefcase, great hair, and tits she's still making monthly payments on." Her smile widened and she crinkled her face at me. "Okay, pooky?"

"How's Someone?" I said.

Her smile faded and she reached into her bag. "Let's get back to David Wetterau and Karen—"

"I hear his name's Trey," I said. "You're dating a guy named Trey, Ange."

"How'd you—"

"We're detectives, remember? Same way you knew I was dating Vanessa."

"Vanessa," she said as if her mouth were filled with onions.

"Trey," I said.

"Shut up." She fumbled with her bag.

I drank some Beck's. "You're questioning my street cred and you're sleeping with a guy named *Trey*."

"I don't sleep with him anymore."

"Well, I don't sleep with her anymore."

"Congratulations."

"Back at you."

There was dead silence between us for a minute as Angie pulled several sheets of thermal fax paper from her bag and smoothed them on the bar. I drank some more Beck's, fingered the cardboard coaster, felt a grin fighting to break across my face. I glanced at Angie. The corners of her mouth twitched, too.

"Don't look at me," she said.

"Why not?"

"I'm telling you—" She lost the battle and closed her eyes as the smile broke across her cheeks.

Mine followed about a half second later.

"I don't know why I'm smiling," Angie said.

"Me, either."

"Prick."

"Bitch."

She laughed and turned on her chair, drink in hand. "Miss me?"

Like you can't imagine.

"Not a bit," I said.

We moved to a long table in the back, ordered some club sandwiches from the kitchen, and ate them as I brought her up to speed, told her in detail about my first meeting with Karen Nichols, my two run-ins with Cody Falk, my conversations with Joella Thomas, Karen's parents, Siobhan, and Holly and Warren Martens.

"Motive," Angie said. "We keep coming back to motive."

"I know."

"Who really vandalized her car, and why?"

"Yup."

"Who wrote the letters to Cody Falk, and why?"

"Why," I said, "did someone feel the need to fuck with this woman's life so completely she jumped off a building rather than take any more of it?"

"And did they go so far as to arrange David Wetterau's accident?"

"Access is an issue, too," I said.

She chewed her sandwich, dabbed the corner of her mouth with a napkin. "How so?"

"Who sent Karen the photos of David and the other woman? Hell, who took the photos?"

"They look professional to me."

"Me, too." I popped a cold french fry in my mouth. "And who gave Karen her own psychiatrist's notes? That's a big one."

Angie nodded. "And why?" she said. "Why, why, why?"

It turned into a long night. We read through all forty-six statements given by the witnesses to David Wetterau's accident, and a good half saw nothing at all, while the other twenty or so backed up the eventual police determination—Wetterau tripped in a pothole, got clipped in the head by a car doing everything in its power *not* to hit him.

Angie had even drawn up a crude diagram of the accident scene. It showed the placement of all forty-six witnesses at the time of the accident, and looked like a rough representation of a football game after a broken play. The majority of the witnesses—twenty-six—had been standing on the southwest corner of Purchase and Congress. Stockbrokers, mostly, heading for South Station after a day in the financial district, they stood waiting for the light to change. Another thirteen stood on the northwest corner, directly across from David Wetterau as he jaywalked toward them. Two more witnesses stood on the northeast corner, and a third drove the car behind Steven Kearns, the driver of the car that eventually clipped Wetterau's head. Of the remaining five witnesses, two had stepped off the curb on the southeast corner as the light turned yellow, and three were in the crosswalk, jaywalking like Wetterau—two heading west into the financial district, one heading east.

The closest witness had been that man, the one

heading east. His name was Miles Brewster, and just after he passed David Wetterau, Wetterau stepped in the pothole. The car was already traveling through the intersection, and when Wetterau fell, Steven Kearns immediately went into his swerve and those in the crosswalk scattered.

"Except for Brewster," I said.

"Huh?" Angie looked up from the photos of David Wetterau and the other woman.

"Why didn't this Brewster guy panic, too?"

She slid her chair over beside mine and looked down at the diagram.

"He's here," I said and placed my finger on the crude stick figure she'd labeled *W#7*. "He's moved past Wetterau, so his back would have been to the car."

"Right."

"He hears tires squeal. He turns *back*, sees the car plowing *toward* him, and yet he's—" I found his statement, read from it. "He's, quote, 'a foot from the guy, reaching toward him, you know, sorta frozen' when Wetterau gets hit."

Angie took the statement from my hand and read it. "Yeah, but you can freeze up in this sort of situation."

"But he's not frozen, he's *reaching*." I pulled my chair in closer to the table, pointed at W#7 in the diagram. "His back was to it, Ange. He had to turn, see it develop. His arm's not frozen, but his legs are? He's standing, by his own admission, a foot, maybe two, from car tires and a rear bumper sliding out of control."

She stared down at the diagram, rubbed her face.

"Our possession of these statements is illegal. We can't reinterview Brewster and let on that we know what his original statement was."

I sighed. "That do make it tougher."

"It do."

"But the guy bears a second look, you agree?"

"Definitely."

She sat back in her chair, raised both hands to her head to push back hair that wasn't there anymore. She caught herself at the same time I did, gave my wide grin her middle finger as she brought her hands back down.

"Okay," she said, and drummed her pen on her notepad. "What's our list of priorities here?"

"First, talk to Karen's psychiatrist."

She nodded. "That's a hell of a leak coming from her office."

"Second, talk to Brewster. You got an address?"

She pulled a piece of paper from the bottom of the thermal fax pile. "Miles Brewster," she said, "Twelve Landsdowne Street." She looked up from the page and her mouth remained open.

"Gee," I said, "what's wrong with this picture?"

"Twelve Landsdowne," she said. "That would make it—"

"Fenway Park."

She groaned. "How's a cop not notice that?"

I shrugged. "A rookie taking the statements at the scene. Forty-six witnesses, he's tired, whatever."

"Shit."

"But Brewster," I said, "is now officially dirty."

Angie dropped the fax paper to the table. "This wasn't an accident."

"Doesn't look like it."

"Your operating theory."

"Brewster's walking east, Wetterau's walking west. Brewster slips out his foot as they pass. Boom."

She nodded, excitement surging past the fatigue in her face. "Brewster says he was reaching down to pick Wetterau back *up*."

"But he was actually holding him down," I said.

Angie lit a cigarette, squinted through the smoke at her diagram. "We've stumbled onto something ugly here, pal."

I nodded. "Big ol' hunk of ugly."

16

Dr. Diane Bourne's office was housed on the second floor of a brownstone on Fairfield Street, in between a gallery specializing in mid-thirteenth-century East African kitchen pottery and a place that stitched bumper stickers on canvas and then sewed them to magnets for easy refrigerator attachment.

The office was done up in some kind of Laura Ashley meets the Spanish Inquisition decor. Plump armchairs and couches with floral stitching bore an inviting sense of softness that was all but overwhelmed by their colors—blood reds and pitch ebonies, carpets that matched, paintings on the wall by Bosch and Blake. I'd always thought a psychiatrist's room was supposed to say Please, tell me your problems, not Please, don't scream.

Diane Bourne was in her late thirties and so svelte I had to resist the urge to call in some takeout, force-feed her lunch. Dressed in a white sleeveless sheath dress that rode high up her throat and low to her knee, she stood out amid all the dark like a ghost floating through the moors. Her hair and skin were so pale it was hard to see where one began and the other ended, and even her eyes were the translucent gray of an ice storm. The tight dress, instead of making her look scrawny, seemed to accentuate the few soft parts of her, the flesh that swelled just slightly over her calves and hips and shoulders. The overall effect, I thought, as she took a seat behind her smoked glass desk, was of an engine— sleek, well-tuned, revving at every red light.

As soon as we took our seats at the desk, Dr. Diane Bourne moved a small metronome to her left, so that her view of us was completely unobstructed, and lit a cigarette.

She gave Angie a small, dark smile. "Now, what can I do for you?"

"We're looking into the death of Karen Nichols," Angie said.

"Yes," she said, and sucked a small white cloud of smoke back into her lungs, "Mr. Kenzie mentioned as much on the phone." She tapped a modicum of ash into a crystal ashtray. "He was rather"—her mist-gray eyes met mine—"cagey about anything else."

"Cagey," I said.

She took another small hit off the cigarette and crossed her long legs. "You like that?"

"Oh, yeah." I raised my eyebrows up and down several times.

She gave me a wisp of a smile and turned back to Angie. "As I hope I made quite clear to Mr. Kenzie, I have no inclination to discuss anything in regards to Miss Nichols's therapy."

Angie snapped her fingers. "Nuts."

Diane Bourne swiveled back to me. "Mr. Kenzie, however, intimated over the—"

"Intimated?" Angie said.

"Intimated, yes, over the phone that he had information which could—do I have this right, Mr. Kenzie?—pose questions as to potential ethical violations in my handling of Ms. Nichols."

I met her arched eyebrow with two of my own. "I wouldn't say I was quite so—"

"Articulate?"

"Verbose," I said. "But, otherwise, Dr. Bourne, that was the gist, yes."

Dr. Bourne moved the ashtray a bit to her left so that we could see the small tape recorder behind it. "It's my legal duty to inform you that this conversation is being recorded."

"Cool," I said. "Let me ask you—where'd you get that? Sharper Image, right? I've never seen one look so chic." I looked at Angie. "You?"

"I'm still back at 'intimated,'" she said.

I nodded. "That was a good one. I've been accused of a lot of things, but jeez."

Diane Bourne shaved some excess ash off against the Waterford crystal. "You two have a very nice act going."

Angie slugged my shoulder and I swept a hand at the back of her head that she ducked at the last moment. Then we both smiled at Dr. Diane Bourne.

She took another tiny toke off her cigarette. "Sort of a Butch and Sundance thing without the homosexual subtext."

"Usually we get the Nick and Nora thing," I said to Angie.

"Or the Chico and Groucho," Angie reminded me.

"With the homosexual subtext, though. But that Butch and Sundance thing."

"Quite the compliment," Angie said.

I turned away from Angie and leaned my elbows on Dr. Bourne's desk, looked past the swing of the metronome and into her pale, pale eyes. "Why would one of your patients have your session notes in her possession, Doctor?"

She didn't say anything. She sat very still, her shoulders hunched very slightly, as if preparing for a sudden bite of cold air.

I leaned back in my chair. "Can you tell me that?"

She cocked her head to the left. "Would you repeat your question, please?"

Angie did so. I provided sign language.

"I don't quite understand what you're driving at." She shaved off another sliver of ash in the crystal.

Angie said, "Is it common practice for you to take notes during sessions with your patients?"

"Yes. It's common with most—"

"And is it your practice, Doctor, to then mail those notes to the patients they concern?"

"Of course not."

"Then how," Angie said, "did your notes for a session with Karen Nichols, dated April the sixth, 1994, end up in Miss Nichols's possession?"

"I have no idea," Dr. Bourne said with the barely patient air of a matron speaking to a child. "Possibly she took them herself during one of her visits."

"You keep your files locked?" I asked.

"Yes."

"Then how could Karen break into them?"

Her chiseled face slackened along the jawline and her lips parted. "She couldn't," she said eventually.

"Which would suggest," Angie said, "that you or someone from your office gave confidential, potentially damaging information to a conceivably unbalanced client."

Dr. Bourne closed her mouth and her jaw tightened. "Hardly, Ms. Gennaro. I seem to remember that we had a break-in here a few—"

"Excuse me?" Angie leaned forward. "You *seem to remember* a break-in?"

"Yes."

"So there'd be a police report."

"A what?"

"A police report," I said.

"No. Nothing of value seemed to be missing."

"Just confidential files," I said.

"No. I never said—"

Angie said, "Because I would think your other clients would expect to be notified if—"

"Ms. Gennaro, I don't think—"

"—confidential documents relating to the most personal aspects of their lives were in the hands of an unknown third party." Angie looked over at me. "Don't you agree?"

"We could let them know," I said. "Purely as a public service."

Dr. Bourne's cigarette had turned to a curled finger of white ash in the crystal tray. As I watched, the finger collapsed.

"Logistically," Angie said, "that would be tough."

"Nah," I said. "We just sit outside in our car. Every time we see someone rich who's approaching the building and looks a little funny in the head, we assume they're a client of Dr. Bourne's and—"

"You will not."

"—we approach and tell them about the break-in."

"In the interest of the public good," Angie said. "People's right to know. Gosh, we're kinda swell that way, aren't we?"

I nodded. "No coal in our stockings this Christmas."

Diane Bourne lit a second cigarette and watched us through the smoke, her pale eyes flat and seemingly nonplussed. "What do you want?" she said, and I detected just the hint of a throb in her vocal cords, a slight ticking not unlike the metronome.

"For starters," I said, "we want to know how those session notes took flight from your office."

"I haven't the faintest."

Angie lit her own cigarette. "Get the faintest, lady."

Diane Bourne uncrossed her legs and tucked them to the side in that effortless way all women can and no man is remotely capable of. She held her cigarette up by her temple and gazed at Blake's *Los* on the east wall, a painting that was about as calming as a plane crash.

"I had a temp secretary a couple of months ago. I sensed—no proof, mind you, just a sense—that she had been going through the files. She was only with me a week, so I didn't give it much thought after she left."

"Her name?"

"I don't remember."

"But you have records."

"Of course. I'll have Miles get them for you on your way out." Then she smiled. "Oh, I forgot, he's not here today. Well, I'll make a note to have him send that information to you."

Angie was sitting two feet away, but I could feel her pulse quicken and her blood warm along with my own.

I indicated the outer office with a backward jerk of my thumb. "Miles would be who?"

She suddenly looked as if she regretted ever mentioning him. "He's, ah, just someone who works for me part-time as a secretary."

"Part-time," I said. "So he has another job?"

She nodded.

"Where?"

"Why?"

"Curious," I said. "It's an occupational hazard. Humor me."

She sighed. "He works at Evanton Hospital in Wellesley."

"The psych hospital?"

"Yes."

"Doing what?" Angie asked.

"He's their records clerk."

"And how long has he worked here?"

"Why do you ask?" Another small cock of the head.

"I'm trying to ascertain who has access to your files, Doctor."

She leaned forward, tapped some ash into the tray.

"Miles Lovell has been in my employ for three and a half years, Mr. Kenzie, and to answer your next question, No, he would have no reason to remove session notes from Karen Nichols's file and mail them to her."

Lovell, I thought. Not Brewster. Uses a false last name, but sticks to his first name out of comfort. Not a bad move if your name is John. Kind of dumb, though, if you name's somewhat less common.

"Okay." I smiled. Picture of the satisfied detective. No more questions here about ol' Miles Lovell. He's right as rain in my book, ma'am.

"He's the most trustworthy assistant I've ever had."

"I'm sure he is."

"Now," she said, "have I answered all your questions?"

My smile widened. "Not even close."

"Tell us about Karen Nichols," Angie said.

"There's very little to tell . . ."

Half an hour later she was still talking, ticking off the details of Karen Nichols's psyche with all the consistency and emotion of that metronome of hers.

Karen, according to Dr. Diane Bourne, had been a classic bipolar manic depressive. She had over the years taken prescriptions for lithium, Depakote, and Tegretol, as well as the Prozac I'd found in Warren's barn. Whether hers was a condition mandated by genetics became largely irrelevant when her father died and his killer shot himself in front of Karen. Following textbook patterns, according to Dr. Bourne, Karen, far from acting out as a child or an adolescent, had been preternaturally well behaved, molding herself into the role of perfect daughter, sister, and eventually, girlfriend.

"She modeled herself," Dr. Bourne said, "like a lot of girls, after television ideals. Repeats mostly in Karen's case. That was part of her pathology—to live as much in the past and an idealized America as she could, so she idolized Mary Tyler Moore's Mary Richards and also all those mothers from fifties and sixties sitcoms—Barbara Billingsley, Donna Reed, Mary Tyler Moore again as Dick Van Dyke's wife. She read Jane Austen and missed the irony and anger of Austen's work entirely. She chose instead to see her work as fantasies of how a good girl's life could be successful if she lived correctly and opted to marry well like Emma or Elinor Dashwood. So this became the goal, and David Wetterau, her Darcy or Rob Petrie, if you will, was the linchpin to a happy life."

"And when he was turned into a vegetable . . ."

"All those demons of hers, repressed for twenty years, came back to roost. I had long suspected that were Karen's model life ever to suffer a serious fissure, her breakdown would manifest sexually."

"Why would you suspect that?" Angie asked.

"You must understand that it was her father's sexual liaisons with the wife of Lieutenant Crowe which predicated Lieutenant Crowe's extreme act of violence and the death of Karen's father."

"So Karen's father had an affair with his best friend's wife."

She nodded. "That's what the shooting was all about. Add in certain aspects of the Electra complex,

which at six years old would have surely been blooming, if not raging, in Karen, her guilt over her father's
death, and her conflicted sexual feelings for her
brother, and you have a recipe for—"

"She had sexual relations with her brother?" I
said.

Diane Bourne shook her head. "No. Emphatically,
no. But, like a lot of women with an older stepbrother,
she did, during adolescence, first recognize symptoms
of her sexual awakening in terms of Wesley. The
male ideal in Karen's world, you see, was a dominating figure. Her natural father was a military man, a
warrior. Her stepfather was domineering in his own
right. Wesley Dawe was given to violent, psychotic
episodes and, until his disappearance, was being
treated with antipsychotic medication."

"You treated Wesley?"

She nodded.

"Tell us about him."

She pursed her lips and shook her head. "I think
not."

Angie looked at me. "Out to the car?"

I nodded. "Need to pick up a thermos of coffee,
but then we're good to go."

We stood.

"Sit down, Ms. Gennaro, Mr. Kenzie." Diane
Bourne waved us down to our seats. "Jesus, you two
don't know when to quit."

"Why we get the big bucks," Angie said.

Dr. Bourne leaned back in her chair, parted the
heavy curtains behind her, and looked out on the
heat-choked brick of the building across Fairfield
from her. The metallic roof of a tall truck bounced

the hard sun back into her eyes. She dropped the curtain and blinked in the darkness of the room.

"Wesley Dawe," she said, her fingers pinched over her eyelids, "was a very confused, angry young man the last time I saw him."

"When was this?"

"Nine years ago."

"And he was how old?"

"Twenty-three. His hatred of his father was total. His hatred of himself was only slightly less so. After he attacked Dr. Dawe that time, I recommended he be involuntarily committed for both his family's well-being and his own."

"Attacked how?"

"He stabbed his father, Mr. Kenzie. With a kitchen knife. Oh, typical of Wesley, he botched the job. He aimed for the neck, I think, but Dr. Dawe managed to raise his shoulder in time, and Wesley ran from the house."

"And when he was caught, you—"

"He was never caught. He disappeared that night. The night of Karen's senior prom, actually."

"And how did that affect Karen?" Angie asked.

"At the time? Not at all." Diane Bourne's eyes caught a glint of light slanting through the gap in the curtains behind her and the flat gray turned shiny alabaster. "Karen Nichols was powerful in her denial. It was her primary shield and her primary weapon. At the time, I think she said something to the effect of, 'Oh, Wesley, he can't seem to stop acting out,' and then went on to speak in great detail about her prom."

"Just like Mary Richards would," Angie said.

"Very astute, Ms. Gennaro. Exactly like Mary

Richards would. Accentuate the positive. Even to the detriment of your own psyche."

"Back to Wesley," I said.

"Wesley Dawe," she said, exhausted now from our questions, "had a genius IQ and a weak, tortured psyche. It's a potentially lethal combination. Maybe if he'd been allowed to mature into his late twenties with proper care, his intelligence would have been allowed to gain dominance over his psychosis and he would have led a so-called normal life. But when he was blamed for his baby sister's death by his father, he snapped, and shortly thereafter, disappeared. It was a tragedy, really. He was such a brilliant boy."

"It sounds like you admired him," Angie said.

She leaned back in her chair, tilted her head toward the ceiling. "Wesley won a national chess tournament when he was nine. Think about that. Nine years old, he was better at something than any other child in the country under the age of fifteen. He had his first nervous breakdown at ten. He never played chess again." She tilted her head forward, held us with those pale eyes. "He never *played*, period, again."

She stood and her shimmering whiteness towered over us for a moment. "Let me see if I can find that temp's name for you."

She led us back into a rear office with a file cabinet and small desk, opened the file cabinet with a key, and riffled through it until she held up a piece of paper. "Pauline Stavaris. Lives—are you ready?"

"Pen in hand," I said.

"Lives at Thirty-five Medford Street."

"In Medford?"

"Everett."

"Phone number?"

She gave it to me.

"I trust we're done," Diane Bourne said.

"Absolutely," Angie said. "It was a pleasure."

She led us back through her main office and then out to the foyer. She shook our hands.

"Karen wouldn't have wanted this, you know."

I stepped back from her. "Really?"

She waved at the foyer. "All this mess you're stirring up. All this sullying of her reputation. She cared deeply about appearances."

"What do you think her appearance was when the cops found her after a twenty-six-story swan dive? You tell me that, Doctor?"

She smiled tightly. "Goodbye, Mr. Kenzie, Ms. Gennaro. I trust I'll never see either of you again."

"Trust all you want," Angie said.

"But don't bet on it," I said.

17

I called Bubba from the car. "What are you doing?"

"Just got off the plane from Mickland," he said.

"Fun time?"

"Bunch of pissed-off midgets, and don't even ask me what language they speak 'cause it don't sound anything like English."

I did my best pure-porridge Northern Irish accent. "Yer man take yew for a sessiun, did he, yah?"

"What?"

"Fer fook's sake, Rogowski, got a fierce amount of cotton in yer ars?"

"Cut it out," Bubba said. "Goddammit."

Angie put her hand on my arm. "Stop torturing the poor fella."

"Angie's with me," I said.

"No shit. Where?"

"Back Bay. We need a delivery man."

"Bomb?" He sounded excited, like he had a few lying around he needed to get rid of.

"Ah, no. Just a tape recorder."

"Oh." He sounded bored.

"Come on," I said. "Remember, Ange is with me. We'll go drinking afterward."

He grunted. "Shakes Dooley says you forgot how."

"Well, school me, brother. School me."

"So we follow Dr. Bourne home," Angie said, "and then we somehow slide a tape recorder into her place?"

"Yeah."

"Dumb plan."

"You got a better one?"

"Not at the moment."

"You think she's dirty?" I said.

"I agree there's something fishy about her."

"So we stick to my plan until we have a better one."

"Oh, there's a better one. I'll come up with it. Trust me. There's a better one."

At four a black BMW pulled up outside of Dr. Bourne's office. The driver sat inside for a bit, smoking, and then he got out and stood on the street, leaned back against the hood of the Beemer. He was a short guy who wore a green silk shirt tucked into tight black jeans.

"He has red hair," I said.

"What?"

I pointed at the guy.

"So? Lotta people with red hair. Particularly in this town."

Diane Bourne appeared on the front landing of her building. The redheaded guy raised his head in recognition of her. Very slightly, she shook her head.

The guy's shoulders rose in confusion as she walked down the stairs and passed him, her head down, her footsteps fast and deliberate.

The guy watched her go, then he turned slowly and looked around the street as if he suddenly sensed he was being watched. He tossed his cigarette to the sidewalk and climbed in his BMW.

I called Bubba, who was parked over on Newbury in his van. "Change of plans," I said. "We're tailing a black Beemer."

"Whatever." He hung up. Mr. Hard-to-Impress.

"Why are we following this guy?" Angie said. I let two cars get in between us and the BMW before I pulled away from the curb.

"Because he's a redhead," I said. "Because Bourne knew him and acted like she didn't. Because he looks hinky."

"Hinky?"

I nodded. "Hinky."

"What's that mean?"

"I don't know. I heard it on *Mannix* once."

We followed the BMW south out of the city with Bubba's black van riding our rear bumper straight into the rush-hour crunch. From Albany Street on, we averaged about six miles a decade as we crawled through Southie, Dorchester, Quincy, and Braintree. Twenty miles, and it took us only an hour and fifteen minutes. Welcome to Boston; we just fucking live for traffic.

He got off the expressway in Hingham and led us through another half an hour of bumper-to-bumper down one humid, crabby lane of Route 228. We passed through Hingham—all white colonials and white picket fences and white people—and then wound past a strip of power plants and mammoth gas tanks under high-tension wire before the black Beemer led us into Nantasket.

Once a grungy beach community with a soiled-neon carny atmosphere that attracted lots of bikers and women with flabby, exposed midriffs and stringy hair, Nantasket Beach slipped into a sterile, picture-postcard loveliness when they tore down the amusement park that once fronted its shores. Gone were the cheesy teacup rides and ratty wooden clowns you'd knock down with a softball to win an anemic guppy in a plastic bag. A roller coaster that, in its time, had been acknowledged as the country's most dangerous had had its twisted dinosaur of a skeleton shattered by wrecking balls and pulled by its roots from the earth so they could build condos overlooking the boardwalk. All that remained of the old days were the ocean itself and a few arcades bathed in sticky orange light along the boardwalk.

Pretty soon they'd replace the arcades with coffee bars, outlaw stringy hair, and as soon as anyone stopped having any fun whatsoever, they could safely call it progress.

It occurred to me, as we wound our way down the beach road past the site of the old amusement park, that if I ever had kids, and I took them to places that had once mattered to me, all there'd be to show for my youth would be the buildings that had replaced it.

The BMW took a quick left just past the end of the boardwalk, then a right, and another left before he pulled into the sandy driveway of a small white

Cape with green awnings and trim. We rolled past, and Angie watched in her sideview mirror.

"What the hell is he doing?"

"Who?"

She shook her head, eyes on the mirror. "Bubba."

I looked in the rearview, saw that Bubba had pulled his black van to a rest on the shoulder about fifty yards before the redhead's house. As I watched, he hopped out of the van and ran up between two Capes that were near identical to the redhead's and disappeared somewhere in the backyards.

"This," I said, "was not part of the plan."

"Carrottop's in his house," Angie said.

I U-turned and drove back down the street, passing the redhead's house as he closed his front door behind him and continuing past Bubba's van. I drove another twenty yards and pulled over on the right shoulder in front of a home construction site, the skeleton of another Cape sitting on bare brown land.

Angie and I got out of the car and walked back toward Bubba's van.

"I hate when he does this," she said.

I nodded. "Sometimes I forget he has a mind of his own."

"I know he has a mind of his own," Angie said. "It's how he uses it that keeps me up nights."

We reached the rear of the van just as Bubba came bounding out from between the two houses, pushed us aside, and opened the rear doors.

"Bubba," Angie said, "what have you done?"

"Sssh. I'm working here." He tossed a pair of

branch cutters into the rear of the van, grabbed a gym bag from the floor, and shut the doors.

"What're you—"

He put a finger to my lips. "Sssh. Trust me. This is good."

"Does it involve heavy explosives?" Angie asked.

"You want it to?" Bubba reached for the van door again.

"No, Bubba. Very much no."

"Oh." He dropped his hand from the door. "No time. Be right back."

He jostled us aside and ran in a crouch across the lawns toward the redhead's house. Even in a crouch, Bubba running across your lawn is about as easy to miss as Sputnik would be. He weighs something less than a piano but something more than a fridge, and he's got that demented newborn's face billowing out from under spikes of brown hair and above a neck the circumference of a rhino's midsection. He kind of moves like a rhino, actually, lumbering and slightly to his right, but oh so quickly.

We watched with mouths slightly ajar as he dropped to his knees by the BMW, slim-jimmed the lock in the time it would take me to do it with a key, and then opened the door.

Angie and I both tensed for the blare of an alarm, but were met with silence as Bubba reached into the car, pulled something out, and slid it in the pocket of his trench coat.

Angie said, "What in the fuck is he doing?"

Bubba reached behind him and unzipped the gym bag by his knees. His hand searched around inside until he found what he was looking for. He removed a small black rectangular object and placed it in the car.

"It's a bomb," I said.

"He promised," Angie said.

"Yeah," I said, "but he's, oh, nuts. Remember?"

Bubba used the sleeve of his trench coat to wipe the places he'd touched in and outside the car, then he gently closed the door and scrambled back across the lawn and over to us.

"I," he said, "am so fucking cool."

"Agreed," I said. "What did you do?"

"I mean, I'm the balls, dude. I'm it. I surprise myself sometimes." He opened the back door of the van, tossed the gym bag on the floor.

"Bubba," Angie said, "what's in the bag?"

Bubba was damn near bursting. He threw the folds of the bag wide, waved us to look inside. "Cell phones!" he said with a ten-year-old's glee.

I looked in the bag. He was right. Ten or twelve of them—Nokias, Ericcsons, Motorolas, most black, a few gray.

"Great," I said. I looked up into his beaming face. "Actually, why is this great, Bubba?"

"'Cause your idea *sucked*, and I came up with this one."

"My idea wasn't bad."

"It sucked!" he said happily. "I mean, it blew, dude. Put a bug in a box, have the guy—or wasn't it some chick at first—take it in the house."

"Yeah, so?"

"So, what if he leaves the box on the dining room table, goes up to the bedrooms to do whatever it is you want to hear?"

"We were kinda hoping he wouldn't."

He gave me a thumbs-up. "Fucking great thinking there."

"So," Angie said, "what was your idea?"

"Replace his cell phone," Bubba said. He pointed into the bag. "These all have bugs already inside. All I had to do was match one of mine"—he pulled a charcoal Nokia flip phone from his pocket—"to his."

"That's his?"

He nodded.

I nodded with him, let my smile match his own, until I dropped it. "Bubba, no offense, but so what? The guy's inside his house."

Bubba rocked back on his heels, raised his eyebrows up and down several times. "Yeah?"

"Yeah," I said. "So—how do I put this?—why the fuck does he need to use his cell phone when he probably has three or four house phones inside?"

"House phones," Bubba said slowly, a frown beginning to replace the smile. "Never thought of those. He can just pick one up and call anywhere he wants, huh?"

"Yeah, Bubba. That's sort of their point. He's probably doing it right now."

"Shit," Bubba said. "Too bad I cut the phone lines out back, huh?"

Angie laughed. She clapped his cherub's face between her hands and kissed his nose.

Bubba blushed and then looked at me, that smile beginning to grow again.

"Ahm . . ."

"Yeah?"

"Sorry," I said.

"For?"

"Doubting you. Okay? Happy?"

"And talking down to me."

"And talking down to you, yes."

"And speaking in a derisive tone of voice," Angie said.

I glared at her.

"What she said." Bubba jerked a thumb at Angie.

Angie looked over her shoulder. "He's coming back out."

We all climbed into the van, and Bubba shut the door behind us, and we looked out through mirrored glass at the redhead as he kicked his front tire, opened his car door, and reached across the seat, pulled his cellular from the console.

"Why didn't he call people during the ride back?" Angie asked. "If the calls were important . . ."

"Roaming," Bubba said. "Someone's moving, it's way easier to tap into their conversation—listen in or clone the phone, whatever."

"But stationary?" I said.

He screwed his face up. "What, you mean like writing something down? What's that got to—"

"Not the paper. Stationary," I said, "as in standing still."

"Oh." He rolled his eyes at Angie. "Showing off the college again." He glanced back at me. "Okay, Joe Word of the Day, yeah, if he's 'stationary' it's way harder to cut into his transmission. Gotta go through land lines and tin roofs and antennas and satellite dishes, microwaves, the whole fucking nine if you know what I mean."

Carrottop walked back into his house.

Bubba used one finger to type on a laptop computer on the floor between us. He pulled a grimy piece of paper from his pocket. In his second-grader's scrawl, he'd listed the cell phone types and serial numbers, and then the frequency numbers for his recording devices beside them. He typed a frequency number into the computer, then sat back on the floor.

"Never tried this before," he said. "Hope it works."

I rolled my eyes and sat back against the side panel.

"I don't hear anything," I said after about thirty seconds.

"Ooops." Bubba raised a finger above his head. "Volume."

He leaned forward and pressed the volume button at the base of the laptop, and after a moment, we heard Diane Bourne's voice through the tiny speakers.

". . . Are you drunk, Miles? Of course it's an issue. They asked all sorts of questions."

I smiled at Angie. "And you didn't want to follow the redhead."

She rolled her eyes and said to Bubba, "One good hunch in three years, he thinks he's a god."

"What questions?" Miles said.

"Who you were, where you worked."

"How did they get onto me?"

Diane Bourne ignored the question. "They wanted to know about Karen, about Wesley, about how the fucking session notes got in Karen's possession, *Miles*."

"All right, all right, just relax."

"Fuck relax! You relax! Oh, Jesus," she said through

a long stream of air. "The two of them are smart. Do you understand?"

Bubba nudged me. "Talking about you two?"

I nodded.

"Shit," Bubba said. "Smart. Oh, sure."

"Yes," Miles Lovell said. "They're smart. We knew that."

"We never knew they'd trace anything to me. Fucking fix it, Miles. Call him."

"Just—"

"Fix it!" she snapped. And then she hung up.

No sooner had Miles hung up than he dialed another number.

A man answered on the other end. "Yeah?"

"Two detectives sniffed around today," Miles said.

"Detectives? You mean cops?"

"No. Private. They know about the session notes."

"Someone forgot to retrieve them?"

"Someone was drunk. What can Someone say?"

"Sure."

"She's rattled."

"The good doctor?"

"Yes."

"Too rattled?" the calm voice asked.

"Definitely."

"She'll need a speaking to?"

"She may need more. She's the weak link here."

"The weak link. Uh-huh."

There was a long pause. I could hear Miles breathing on his end, static and hiss on the other.

"You there?" Miles asked.

"I find it boring."

"Which?"

"Working that way."

"We may not have time for your way. Look, we—"

"Not over the phone."

"Fine. The usual, then."

"The usual. Don't worry so much."

"I'm not worried. I just want this dealt with faster than your usual inclinations allow."

"Absolutely."

"I'm serious."

"I recognize that," the calm voice said, and then he broke the connection.

Miles hung up, immediately dialed a third number.

A woman picked up a phone on the fourth ring, her voice thick and sluggish. "Yeah."

"It's me," Miles said.

"Uh-huh."

"'Member that time we were supposed to pick something up at Karen's?"

"What?"

"The notes. Remember?"

"Hey, it was your deal."

"He's pissed."

"So? It was *your* deal."

"That's not the way he sees it."

"What are you saying?"

"I'm saying he could go on another of his warpaths. Be careful."

"Aww, Jesus," the woman said. "You . . . you fucking kidding me? Jesus, Miles!"

"Calm down."

"No! Okay? Jesus! He owns us, Miles. He owns us."

"He owns everyone," Miles said. "Just . . ."

"What? Just what, Miles? Huh?"

"I dunno. Watch your back."

"Thanks. Thanks a lot. Shit." She hung up.

Miles broke the connection and we sat in the van and watched his house, waited for him to pop his head out and take us wherever it was he intended to go.

"That woman sound like Dr. Bourne to you?"

Angie shook her head. "No. Definitely younger."

I nodded.

Bubba said, "So this guy in the house, he did something heinous?"

"Yeah. I think so."

Bubba reached under his trench coat, pulled out a .22 and screwed on a silencer. "So, okay. Let's go."

"What?"

He looked at me. "Let's just kick in the door and shoot him."

"Why?"

He shrugged. "You said he did something heinous. So, okay, let's shoot him. Come on. It'll be fun."

"Bubba," I said, and placed my hand over his so he lowered the gun, "we don't know what we're dealing with yet. We need this guy to lead us to whoever he's working with."

Bubba's eyes widened and his mouth dropped open and he stared at the van wall like a child whose birthday balloon just popped in front of his face.

"Man," he said to Angie, "why's he bring me along if I can't shoot someone?"

Angie put a hand on his neck. "There, there, fella. All good things come to those who wait."

Bubba shook his head. "You know what comes to those who wait?"

"What?"

"More waiting." He frowned. "And still no one gets shot." He pulled a bottle of vodka from his trench coat, took a long pull, and shook his massive head. "Don't seem fair sometimes."

Poor Bubba. Always showing up for the party in the wrong clothes.

18

Miles Lovell left his house shortly after sundown as the sky saturated itself in tomato red and the smell of low tide rode the breeze inland.

We let him get a few blocks away before we turned out onto the beach road and picked him back up again near the gas tanks on that industrial-refuse stretch of 228. Traffic was much lighter now, and what there was of it headed toward the beach, not away from it, so we hung a quarter mile back, waiting for the light to leave the sky.

The red only deepened, though, and plumes of deep blue feathered up around it. Angie rode with Bubba in the van and I rode ahead of them in the Porsche as Lovell led us back through Hingham and onto Route 3 again, heading farther south.

It wasn't a long ride. A few exits later, he pulled off by Plymouth Rock, and then, a mile later, turned down several smaller dirt roads, each getting dustier and less developed as we hung way back and hoped we didn't lose him in any switch-backs or small lanes shrouded by thick vegation and low tree limbs.

I had my windows rolled down and the radio off, and I could hear him occasionally, the crunch of his tires on rutted road up ahead, a strain of the jazz on his stereo flowing through his sunroof. We were deep in the Myles Standish forest, as far as I could tell, the pine and white maple and larch towering over us under the red sky, and I smelled the cranberries long before I saw them.

It was a sweet, sharp smell, hot with a secondary odor of fermenting fruit laid bare to a day's sun. White vapors rose and drifted through the trees as the night cooled the bog, and I pulled over in the last clearing before the bog itself, watching Lovell's taillights wind down the final small lane that led to the soft banks.

Bubba's van pulled in beside the Porsche, and the three of us exited our vehicles and carefully shut our doors behind us so that the only noises they made were soft clicks as the locks caught. Fifty yards through thin trees we heard Miles Lovell's door open, followed by the snap of it shutting. The sounds were hard and clear out here, traveling over the misty bogs and through the thin tree line as if they were occurring beside us.

We walked down the damp, dark lane that led to the bog, and through the thin trees we caught glimpses of the sea of cranberry, green at this stage of their growth, the knobby surfaces of the fruit bobbing in the moisture and white vapor, lapping gently against themselves.

Footsteps echoed off wood and a crow cawed in the deepening night air and the treetops rustled in a soft humid kiss of wind. We reached the edge of the tree line by the rear bumper of the BMW, and I peeked my head around the final tree trunk.

The cranberry bog lay wide and undulating before me. The white vapor hung like cold breath an inch over the crop, and a cross of dark plank wood divided the entire bog into four long rectangles. Miles Lovell walked up one of the shorter planks. In the center of the cross was a small wood pump shed, and Lovell opened its door, walked inside, and shut the door behind him.

I crept out along the shoreline, used Lovell's car to block me, I hoped, from the view of anyone on the far side of the bog, and looked at the shed. It was barely big enough to qualify as a Porta Potti, and there was one window on the right side facing the long plank that stretched north across the bog. A muslin curtain hung down on the other side of the glass, and as I watched, the panes turned muted orange with light and Lovell's muddy silhouette passed by and vanished on the other side.

Save for the car, there was no cover out here—just soggy shore and marshy ground to my right that buzzed gently with bees, mosquitoes, and crickets rousing themselves for the night shift. I crept back to the tree line. Angie, Bubba, and I worked our way through the thin trunks to the last group fronting the bog. From there we could see the front and left side of the hut and a portion of the cross that stretched over to the opposite shore and disappeared in a black thicket of trees.

"Shit," I said. "Wish I'd brought the binoculars."

Bubba sighed, pulled a pair from his trench coat, and handed them to me. Bubba and his trench coat—

sometimes you'd swear he carried a Kmart in the thing.

"You're like Harpo Marx with that coat. I ever tell you that?"

"Seven, maybe eight hundred times."

"Oh." My cool quotient was definitely slipping.

I trained the binoculars on the shed, racked the focus, and got nothing for my efforts but a clear view of wood. I doubted there was a window on the far side, and the one I'd seen on the right wall had been curtained, so it appeared for the moment that all there was to do was wait for the mystery man to appear for his meeting with Lovell and hope the mosquitoes or bees didn't come out in force. Of course, if they did, Bubba probably had a can of repellent in his trench coat, maybe a bug light.

Around us, the sky bled free of red and gradually painted itself dark blue, and the green cranberries brightened against the fresh backdrop while the mist changed from white to mossy gray and the trees turned black.

"You think the guy Miles is meeting could've shown up first?" I asked Angie after a while.

She looked out at the hut. "Anything's possible. He would have had to approach from another way, though. Lovell made the only tracks over there, and we're parked to the north."

I panned the binoculars to the southern tip of the cross where it disappeared in tall stalks of withered yellow vegetation rising out of a gaseous marsh teeming with mosquitoes. That definitely seemed the least appealing and most difficult direction from which to approach, unless you really dug malarial infections.

Behind me, Bubba snorted and kicked at the ground, snapped a few thick twigs off a tree.

I turned the lenses on the opposite shore, the eastern tip of the cross. There, the shore looked firmer and the trees were thick and dry and tall. So thick, in fact, that no matter how much I adjusted and readjusted the focus, I could see nothing but black trunks and green moss going back fifty yards.

"If he's in there, he came from the other side." I pointed, then shrugged. "I guess we get a glimpse of him on the way out. You got a camera?"

Angie nodded, pulled from her bag a small Pentax with built-in auto lenses and flash adjustments for night shooting.

I smiled. "One of my Christmas presents."

"Christmas '97." She chuckled. "The only one I can safely show in public."

I caught her eyes, and she held my gaze for a moment in which I felt a stab of sudden, overpowering yearning. Then she dropped her eyes, a flush of heat rose up my face, and I went back to the binoculars.

"You guys do this sort of shit every day, don't you?" Bubba said after about another ten minutes. He took another pull from his vodka bottle and burped.

"Oh, sometimes we get car chases," Angie said.

"What a godawful boring fucking life." Bubba fidgeted, then absently punched a tree trunk.

I heard a muffled thump from the shed, and a line of lower shingles shook. Miles Lovell, stuck in a pump shed, kicking the walls, as bored as Bubba.

A crow, maybe the same one we'd heard earlier, cawed as it glided low over the bog, swept gracefully around the front of the hut, skimmed its beak over the water, then swooped up and away into the dark trees.

Bubba yawned. "I'm gonna leave."

"Okay," Angie said.

His hand swept the trees around him. "I mean, this is great and all, but there's pro wrestling on tonight."

"Of course," Angie said.

"Ugly Bob Brutal versus Sweet Sammy Studbar."

"Where I'd be," Angie said, "but, alas, I have a job."

"I'll tape it for you," Bubba promised.

Angie smiled. "Would ya? Gosh, that'd be just super."

The sarcasm completely eluded Bubba. His spirits picked up and he rubbed his hands together. "Sure. Look, I got a whole bunch of old ones on tape. Sometime we could—"

"Sssh," Angie said suddenly, and put a finger to her lips.

I turned my head back toward the hut, heard a door close quietly from the far side. I raised the binoculars and stared through them as a man exited the far side of the shed and walked along the plankwood toward the stand of thick trees.

I could only see the back of him. He had blond hair and stood maybe six-two. He was slim and moved with a casual fluid ease, one hand in the pocket of his trousers, the other swaying languidly at his side. He wore light gray trousers and a white long-sleeved shirt rolled up to the elbows. His head was tilted back slightly, and the sound of his soft whistling carried back over the mist and bogs to us.

"Sounds like 'Camp Town Ladies,'" Bubba said.

"Nah," Angie said. "That's not it."

"Then what is it, you know so much?"

"I don't know. I just know what it isn't."

"Oh, sure," Bubba said.

The man had almost reached the middle of the planks and I waited for him to turn and look back so I could see his face. The whole point of coming here had been to see who Miles was meeting, and if the blond guy had a car in those trees, he'd be long gone even if we gave chase right now.

I picked a rock up off the ground and arced it out through the trees and over the bog. It dropped into the watery mass of bobbing fruit about six feet to the blond guy's left and made a distinct plunking sound that we could hear thirty yards away.

The man didn't seem to notice. He didn't break stride. He kept whistling.

"I'm telling you," Bubba said, picking up his own rock, "it's 'Camp Town Ladies.'"

Bubba threw his rock, a hefty two-pounder that only reached halfway across the bog but made twice as much noise. Instead of a plunk, we got a heavy splash, and still the blond man showed no visible reaction.

He'd reached the end of the planks, and I made a decision. If he knew someone was following him, he might vanish, but he was going to vanish anyway, and I needed to see his face.

I screamed, "Hey!" and my voice ripped the mist

and sullen bog air, sent birds shredding upward through the trees.

The man stopped at the tree line. His back tensed. His shoulder turned ever so slightly to the left. Then he raised his arm so that his hand was held up at a ninety-degree angle from his body, as if he were a traffic cop halting the flow, or a party guest waving goodbye as he left the party.

He'd known we were there. And he wanted us to know it.

He lowered his hand and disappeared into the dark tree line.

I bolted from our stand of thin trees and out onto the soggy shore, with Angie and Bubba right behind me. I'd been loud enough that Miles Lovell would have heard my call across the bog, so our cover was blown in either case. Now our only hope was to get to Lovell while he was alone on a bog, before *he* could bolt, and scare the truth out of him.

As our heels hammered the plank wood and the sharp scent of the bog turned bitter in my nostrils, Bubba said, "Come on. Back me up, man. It was 'Camp Town,' right?"

"It was 'We're the Boys of Chorus,'" I said.

"What?"

I picked up my pace and the hut canted from side to side as we bounded toward it; the planks felt like they'd give way underfoot.

"From the Looney Tunes cartoon," I said.

"Oh, yeah!" Bubba said, and then he sang it: "Oh, we're the boys of chorus. We hope you like our show. We know you're rooting for us. But now we have to go-oh-oh!"

The words, as they boomed from Bubba's mouth over the still, silent bog, rode up my spine like insects.

As I reached the hut, I grasped the doorknob.

Angie said, "Patrick!"

I looked back at her and froze in her glare. I couldn't believe what I'd almost done—run up to a closed door with a potentially armed stranger waiting on the other side and been about to throw open the door like I was going home.

Angie's mouth remained open, her head cocked and her eyes blazing, stunned, I think, by my almost criminal mental lapse.

I shook my head at my own stupidity and stepped back from the door as Angie pulled her .38 and stood to the left, pointed it at the center of the door. Bubba had already pulled his gun—a sawed-off shotgun with a pistol grip—and he stood to the right, pointing it at the door with all the trepidation of a geography teacher pointing out Burma on a dated classroom map.

He said, "Uh, we're ready now, genius."

I pulled my Colt Commander, stepped to the left of the doorjamb, and rapped the wood with my knuckles. "Miles, open up!"

Nothing.

I rapped again. "Hey, Miles, it's Patrick Kenzie. I'm a private detective. I just want to talk.

I heard the sound of something hitting cheap wood inside, followed by the rattle of tools or some metal in a corner.

I knocked a last time. "Miles, we're going to come in. Okay?"

Something banged up and down against the floorboards inside.

I flattened my back against the wall and reached
around to the knob, looked at Angie and Bubba.
They both nodded. A bullfrog croaked from somewhere out on the bog. The breeze died and the trees
were still and dark.

I turned the knob and threw open the door and
Angie said, "Jesus Christ!"

Bubba said, "Wow," with a touch of admiration,
if not awe, in his voice, and lowered his shotgun.

Angie lowered her .38, and I stepped in front of
the doorway and looked in the shed. It took me a
second or two to realize what I was looking at because there was so much to digest and yet nothing
you really wanted to.

Miles Lovell sat tied to the motor of a septic
pump in the center of the shed. He'd been fastened
to the motor by a thick electrical cord wrapped tight
around his waist and tied off behind his back.

The gag in his mouth had darkened with blood
that seeped past the corners of his mouth and down
his chin.

His arms and legs had been left untied, and his
heels kicked the floorboards as he writhed against
the metal block.

His arms, however, hung immobile by his sides,
and the man who'd done this to him hadn't been
worried Miles would use them to untie himself because Miles no longer had possession of his own
hands.

They were on the floor to the left of the silent
motor, chopped off above the wrists and neatly laid,

palms down, on the floorboards. The blond man had applied tourniquets over both stumps and left the ax embedded in the wood between the hands.

We approached Lovell as his eyes rolled back to whites and the hammering of his heels began to seem less like pain and more like shock. Even with the tourniquets, I doubted he could live much longer, and I willed myself to put the horror of his maiming in the back of my mind and try to get him to answer a question or two before either the shock or death set in permanently.

I pulled the gag from between his lips and jumped back as a mouthful of dark blood spilled out onto his chest.

Angie said, "Oh, no. No fucking way. You have got to be kidding."

My stomach slid east, then west, then back east again, and a soft, warm buzzing found my brain.

Bubba said, "Wow," again, and this time I was sure I detected awe in his voice.

Miles, shock or no shock, death or no death, wouldn't be answering my questions.

He wouldn't be answering anyone's questions for a long, long time.

And even if he lived, I wasn't sure he'd be happy about it.

While we'd waited in the trees and the mist had ridden gently over the cranberry bog and his BMW had sat waiting on the shore, Miles Lovell's tongue had gone the way of his hands.

19

Three days after Miles Lovell was admitted to ICU, Dr. Diane Bourne walked into her Admiral Hill town house and found Angie, Bubba, and me cooking a very early Thanksgiving dinner in her kitchen.

I was in charge of the thirteen-pound turkey because I was the only one of us who liked to cook. Angie lived in restaurants and Bubba was strictly takeout, but I'd been cooking since I was twelve. Nothing spectacular, mind you—after all, there's a reason you rarely hear "Irish" and "cuisine" mentioned in the same sentence—but I can handle most fowl, beef, and pasta dishes, and I can blacken hell out of any fish known to man.

So I cleaned and roasted and basted and spiced the turkey, then prepared the mashed potatoes with diced onions, while Angie assigned herself to the preparation of the Stove Top stuffing and this green-beans-and-garlic recipe she'd found on the inside of a soup can label. Bubba had no official duties, but he'd brought plenty of beer and several bags of chips for us and a bottle of vodka for him-

self, and when he came upon Diane Bourne's blue
Persian cat, he was nice enough not to kill it.

Roasting a turkey takes a while, with very little
to do during the downtime, so Angie and I availed
ourselves of the upstairs quarters and ransacked
Diane Bourne's house until we found one thing of
particular interest.

Miles Lovell had gone into shock not long after
we called the ambulance. He'd been rushed to Jordan Hospital in Plymouth, where he was stabilized
and airlifted to Mass General. After they'd worked
on him there for nine hours, he'd been placed in
ICU. They'd been unable to reattach his hands, but
they would have had a shot at reattaching his tongue
if the blond man hadn't either taken it with him or
tossed it into the bog.

My gut feeling was that the blond man had
taken it with him. I didn't know much about him—
not his name or even what he looked like—but I was
getting a sense for him. He was, I was sure, the man
Warren Martens had seen at the motel and described
as the man in charge. He had destroyed Karen Nichols, and now he'd destroyed Miles Lovell. Merely
killing his victims seemed to bore him—instead, he
preferred to leave them wishing they were dead.

Angie and I returned downstairs with the treat
we'd found in Dr. Bourne's bedroom, and the plastic
thermometer popped up from the turkey just as Diane Bourne let herself into the town house.

"Talk about your timing," I said.

"Sure," Angie said, "we do all the work, she reaps
the rewards."

Diane Bourne turned into the dining room,

separated from the kitchen by nothing but an open portico, and Bubba gave her a big three-finger wave with the same hand that held his bottle of Absolut.

Bubba said, "What's shaking, sister?"

Diane Bourne dropped her leather bag and opened her mouth as if about to scream.

Angie said, "Now, now. There, there." She crouched on the kitchen floor and slid the videocassette we'd found in the master bedroom into the dining room, where it came to rest at Diane Bourne's feet.

She looked down at the videocassette and closed her mouth.

Angie hoisted herself up onto the counter and lit a cigarette. "Correct me if I'm wrong, Doctor, but isn't it unethical to have sex with a client?"

I would have raised my eyebrows at Dr. Bourne, but I was busy pulling the roasting pan from the oven.

"Damn," Bubba said. "Smells good."

"Shit," I said.

"What?"

"Anyone remember cranberry sauce?"

Angie snapped her fingers and shook her head.

"Not that I particularly care for the stuff. Ange?"

"Never liked the cranberry sauce," she said, her eyes on Diane Bourne.

"Bubba?"

He belched. "Gets in the way of the booze."

I turned my head. Diane Bourne was frozen in the dining room over her dropped bag and the videocassette.

"Dr. Bourne?" I said and her eyes snapped my way. "You a fan of the cranberry?"

She took a long, deep breath and closed her eyes as she let it back out. "What are you people doing here?"

I held up the roasting pan. "Cooking."

"Stirring," Angie said.

"Drinking," Bubba said, and pointed the bottle in Dr. Bourne's direction. "Taste?"

Diane Bourne gave us all a tight shake of the head and closed her eyes again as if we'd disappear by the time she reopened them.

"You," she said, "are breaking and entering. That's a felony."

"Actually," I said, "the breaking on its own is just misdemeanor vandalism."

"But, yeah," Angie said, "the entering part is definitely wrong."

"Bad," Bubba agreed, and swiped one index finger off the other several times. "Bad, bad, bad."

I placed the bird on top of the stove. "We brought food, though."

"And chips," Bubba said.

"Yeah." I nodded at him. "The chips alone should balance out the B and E thing."

Diane Bourne looked at the videocassette between her feet and held up a silencing hand. "What do we do now?"

I looked at Bubba. He shot a confused look at Angie. Angie passed it on to Diane Bourne. Diane Bourne looked at me.

"We eat," I said.

Diane Bourne actually helped carve the turkey with me and showed us the locations of all the

ceramic bowls and serving dishes we'd have probably busted the place up looking for.

By the time we all sat down at her hammered-
copper dining room table, the color had returned to
her face and she'd helped herself to a glass of white
wine and brought the bottle to the table with her.

Bubba had called dibs on both legs and a wing, so
the rest of us ate white meat, politely passed around
the bowls of green beans and spuds, and buttered
our rolls with pinkies extended.

"So," I said over the volume of Bubba's teeth tear-
ing a Hyundai's worth of meat off the bone, "I hear
you're short a part-time secretary, Doctor."

She took a sip of wine. "Unfortunate, yes." She
took a miserly bite of turkey and then another sip of
wine.

"Police talk to you?" Angie asked.

She nodded. "I understand they got my name from
you."

"Did you tell them anything?"

"I told them Miles was a valued employee, but
I knew little of his private life."

"Uh-huh," Angie said, and drank some of the beer
she'd poured into one of Diane Bourne's wine goblets. "Did you mention the phone call Lovell placed
to you about an hour before he was attacked?"

Diane Bourne didn't miss a beat. She smiled
around her wineglass, took a delicate sip. "No, I'm
afraid that slipped my mind."

Bubba poured a gallon of gravy over his plate,
added half a shaker of salt, and said, "You're a
drunk."

Diane Bourne's pale face turned the color of a cue ball. "What did you just say?"

Bubba used his fork to point at her wine bottle. "You're a drunk. Sister, you're taking tiny sips, but you're taking a lot of them."

"I'm nervous."

Bubba gave her the grin of one shark to another. "Right, sister. Right. You're a drunk. I can see it in you." He took a pull from his Absolut bottle, looked at me. "Lock her in a room, buddy. Thirty-six hours tops, she'll be screaming for it. She'd blow an orangutan, he'd give her a drink."

I watched Diane Bourne while Bubba spoke. The videocassette hadn't rattled her. Our knowledge of the phone call hadn't rattled her. Even our being here, in her home, hadn't shocked her too much. But Bubba's words sent tremors up her fine throat, tiny spasms through her fingers.

"Don't worry," Bubba said, his eyes on his food, fork and knife hovering above the mess like hawks about to descend, "I respect a woman likes to drink. Kinda respect that nympho-lesbian action you got going on the tape, too."

Bubba dove back into his food, and for a few moments the only sounds in that room came from his shoveling and snarfing.

"About the videotape," I said.

Diane Bourne tore her eyes away from Bubba and gulped the rest of her wine. She poured another half goblet, looked at me as a brazen pride swept over the unsettlement Bubba had placed there.

"Are you angry with me, Patrick?"

"No."

She took another meager bite of turkey. "But I thought Karen Nichols's death was a personal crusade for you, Patrick."

I smiled. "Classic interrogation technique, Diane. Kudos."

"Which?" All wide-eyed innocence.

"Using the subject's first name as much as possible. Unnerves him, supposedly, forces intimacy."

"I'm sorry."

"No, you're not."

"Ah, well, maybe not, but—"

"Doctor," Angie said, "you're fucking both Karen Nichols and Miles Lovell on that tape. Care to explain?"

She turned her head, locked Angie in her calm gaze. "Did it turn you on, Angie?"

"Not particularly, Diane."

"Did it repulse you?"

"Not particularly, Diane."

Bubba looked up from his second turkey leg. "I got major wood, though, sister. Keep it in mind."

She ignored him, though another of those tremors found her throat for a moment. "Come, Angie, no latent desires to experiment sexually with another woman?"

Angie drank some beer. "If I did, Doctor, I'd pick a woman with a better body. Call me shallow."

"Yeah," Bubba said, "you need to get some meat on those bones, Doc."

Diane Bourne turned her eyes on me again, but they were less calm, less certain. "You, Patrick, did you enjoy watching?"

"Two girls and a guy?"

She nodded.

I shrugged. "It was a lighting issue, really. I like my porn with higher production values, to tell the truth."

"Plus the hairy ass factor," Bubba reminded me.

"Good point, Ebert." I smiled at Diane Bourne. "Lovell had a hairy ass. We don't be digging hairy asses. Doctor, who shot that video?"

She drank some more wine. In the face of her probes into our psyches, we'd grown more glib. One of us she might have been able to make progress with, but all three of us together could outglib the Marx Brothers, the Three Stooges, and Neil Simon combined.

"Doctor?" I said.

"The video was on a tripod. We shot it."

I shook my head. "Sorry. Won't wash. There's four different angles on that tape, and I don't think any of you three got up to move the tripod."

"Maybe we—"

"There's also a shadow," Angie said. "A man's shadow, Diane, against the east wall during foreplay."

Diane Bourne closed her mouth, reached for her wineglass.

"We can burn you down, Diane," I said. "And you know it. So don't fuck around with us anymore. Who shot the tape? The blond guy?"

Her eyes snapped up and then dropped just as quickly.

"Who is he?" I said. "We know he maimed Lovell. We know he's six-two, weighs about one-ninety, dresses well, and whistles when he walks.

We've placed him with both Karen Nichols and Lovell at the Holly Martens Inn. We go back and ask questions, I'm sure we'll get a description of you there as well. What we need is his name."

She shook her head.

"You're not in a position to negotiate, Diane."

Another shake of the head, another draining of her goblet. "I won't under any circumstances discuss this man."

"You don't have a choice."

"Yes, I do, Patrick. Oh, yes, I do. It may not be an easy choice, but it's a choice. And I will not cross this man. Ever. And should the police question me, I will deny he even exists." She emptied the wine bottle into her goblet with a shaky hand. "You have no idea what this man is capable of."

"Sure, we do," I said. "We found Lovell."

"That was spur-of-the-moment," she said with a bitter grin. "You should see what he's capable of when he has time to plan."

"Karen Nichols?" Angie said. "Is that what he's capable of?"

Diane Bourne gave her bitter grin a derisive turn downward as she looked at Angie. "Karen was weak. Next time, he's choosing someone strong. Add to the challenge." She gave Angie a flat, contemptuous smile, and Angie damn near knocked it off when she slapped her.

The wine goblet shattered against the serving dish and a red mark the shape of a salmon steak obscured Diane Bourne's left cheekbone and ear.

"Damn," I said, "no leftovers for this house."

"Don't get the wrong impression of us, bitch,"

Angie said. "Just because you're a woman doesn't mean things can't get physical."

"Very physical," Bubba said.

Diane Bourne looked at the shards of her glass sticking out of the plate of carved white meat. She watched as her wine pooled in the divots of her hammered copper.

She jerked a thumb at Bubba. "*He'd* torture me, maybe even rape me. But you don't have the stomach for it, Patrick."

"Amazing how your stomach feels when you walk outside," I said. "Come back after it's all done."

She sighed and settled back into her chair. "Well, you're just going to have to do it. Because I won't betray this man."

"Out of fear or love?" I asked.

"Both. He engenders both, Patrick. As all worthy beings do."

"You're done as a psychiatrist," I said. "You know that, don't you?"

She shook her head. "I think not. You release that tape to anyone, I'll file breaking and entering charges against the three of you."

Angie laughed.

Diane Bourne looked at her. "You are breaking and entering."

"You should have fun explaining this," Angie said and swept her hand over the table.

"Officer, they were *cooking*!" I said.

"Basting!" Angie said.

"And, madam, how did you respond?"

"I helped carve," Angie said. "And, of course, I showed them to my china."

"Did you go with the light meat or the dark?"

Diane Bourne lowered her head and shook it.

"Last chance," I said.

She kept her head down, shook it again.

I pushed my chair back from the table, held up the videotape. "We'll make copies and it's going out, Doctor, to every psychiatrist and psychologist listed in the yellow pages."

"And the media," Angie said.

"Oh, God, yeah," I said. "They'll go nuts."

She looked up and tears filled her eyes and her voice cracked when she spoke. "You'd take my career?"

"You took her life," I said. "Have you watched this tape? Did you look in her eyes, Diane? There's nothing there but self-hatred. You put that there. You and Miles and this blond guy."

"It was an experiment," she said, and her voice was clogged. "It was just an idea. I never thought she'd kill herself."

"He did, though," I said. "The blond guy. Didn't he?"

She nodded.

"Give me his name."

A hard shake of the head that sent her tears to the table.

I held up the tape. "It's his name or your reputation and career."

She continued to shake her head, softer now but continuous.

We gathered our things from the kitchen, took what was left of our beer from the fridge. Bubba found a Ziploc storage bag and dumped the remainder of

the stuffing and potatoes in there, then took another one and filled it with turkey.

"What are you doing?" I said. "There's glass in
there."

He gave me a look like I was autistic. "I'll pick it
out."

We walked back into the dining room. Diane
Bourne stared at her reflection in the copper, elbows
on the table, the heels of both hands pressed to her
forehead.

As we reached the foyer, she said, "You don't want
him in your life."

I turned back and looked in her hollow eyes. She
suddenly looked twice her age, and I could see her
in a nursing home forty years from now, alone,
spending her days lost in the bitter smoke of her
memories.

"Let me decide that," I said.

"He'll destroy you. Or someone you love. For fun."

"His name, Doctor."

She lit a cigarette, exhaled loudly. She shook her
head, lips tight and pale.

I started to leave, but Angie stopped me. She raised
a finger, her gaze locked on Diane Bourne, her body
very still.

"You're ice," Angie said. "Isn't that right, Doctor?"

Diane Bourne's pale eyes followed the trail of her
smoke.

"I mean, you have this cool, patrician thing down
pat." Angie placed her hands on the back of a chair,
leaned into the table slightly. "You never lose your
poise, and you *never* get emotional."

Diane Bourne took another hit off her cigarette.

It was like watching a statue smoke. She gave no indication that we were still in the room.

Angie said, "But you did once, didn't you?"

Diane Bourne blinked.

Angie looked over at me. "In her office, remember? The first time we spoke to her."

Diane Bourne flicked some ash and missed the ashtray.

"And it wasn't when she spoke about Karen," Angie said. "It wasn't when she spoke about Miles. Do you remember, Diane?"

Diane Bourne raised her eyes and they were pink, angry.

"It was when you spoke about Wesley Dawe."

Diane Bourne cleared her throat. "Get the fuck out of my home."

Angie smiled. "Wesley Dawe, who killed his little sister. Who—"

"He didn't kill her," she said. "You get that. Wesley wasn't anywhere near her. But he was blamed. He was—"

"It's him, isn't it?" Angie's smile broadened. "That's who you're protecting. That was the blond man on the bog. Wesley Dawe."

She said nothing, just stared at the smoke as it flowed from her mouth.

"Why did he want to destroy Karen?"

She shook her head. "You've gotten the name, Mr. Kenzie. That's all you get. And he already knows who you are." She turned her head, gave me her pale, desolate eyes. "And he doesn't like you, Patrick. He thinks you're a meddler. He thinks you should have walked away from this when it was proven Karen's death was by her own hand." She held out her hand. "My tape, please."

"No."

She dropped her hand. "I gave you what you wanted."

Angie shook her head. "I drew it out of you. Not the same thing."

I said, "You're the master of the psyche, Doctor, so turn your gaze inward for a moment. Which is more important to you—your reputation or your career?"

"I don't see—"

"Pick," I said sharply.

Her jaw set as if it were on steel pins, and she spoke through gritted teeth. "My reputation."

I nodded. "You can keep it."

Her jaw loosened and her eyes were bewildered behind her glowing cigarette coal as she took another long haul of smoke into her lungs. "What's the catch?"

"Your career is over."

"You can't end my career."

"I'm not going to. You're going to."

She laughed, but it was a nervous one. "Don't overestimate yourself, Mr. Kenzie. I have no intention of—"

"You'll close your office tomorrow," I said. "You'll refer all your clients to other doctors, and you'll never practice in this state again."

Her "Ha!" was louder, but sounded even less sure.

"You'll do this, Doctor, and you'll keep your reputation. Maybe you can write books, line up a talk show. But you'll never work one-on-one with a patient again."

"Or?" she said.

I held up the videocassette. "Or this thing starts playing cocktail parties."

We left her there and as we opened the door, Angie said, "Tell Wesley we're coming for him."

"He already knows," she said. "He already knows."

20

Rain fell softly on sun-drenched streets the afternoon I met Vanessa Moore at a sidewalk cafe in Back Bay. She'd called and asked to meet so we could discuss Tony Traverna's case. Vanessa was Tony T's attorney; we'd first met the last time Tony jumped bail, and I had appeared as a witness for the prosecution. Vanessa had cross-examined me the same way she made love—with a cool hunger and sharpened nails.

I could have declined Vanessa's invite, I suppose, but it had been a week since the night we'd cooked for Diane Bourne, and in that week, we seemed to have taken four steps back. Wesley Dawe did not exist. He wasn't listed in census records or with the Registry of Motor Vehicles. He did not own a credit card. He had no bank account in the city of Boston or the state of Massachusetts, and after getting slightly desperate, Angie discovered no one by that name existed in New Hampshire, Maine, or Vermont.

We'd gone back to Diane Bourne's office, but apparently she'd taken our advice to heart. The office was closed. Her town house, we soon discovered, was abandoned. In a week, she hadn't shown up there, and a cursory search of the place revealed only that she may have taken enough clothing to get by for a week before she had to either do laundry or shop for more.

The Dawes went fishing. Literally, I found out, after I'd impersonated a patient of the doctor's and learned they were at their summer home in Cape Breton, Nova Scotia.

We lost Angie's help when she was assigned by Sallis & Salk to join a team of bodyguards watching an oily South African diamond merchant around the clock as he did whatever it was oily diamond merchants do when they come to our little hamlet.

And Bubba went back to doing whatever it is Bubba does when he isn't out of the country buying things that could blow up the Eastern Seaboard.

So I was a bit adrift, and caseless, it seemed, when I found Vanessa sitting outdoors under a large Cinzano umbrella, the gentle drizzle bouncing off the cobblestone and spraying her ankles, but leaving the wrought-iron table and rest of Vanessa untouched.

"Hey." I leaned in to kiss her cheek and she slid a hand along my rib cage as she accepted it.

"Hi." She watched me take my seat with the amusement that lived in her eyes like twin birthmarks, a lusty vivacity that said just about anything was hers for the taking. It was just a matter of her choosing.

"How you doing?"

"I'm good, Patrick. You're damp." She patted a napkin to dry her palm.

I rolled my eyes and raised a hand to the heavens. The shower had come suddenly as I'd walked from my car, broke from a tear in a lone cloud that floated through an otherwise glossy sky.

"I'm not complaining," she said. "Nothing looks better on a handsome man in a white shirt than a little rain."

I chuckled. The thing with Vanessa was that even if you saw her coming, she kept coming. Ran right at you and then through you, made you wonder why you'd even tried to ward her off in the first place.

We may have agreed months ago that the sexual component of our relationship was over, but today Vanessa seemed to have changed her mind. And when Vanessa changed her mind, the rest of the world changed theirs with her.

Either that, or she was just trying to work me into a lather, leave me standing alone after I'd made my move so she'd have something even better than sex to get her off that night. With her, you never knew. And I'd learned in the past that the only way to play it safe with her was not to play at all.

"So," I said, "why do you think I can help you with Tony T?"

She used her fingers to pick a pineapple chunk off her fruit plate, tossed it back in her mouth, and chewed it to pure pulp before speaking.

"I'm working on a diminished capacity defense," she said.

"What?" I said. "'Your Honor, my client's a moron so let him go'?"

The tip of her tongue ran lightly under her upper teeth. "No, Patrick. No. I was thinking more along the lines of: 'Your Honor, my client believes himself to be under a very real threat of death from members of the Russian crime syndicate, and his actions have stemmed from this fear.'"

"The Russian syndicate?"

She nodded.

I laughed.

She didn't. "He's honestly quite afraid of them, Patrick."

"Why?"

"His last job, he robbed the wrong safe."

"Belonging to a member of the syndicate?"

She nodded.

I tried to follow the logic of her proposed defense. "So he was so terrified, he blew town and went to Maine?"

Another nod.

"That'll help on the bail jumping," I said. "What about the other stuff?"

"Building blocks, Patrick. All I need is to get the illegal flight thrown out and everything can build from there. See, he crossed state lines again. That's federal. I get the federal charges tossed, the state stuff will fall in line."

"And you want me to . . ."

She wiped a thin drop of rain from her temple and gave me a chuckle so dry you could hang a nail on it. She leaned in to the table. "Oh, Patrick, there are several things I could possibly want from you, but in terms of Anthony Traverna, I just need you to attest under oath to his fear of the Russians."

"But I wasn't aware of it."

"But maybe, in hindsight, you remember how fearful in general he seemed during the ride back from Maine."

She speared a grape with her fork, sucked it off the tines.

She was dressed down this afternoon in a simple black skirt, dark cherry tank top, and black sandals. Her long walnut hair was tied back in a ponytail, and she'd foresaken her contacts for wafer-thin eyeglasses with red rims. And still the sensual power pouring from her limbs and flesh would have blown me out into the street if I hadn't been used to it.

"Vanessa," I said.

She speared another grape, propped her elbow on the table, and let the grape hover an inch from her lips as she stared over it at me. "Yes?"

"You know the DA will call me."

"Well, actually the bail jump's federal, so it'll be the AG's office."

"Fine. But they'll call me."

"Yes."

"And you'll try to get what you need on cross."

"Yes, again."

"So why ask me down here today?"

She considered the grape, but still didn't eat it. "If I told you Tony was scared? I mean, terrified. And that I believe him when he says there's an open contract on him?"

"I'd say you'd attach garnishing to his estate and go on about your business."

She smiled. "So cold, Patrick. He is, though, you know."

"I know. But I also know that wouldn't be reason enough to ask me here."

"Point taken." She flicked her tongue and the grape disappeared from the fork. She chewed and swallowed, took a sip of mineral water. "Clarence misses you, by the way."

Clarence was Vanessa's dog, a chocolate Lab she'd bought on impulse six months ago and, last time I'd noticed, didn't have a clue how to raise. You said, "Clarence, sit," and Clarence ran away. You said, "Here," and he shit on the rug. There was something likable about him, though. Maybe it was the puppy innocence in his eyes, a wide aiming-to-please that filled his brown pupils even as he pissed on your foot.

"How's he doing?" I asked. "Housebroken yet?"

Vanessa held her forefinger and thumb a hair's width apart. "So, so, close."

"Eaten any more of your shoes?"

She shook her head. "I keep them on a high shelf. Besides, he's more into underwear these days. Last week he puked up a bra I'd been missing."

"Least he gave it back."

She smiled, speared another chunk of fruit. "Remember that morning in Bermuda we woke to the rain?"

I nodded.

"Sheets of it, like walls really, vibrating off the windows and you couldn't even see the sea from our room."

I nodded again, tried to hurry her through it. "And we stayed in bed all day and drank wine and messed up the sheets."

"Burned the sheets," she said. "Broke that arm-chair."

"I got the credit card bill," I said. "I remember, Vanessa."

She cut off a small piece of her watermelon wedge, slid it between her lips. "It's raining now."

I looked out at the small puddles on the sidewalk. Barely teardrops, their surfaces streaked gold with sun.

"It'll pass," I said.

Another dry chuckle and she sipped some more mineral water and stood. "I'll use the powder room. Take the time to refresh your memory, Patrick. Remember the bottle of Chardonnay. I have a few more at home."

She walked into the restaurant and I tried not to watch her because a glimpse of her exposed skin and I could all too easily conjure up what hid under her clothes, could see the rivulets of white wine that had splashed over her torso in Bermuda when she'd lain back on the white sheets and poured half the bottle over her body, asked if I was a bit parched.

I watched anyway, as she knew I would, but then my vision was blocked by a man's body as he stepped from the restuarant out onto the patio and put his hand on the back of Vanessa's chair.

He was tall and slim, with sandy brown hair, and he gave me a distant smile as he pulled back on Vanessa's chair and seemed about to drag it back into the restaurant with him.

"What are you doing?" I said.

"I need this seat," he said.

I looked around at the dozen or so other chairs

on the patio, the twenty more inside that weren't occupied.

"It's taken," I said.

The man looked down at it. "Is it taken? Is this seat taken?"

"It's taken," I repeated.

He was very well dressed in off-white linen trousers and Gucci loafers, a cashmere black vest over a white T-shirt. His watch was a Movado, and his hands looked like they'd never touched a piece of dirt or work in his life.

"You're sure?" he asked, still talking down to the chair. "I heard this seat was unoccupied."

"It's not. You see the plate of food in front of it? It's occupied. Trust me."

He looked over at me and there was something loose and afire in his ice blue eyes. "So I can take it? It's okay?"

I stood. "No, you can't take it. It's taken."

The man swept his hands out at the patio. "There are plenty of other ones. You get one of those. I'll take this. She'll never know the difference."

"You get one of those," I said.

"I want this one." He spoke reasonably, carefully, as if discussing something with a child that was beyond the child's grasp. "I'll just take it. Okay?"

I took a step toward him. "No. You won't. It's spoken for."

"I'd heard it wasn't," he said gently.

"You heard wrong."

He looked down at the chair again, then nodded. "So you say, so you say."

He held up an apologetic hand that matched his smile and walked back into the restaurant as Vanessa stepped past him onto the patio.

She looked back over her shoulder. "Friend of yours?"

"No."

She noticed a small splatter of rain on her chair. "How'd my chair get wet?"

"Long story."

She gave me a curious frown and pushed the chair aside, pulled another one out from the closest table and settled back into her original place.

Through the small crowd of patrons, I saw the guy take a seat at the bar and smile at me as Vanessa pulled her replacement chair over to our table. The smile seemed to say, I guess it wasn't taken after all, and then he turned his back to us.

The interior of the restaurant filled as the rain picked up, and I lost sight of the guy at the bar. The next time I had a clear view, he was gone.

Vanessa and I stayed out in the rain, drinking mineral water as she picked at her fruit and the rain found the back of my shirt and neck.

We'd reverted to harmless small talk when she returned from the bathroom—Tony T's fear, the Middlesex ADA with the ferret's head who was rumored to keep mothballs and carefully folded women's underwear at the bottom of his attaché case, how pathetic it felt to live in an alleged sports town that couldn't hold on to either Mo Vaughn or Curtis Martin.

But underneath the small talk was the constant hum of our shared want, the echoes of surf and sheets of rain in Bermuda, the hoarse sounds of our voices in that room, the smell of grapes on skin.

"So," Vanessa said after a particularly pregnant lull in the chitchat, "Chardonnay and me, or what?"

I could have wept from lust, but then I forced myself to conjure up the aftermath, the sterile walk down her stairs and back to my car, the empty reverberations of our approximated passion ringing in my head.

"Not today," I said.

"It might not be an open-ended offer."

"I understand that."

She sighed and handed her credit card over her shoulder as the waitress stepped out onto the patio.

"Find a girl, Patrick?" she asked as the waitress went back inside.

I said nothing.

"A good, low-maintenance woman of hardy stock who won't give you any trouble? Cook for you, clean for you, laugh at your jokes, and never look at another man?"

"Sure," I said. "That's it."

"Ah." Vanessa nodded and the waitress came back with her credit card and bill. Vanessa signed and handed the receipt copy to the waitress with a flick of the wrist that was, in itself, dismissal. "But, Patrick, I'm curious."

I resisted the urge to lean back from the carnal force of her. "Pray tell."

"Does your new woman do the real wicked things? You know, those things we've done with—"

"Vanessa."

"Hmm?"

"There is no new woman. I'm just not interested."

She placed a hand to her breast. "In me?"

I nodded.

"Really?" She held her hand out to the rain, caught a few drops, and wiped them on her throat as she arched her head back. "Let me hear you say it."

"I just did."

"The whole sentence." She lowered her chin, caught me in the full impact of her gaze.

I shifted in my chair, tried to wish my way out of this situation. When that didn't work, I just said it, flat and cold.

"I'm not interested in you, Vanessa."

The loneliness of another can be shocking when it lays itself bare without warning.

A dire abandonment broke Vanessa's features into pieces, and I could feel the hollow chill of her beautiful apartment, the ache of her sitting alone at 3 A.M., lover gone, law books and yellow legal pads spread before her at her dining room table, pen in hand, the pictures of a much younger Vanessa that adorned her mantel staring down at her like ghosts of a life unlived. I could see a tiny flicker of hungry light in her chest, and not the hunger of her sexual appetite, but the conflicted hunger of her other selves.

In that moment, her features went skeletal, and her beauty vanished, and she looked like she'd fallen to scraped knees under the weight of the rain.

"Fuck you too, Patrick." She smiled as she said it. Smiled with lips that twitched at the corners. "Okay?"

"Okay," I said.

"Just . . ." She stood, a fist clenched around her bag strap. "Just . . . fuck you."

She left the restuarant, and I stayed where I was, turned my chair and watched her walk up the street through the drizzle, bag swinging back and forth against her hip, her steps stripped of grace.

Why, I wondered, does it all have to be so messy?

My cell phone rang, and I pulled it from my shirt pocket, wiped the condensation from its surface as I lost Vanessa in a crowd.

"Hello."

"Hello," the man's voice said. "Can I assume that chair's free now?"

21

I turned in my chair, looked into the restaurant for the sandy-haired man. He wasn't at a table. He wasn't at the bar as far as I could see.

"Who is this?" I said.

"What a tearful breakup scene, Pat. For a minute, I was pretty sure she'd toss a drink in your face."

He knew my name.

I turned again in the chair, looked along the sidewalk for him, for anyone with a cellular phone.

"You're right," I said. "The chair's free. Come on back and get it."

His voice was the same gentle monotone I'd heard on the patio when he'd tried to take the chair. "She has incredible lips, that attorney. Incredible. I don't think they're implants either. Do you?"

"Yeah," I said, scanning the other side of the street, "they're nice lips. Come on back for the chair."

"And she's asking you, Pat—*she's* asking *you*—to

come slide your dick through those lips and you say *no*? What're you, gay?"

"You bet," I said. "Come on back and fag-bash me. Use the chair."

I peered through the rain at the windows on the other side of the street.

"And she picked up the check," he said, his soft monotone like a whisper in a dark room. "She picked up the check, wanted to blow you, looks like six or seven million bucks—fake tits, true, but nice fake tits, and hey, no one's perfect—and you still say no. Hats off to you, buddy. You're a stronger man than me."

A man with a baseball cap on his head and an umbrella raised above him walked through the mist toward me, a cellular pressed to his ear, his strides loose and confident.

"Me," the voice said, "I'd figure her for a screamer. Lots of 'Oh, Gods' and 'Harder, harders.'"

I said nothing. The man with the baseball cap was still too far away for me to see his face, but he was getting closer.

"Can I be frank with you, Pat? A piece of ass like that comes along so seldom that if I were in your place—and I'm not, I know that, but if I were—I'd just feel compelled to go back with her to that apartment on Exeter, and I gotta be honest with you, Pat, I'd hump her till the blood ran down her thighs."

I felt cold moisture that didn't come from the rain seep down behind my ear.

"Really?" I said.

The man with the baseball cap was close enough

for me to see his mouth, and his lips moved as he approached.

The guy on the other end of the line was silent, but somewhere on his end, I could hear a truck grind its gears, the patter of rain off a car hood.

". . . and I can't *do* that, Melvin, if you've got half my shit tied up offshore." The man in the baseball cap passed me, and I could see he was at least twice the age of the guy from the patio.

I stood, looked as far up and down the street as I could.

"Pat," the guy on the phone said.

"Yeah?"

"Your life is about to get . . ." He paused and I could hear him breathing.

"My life's about to get what?" I said.

He smacked his lips. "Interesting."

And he hung up.

I swung my body over the wrought-iron fence that separated the patio from the sidewalk, and the rain found my head and chest as I stood on the side-walk for a while with people walking around me and occasionally jostling a shoulder. Eventually, I realized standing there did no good. The guy could be anywhere. He could have called from the next county. The truck that had ground its gears in the background hadn't been in my immediate vicinity or I would have heard it on my end.

But he'd been close enough to know when Vanessa left and to call within a minute of her abrupt departure.

So, no, he wasn't in another county. He was here

in Back Bay. But even so, that was a lot of ground to cover.

I started walking again, my eyes searching the streets for a glimpse of him. I dialed Vanessa's number and when she answered, I said, "Don't hang up."

"Okay."

She hung up.

I gritted my teeth and pressed redial.

"Vanessa, please listen a sec. Someone just threatened you."

"What?"

"That guy you thought was a friend of mine on the patio?"

"Yes . . ." she said slowly, and I heard Clarence yip in the background.

"He called me when you left. He's a total stranger, Vanessa, but he knew my name, and your occupation, and he made it clear to me that he knew where you lived."

She gave me that martini chuckle of hers. "And let me see, you need to come over here to protect me? Jesus, Patrick, we don't need these games. You want to fuck me, you should have said yes on the patio."

"Vanessa, no. I want you to go to a hotel for a while. Now. Send my office the bill."

The chuckle was replaced by a mean laugh. "Because some weirdo knows where I live?"

"This guy's not your average weirdo."

I turned on Hereford, walked toward Commonwealth Avenue. The rain had lessened, but the mist had thickened around it, turned the air to warm onion soup.

"Patrick, I'm a defense attorney. Hang on—

Clarence, down! Down, now! Sorry," she said to me. "Where was I? Oh, yeah. Do you know how many gangbangers and petty sociopaths and freaks in general have threatened my life when I've failed to get them Get Out of Jail Free cards? Are you serious?"

"This may be a little different."

"According to a screw I know at Cedar Junction, Karl Kroft—whom I unsuccessfully defended on murder one and ag rape—drew up a shit list—and I'm being quite literal here—in his cell. And before—"

"Vanessa."

"And before they wiped it off, Patrick, and put dear Karl under twenty-four-hour watch, my friend the guard said he saw the list. He said my name was number one. *Above* Karl's ex-wife, who he'd already tried to kill once with a saw."

I wiped thick condensation from my eyes, wished I'd worn a hat. "Vanessa, just listen a second. I think this—"

"I live in a building with twenty-four-hour security and two doormen, Patrick. You've seen how hard it is to get in. I have six locks on my front door, and even if you could reach my windows on the fourteenth floor, they're impenetrable. I have Mace, Patrick. I have a stun gun. And if that doesn't work, I have a real gun, fully loaded, and always within reach."

"Listen. That guy they found in the cranberry bog last week with his tongue and hands cut off. He was—"

Her voice rose. "And if anyone can get past all *that*, then, Patrick, fuck it, they can have me. Hell, they certainly put in the effort."

"I understand, but—"

"Ta, sweetie. Good luck with your latest weirdo."

She hung up, and I clenched the phone in my hand as I crossed into the Commonwealth Avenue mall, a mile-long stretch of green grass and ebony trees, small benches and tall statues, that cuts up the center of the avenue between the east- and westbound lanes.

Warren Martens had said that Miles Lovell's friend dressed shabby-rich. That he had an air about him that suggested power or at least a power complex.

That pretty much described the guy on the patio.

Wesley Dawe, I wondered. Could this be Wesley? Wesley was blond, but the height and build were right, and hair dye is cheap and easily obtained.

My car was parked four blocks down Commonwealth, and while the rain was light, it was steady, and the mist was threatening to turn into a fog. Whoever the guy was, I decided, he'd either chosen or been sent to rattle my cage, to let me know that he knew me, and I didn't know him, and that made me vulnerable and gave him a semblance of omnipotence.

I've had my cage rattled by pros, though—wiseguys, cops, gangbangers, and in one case a pair of bona fide serial killers—so the days when a disembodied voice on the other end of a phone line could give me the shakes and a dry mouth were gone. Still, it did have me guessing, which may have been the point.

My cell phone rang. I stopped under the canopy of a tree, and it rang a second time. No shakes or dry mouth. Just a small quickening of the pulse. Midway through the third ring, I answered.

"Hello."

"Hey, pal. Where you at?"

Angie. My pulse slowed.

"Comm Ave., heading to my car. You?"

"Outside an office in the Jeweler's Exchange."

"Fun with your diamond merchant?"

"Oh, yeah. He's aces. When he isn't hitting on me, he's telling racist jokes to his male bodyguards."

"Some girls have all the luck."

"Yeah. Well, just thought I'd check in. I meant to tell you something, but I can't remember what it was."

"That's helpful."

"No, it's right on the tip of my tongue, but . . . Well, whatever, he's coming out again. I'll call you back when I think of it."

"Cool."

"Okay. McGarrett out." She hung up.

I stepped out from under the tree and had taken all of four steps when Angie remembered what she'd forgotten and called back.

"You remember?" I said.

"Hi, Pat," the sandy-haired guy said. "Enjoying the rain?"

An extra heart appeared in the center of my chest and began to thump. "Loving it. You?"

"I've always liked rain, myself. Let me ask you— was that your partner you were talking to?"

I'd been under a large tree on the southern side of the mall. No way he could have seen me from the north. That left east, west, and south.

"Don't have a partner, Wesley." I looked south. The sidewalk across from me was empty except for a young woman being pulled across the slick concrete by three large dogs.

"Ha!" he shouted. "Very quick, Pat. You're good, buddy. Or was that a lucky guess?"

I looked east to Clarendon Street. Just street traffic crossing at the light, no one on a cellular that I could see.

"Little of both, Wesley. Little of both."

"Well, I'm real proud of you, Pat."

I turned very slowly to my right and through the thick mist and drizzle, I saw him.

He stood on the southeast corner of Dartmouth and Commonwealth. He'd covered his upper half with a hooded, transparent slicker. When our eyes met, he gave me a wide grin and waved.

"Now you see me . . ." he said.

I took a step off the curb and cars that had just jumped off the light at Dartmouth screamed past. A Karmann Ghia almost clipped my kneecap as its horn blared and it jerked a hair to its right.

"Oooh," Wesley said. "Close one. Careful, Pat. Careful."

I walked along the edge of the mall toward Dartmouth, my eyes on Wesley as he took several casual steps backward.

"I knew a guy who got hit by a car once," Wesley said as I lost him around the corner.

I broke into a trot and reached Dartmouth. The traffic continued to smoke the road in front of me, rain hissing off the tires. Wesley stood at the mouth of the public alley that ran parallel to Commonwealth Avenue from the Public Garden to the Fens a mile west.

"This guy tripped and a car fender hit his head while he was down. Turned his frontal lobe to egg salad."

The light turned yellow, but this was merely an excuse for eight cars in two lanes to speed up as they broke through the intersection.

Wesley gave me another wave and disappeared into the alley.

"Always be careful, Pat. Always."

I bolted across the avenue as a Volvo turned right onto Commonwealth and cut me off. The driver, a woman, shook her head at me, and then roared down the avenue.

I reached the sidewalk, spoke into the phone as I ran toward the mouth of the alley. "Wesley, you still there, buddy?"

"I'm not your buddy," he whispered.

"But you said you were."

"I lied, Pat."

I reached the alley and slid on the sole strip of cobblestone at its mouth, banged into an overflowing Dumpster. A soaked paper bag exploded upward from the Dumpster and a rat surged up and over the edge, dropped to the alley. A cat that had been lying in wait under the Dumpster took off after it, and the two of them bolted the length of a city block in about six seconds. The cat looked big and mean, but so did the rat, and I wondered who exactly was controlling the chase. If I'd been betting, I'd have to have given a slight edge to the rat.

"You ever play Bronco Buster?" Wesley whispered.

"Which?" I looked up at the fire escapes dripping water from chipped iron. Nothing.

"Bronco Buster," Wesley whispered. "It's a game. Try it with Vanessa Moore some night. What you do is you mount the woman from behind, doggie style. You with me?"

"Sure." I walked down the center of the alley, peering through the fog and drizzle at the rear doorways of opulent town houses, the small garages, and the shadowed places where buildings met buildings and some jutted out and others didn't.

"So you have her from behind and you slip your dick in there so it's good and firm, as deep as it can go. How deep would that be in your case, Pat?"

"I'm Irish, Wesley. You figure it out."

"None too deep, then," he said, and a low "ha-ha" rode his whisper.

I craned my head up at the odd collection of small wooden decks that protruded from the brick, like lean-tos for those underneath. I peered up at the cracks between the wood slats, looking for any shape resembling feet.

"Well, anyway," he said, "once the two of you are attached good and snug, you whisper another woman's name in her ear and then hold on tight like a bronco buster as the bitch goes wild."

I spotted a few roof gardens, but they were too high up to tell if anyone was in them, and besides, none of the fire escapes looked close enough for easy access.

"Think you'd like that game, Pat?"

I turned a slow 360, willed my eyes to relax, to glide over the surface and see if anything incongruous showed itself.

"I asked if you'd like that game, Pat."

"No, Wes."

"Too bad. Oh, Pat?"

"What, Wes?"

"Take another look due east."

I turned 180 degrees to my right and saw him down the far end of the alley, a tall figure made opaque by the fog, silhouette of a phone held to his ear.

"Whattaya say?" he said. "Let's play."

I broke into a run and he bolted as soon as I did. I heard the slap and clatter of his feet on wet cement and then he broke the connection.

By the time I reached the Clarendon Street end of the alley, he was gone. Shoppers and tourists and high school students filled the sidewalks. I saw men in trench coats and yellow macs and construction workers drenched to the bone. I saw steam rising from the sewer grates and enveloping taxis as they rolled past. I saw a kid on Rollerblades wipe out in front of a parking lot on Newbury. But not Wesley.

Just the mist and rain he'd left behind.

22

The morning after I had my encounter with Wesley in the rain, I got a call from Bubba telling me to be outside my house in half an hour because he was coming to pick me up.

"Where we going?"

"To see Stevie Zambuca."

I stepped back from the small telephone table, took a long breath. Stevie Zambuca? Why the hell would he want to see me? I'd never met the man. I would have assumed the man had never heard of me. I'd been kind of hoping to keep it that way.

"Why?"

"Dunno. He called me, said to come to his house and bring you."

"I was requested."

"You wanna call it that, sure. You were requested." Bubba hung up.

I went back out into the kitchen and sat at the table, drank my morning coffee, and tried to breathe steadily enough to avoid a panic attack. Yes, Stevie Zambuca scared me, but that wasn't rare. Stevie Zambuca scared most people.

Stevie "The Pick" Zambuca ran a crew out of East Boston and Revere that, among other things, controlled most North Shore gambling, prostitution, narcotics, and chop-shop operations. Stevie was called "The Pick" not because he carried an ice pick or because he was skinny or knew his way around a lock, but because he was famous for giving his victims a choice on how they'd die. Stevie would enter a room where three or four of his goons held a guy to a chair, and he'd place an ax and a hacksaw in front of the guy and tell the guy to pick. Ax or saw. Knife or sword. Garrote or hammer. If the victim couldn't pick, or didn't do so in time, Stevie was rumored to use a drill, his weapon of choice. This was one of the reasons why newspapers sometimes erroneously called Stevie "The Drill," which, according to rumor, pissed off a Somerville made guy named Frankie DiFalco who had a really big dick.

For half a second I wondered if Cody Falk's bodyguard, Leonard, could be connected to this. I'd made him for a North Shore guy, after all. But that was just the panic. If Leonard had enough pull to get Stevie Zambuca to call me to his house, then Leonard wouldn't have needed to hire himself out to Cody Falk.

This didn't make sense. Bubba traveled in mob circles. I didn't.

So why did Stevie Zambuca want to see me? What had I done? And how could I undo it? Quickly. Really quickly. By yesterday, perhaps.

Stevie Zambuca's house was a small, unprepossessing split-level ranch that sat on the end of a dead-end street on top of a hill that looked down over Route 1 and Logan Airport in East Boston. He could even see the harbor from there, though I doubt he looked much. All Stevie needed to see was the airport; half his crew's income came from there—baggage handlers' unions, transport unions, shit that fell off the back of trucks and planes and landed in Stevie's lap.

The house had an above-ground pool and a chain-link fence surrounding a small front yard. The backyard was bigger, but not by much, and kerosene torches were staked into the ground every ten feet, throwing light on a summer morning made blue by fog and a temperature dip that felt more like October than August.

"It's his Saturday brunch," Bubba said as we exited his Humvee and headed for the house. "He does it every week."

"A wise guy brunch," I said. "How quaint."

"The mimosas are good," Bubba said. "But stay away from the canoli, or the rest of the day your best friend will be your fucking toilet seat."

A fifteen-year-old girl with a waterfall of orange-highlighted black hair pushed up off her forehead opened the door, her face a mask of fifteen-year-old fuck-you apathy and repressed anger she had no idea what to do with yet.

Then she recognized Bubba and a shy smile fought its way across her dim lips. "Mr. Rogowski. Hi."

"Hey, Josephina. Nice streaks."

She touched her hair nervously. "The orange? You like it?"

"It kicks," Bubba said.

Josephina looked down at her knees and twisted her ankles together, swayed slightly in the doorway. "My dad hates it."

"Hey," Bubba said, "that's what dads do."

Josephina absently pulled a strand of hair into her mouth, continued to sway a bit under Bubba's open gaze and wide smile.

Bubba as sex symbol. Now I'd seen it all.

"Your dad around?" Bubba asked.

"He's in back?" Josephina said as if asking Bubba if that were okay.

"We'll find him." Bubba kissed her cheek. "How's your mom?"

"On my ass," Josephina said. "Like, constantly."

"And that's what moms do," Bubba said. "Fun being fifteen, huh?"

Josephina looked up at him and for a moment I feared she'd grab his face right there and plant one on his oversized lips.

Instead, she pivoted on her toes like a dancer and said, "I gotta go," and ran out of the room.

"Weird kid," Bubba said.

"She's got a crush on you."

"Fuck off."

"She does, you idiot. Are you blind?"

"Fuck off or I'll kill you."

"Oh," I said. "In that case never mind."

"Better," Bubba said as we worked our way through a crowd in the kitchen.

"She does, though."

"You're dead."

"Kill me later."

"If there's anything left after Stevie gets through."

"Thanks," I said. "You're pissa."

The small house was jammed. Everywhere you looked, you saw a wise guy or a wise guy's wife or a wise guy's kid. It was a crowd of crushed velour jogging suits and Champion sweatshirts on the men, black nylon stretch pants and loud yellow-and-black or purple-and-black or white-and-silver blouses on the women. The kids wore mostly pro sports team apparel, the brighter the better, and all of it loose and baggy and uniform so that a Cincinnati Bengals red-and-black zebra-striped hat gave way to an identical jersey and sweatpants.

The interior of the house was one of the ugliest I'd ever seen. White marble steps dropped off the kitchen and into a living room covered in white shag carpeting so deep you couldn't see anyone's shoes. Running through the white shag were what appeared to be sparkling pinstripes the color of pearl. The couches and armchairs were white leather, but the coffee table, end tables, and enormous home entertainment armoire were a shiny metallic black. The lower half of the walls was covered by an industrial plastic shell made to look like cave rock, and the upper half was clad in red silk wallpaper. A wet bar, encased in mirrored glass and lit by 150-watt bulbs, was built into the far corner of all that red and cave rock, and painted black to match the armoire. Amid pictures of Stevie and his family hanging from the walls, the Zambucas had placed framed photos of their favorite Italians—John Travolta as Tony Manero, Al Pacino as Michael Corleone, Frank Sinatra, Dino, Sophia Loren, Vince Lombardi, and, inexplicably, Elvis. I guess with the dark hair and the questionable taste in clothing, the King was an honorary goomba, kind of guy you could've trusted to do a hit and keep his mouth shut, make you a nice sausage-and-peppers hoagie afterward.

Bubba shook a bunch of hands, kissed a few cheeks, but didn't pause for conversation, and no one looked like they wanted to engage him in one anyway. Even in a room full of second-story men, bank robbers, bookies, and killers, Bubba sent an electric trill through the house, a distinct aura of threat and otherworldliness. The men's smiles were fragmented and slightly shaky when they saw him, and the women's reconstructed faces bore an odd mixture of fear and arousal.

As we neared the edge of the living room, a middle-aged woman with bleached-blond hair and tanning-lamp flesh threw out her arms and screamed, "Aaah, Bubba!"

He lifted her off her feet when he hugged her and she smacked a kiss as loud as her greeting onto the side of his face.

He deposited her gently back to the shag carpet and said, "Mira, how are ya, hon?"

"Great, big fella!" She leaned back and cupped her elbow in her hand as she took a drag from a white cigarette so long it could have hit somebody in the kitchen if she'd turned without warning. She wore a bright blue blouse over matching blue pants and blue open-toed heels with four-inch spikes. Her face and body were a miracle of modern medicine—tiny tuck marks where the jaw line met the ears, jutting ass and breasts an eighteen-year-old would envy, hands as creamy porcelain as a doll's. "Where you been hiding? You seen Josephina?"

Bubba answered the second question. "She let us in, yeah. She looks great."

"Pain in my patootie," Mira said, and laughed through a burst of smoke. "Stevie wants to put her in a convent."

"Sister Josephina?" Bubba asked with a cocked eyebrow.

Mira's cackle ripped through the room. "Wouldn't that be a sight? Ha!"

She looked at me suddenly and her bright eyes dulled with suspicion.

"Mira," Bubba said, "this is my friend Patrick. Stevie has some business with him."

Mira slid a smooth hand into mine. "Mira Zambuca. Pleased to meet you, Pat."

I hate being called Pat, but I decided not to mention it.

"Mrs. Zambuca," I said, "a pleasure."

Mira didn't look all that pleased having a pale-faced Mick in her living room, but she gave me a distant smile that told me she'd bear it as long I stayed away from the silverware.

"Stevie's out by the grill." She cocked her head in the direction of streams of smoke billowing by the glass doors that led out back. "Making them veal and pork sausages everyone loves so much."

Particularly for brunch, I thought.

"Thanks, hon," Bubba said. "You look dynamite, by the way."

"Aw, thanks, sweetie. Ain't you a caution?" She turned away from us and almost ignited sixteen pounds of another woman's hair with her cigarette before the woman saw it coming and leaned back.

Bubba and I worked our way through the rest of the crowd and out through the back. We closed the door behind us and waved at the clouds of smoke filling the back deck.

Out here, it was strictly men, and a master blaster propped up on the deck rail played Springsteen, another honorary goomba, and most of the guys were fatter than the ones inside, stuffing their mouths even now with cheeseburgers and hot dogs piled high with peppers and onions and relish chunks the size of bricks.

A short guy worked the grill, his jet-black pompadour adding three inches to his height. He wore jeans over white running shoes and sported a T-shirt emblazoned with the words WORLD'S GREATEST DAD on the back. A red-and-white-checkered apron covered the front of him as he worked a steel spatula over a two-tiered grill stuffed from end to end with sausages, hamburgers, marinated chicken breasts, hot dogs, red and green peppers, onions, and a small pile of garlic chunks in a nest of foil.

"Hey, Charlie," the short guy called out, "you like your burger black, right?"

"Black as Michael Jordan," a greasy sea of flesh called back as several men laughed.

"That's some black." The short guy nodded and lifted a cigar from an ashtray beside the grill and popped it in his mouth.

"Stevie," Bubba said.

The guy turned and smiled around his cigar. "Hey, Rogowski! Hey, everyone, the Polack's here!"

There were calls of "Bub-ba!" and "Rogowski!" and "Kill-a!" and several men slapped Bubba's broad back or shook his hand, but no one acknowledged my presence, because Stevie hadn't. It was as if I wouldn't exist until he said so.

"That thing last week," Stevie Zambuca said to Bubba. "You have any problems?"

"Nope."

"That guy was talking shit? He give you any headaches?"

"Nope," Bubba said again.

"Heard that suit in Norfolk is looking to give you grief."

"Heard that, too," Bubba said.

"You want a hand with it?"

"No, thanks," Bubba said.

"You sure? Be the least we could do."

"Thanks," Bubba said, "but I got it covered."

Stevie Zambuca looked up from the grill and smiled at Bubba. "You don't ever ask for nothing, Rogowski. It makes people nervous."

"You, Stevie?"

"Me?" He shook his head. "No. It's old school, far as I'm concerned. Something most of these fucking guys could learn from. Me and you, Rogowski, we're almost all that's left of the old days and we ain't that old. The rest of these fucking guys?" He looked back over his shoulder at the fat farm on his porch. "They're hoping for movie deals, shopping book ideas to agents."

Bubba glanced at the men with complete disinterest. "Freddy's got it bad, I hear."

Fat Freddy Constantine ran the mob here, but

word was he wouldn't be around much longer. The guy favored to take his seat was currently grilling sausage in front of us.

Stevie nodded. "His entire prostate's in a biohazard bag at Brigham and Women's. I hear his intestinal tract's next."

"Too bad," Bubba said.

Stevie shrugged. "Hey, it's nature, right? You live, you die, people cry, and then they think about where they're gonna eat." Stevie shoveled five burgers onto a plate the size of a gladiator's shield, followed them with a half dozen hot dogs and some chicken. He held the plate over his shoulder and said, "Come get it, you fat fucking humps."

Bubba leaned back on his heels and dug his hands into his trench coat as one of the blobs took the plate from Stevie's hand and walked it back to the condiment table.

Stevie closed the grill cover. He placed the spatula on the grill tray and took a long puff on his cigar.

"Bubba, you go mingle, get something to eat. Me and your friend going to take a walk around the yard."

Bubba shrugged and stayed where he was.

Stevie Zambuca held out a hand. "Kenzie, right? Walk with me."

We walked off the small porch and down into the yard, made our way between empty white tables and lawn sprinklers that were shut off, down to a small garden encased in brick that hosted a sickly array of dandelions and crocuses.

Beside the garden was a wooden porch swing hanging from metal posts and a rod that had once supported a clothesline. Stevie Zambuca sat on the right side of the porch swing and patted the wood.

"Have a seat, Kenzie."

I sat.

Stevie leaned back and took a long toke from his cigar, blew the smoke back out as he lifted his legs off the ground, held his heels over the grass for a moment, seemed fascinated by his white running shoes.

"You known Rogowski, what, your whole life?"

"Yeah," I said.

"He always crazy?"

I looked up at Bubba as he crossed the porch and fixed himself a cheeseburger at the condiment table.

"He's always followed the beat of his own drummer," I said.

Stevie Zambuca nodded. "I heard all the stories," he said. "Lived on the streets since he was, what, eight or something, you and some of your friends used to bring him food, shit like that. Then Morty Schwartz, the old Jew bookie, took him in, raised him till he died."

I nodded.

"They say the only things he cares about are dogs, Vincent Patriso's granddaughter, the ghost of Morty Schwartz, and you."

I watched Bubba take a seat away from the rest of the men and eat his burger.

"Is that true?" Stevie Zambuca asked.

"I guess," I said.

He patted my knee. "You remember Jack Rouse?"

Jack Rouse had been the kingpin of the Irish mob until he disappeared a few years back.

"Sure."

"He put a hit on you not long before he disappeared. An open hit, Kenzie. And you know why it didn't go down?"

I shook my head.

Stevie Zambuca tilted his chin up in the direction of the porch. "Rogowski. He walked into a card game filled with capos and said anything happened to you, he'd hit the streets armed, kill every soldier he saw until someone killed him."

Bubba finished his hamburger and carried his paper plate back for a second. The men near the condiment table drifted away and left him alone. Bubba was always alone. It was his choice but his price, too, for being so unlike the rest of his species.

"Now that's loyalty," Stevie Zambuca said. "I try and instill that in my men, but I can't. They're only as loyal as their wallets are thick. See, you can't teach loyalty. You can't instill it. It's like trying to teach love. Can't be done. It's either in your heart, or it ain't. You ever get caught bringing him food?"

"By my parents?"

"Yeah."

"Sure."

"You catch an ass-whipping?"

"Oh, yeah," I said. "Several."

"But you kept stealing food from your family's table, right?"

"Yeah," I said.

"Why?"

I shrugged. "It's just what we did. We were kids."

"See, that's what I'm talking about. That's loyalty.

That's love, Kenzie. You can't put that in someone. And," he said with a stretch and a sigh, "you can't take it out, either."

I waited. The point, I was pretty sure, was coming.

"You can't take it out," Stevie Zambuca repeated. He leaned back and put his arm around my shoulder. "We got this guy does some work for us. Sort of like private contracting, if you know what I mean. He isn't employed by the organization, but he provides things sometimes. You follow?"

"I guess."

"This guy? He's important to me. I really can't over-stress how important."

He took a few puffs off his cigar, kept his arm around me, and gazed out at his small yard.

"You're bothering this guy," he said eventually. "You're annoying him. That annoys me."

"Wesley," I said.

"Oh, his fucking name? That don't matter. You know who I'm talking about. And I'm telling you, you're going to stop. You're going to stop now. If he decides to walk up to you and piss on your head, you're not even going to reach for a towel. You're gonna say, 'Thanks,' and wait to see if he's got anything more to give you."

"This guy," I said, "destroyed the life of—"

"Shut the fuck up," Stevie said mildly, and tightened his hand against my shoulder. "I don't give a shit about you or your problems. My problems are the only thing that matter here. You are an annoyance. I'm not asking you to stop. I'm telling you. Take a good look at your friend up there, Kenzie."

I looked. Bubba sat down again, bit into his burger.

"He's a great earner. I'd miss a guy like that. But if I hear you're bothering this independent contractor friend of mine? Making inquiries? Mentioning his name to people? I hear any of that, and I'll whack out your buddy. I'll cut his fucking head off and mail it to you. And then I'll kill you, Kenzie." He patted my shoulder several times. "We clear?"

"We're clear," I said.

He withdrew his arm, puffed his cigar, leaned forward with elbows on his knees. "That's great. When he finishes his burger, you take your Irish ass out of my home." He stood and began to walk toward the deck. "And wipe your feet on the mat before you walk back through the house. Fucking rug in the living room is a bitch to clean."

23

Bubba can barely read or write. He has just enough rudimentary skills in that area to decipher weapons manuals and other simple instruction texts as long as they're accompanied by diagrams. He can read his own press clippings, but it takes him half an hour, and he runs into trouble if he can't sound out the words phonetically. He has no grasp of complex dynamics in any type of human intercourse, knows so little about politics that as recently as last year I had to explain to him what the difference between the House and the Senate was, and his ignorance of current events is so total that the only thing he understands about Lewinsky is as a verb.

But he is not stupid.

There are those who have assumed, fatally as it turned out, that he was, and countless cops and DAs have managed through all their concerted effort to imprison him only twice, both times on weapons infractions so minor compared to what he was truly guilty of that the terms seemed more like vacation time than punishment.

Bubba has traversed the world a few times over and can tell you where to get the best vodka in former Eastern bloc villages you've never heard of, how to find a clean brothel in West Africa, and where to get a cheeseburger in Laos. Sitting atop tables scattered throughout the three-story warehouse he calls home, Bubba has constructed from memory Popsicle-stick models of several cities he's visited; I once checked his version of Beirut against a map and found a small street in Bubba's model the mapmakers had missed.

But where Bubba's intelligence is most prominent and most unnerving is in his innate ability to read people without having appeared to even notice them. Bubba can smell an undercover cop from a mile away; he can find a lie in the quiver of an eyelash; and his knack for sensing an ambush is so legendary in his circles that his competitors long ago quit trying and simply allowed him to carve out his slice of pie.

Bubba, Morty Schwartz told me not long before he died, was an animal. Morty meant it as a compliment. Bubba had flawless reflexes, unswerving instinct, and primal focus, and none of these skills were diluted or compromised by conscience. If Bubba had ever had conscience or guilt, he'd left them back in Poland along with his mother tongue when he was five years old.

"So what'd Stevie say?" Bubba asked as we drove through Maverick Square and headed for the tunnel.

I had to be careful here. If Bubba suspected Stevie was using him against me, he'd kill Stevie and half his crew, consequences be damned.

"Nothing much."

Bubba nodded. "He just called you to his house to shoot the shit?"

"Something like that."

"Sure," Bubba said.

I cleared my throat. "He told me Wesley Dawe has diplomatic immunity. I'm to stay away."

Bubba rolled down his window as we approached the tollbooths outside the Sumner Tunnel. "What could some yuppie psycho be worth to Stevie Zambuca?"

"Apparently a lot."

Somehow Bubba managed to squeeze his Hummer in between the tollbooths, handed the operator three bucks, and rolled his window back up as we joined the eight lanes trying to cram their way into two.

"But how?" he said, and maneuvered the double-wide freakish machine through the throng of metal like it was a letter opener.

I shrugged as we entered the tunnel. "Wesley's already proven he has access to one psychiatrist's files. Maybe he has access to others."

"And?"

"And," I said, "that access could give him private information on judges, cops, contractors, you name it."

"So what are you gonna do?" Bubba asked.

"Back off," I said.

His faced was bathed in the sickly yellow wash of the tunnel lights when he turned his head and looked at me. "You?"

"Yeah," I said. "I'm no dummy."

"Huh," Bubba said softly, and looked back out the windshield.

"I'll just let things cool down," I said, hating the hint of desperation I heard in my voice. "Figure out another way to come at Wesley."

"There ain't no other way," Bubba said. "You either take this guy down or you don't. You do, and Stevie'll figure out it was you no matter how you cover your tracks."

"So, what, you're saying I should take down Wesley and hand over the rest of my life to Stevie Zambuca?"

"I can talk to him," Bubba said. "Reason with him."

"No."

"No?"

"Yeah, no. You talk to him, right? And let's say his position doesn't change. Where's that put you? Asking for something he ain't going to give."

"So then I ice his ass."

"And then? You whack a made guy, everyone's going to say, No problem?"

Bubba shrugged as we rolled through the mouth of the tunnel and out into the North End. "I don't think that far ahead."

"I do."

He gave me another shrug, a harder one. "So you're just going to back down?"

"Yeah. That okay with you?"

"Fine," he said distantly. "Fine, man. Whatever."

He didn't look at me when he dropped me off. He kept his eyes on the road, his head moving slightly in time with the chug of the engine.

I got out of the Hummer and Bubba spoke with

his eyes still locked on the avenue. "Maybe you should get out."

"Get out of where?"

"This business."

"Why's that?"

"Fear kills, man. Shut the door, will you?"

I closed the door and watched him drive off.

When he reached the light, he slammed on the brakes and then the Hummer was suddenly careening back toward me in reverse. I looked down the avenue, saw a red Escort moving forward in Bubba's lane. The driver looked up, saw the Hummer hurtling backward toward her. She veered left into the passing lane put her hand on the horn, and passed Bubba in a blare of indignant noise, middle finger predictably extended so that for a moment neither of her hands were steering.

Bubba flipped his own bird at the rear of the Escort as he hopped out of the Hummer and slammed his hand on the hood.

"It's me."

"What?"

"It's me!" he bellowed. "That piece of shit is using me, ain't he?"

"No, he—"

"He can't threaten Angie, 'cause she's connected. So it was me."

"Bubba, he threatened me. Okay?"

He threw back his head and screamed, "Bullshit!" at the sky. He dropped his head and came around the car, and for a moment I was pretty sure he was going to pummel me.

"You," he screamed, shoving a finger in my face,

"don't back down. You never have, which is why my second fucking career has been saving your ass."

"Bubba—"

"And I don't mind!" he yelled.

A group of kids turned the corner, saw Bubba in full horror tilt, and made a beeline for the other side of the avenue.

"Don't fucking lie to me anymore," Bubba said. "Don't. If you or her lie to me, it fucking hurts. It makes me want to go maim someone. Anyone!" He punched his own chest so hard that if it had belonged to anyone else the sternum would have shattered like crockery. "Stevie threatened me, didn't he?"

"What if he did?"

Bubba wheeled at the air with his huge flailing arms and spittle shot from his mouth. "I'll fucking kill him. I'll fucking rip his goddamn large intestine out and strangle him with it. I'll squeeze his fucking head until—"

"No," I said. "Don't you get it?"

"Get what?"

"That's the bind. That's what Wesley wants. This threat didn't come from Stevie, it came from Wesley. That's how the fucker works."

Bubba bent, took a long breath. He looked like a hunk of granite about to come gradually to life.

"You lost me," he said eventually.

"I'll bet," I said slowly, "that Wesley knows Angie's connected, knows the only way to get to me is through you. I'm telling you, he gave Stevie the idea to threaten you, knowing that, worst-case scenario, you'd find out, flip out, and get us all killed."

"Huh," he said softly. "This guy's smart."

A blue and white pulled alongside us and the cop riding shotgun rolled down his window.

"Everything okay, gents?" He looked vaguely familiar.

"Fine," I said.

"Hey, you, big fella."

Bubba turned his head, met the cop's gaze with a grimace.

"You're Bubba Rogowski, ain't you?"

Bubba looked off down the avenue.

"Kill anyone lately, Bubba?"

"It's been, like, hours, Officer."

The cop chuckled. "That your Hummer?"

Bubba nodded.

"Move it into a space, or I'll ticket it."

"Fine." Bubba turned back to me.

"Now, Rogowski," the cop said.

Bubba gave me a bitter smile and shook his head. Then he walked out past the cruiser and climbed in the Hummer as the cops watched with wide, satisfied grins. Bubba pulled forward and found a spot large enough to accommodate him about a hundred yards down the avenue.

"You know your friend's a scumbag?" the cop asked me.

I shrugged.

"That could make you a scumbag by association if you're not careful."

I recognized the cop now. Mike Gourgouras, allegedly a bagman for Stevie Zambuca, Stevie sending him by to make sure the message sank in.

"Might wanna consider distancing yourself from a guy like that."

"Okay." I held up a hand, smiled. "Good advice."

Gourgouras narrowed his small dark eyes at me. "You busting my balls?"

"No, sir."

He gave me a smile. "Be careful in your choices, Mr. Kenzie." His window rolled up with a whir and then the cruiser pulled down the avenue, beeped once at Bubba as he walked back down the sidewalk toward me, then turned the corner.

"Stevie's boys," Bubba said.

"You noticed?"

"Yeah."

"You calm?"

He shrugged. "I'm getting there, maybe."

"All right," I said. "How do we get Stevie off our ass?"

"Angie."

"She's not going to like calling in that marker."

"She has no choice."

"How do you figure?"

"With us dead, you know how boring her life would be? Shit, man, she'd about shrivel up and die."

He had a point.

I called Sallis & Salk, only to be told Angie didn't work there anymore.

"Why not?" I asked the receptionist.

"There was, I believe, an incident."

"What kind of incident?"

"That, I'm not at liberty to discuss."

"Well, could you tell me whether she quit or got fired?"

"No, I cannot."

"Wow. You can't tell me much of anything, can you?"

"I can tell you this phone conversation is over," she said, and hung up.

I called Angie at home, got her voice mail. She could still be home, though. She turns her ringer off a lot when feeling antisocial.

"Incident?" Bubba said as we drove over to the South End. "Like an international incident?"

I shrugged. "With Ange, I wouldn't rule it out."

"Wow," Bubba said. "How cool would that be?"

We found her at home, as I'd expected. She'd been cleaning, scrubbing her hardwood floors with Murphy's Oil Soap, blasting Patti Smith's *Horses* through the apartment so loud, we'd had to shout at her through an open window because she couldn't hear the bell.

She turned down the music, let us in, and said, "Don't step on the living room floor or it's your ass."

We followed her into the kitchen and Bubba said, "Incident?"

"It was nothing," she said. "I was sick of working for them anyway. They use women for window dressing, think we look hot in our Ann Taylor suits, packing heat."

"Incident?" I said.

She let out a half scream of frustration and opened the fridge.

"The diamond merchant pinched my ass. Okay?"

She tossed a can of Coke at me, then handed one to Bubba, took her own to the kitchen counter, and leaned against the dishwasher.

"Hospital?" I said.

She raised her eyebrows over the Coke, took a swig. "It's not like he really needed it, little crybaby. I just backhanded him. A tap. With my fingers." She held up the backs of her fingers. "How was I to know he was a bleeder?"

"Nose?" Bubba asked.

She nodded. "One tap."

"Lawsuit?"

She snorted. "He can try. I went to my own doctor and she took a photo of the bruise."

"She photographed your ass?" Bubba said.

"Yes, Ruprecht, she did."

"Damn, I woulda done it."

"Me, too."

"Oh, thanks, guys. Should I swoon now?"

"We need you to call Grandpa Vincent," Bubba said abruptly.

Angie almost dropped her Coke. "Are you doped to the gills or something?"

"No," I said. "Unfortunately, we're serious."

"Why?"

We told her.

"How've you two managed to stay alive this long?" she asked when we finished.

"It's a mystery," I said.

"Stevie Zambuca," she said. "Little homicidal wackjob. He still have the Frankie Avalon 'do?"

Bubba nodded.

Angie swigged some Coke. "Wears lifts."

"What?" Bubba said.

"Oh, yeah. Lifts. In his shoes. Has them done special by this old cobbler in Lynn."

Angie's grandfather, Vincent Patriso, had once (and some said still did) run the mob north of Delaware. He'd always been one of the quiet guys, never mentioned in the papers, never labeled *Don* by anyone in the legitimate press. He'd owned a bakery and a few clothing stores in Staten Island, sold them a few years back, and divided his time between a new house in Enfield, New Jersey, and one in Florida. So Angie knew her way around the cast list of Boston wise guys pretty well—could, in fact, probably tell you more about most of them than their own capos.

Angie hoisted herself up on the counter, drained her Coke, brought one leg up on the counter, placed her chin on her knee.

"Call my grandfather," she said eventually.

"We wouldn't ask," Bubba said, "except, like, Patrick's real scared."

"Oh, sure, blame me."

"Crying on the way over," Bubba said. "Blubbering, really. 'I don't wanna die. I don't wanna die.' It was embarrassing."

Angie tilted her chin so that her cheek rested on her knee and smiled at him. She closed her eyes for a moment.

Bubba looked at me. I shrugged. He shrugged.

Angie lifted her head and lowered her leg. She groaned. She ran her fingers back along her temples. She groaned again.

"All the years I was married and Phil beat me, I never called my grandfather. All the scary shit," she looked at me, "that you and I have gotten ourselves into, I've never called my grandfather. This"—she raised her tank top and exposed the puckered scar of

a bullet that had torn through her small intestines—
"and I never called."

"Sure," Bubba said, "but this is important."

She hummed her empty Coke can off his forehead.

She looked over at me. "How serious was Stevie?"

"As the plague," I said. "He'll kill us both." I
jerked a thumb at Bubba. "Him first."

Bubba snorted.

Angie stared at us both for a long time and her
face gradually softened.

"Well, I don't have a job anymore. Which means
I probably can't afford this apartment much longer.
Can't hold on to a boyfriend, and I don't like pets.
So, I guess you two morons are all I got."

"Stop it," Bubba said. "I'm getting all choked up
and shit."

She dropped off the counter. "All right, who's
driving me to a safe phone?"

She used one off the lobby of the Park Plaza
Hotel and I gave her plenty of room, wandered
around the marble floors, admired the old elevators
with their brass doors and the brass ashtrays standing to the left of the doors, wished it was still cool to
wear fedoras and knock back scotch for lunch,
light wooden matches with your thumbnail, and
call people "mugs."

Where have you gone, Burt Lancaster, and why'd
you take most of the cool shit with you?

She hung up the phone, walked toward me, completely out of place among the brass fixtures and
red Orientals, marble floors and people in silks and

linens and Malaysian cotton, in her faded white tank top, gray shorts, and Nike thongs, no makeup, smelling like Murphy's Oil Soap, and all she had to do was give me that loopy grin she was giving me now, and I was pretty certain I'd never seen anyone look half as tremendous.

"Looks like you'll live," she said. "He said to give him the weekend, steer clear of Stevie till then."

"What'd it cost you?"

She shrugged, started heading for the exit. "I got to make him a plate of chicken piccata next time he's up this way and, oh yeah, make sure Luca Brasi sleeps with the fishes."

"Every time you think you're out," I said.

"They pull me back in."

24

On Monday we went to work in earnest. Angie planned to spend the day trying to contact a friend at the IRS in Pittsburgh, see if she could get any hits on Wesley Dawe's revenue info for the years before he disappeared, and Bubba promised he'd try the same with a guy he knew at the Massachusetts Department of Revenue, though he seemed to remember something shady happened concerning his friend but couldn't recall what that was.

I used the computer in the office to search the Net's national phone books and any other databases I could think of. Typing in *Wesley Dawe* over and over and over and getting nothing, nothing, and nothing.

Angie's friend at the IRS kept her hanging all afternoon, and Bubba never called to report on his progress, and finally, sick of brick walls, I drove downtown to check out Naomi Dawe at the Hall of Records.

There was nothing out of the ordinary in either her birth or death records, but I copied all the info down in a notepad anyway and stuck it in my back pocket as I left City Hall.

I stepped out onto the rear of City Hall Plaza and two beefy guys, both balding, both wearing aviator glasses and thin Hawaiian shirts untucked over jeans, fell into step beside me.

"We're going to take a little walk," the guy on my right said.

"Cool," I said. "If we go to the park, will you buy me an ice cream?"

"Guy's a comedian," the one on my left said.

"Sure," the other guy said. "He's fucking Jay Leno over here."

We crossed the plaza toward Cambridge Street and a small gang of pigeons took flight in front of us. I could hear both guys breathing a little heavy, a daily constitutional apparently not something they worked into their schedules.

It was hot, but a colder than normal sweat broke out on my forehead as I noticed the dark pink Lincoln double-parked on Cambridge. I'd seen the same Lincoln parked in Stevie Zambuca's driveway on Saturday.

"Stevie felt like chatting," I said. "How nice."

"You notice his delivery was a little shaky on that one?" the guy on my right side said.

"Maybe this ain't so funny no more," the other guy said, and with an amazingly smooth and swift move for a guy his size, his hand slipped under my own shirt and removed my gun.

"Don't worry," he told me, "I'll keep it in a safe place."

The back door of the Lincoln opened as we ap-

proached and a thin young guy got out of the car
and held the door open for me.

I could make a scene, and the two guys beside me
would kneecap me and shove me in anyway, broad
daylight or not.

I decided to proceed with grace.

I climbed in the car beside Stevie Zambuca and
they shut the door behind me.

The front seats were empty. Apparently my beefy
handlers did the driving.

Stevie Zambuca said, "Someday that old guy? He's
gonna die. He's, what, eighty-four now, right?"

I nodded.

"So he dies someday, I'll fly out to his funeral, pay
my respects, and come back and take a pipe to your
fucking elbows, Kenzie. You just be ready for that
day, because I will be."

"Okay."

"Okay?" He smiled. "Think you're pretty fucking cool, don't you?"

I didn't say anything.

"Well, you ain't. But for now, I'll play ball." He
tossed a brown paper bag on my lap. "There's eight
thou in there. This guy, he paid me ten to back you
off."

"So you've done business with him?"

"No. It was a straight job. Ten grand to keep you
off his back. Never met the guy until Friday night.
He approached one of my people, made his pitch."

"Did he tell you to threaten Bubba to get to me?"

Stevie stroked his chin. "Matter of fact, yeah. He
knows a lot about you, Kenzie. A lot. And he don't
like you. At all, motherfucker. At all."

"You know anything about where he lives, works, that sort of thing?"

Stevie shook his head. "No. Guy I know in K.C. vouched for him. Heard he was stand-up."

"K.C.?"

Stevie's eyes met my own. "K.C. Why's that bother you?"

I shrugged. "It just doesn't seem to fit."

"Yeah, well, whatever. When you see him, give him the eight Gs, tell him the other two Gs are for my aggravation."

"How do you know I'll see him?"

"He's got a real hard-on for you, Kenzie. Like diamond-cutter hard. He kept saying you 'interfered.' And Vincent Patriso might be able to back me off, but he can't back this guy off. He wants you dead."

"No. He wants me to wish I were."

Stevie chuckled. "Maybe you got something there. This guy? He's smart, speaks real well, but in there with all that brain power, there's disease, Kenzie. Personally, I think he's got rocks in his head, and the rocks got little birds flying around in 'em." He laughed, brought his hand down on my knee. "And you pissed him off. Ain't that great?" He pressed a button on his door console and the locks popped up. "See you later, Kenzie."

"See you, Stevie."

I opened the door, blinked in the sun.

"Yeah, you'll see me," Stevie said as I stepped out of the car. "After the old guy's funeral. Up close. In Technicolor."

One of the beefy guys handed me my gun. "Take it easy, comedian. Try not to shoot off your own foot."

My cell phone rang as I walked back across City Hall Plaza toward the parking garage where I'd left my car.

I knew it was him before I even said, "Hello."

"Pat, buddy. How are you?"

"Not bad, Wes. Yourself?"

"Hanging to the left, my friend. Say, Pat?"

"Yeah, Wes?"

"When you get to the parking garage, go up to the roof, will you?"

"We going to meet, Wes?"

"Bring the envelope Don Guido gave you."

"But of course."

"Don't waste our time contacting the police, okay, Pat? There's nothing to hold me on."

He hung up.

I waited until I was in the shadows of the garage itself, unseeable to anyone inside or on the roof, before I called Angie.

"How fast can you get down by Haymarket?"

"The way I drive?"

"So about five minutes," I said. "I'll be on the roof of the garage at the base of New Sudbury. You know the one?"

"Yup."

I looked around me. "I need a picture of the guy, Ange."

"That garage roof? How'm I gonna shoot down on that? All the buildings around it are shorter."

I found one. "The antiques co-op at the end of Friend Street. Get on the roof."

"How?"

"I don't know. Outside of the friggin' expressway, I don't see any other place you could shoot from."

"Okay, okay. I'm on my way."

She hung up and I took the stairs eight stories to the roof, the stairwell dark and dank and reeking of urine.

He was leaning with his arms up on the wall, looking down at City Hall Plaza, Faneuil Hall, the sudden towering eruption of the financial district where Congress met State. For a moment, I considered rushing him, giving his legs a quick lift and chuck, seeing what sounds he'd make as he tumbled end over end and splattered all over the street. With any luck, it'd be ruled a suicide, and if he had a soul, it would choke on the irony all the way down to hell.

He turned to me when I was a good fifteen yards away. He smiled.

"Tempting, isn't it?"

"What's that?"

"The thought of throwing me off the roof."

"A bit."

"But the police would quickly ascertain that the last call I made from my cell phone was to your cell phone, and they'd triangulate the source of the signals and place you at City Hall, six or seven minutes before I died."

"That'd be a bummer," I said. "Sure." I pulled my gun from my waistband. "On your knees, Wes."

"Oh, come on."

"Hands behind your head and lace the fingers."

He laughed. "Or what? You'll shoot me?"

I was ten feet away now. "No. But I'll pistol-whip your nose beyond recognition. Would you like that?"

He grimaced, looked at his linen trousers and the dirty ground at his feet.

"How about I just hold up my hands, you frisk me, and I remain standing?"

"Sure," I said. "Why not?" I kicked him in the back of the left knee and he dropped to the ground.

"This is not what you want to do!" He looked back at me, his face scarlet.

"Oooh," I said. "Wesley gets angry."

"You have no idea."

"Hey, psycho, put your fucking hands behind your head. Okay?"

He did.

"Lace the fingers."

He did.

I ran my hands along his chest, under the flaps of his untucked black silk shirt, along his waistband, crotch, and ankles. He wore black golf gloves in the dead of summer, but they were too tight and too small to conceal even a razor, so I let them be.

"The irony is," he said as I searched him, "that even as your hand is running all over my body, you can't touch me, Pat."

"Miles Lovell," I said. "David Wetterau."

"You can place me at the sites of either of their accidents?"

Nope. Son of a bitch.

I said, "Your stepsister, Wesley."

"Committed suicide, last I heard."

"I can place you at the Holly Martens Inn."

"Where I provided aid and sustenance to my clinically depressed sister? Is that what you're talking about?"

I finished frisking him and stepped back. He was right. I had nothing on him.

He looked back over his shoulder at me. "Oh," he said, "you're done?"

He unlaced his fingers and stood, brushed at the dark ovals on each knee, the oily, sunbaked tar permanently imprinted in the linen.

"I'll send you the bill," he said.

"Do that."

He leaned back against the wall, studied me, and I again felt the irrational urge to push him over. Just to hear his scream.

Up close for the first time, I could feel the casual combination of power and cruelty that he wore like a cloak draped over his shoulders. His face was a strange mix of hard angles and ripeness—hard jawline under fleshy red lips, a doughy, pudding softness to his ivory skin interrupted by jutting cheekbones and eyebrows. His hair was blond again, and combined with those fleshy lips and eyes so blue and vibrant and mean, the total effect of his face was defiantly Aryan.

As I studied him, he studied me, cocking his head ever so slightly to the right, his blue eyes narrowing, the hint of a knowing grin curling the corners of his ample mouth.

"That partner of yours," he said, "is a real babe. You fuck her, too?"

It was as if he wanted me to throw him off the roof.

"I bet you have," he said, and glanced over his shoulder at the city below. "You bang Vanessa Moore—who by the way I caught in court the other day, quite good—and you're banging your hot little partner and God knows who else. You're quite the swordsman, Pat."

He turned his head back to me and I placed my gun in its holster at the small of my back for fear I'd use it.

"Wes."

"Yeah, Pat?"

"Don't call me Pat."

"Oh." He nodded. "Found a sore spot. Always interesting. People, you know, you can never be sure where their weaknesses lie until you prod a bit."

"It's not a weakness, it's a preference."

"Sure." His eyes glittered. "You keep telling yourself that, Pat, er, rick."

I chuckled in spite of myself. The guy didn't quit.

A traffic helicopter from one of the news stations flew over us and then made an arc over the expressway as the crush of rush hour began to swell on the elevated girders to my left.

"I really hate women," Wesley said evenly, his eyes following the path of the helicopter. "As a species, intellectually, I find them . . ." He shrugged ". . . silly. But physically"—he smiled, rolled his eyes—"Christ, it's all I can do to keep from genuflecting when a really gorgeous one walks by. Interesting paradox, don't you think?"

"No," I said. "You're a misogynist, Wesley."

He chuckled. "You mean like Cody Falk?" He clucked his tongue. "You couldn't get me out of bed for rape. It's pedestrian."

"You'd prefer to reduce people to shells, that it?"

He raised an eyebrow.

"Like your stepsister. Reduce her to nothing, so that the only way she can express her horror is sexually."

He raised the eyebrow another notch. "She loved it. Are you kidding? Christ, Pat—whatever the fuck your name is—isn't that what sex is all about? Oblivion. And don't give me this PC rhetoric about spiritual commingling and making love. Sex is about fucking. Sex is about regressing to our most animalistic state. Caveman. Private. Pre-Ur. We slurp and scratch and bite and groan like animals. All the drugs and marital aids and whips and chains and variances we add to the stew are all just extras meant to heighten—no, accomplish—the same thing. Oblivion. A regressive state that transports us back centuries and de-evolves us. It's fucking, Pat. It's oblivion."

I clapped. "Terrific speech."

He took a bow. "You like that?"

"You've practiced it."

"It's been tweaked over the years, sure."

"Thing is, Wes—"

"What's 'the thing,' Pat? Tell me."

"You can't explain poetry to a computer. You can teach it rhyme or meter, but it doesn't understand beauty. Nuance. Essence. You don't understand making love. That doesn't mean a higher state—beyond fucking—doesn't exist."

"Is that what you're shooting for with Vanessa

Moore? A higher sexual state? The spirituality inherent in making love?"

"No," I said, "we're just fuck buddies."

He chuckled. "You ever felt love, Pat? For a woman?"

"Sure."

"Ever achieved that spiritual state you speak of?"

"Yup."

He nodded. "So where is she now? Or were there more than one? Where are they now? I mean, if it was so great, so fucking spiritual, why aren't you with one of them instead of talking to me and occasionally dipping your wick in Vanessa Moore?"

I didn't have an answer. At least not one I felt like attempting to explain to Wesley.

It was a hell of a point, though. If love dies, if relationships deteriorate, if what was making love reverts back to having sex, then was it ever love to begin with? Or just something we sell ourselves on to distance ourselves from the beasts?

"When I came in my own stepsister," Wesley said, "it purified her. It was voluntary, consensual sex, Pat, I assure you. And she loved it. And thereby found her essence, her true self." He turned his back to me, looked out as the helicopter made a wide circle over the Broadway Bridge and headed back toward us. "By facing her true self, all the illusions she'd used to prop herself up shattered. And she shattered. It broke her. It could have built her, if she'd been strong enough, brave enough, but it broke her." He turned back to me.

"Or you did," I said. "Some would say Karen was destroyed by you, Wes."

He shrugged. "We all have points we reach where either we break or we build. Karen found hers."

"With your help."

"Possibly. And if she'd built from there, who's to say she wouldn't be a happier person? What's your breaking point, Pat? Have you ever wondered just which elements of your current version of happiness you could stand to lose before you were reduced to a glimmer of yourself? Which elements, eh? Your family? Your partner? Your car? Your friends? Your home? How soon before you'd be natal again? Stripped of embroidery? And then—*then*, Pat—who would you be? What would you do?"

"After I killed you, or before?"

"Why would you kill me?"

I held out my arms, stepped close to him. "Gee, I dunno, Wes. You take everything from some guys, they just figure they got nothing to lose."

"Sure, Pat. Sure." He placed a hand to his chest. "But don't you think I'd have planned for contingencies like that?"

"You mean like hiring Stevie Zambuca to back me off?"

He dropped his eyes, looked at the bag in my hand.

"I presume Stevie's services are no longer at my disposal."

I tossed the bag between his feet. "That's about the size of it. By the way, he took out a two-grand aggravation fee for himself. These mob guys, Wes, you know what I'm saying?"

He shook his head. "Patrick, Patrick, I hope you

understand that I've been speaking hypothetically. I bear no animosity toward you."

"Cool. Too bad I can't say the same thing, Wes."

He lowered his head until his chin touched his chest. "Patrick, trust me on this: You don't want to play chess with me."

I flicked the fingers of my right hand off his chin.

When he raised his head, the blithe cruelty in his eyes had been replaced by raw rage.

"Ah, yes, I do, Wes."

"Tell you what—take that money, Pat." His teeth were gritted, his face suddenly damp. "Take it and forget about me. I don't feel like dealing with you now."

"But I feel like dealing with you, Wes. A whole lot."

He laughed. "Take the money, buddy."

I met his laugh with my own. "I thought you could destroy me, pal. What's up with that?"

The sleepy malevolence zapped the blue in his eyes again. "I can, Pat. It's just a time issue at the moment."

"A time issue? Wes, buddy, I got plenty of time. I've cleared my decks for you."

Wesley's jaw tightened and he pursed his lips and nodded several times to himself.

"Okay," he said. "Okay."

I glanced to my left, spotted a Honda sitting on the expressway, fifty yards off and a few feet above us, the hood up. The hazards blinked and cars beeped and honked and a few people threw the finger as Angie kept her head under the hood, fiddled with some cables, and shot pictures of me and Wesley from the camera sitting atop the oil filter cover.

Wesley raised his head and stuck out his gloved hand. Bright green homicide shone in his eyes.

"War?" he asked.

I shook his gloved hand. "War," I said. "You bet."

25

"So where you parked, Wes?" I asked as we left the roof and descended the stairwell.

"Not in the garage, Pat. You're on six, I believe."

We reached the sixth-floor landing. Wesley stepped back from me a few feet. I leaned in the doorway.

"Your floor," he said.

"Yup."

"Thinking of trying to stick with me?"

"It crossed my mind, yeah, Wes."

He nodded, rubbed his chin, and parts of him moved with a sudden, blurry explosion of speed. One of his loafers connected with my jaw and knocked me back into the garage.

I scrambled to my feet between two cars, reached for my gun, and had it out of the holster and swinging around toward him when he exploded all over me again. It seemed like I took about six punches and six kicks in roughly four seconds, and my gun clattered across the garage and disappeared under a car.

"You frisked me on the roof because I allowed you to, Pat."

I hit my hands and knees and he booted me in the stomach.

"You're alive right now because I'm allowing it. But, I don't know—maybe I'm changing my mind."

He telegraphed the next kick. Out of the corner of my eye, I saw his ankle flex and his foot leave the ground, and I took the kick in the ribs and held on to the ankle.

I heard the sound of a car approaching from the fifth level, moving up one ramp toward the next, a torn muffler chugging loudly, and Wesley heard it, too.

He kicked me in the chest with his free foot, and I let go of his ankle.

Headlights arced against the wall at the bottom of the ramp.

"Be seeing you, Pat."

His footsteps clanged down the metal staircase, and I tried to get back on my feet, but my body decided to roll over and lie on its back instead as the approaching car screeched to a halt.

"Jesus," a woman said as she hopped out of the passenger side. "Oh, my God."

A guy stepped out of the driver's side, put his hand on the roof. "Buddy, you all right?"

I raised an index finger as the woman's feet approached. "One sec, okay?" I pulled my cell phone out and dialed Angie's cell phone.

"Yeah?"

"He should be exiting the garage any second. You see him?"

"What? No. Wait. There he is." Horns blared behind her.

"You see a black Mustang anywhere near him?"

"Yup. He's crossing to it."

"Get the plate number, Ange."

"Okay. Kirk, out."

I hung up and looked up at the couple standing over me. They wore matching black Metallica T-shirts.

I said, "Metallica's playing the Fleet Center tonight?"

"Uh, yeah."

"I thought they broke up."

"No." The guy's upside-down face blanched as if I'd just predicted one of the signs of the apocalypse. "No, no, no."

I put my cell phone back in my pocket, raised both hands. "A little help?"

They stepped over me and arranged themselves in position, grasped my hands.

"Gently," I said.

They pulled me to my feet and the garage lurched up and down several times and the light went all greasy in my head. I touched my ribs, then my upper chest and shoulders, finally my jaw. Nothing seemed broken. Everything, however, hurt. A lot.

"You want us to call security?" the guy said.

I leaned back against a parked car, checked each tooth with my tongue. "No. It's okay. You might want to step away kinda fast, though."

"Why?"

"Because I'm definitely going to puke."

They moved almost as fast as Wesley had.

* * *

"Let me get this straight," Bubba said as he swabbed rubbing alcohol on my scraped forehead. "You got your ass handed to you like a *hat* by a guy looks like Niles Crane."

"Uh-huh," I managed, an ice pack the size of a football pressed to my swollen jaw.

"I don't know," Bubba said to Angie. "Can we hang out with him anymore?"

Angie looked up from the photos she'd had developed of Wesley at Foto-Fast while Bubba had checked me for breaks or sprains, taped up my bruised ribs, cleaned the wounds and scrapes from the garage floor and the ring on Wesley's right hand. Say what you will about Bubba's intelligence or lack thereof, but he's a hell of a field medic. Has better drugs, too.

Angie smiled. "You do become more of a liability with every passing day."

"Ha," I said. "Nice hair."

Angie touched the sides of her head and scowled. The portable phone by her elbow rang, and she picked it up.

"Hey, Devin," she said after a few seconds. "Huh?" She looked at me. "His jaw looks like a pink grapefruit, but otherwise I think he's okay. Huh? Sure." She lowered the phone. "Devin wants to know when you turned into such a Sally."

"The guy knew fucking kung fu," I said through gritted teeth, "judo, some goddamn fly-in-the-air, kick-your-head-off shit."

She rolled her eyes. "What's that?" she said into

the phone. "Oh, okay." Back to me: "Devin asks why you didn't just shoot him?"

"Good question," Bubba said.

"I *tried*," I said.

"He tried," she told Devin. She listened, nodded, said to me, "Devin said next time? Try harder."

I gave her a bitter smile.

"He's giving your advice due consideration," she told Devin. "And those plates?" She listened. "Okay, thanks. Yeah, let's do that soon. Okay. Bye."

She hung up. "The plates were stolen from a Mercury Cougar last night."

"Last night," I said.

She nodded. "Methinks our Wesley plans ahead for all eventualities."

"And can high-step like a chorus girl!" Bubba said.

I leaned back in my chair, gave them a "bring it on" gesture with my free hand. "Let's get it over with. All the jokes. Let's go."

"You kidding?" Angie said. "No way."

"Months," Bubba said. "Months we'll be milking this."

Bubba's friend at the state revenue office had been indicted last year on multiple fraud charges, so that turned into a dead end, but Angie finally got a call from her IRS contact and started scribbling notes as she listened to him, saying, "Uh-huh, uh-huh," over and over as I nursed my swollen jaw and Bubba spooned cayenne pepper into a collection of hollow-point bullets.

"Stop that," I said.

"What? I'm bored."

"You're bored a lot lately."

"Well, look at the company I've been keeping."

Angie looked up from the table as she hung up the phone and smiled at me. "We got him."

"Wesley?"

She nodded. "Paid taxes from 1984 until '89, when he disappeared."

"Okay."

"It gets better. Guess where he worked?"

"I haven't a clue."

Bubba spooned some more cayenne into a metal jacket. "Hospitals."

Angie tossed her pen at his head. "You're stomping my lines again."

"Lucky guess. Back off." Bubba frowned, rubbed his head, went back to his bullets.

"Psych hospitals?" I said.

Angie nodded. "Among others, yeah. He did a summer at McLean. He did a year at Brigham and Women's. A year at Mass General. Six months at Beth Israel. Apparently, he wasn't very good at his jobs, but his father kept getting him others."

"What departments?"

Bubba raised his head, opened his mouth, caught Angie's glare, and dropped his head again.

"Custodial," Angie said. "Then Records."

I sat at the table, looked down at my notes from the Hall of Records. "Where was he working in '89?"

Angie glanced at her notes. "Brigham and Women's. Records Department."

I nodded, held up my notes so she could see them.

" 'Naomi Dawe,' " she read. " 'Born, Brigham and

Women's, December eleven, 1985. Died, Brigham and Women's, November seventeen, 1989.'"

I dropped the notes and stood, walked toward the kitchen.

"Where you going?"

"Making a phone call."

"To who?"

"Old girlfriend," I said.

"We're working," Bubba said, "all he's thinking about is getting some."

I met Grace Cole on Francis Street in Brookline, in the heart of the Longwood Hospital district. The rain had stopped and we walked down Francis and crossed Brookline Avenue, worked our way down to the river.

"You look . . . bad," she said, and tilted her head, considering my jaw. "Still doing the same work, I take it."

"You look stupendous," I said.

She smiled. "Always the flirt."

"Just honest. How's Mae?"

Mae was Grace's daughter. Three years ago, the violence in my life had driven them into an FBI safe house, almost derailed Grace's surgical residency, and pretty much slammed the door on what remained of our relationship. Mae had been four. She'd been smart and pretty and liked to watch the Marx Brothers with me. I couldn't think of her without it eliciting a scraping sensation under my ribs.

"She's good. She's in second grade, doing well. She likes math, hates boys. I saw you on TV last year, when those men were killed near the Quincy Quarries. You were in a crowd shot."

"Mmm."

Water dripped from the weeping willows along the river path, and the river itself was a hard chrome in the wake of the dull rain.

"Still mixing it up with dangerous people?" Grace pointed at my jaw, the scrapes on my forehead.

"Me? Nah. Fell in the shower."

"Into a tub full of rocks?"

I smiled, shook my head.

We stepped aside for a pair of joggers, their legs pumping, their cheeks puffing, the air around them filled with fury.

Our elbows touched as we stepped back, and Grace said, "I took a job in Houston. I leave in two weeks."

"Houston," I said.

"Ever been?"

I nodded. "Big," I said. "Hot. Industrial."

"Cutting edge in medical technology," Grace said.

"Congratulations," I said. "I mean it."

Grace chewed her lower lip, looked out at the cars gliding past on slick roads. "I've almost called you a thousand times."

"What stopped you?"

She gave me a small shrug, her eyes on the road. "News footage of you near corpses in the quarries, I guess."

I followed her gaze out onto the road because there was nothing to say.

"You with someone?"

"Not really."

She looked in my eyes, smiled. "But you're hoping?"

"I'm hoping, yeah," I said. "You?"

She looked back at the hospital. "A fellow doctor, yeah. I'm not sure how Houston's going to affect it. It's amazing what it takes."

"How's that?"

She raised her hand to the road, then dropped it. "Oh, you know, holding down a career, holding down a relationship, second-guessing your choices. Then one day your path is decided, you know? Your choices have been made. For better or worse, it's your life."

Grace in Houston. Grace gone from this city. I hadn't spoken to her in nearly three years, but it'd been comforting, somehow, knowing she was around. A month from now, she wouldn't be. I wondered if I'd feel the lack like a tiny hole in the fabric of the cityscape.

Grace reached into her bag. "Here's what you asked for. I didn't see anything odd. The girl drowned. The fluid in her lungs was consistent with the fluid from a pond. Time of death was consistent with a girl that age who'd fallen in icy water and been rushed to us."

"She die at the home?"

She shook her head. "In the OR. Her father resuscitated her at the accident scene, got her heart pumping. But it was too late."

"Do you know him?"

"Christopher Dawe?" She shook her head. "Only by reputation."

"And what's his reputation?"

"Brilliant surgeon, weird man." She handed me

the manila folder, looked down the river, then out at the street. "So, okay, well . . . Look, I . . . I have to go. It was nice seeing you."

"I'll walk you back."

She put a hand to my chest. "I'd be grateful if you didn't."

I looked in her eyes and saw regret and maybe a kind of wild nervousness over the uncertainty of her future, a sense of the buildings that rose behind us closing in.

"We did love each other, didn't we?" she said.

"Yeah, we sure did."

"That's too bad, isn't it?"

I stood by the river and watched her walk up to the light in her blue scrubs and white lab jacket, her ash-blond hair damp with the moisture that still hung in the air.

I loved Angie. Probably always had. Some part of me still loved Grace Cole, though. Some ghost of myself still lived back in the days when we'd shared a bed and talked of the future. But that love we'd had and those selves we'd been were gone, placed in a box like old photographs and letters you'd never read again.

As she disappeared in the throng of medical people and medical buildings, I found myself agreeing with her. It was too bad. It was a fucking shame.

Bubba had placed his bullets in stacked white cases beside his chair by the time I got back to the apartment. He and Angie played Stratego on the dining room table, shared some vodka, and had Muddy Waters playing on my stereo.

Bubba's rarely good at games. He gets frustrated

and usually ends up dumping the board in your lap, but at Stratego, he's tough to beat. Must be all those bombs. He places them in the last place you'd suspect, and gets downright kamikaze with his scouts, wading into certain death with glee in his baby's face.

I waited till Bubba took Angie's flag, studying the intake and birth and death forms on Naomi Dawe, and finding absolutely nothing unusual.

Bubba shouted, "Ha! Now take me to your daughters," and Angie swept her hand across the board, knocked the pieces to the floor.

"Man, she's a sore loser."

"I'm competitive," Angie said, and bent to pick up the pieces. "There's a difference."

Bubba rolled his eyes and then looked at the papers I'd spread across my side of the table. He got out of his chair, stretched, and looked over my shoulder. "What're those?"

"Hospital records," I said. "Mother's intake when she came to give birth. Daughter's birth. Daughter's death."

He looked down at the forms. "They don't make sense."

"They make perfect sense. Which word's giving you trouble?"

He slapped the back of my head. "How come she's got two blood types?"

Angie raised her head from the other side of the table. "What?"

Bubba pointed down at Naomi's birth record, and then her death record. "She's O neg in that one."

I looked at the death record. "And B positive in this one."

Angie came over to our side of the table. "What are you two talking about?"

We showed her.

"What the hell could it mean?" I said.

Bubba snorted. "Means only one thing. The kid who was born on that day"—he stabbed the birth record with his finger—"ain't the same kid who died"—he stabbed the death record—"on this day. Man, you guys are slow sometimes."

26

"That's her," I said as Siobhan walked down the Dawes' street, her small head and body hunched as if she expected hail.

"Hi," I said as she passed the Porsche.

"Hello." Her flat gaze said she wasn't particularly surprised to see me.

"We need to see the Dawes."

She nodded. "He spoke of a restraining order against you."

"Just talk," I said. "I haven't done anything."

"Yet," she said.

"Yet. I understand they're in Nova Scotia. I need an address."

"And why should I help you?"

"Because he treats you like the help."

"I am the help."

"It's your job," I said. "Not who you are."

She nodded to herself, looked at Angie. "You're the partner then?"

Angie held out her hand, introduced herself. Siobhan shook it, said, "Well, they're not in Nova Scotia."

"No?"

She shook her head. "There right back there. In the house."

"They never left?"

"They left." She looked over her shoulder at the house. "They came back. I'd say your partner there, pretty as she is, could ring the bell, get them to open the door, as long as you're nowhere to be seen, Mr. Kenzie."

"Thanks," I said.

"Don't thank me. Just, for fuck's sake, don't kill them. I need the job."

She lowered her head, hunched into herself, and walked away.

"That's one hard chick," Angie said.

"Talks cool, though."

"'For fook's saik,'" Angie said with a grin.

We parked up the street, walked back to the Dawes' house, and walked swiftly up the path leading to the door, hoping no one was watching from the window, because there was no alternative but to just gut it out and hope they didn't spot me from inside, bolt the door, and call the Weston police.

We reached the front door and I stood to the right of it as Angie swung the screen door wide and rang the bell.

It took a minute, but then the front door opened and I heard Christopher Dawe say, "Yes?"

"Dr. Dawe?" Angie asked.

"How can I help you, miss?"

"My name is Angela Gennaro. I'm here to speak to you about your daughter."

"Karen? Good God, are you from a paper? It was a tragedy that happened over—"

"Naomi," Angie said. "Not Karen."

I stepped around the door and met Christopher Dawe's eyes. His mouth was open and his face was bone white and he held a shaky hand to his goatee.

"Hi," I said. "Remember me?"

Christopher Dawe led us out to an enclosed rear porch that looked out upon his expansive swimming pool, expansive lawn, and a small liquid dime of a pond far off through a small stand of trees. He grimaced as we settled into the seats across from him.

Dr. Dawe placed a hand over his eyes and peered through the gaps between fingers at us. When he spoke he sounded as if he hadn't slept that week. "My wife is at the club. How much do you want?"

"A ton," I said. "How much you got?"

"So," he said, "you *are* working with Wesley."

Angie shook her head. "Against. Definitely against." She pointed at my swollen jaw.

Christopher Dawe dropped his hand from his eyes. "Wesley did that to you?"

I nodded.

"Wesley," he said.

"Apparently he knows his way around a dojo."

He studied my face. "How exactly did he do this to you, Mr. Kenzie?"

"The jaw, I think, was a spin kick. I'm not real sure. He was moving pretty fast. Then he just went all David Carradine on me and chopped me up."

"My son doesn't know karate."

"When's the last time you saw him?" Angie asked.

"Ten years ago."

"Let's assume," I said, "he picked it up. Back to Naomi."

Christopher Dawe held up a hand. "Just one moment. Tell me how he moves."

"How he moves?"

He spread his hands. "How he moves. Walks, for example."

"Fluidly," Angie said. "You could say he almost glides."

Christopher Dawe opened his mouth, then covered it with his fingers, bewildered.

"What?" Angie said.

"My son," Christopher Dawe said, "was born with one leg a full two and a half inches shorter than the other. There are a lot of things distinctive about my son's gait, but grace isn't one of them."

Angie reached in her bag, pulled out a photo of Wesley and me on the roof. She handed it to Dr. Dawe. "This is Wesley Dawe."

Dr. Dawe looked at the photo, then placed it on the coffee table between us.

"That man," Christopher Dawe said, "is not my son."

From the porch, and through the small stand of trees, the pond where Naomi Dawe died looked like a blue puddle. It was flat and seemed shriveled by the heat, as if it might disappear as you watched, be sucked back into the earth and replaced by dark mud. It seemed far too inconsequential a pockmark of nature to have taken a life.

I turned from the screen, glanced down at the photo on the coffee table. "Then who is this guy?"

"I haven't the faintest idea."

I stabbed the photo with my index finger. "You're sure?"

"We're talking about my son," Christopher Dawe said.

"It's been ten years."

"My *son*," he said. "There's barely a resemblance. Maybe in the chin, perhaps, but that's all."

I threw up my hands, walked back to the screen, watched the great house's reflection undulate in the swimming pool.

"How long has he been blackmailing you?"

"For five years."

"But he's been gone for ten."

He nodded. "The first five years, he drew off a trust. When that ran out, he contacted me."

"How?"

"He called."

"Did you recognize his voice?"

He shrugged. "He whispered. But he spoke of things—childhood memories—only Wesley would know. He instructed me to send ten thousand in cash every two weeks by regular mail. The addresses I sent it to changed frequently—sometimes post office boxes, other times hotels, occasionally street addresses. Different cities, different towns, different states."

"Was there any sort of consistency?" I asked.

"The amount of money. For four years, ten thousand every two weeks, and the mailboxes where I was instructed to drop the money were always somewhere in Back Bay. Beyond that, no."

"You said it was consistent for four years," Angie said. "What happened within the last year?"

He spoke in a hoarse voice. "He decided he wanted half."

"Half your fortune?"

He nodded.

"How much would that be, Doctor?"

"I don't feel the need to divulge the size of my family fortune to you, Mr. Kenzie."

"Doctor, I have hospital intake records that show pretty conclusively that the girl who drowned in your pond was not the girl your wife gave birth to. You'll tell me anything I want to know."

He sighed. "Six-point-seven million, roughly. A sum whose foundation was laid ninety-six years ago by my grandfather when he came to these shores and—"

I waved him off. I didn't give a shit about his family history, his sense of legend.

"Is that figure exclusive of real estate?"

He nodded. "Six-point-seven in stocks, bonds, negotiable securities, T-bills, and cash reserves."

"And Wesley—or Wesley's impersonator, go-between, whoever the hell he is—demanded half."

"Yes. Said he'd never bother us again."

"Did you believe him?"

"No. As he saw it, however, I had no choice but to comply. Unfortunately, as it turned out, I didn't agree. I thought I had one simple option." He sighed. "*We* felt we had an option. My wife and I. We called Wesley's bluff, Mr. Kenzie, Miss Gennaro. We decided not to pay him anything, not one more dime. If he chose to go to the police, he could, and he'd get nothing still. Either way, we were tired of hiding and tired of paying."

"How did Wesley respond?" Angie asked.

"He laughed," Christopher Dawe said. "He said, and I quote, 'Money's not the only commodity I can strip you of.'" He shook his head. "I thought he was talking about this house or the vacation house, some classic antiques and art we own. But he wasn't."

"Karen," Angie said.

Christopher Dawe nodded wearily. "Karen," he whispered. "We didn't so much as suspect until near the very, very end. She'd always been . . ." He raised his hand, grasped for the word.

"Weak?" I said.

"Weak," he agreed. "And then her life took a bad turn. What happened to David was an accident, and we believed she simply wasn't strong enough to bear up. I hated her failure. Despised it. The more she slipped downward, the more scorn I felt."

"When she came to you for help, though?"

"She was on drugs. She acted like a whore. She—" He raised his hands to his head. "How were we to know it was Wesley behind it? How could one begin to assume a person would consciously set out to drive another person mad? His sister? How? How were we to know?"

He pulled his hands down from his head, covered his face with them, stared at me from between the fingers again.

"Naomi," Angie said. "Switched at birth."

A nod.

"Why?"

He dropped his hands. "She had a heart condition known as Truncus Arteriosis. Not something anyone picked up on in the delivery room, but she was my child, I did my own exams. I discovered a murmur and ran a few more tests. In those days, Truncus Arteriosis was thought to be inoperable. Even now, it's often fatal."

"So you traded your child in," Angie said, "for a better model?"

"It was hardly a snap decision," he said, eyes wide. "I agonized. I did. But once the idea took hold, I . . . You don't have children. I can tell. You have no idea what it takes to raise a healthy one, never mind a terminally sick one. The mother, the birth mother of the child I switched, had hemmorhaged in labor. She'd died in childbirth in the ambulance. The child had no relatives. It all seemed as if God were telling me—no, *directing* me—to do it. So I did."

"How?" I asked.

He gave me a shaky smile. "You'd be saddened to realize how easy it was. I'm a renowned cardiologist, Mr. Kenzie, with an international reputation. No nurse or intern is going to question my presence in a maternity ward, especially when my wife has just given birth." He shrugged. "I switched the charts."

"And the computer files," I said.

He nodded. "But I forgot about the intake form."

"And," Angie paused, shaking slightly, tremors of outrage coursing under her skin as she clenched a fist on her knee, "when your real child was adopted, how were her parents supposed to feel when she died?"

"She lived," he said quietly as tears fell silently from under his hand and down his face. "She was adopted by a Brookline family. Her name is," he choked on it, "Alexandra. She's thirteen, and I understand she sees a heart specialist at Beth Israel who seems to have done amazing things, because *Alexandra* swims, she plays volleyball, she runs, she rides a bicycle." The tears came in torrents now, but still silently, like rain from a summer cloud. "She didn't fall through a frozen pond and drown. You see? She didn't. She lives."

He tilted his chin up and smiled brightly as the tears leaked into his mouth. "That's irony, Mr. Kenzie, Miss Gennaro. That's titanic irony, don't you think?"

Angie shook her head. "With all due respect, Dr. Dawe, it sounds more like justice."

He gave her a bitter nod, then wiped the tears from his face. He stood.

We looked up at him. Eventually, we stood, too.

He walked us back to the foyer, and as we had the first time I'd been here, we stopped by the shrine they'd erected to their daughter. This time, however, Christopher Dawe acknowledged it. He squared his shoulders to it and placed his hands in his pockets and glanced at the photographs one by one, his head moving in shifts so slight they were nearly imperceptible.

I studied the ones in which Wesley appeared, and I realized that except for the height and the blond hair, he didn't look much like the man I'd come to believe was him. The young Wesley in these photos had small eyes, weak lips, a tremulous sag to his entire face, as if it were sinking under the combined weight of genius and psychosis.

"A couple of mornings before she died," Christopher Dawe said, "Naomi came in the kitchen and asked me what doctors did. I said we healed sick people. She asked why people got sick. Was God punishing them for being bad? I said no. She said, 'Then why?'" He looked over his shoulder at us, gave us a faint smile. "I didn't have an answer. I stalled. I smiled like an idiot and still had the dumb smile on my face when her mother called her and she ran out of the room." He turned his head back to the pictures of the small, dark-haired girl. "I wonder if that's what she thought as her lungs filled with water—that she'd done something bad, and God was punishing her."

He sucked a breath loudly through his nostrils and his shoulders tensed for a moment.

"He seldom calls anymore. He usually writes. When he does call, he whispers. Maybe it's not my son."

"Maybe," I said.

"I won't pay him another dime. I've told him. I've told him he has nothing left to threaten me with."

"How'd he react?"

"He hung up." Dr. Dawe turned away from the photos. "I suspect he'll come after Carrie soon."

"And then what will you do?"

He shrugged. "Bear up. Find out how strong we really are. You see, even if we pay him, he'll destroy us anyway. I think he's drunk with it, this power he seems to have. I think he'd do it whether it brought him financial gain or not. This man—whoever he is, my son, my son's friend, my son's captor, *whoever*—he sees this as his life's work, I think." He gave us a dead, hopeless smile. "And he really loves his job."

27

Information about Wesley, or the man who called himself Wesley, had the character of Wesley himself: It appeared in scant flashes, bright and fast, and then disappeared. For three days we worked out of the belfry office and my apartment trying to glean, from notes, photos, and rough transcripts of the interviews we'd conducted, any tangible proof of who this guy was. Using contacts at the Registry of Motor Vehicles, BPD, and even agents I'd once worked with from both the FBI and the Justice Department, we ran the photos of Wesley through computers that interfaced with every known justice agency, including Interpol, and got zip.

"Whoever this guy is," Neal Ryerson at Justice told me, "he keeps the lowest profile since D. B. Cooper."

Through Ryerson we also acquired a list of the owners of every 1968 Shelby Mustang GT-500 convertible still in existence in the U.S. Three were registered to owners in Massachusetts. One was a woman, two men. Posing as a writer from a car magazine, Angie visited all three at their homes. None was Wesley.

Hell, Wesley wasn't even Wesley.

I considered what Stevie Zambuca had said about Wesley being vouched for by someone in Kansas City, but based on our list, no one in the entire city of K.C. owned a '68 Shelby.

"What's the oddest thing?" Angie asked on Friday morning, panning her hand over the mountain of paper on my dining room table. "About all of this? What jumps out?"

"Oh, I dunno," I said. "Everything?"

Angie grimaced, sipped from her Dunkin' Donuts coffee cup. She picked up the list the Dawes had compiled for us, as best they could remember, of addresses where they'd sent the bimonthly cash deposits.

"This bugs me," she said.

"Okay." I nodded. It bugged me, too.

"Instead of trying to find Wesley, maybe we should see where the money takes us."

"Fine. But I bet they're bullshit drops. I bet they're big homes where he knew no one was home and the postman would have to leave the packages on the porch, and once he'd left, Wesley just swooped in and picked them up."

"Possibly," she said. "But if just one of them is the address of someone who knows Wesley, or whoever the hell this guy is?"

"Then it's worth the effort. You're right."

She placed the list down directly in front of her. "Most of these are local. We got Brookline once,

Newton twice, Norwell once, Swampscott, Manchester-by-the-Sea . . ."

The phone rang and I picked it up. "Hello."

"Patrick," Vanessa Moore said.

"Vanessa, what's up?"

Angie looked up from the list, rolled her eyes.

"I think you were right," Vanessa said.

"About what?"

"That guy on the patio."

"What about him?"

"I think he's trying to hurt me."

Her nose was broken and a sallow brown bruise fringed the orbital bone of her left eye while a streak of hard black ran underneath it. Her hair was unkempt, the ends split and frizzy, and her good eye had a bag underneath it as dark as the bruise. Her normally ivory skin was gray and faded. She was chain-smoking, even though she'd once told me she'd quit five years ago and never missed it.

"What's this," she said, "Friday?"

"Yeah."

"One week," she said. "My life has fallen apart in one week."

"What happened to your face, Vanessa?"

She turned it up to me as we walked. "Pretty, huh?" She shook her head and the tangled hair fell in her face. "I never saw him. The guy who did it. Never saw him." She yanked the leash in her hand. "Come on, Clarence. Keep up."

We were in Cambridge, along the Charles. Twice a week, Vanessa taught a law class at Radcliffe. I'd been dating her when she was offered the job, and was initially surprised she'd accepted it. The stipend Radcliffe paid wouldn't cover her annual dry cleaning bill, and it wasn't like she needed more work. She'd jumped at it, though. Even with all her other work, the part-time teaching offer had validated something in her she couldn't completely articulate, and besides, she got to take Clarence into the classroom with her and have it chalked up as the eccentricity of a brilliant mind.

We'd walked down Brattle from her classroom and crossed over the river to let Clarence run wild for a bit on the grass. Vanessa hadn't spoken for a long time. She'd been busy smoking.

When we began working our way west along the jogging path, she finally began to speak. We made slow progress because Clarence stopped to sniff every tree, chew every fallen branch, lick every discarded coffee cup or soda can. The squirrels, seeing he was on a leash, started fucking with him, darting in far closer than they'd normally dare, and I swear one smiled when Clarence lunged only to be jerked back against his leash, fell to the grass on his belly, and covered his eyes with his paws as if humiliated by it all.

Now, though, we'd left the squirrels behind, and he simply dawdled, chewing grass like a calf, while Vanessa was having none of it.

"Clarence," she snapped, "here!"

Clarence looked at her, seemed to acknowledge the command, then started walking the other way.

Vanessa clenched the leash in her hand and seemed ready to yank back so hard she'd decapitate the dumb bastard.

"Clarence," I said in a firm, normal tone I'd heard Bubba use a thousand times with his dogs, and then I followed it with a whistle. "Here, boy. Stop fucking around."

Clarence trotted over to us and then fell into step a few feet ahead of Vanessa, his little butt wiggling like a Parisian hooker's on Bastille Day.

"How come he listens to you?" Vanessa said.

"He can hear the tension in your voice. It's making him nervous."

"Yeah, well, I got reason to be tense. He's a dog, what's he got to be tense about—missing a nap?"

I put a hand on the back of her neck, kneaded the muscles and tendons between my fingers. It was as stiff and gnarled back there as one of the tree trunks.

Vanessa let out a long breath. "Thanks."

I kneaded the flesh some more, felt it starting to loosen a bit. "Keep going?"

"As long as you can."

"You got it."

She gave me a tiny smile. "You'd be a good friend, Patrick. Wouldn't you?"

"I am your friend," I said, not sure it was true, but then, sometimes just saying something plants the seed that allows it to become truth.

"Good," she said. "I need one."

"So this guy who hit you?"

Hard pebbles sprouted under the skin at the back of her neck again.

"I was walking up to the door of a coffee shop. He was apparently waiting on the other side. The door was smoked glass. He could see out. I couldn't see in. Just as I reached for the door, he slammed it open into my face. Then he just hopped over me as I was lying on the pavement and walked away."

"Witnesses?"

"Inside the coffee shop, yeah. Two people remembered seeing a tall, slim guy wearing a baseball cap and RayBans—they couldn't agree on his age, but they both knew what kind of sunglasses he wore—who stood by the door, looking down at a leaflet in his hand."

"Anything else they remember about him?"

"Yeah. He wore driving gloves. Black. Middle of the summer, guy's wearing gloves, nobody finds him suspicious. Jesus."

She stopped to light her third cigarette of the walk. Clarence took that as his signal to go off the path again and sniff a pile of shit left by another dog. Probably the primary reason I've never owned a dog is because of this colorful aspect of their personalities. Give Clarence another thirty seconds, he'd try to eat it.

I snapped my fingers. He looked up at me with that slightly confused, slightly guilty look that to me is the most defining characteristic of his species.

"Leave it," I said, again relying on recollections of Bubba for my tone of voice.

Clarence turned his head sadly and then wiggled his butt away from it, and we all resumed walking.

It was another dull August day, humid and clammy without being particularly hot. The sun was somewhere behind slate clouds and the mercury hovered in the high seventies. The bicyclists and joggers and speed-walkers and Rollerbladers all seemed to be moving past us through a jungle of thin, transparent cobwebs.

Along this stretch of the river path, small tunnels cropped up every now and then. No more than sixty feet long and fifteen wide, they formed the bases of the footbridges that led pedestrians over from the other side of the Soldiers Field Road/Storrow Drive split. Walking through the tunnels, stooping slightly, felt like walking through a child's fun house. I felt huge and a bit silly.

"My car was stolen," Vanessa said.

"When?"

"Sunday night. I still can't believe this has been only a week. You want to hear about Monday through Thursday?"

"Very much."

"Monday night," she said, "someone managed to slip past building security and throw the main circuit breaker in the basement. Power was off for about ten minutes. No big deal unless your alarm clock is electric and fails to go off in the morning and you end up being seventy-five minutes late for opening arguments in a fucking murder trial." A small gasp escaped her lips, and she bit down on it and wiped the back of her hand across her eyes.

"Tuesday night, I come home to a series of pornographic recordings on my answering machine."

"Guy's voice, I assume."

She shook her head. "No. The caller had placed the phone up to a TV playing pornographic movies. Lots of moaning and 'Take that, bitch,' and 'Come in my face,' shit like that." She flicked her cigarette into the damp sand to the left of the path. "Normally, I guess I'd have shrugged it off, but I was starting to get a feeling of dread in my stomach, and the message total was twenty."

"Twenty," I said.

"Yup. Twenty different recordings of porno movies. Wednesday," she said with a long sigh, "someone pickpockets my wallet from my bag as I eat lunch in the courtyard of the federal courthouse." She patted the bag slung over her shoulder. "All I have in here is cash and whatever credit cards I was smart enough to leave in the drawer back home because they'd made my wallet bulge."

Just to my left, Clarence suddenly stopped and cocked his head high and to his left.

Vanessa stopped, too weary to pull him forward, and I stopped with her.

"Any activity on the stolen credit cards before you noticed they were gone?"

She nodded. "At a hunting and fishing store in Peabody. A man—the fucking clerks remember he was a man, but they never noticed he was using a fucking woman's credit card—purchased several lengths of rope and a buck knife."

About 150 yards ahead of us, three teenage boys broke from a tunnel on Rollerblades, their feet slashing expertly back and forth in front of one another, bodies low, arms swinging in tandem with their feet. It looked like they were talking shit to one another, laughing, goading one another on.

"Thursday," Vanessa said, "I got hit with the door. Had to walk back into court with an ice pack on my nose and ask for an emergency continuance until Monday."

An ice pack, I thought, and gingerly touched my jaw. Wesley should have his own patent on the things.

"This morning," Vanessa said, "I start receiving phone calls about mail that never arrived at its destination."

Clarence let out a low growl, his head still cocked, body a single tensed muscle.

"What did you just say?" I looked away from Clarence and hard at Vanessa, my body beginning to tingle with the connection Angie and I had kept missing.

"I said some of my mail never reached its destination. No big deal, unto itself, but piled on top of everything else."

We stepped to the side of the path as the Rollerbladers approached, their skates hissing off asphalt, and I kept one eye on Vanessa and one on Clarence, because he's been known to take off without warning after anything moving faster than he can.

"Your mail," I said, "didn't get through."

Clarence barked, but not at the Rollerbladers; his nose pointed up and far off, down toward the tunnel.

"No."

"Where'd you mail it from?"

"The mailbox in front of my building."

"Back Bay," I said, stunned it had taken me this long to see it.

The first two kids whizzed past us, and then I saw the elbow of the third one rise. I reached for Vanessa and pulled her toward me, saw the flash of a grin on the kid's face as he dropped the elbow and grabbed the strap of Vanessa's bag.

The kid's speed, the force of his pull, and the way I'd twisted Vanessa's body awkwardly toward me combined to create a mess of bad balance and flailing limbs. When the bag was ripped from Vanessa's shoulder, she instinctively tried to grasp it, her arm going back and twisting up as I put my foot out to trip the kid, all of this happening in less than a second before Vanessa was wrenched back forward again, slamming into me and knocking me over onto my back.

The kid's skates left the ground and flew over my reaching fingers, and Vanessa dropped the leash as her hip slammed off the pavement and her abdomen slammed into my knee. I heard the air leave her in a burst, cut off a yelp of pain from the impact of her hip, and the kid looked back over his shoulder at me as his skates returned to earth. He laughed.

Vanessa rolled off me.

"You okay?"

"No breath," she managed.

"Wind got knocked out of you. Stay here. I'll be right back."

She nodded, gulping for air, and I took off after the kid.

He'd caught up with the group and they had twenty yards on me, easy, by the time I gave chase. Every ten yards I ran, they clocked an extra five. I was running full out, and I'm pretty fast in the first place, but I was losing ground steadily as they reached a straightaway, no curves, no tunnels.

I dipped my hand as I ran, scooped up a rock, and took another four steps as I zeroed in on the back of the kid with Vanessa's bag. I threw sidearm, putting my whole body into it, my feet leaving the ground like Ripken throwing from third to first.

The rock hit the kid high on the back between the shoulder blades, and he doubled over like he'd been punched in the stomach. His gangly body canted hard to the left, and one skate left the pavement. His arms pin-wheeled, with Vanessa's bag jerking in his left hand, and then he lost it all at once. He pitched forward, with his head surging for the pavement and his hands coming around too late, the bag swinging out and away, falling to the grass to his left as he performed a triple somersault on asphalt.

His friends gave one shocked glance back over their shoulders and then accelerated. They reached a bend and disappeared just as I caught up with the acrobat.

Even with knee and elbow pads, he looked like he'd been thrown from a plane. His arms, legs, and chin were a raw, pink mess of scrapes and contusions. He rolled over on his back and I was grateful to see that he was older than I'd first guessed—twenty, at least.

I picked up Vanessa's bag, and the kid said, "I'm bleeding all over, motherfucker."

I spied a compact, a set of keys, and a box of Altoids on the grass, but otherwise the contents of Vanessa's bag seemed intact. Bills in a silver money clip and credit cards bound by a rubber band sat at the bottom amid cigarettes, lighter, and makeup.

"You're bleeding?" I said. "Oh. Whoops."

The kid tried to sit up, then decided against it and flopped back down.

My cell phone rang.

"That would be him," the kid said through huffing breaths.

Humid as all hell out here, and my spine turned to dry ice.

"What?"

"The guy who gave us a hundred bucks to take you off. He said he'd be calling." The kid closed his eyes and hissed at the pain.

I pulled the cell phone from the front pocket of my jeans, looked back up at the bend where I'd left Vanessa. Fuck the kid, I thought. He wouldn't be able to tell me anything.

And I broke into a run as I put the cell phone to my ear.

"Wesley."

I heard snorts and liquid chewing close to the receiver, Wesley's voice echoing in the background like he was in a bathroom.

"Aww, who's a good doggie? Yeah. That's it, boy. Good boy. Yeah. Mmm. Chow down, fella."

"Wesley."

"Don't they feed you at home?" Wesley said in the background as Clarence's greedy chewing continued.

I turned the bend, saw Vanessa getting to her feet, her back to the tunnel 150 yards beyond her, where I could see the dark shapes of a short dog and a tall man bending over him, hand below his snout.

"Wesley!" I shouted.

The man in the tunnel straightened, and Vanessa spun and looked toward the tunnel as Wesley's voice came directly into the phone.

"Gotta love a dog whistle, Pat. We don't hear a fucking thing, but those pooches go wild."

"Wesley, listen to—"

"You're never sure which thing will make a woman crack like a fucking egg, Pat. The fun lies in trying."

He broke the connection and the man in the tunnel stepped out the far side and disappeared.

I reached Vanessa, pointed at her wild face as I passed. "Stay here. You hear me?"

She tried to catch up. "Patrick?" She grasped her hip, wincing, kept trying to run.

"Stay here!" I screamed it, could hear the echoes of desperation in my voice as I ran forward with my torso twisted back toward her.

"No. What're you—"

"Don't take another fucking step!" I tossed her bag so that it exploded all over the pavement in front of her and she followed the bounce and slide of her money clip. She bent by it and I turned my torso forward, willed myself to run even faster.

I slowed, though, as I neared the tunnel, felt something build in my chest, rise up my esophagus, and catch there, burning, even before I saw him.

Clarence wobbled out of the darkness toward me, his normally sad dog eyes now confused and afraid.

"Here, boy," I said softly, and dropped to my knees, felt the liquid burning in my throat find my eyes.

He took another four steps on quaking legs and then sat back on his haunches. He stared at me through drooping eyelids. He seemed to be trying to ask me something.

"Hey," I whispered. "Hey, guy. It's okay. It's okay."

I willed myself not to look away from the bewildered pain in his face, that searching question.

He lowered his head slowly and vomited a stream of pure black.

"Oh, Jesus." It came out of me in a hoarse whisper.

I crawled over to him, and when I touched his head, I felt the fire there, the scorch of fever. He rolled over and lay on his side and panted. I turned on my side with him and he looked up at me as I caressed his trembling rib cage and sweaty, feverish brow.

"Hey," I whispered as his eyes rolled up to whites. "Hey, you're not alone, Clarence. Okay? You're not alone."

His mouth opened wide as if he were about to yawn and a racking shudder thrust its way through his body from his back paws to his burning head.

"Goddammit," I said when he died. "Goddammit."

28

"I want to burn him alive," I said to Angie over the cell phone. "I want to kneecap the sick prick."

"Calm down."

I sat in the waiting room of the veterinarian's office where Vanessa had demanded we take Clarence. I'd carried the soft corpse in and laid it on a cold metal table. Then I'd seen a request that I leave in Vanessa's eyes and I'd followed it back out into the waiting room.

"I want to cut off his fucking head and piss down his neck."

"Now you sound like Bubba."

"I feel like Bubba. I want him dead, Ange. I want him gone. I want this to stop now."

"Then *think*," she said. "Don't go caveman on me. Think. Where is he? How do we find him? I checked the houses on the list. He's not—"

"He's a mailman," I said.

"What?"

"He's a mailman," I repeated. "Right here in the city. Back Bay."

"You're not kidding," she said.

"Nope. Wetterau lived in Back Bay. Karen was always at his place, according to her roommate, only came home to pick up clothes and mail."

"So you think she *sent* her mail . . ." Angie said.

"From Wetterau's. In Back Bay. Dr. Dawe makes all his drops to Back Bay mailboxes. The destinations don't matter because the mail is intercepted before it even gets there. Vanessa lives in Back Bay. Suddenly her mail's not getting through. We've been giving this douchebag too much credit. He's not running around all over creation with crack timing to fuck with people's mail. He's stealing it at the source."

"A goddamn mailman," Angie said.

The door to the vet's office opened, and I saw Vanessa lean against the doorjamb, listen to something the doctor said.

"I gotta go," I told Angie. "See you in a bit."

Vanessa's bruised face was blank, her steps stiff as she walked out into the waiting room.

"Strychnine," she said as I approached. "Injected into chunks of prime rib. That's how they think he killed my dog."

I placed a tentative hand on her shoulder, but she shrugged it off.

"Strychnine," she said again and walked toward the exit. "He killed my dog with poison."

"I'm close," I said as we stepped outside. "I'm going to get him."

She stood on the stone steps, looked up at me with a ghost's smile—weightless and floating. "Good for you, Patrick, because I got nothing left for him to take. Mention that to him the next time you two chat, would you? I got nothing left."

* * *

"A mailman," Bubba said.

"Think about it," I said. "We give him credit for being practically omnipotent, but he's actually limited. Files he had access to through Diane Bourne and Miles Lovell only, and the correspondence of people who lived in Back Bay. He fucked with Karen's mail and Vanessa's and made sure the money drops went through Back Bay mailboxes. That means he's either Central Post Office in the sorting department—in which case he's gotta sort through a few hundred thousand pieces of mail a night to find the right ones, or—"

"It's his route," Bubba said.

I shook my head. "No. He'd have to stand around in public going through the mail. That doesn't work."

"He drives the pickup route," Angie said.

I nodded. "Drives around in a truck, empties the blue mailboxes, fills the green ones. Yup. That's our boy."

"I hate mailmen," Bubba said.

"That's because they hate your dogs," Angie said.

"Maybe it's time to teach the dogs to hate 'em back," I said.

Bubba shook his head. "He poisoned the fucking *dog*?"

I nodded. "I've seen humans die, and it still got to me."

"Humans don't love like dogs," Bubba said. "Shit. Dogs?" His voice was as close to tender as I'd ever heard it. "All they know how to do if they're treated right is love you."

Angie reached out and patted his hand and he gave her that soft, disarming smile of his.

Then he looked at me and the smile turned mean and he chuckled. "Oh boy oh boy oh boy. How many ways we gonna fuck Wesley up, my brutha?" He held up his hand.

I high-fived him. "Couple thousand," I said. "For starters."

You can sit on one of the prettiest streets in the country, and if you've been sitting long enough, it begins to look ugly. Angie and I had been sitting on Beacon Street, halfway between Exeter and Fairfield, for two hours, the mailboxes fifty yards up on our right, and in that time I'd had plenty of opportunity to appreciate the dusky charcoal town houses and black wrought-iron trellises hanging beneath bright white dormer windows. I'd enjoyed the sharp summer smell of abundant flora in the air and the way the fat raindrops dripped through the trees and clattered on the pavement like coins. I could tell you how many of the buildings had roof gardens or just flower boxes jutting from windowsills, which were occupied by businessmen and -women, tennis players, joggers, pet owners, and artists running out with paint-splattered shirts only to return ten minutes later with Charrette bags filled with sable brushes.

Unfortunately, after about twenty minutes, I didn't really care.

A mailman passed us, bulging bag bouncing off his outer thigh, shrouded in rain gear, and Angie said, "Hell with it. Let's just get out and ask him."

"Sure," I said. "Not like he'd mention to Wesley that people were asking about him."

The mailman climbed some slick stairs with careful steps, reached the landing, and swung his bag around to the front of his thighs and dug into it.

"His name's not Wesley," Angie reminded me.

"It's the only name I got right now," I said. "You know how much I hate change."

Angie drummed her fingers on the dashboard, then said, "Shit, and I hate waiting," and tipped her head out the window, let the rain fall on her face.

The serpentine twist of her legs and waist coupled with the arch of her back as she did so made me recall images of her from our days as lovers that made the car seem about four times as small, and I turned my head and stared back through the windshield at the street.

When she pulled herself back in, she said, "When's the last time we had a sunny day?"

"July," I said.

"El Niño, you think?"

"Global warming."

"Signs of a second shift in the polar ice caps," she offered.

"Beginnings of a biblical flood. Break out the ark."

"If you were Noah and God gave you the head's up, what would you bring?"

"On said ark?"

"*Sí.*"

"A VCR and all my Marx Brothers movies. Couldn't survive long without my Stones or Nirvana CDs, I suppose."

"It's an *ark*," she said. "Where you going to get electricity at the end of the world?"

"Portable generators aren't an option?"

She shook her head.

"Shit," I said. "I'm not sure I'd want to live then."

"People," she said wearily. "Who would you take?"

"Oh, *people*," I said. "You should have made that clear. Without the Marx Brothers tapes and the tunes? They'd have to be people who knew how to party."

"Goes without saying."

"Let's see," I said. "Chris Rock to keep me laughing. Shirley Manson to sing . . ."

"Not Jagger?"

I shook my head hard. "No way. He's too good-looking. He'd hurt my chances with the chicks."

"Oh, there'll be chicks?"

"Gotta be chicks," I said.

"And you the only guy?"

"I'm going to share?" I frowned.

"Men." She shook her head.

"What? It's my ark. I built the damn thing."

"I've seen your carpentry skills. It won't get out of the harbor." She chuckled, turned on the seat. "So what about me? What about Bubba and Devin and Oscar and Richie and Sherilynn? You're just going to leave us to drown while you play Robinson Crusoe with the bimbos?"

I turned, caught the malicious gaiety in her eyes. Here we were stuck on a grindingly boring stake-out, having one of our more inane conversations, and suddenly the job was fun again.

"I didn't realize you wanted to come along for the ride," I said.

"I'm going to drown?"

"So," I said, and shifted on the seat, brought one leg up off the floor, and our knees touched. "You're saying if I was one of the last guys on the planet . . ."

She laughed. "You still wouldn't have a chance with me."

But she didn't pull away when she said it. She moved her head in another inch.

I could suddenly feel it in my chest, a cool funnel of air that loosened as it twirled—loosened everything that had been clenched and sore since Angie walked out of my apartment with the last of her suitcases in hand.

The gaiety left her eyes and was replaced by something warmer, but unsettled, still questioning.

"I'm sorry," I said.

"What?"

"About what happened in the woods last year. About that child."

She held my eyes. "I'm not sure any longer that I was right."

"Why's that?"

"Maybe nobody has the right to play God. Look at the Dawes."

I smiled.

"What's funny?"

"Just . . ." I took the fingers of her right hand in mine, and she blinked, but didn't pull them away. "Just that over the last nine months I've been seeing it more your way. Maybe it *was* a relative situation.

Maybe we should have left her there. Five years old, and she was happy."

She shrugged, squeezed my hand. "We'll never know, will we?"

"About Amanda McCready?"

"About anything. I think sometimes when we're old and gray, will we finally be settled about the things we've done, all the choices we made, or will we look back and think about all the things we could've done?"

I kept my head very still, my eyes on hers, waiting for the searching to settle, for her to see whatever answers she was looking for in my face.

She tilted her head slightly, and her lips parted a tenth of an inch.

And a white post office truck sluiced through the rain on my left, glided in front of us, clicked on its hazards, and double-parked in front of the mailboxes fifty yards ahead.

Angie pulled away and I turned forward in my seat.

A man in a clear, hooded slicker over his blue and white postal uniform jumped from the right side of the truck. He held a white plastic carton in his hands, its contents protected from the rain by a plastic trash bag taped loosely on top. The man came around to the front of the mailboxes, placed the crate by his feet, and used a key to open the green mailbox.

Most of his face was obscured by the rain and the hood, but as he emptied the carton of mail into the box, I could still see his lips—thick and red and cruel.

"It's him," I said.

"You're sure?"

I nodded. "A hundred percent. It's Wesley."

"Or the Artist Formerly Known as Wesley, as I like to call him."

"That's because you need psychiatric care."

As we watched him fill the green box, the postman descended the stairs of a brownstone and called out to him. He joined him at the boxes and they chatted, raised their heads to the rain, then down again, laughed about something.

They bullshitted for another minute and then Wesley waved, hopped in the truck and drove off.

I opened my door and left Angie's sudden, surprised "Hey!" behind as I ran down the sidewalk, my hand raised and yelled, "Wait up! Wait!" as Wesley's truck reached the green light at Fairfield and kept going, drifting into the far left lane for a turn onto Gloucester.

The postman narrowed his eyes at me as I reached him.

"Trying to catch a bus, buddy?"

I bent over as if out of breath. "No, that truck."

He held out his hand. "I'll take it."

"What?"

"Your letter. You trying to send something, right?"

"Huh? No." I shook my head, then gestured with it up Beacon as Wesley made the turn onto Gloucester. "I saw you two talking here, and I think that's my old roommate. Haven't seen him in ten years."

"Scott?"

Scott.

"Yeah," I said. "Scottie Simon!" I clapped my hands as if elated.

The postman shook his head. "Sorry, pal."

"What?"

"That ain't your buddy."

"It was," I said. "That was Scott Simon, no question. I'd recognize him anywhere."

The postman snorted. "No offense, mister, but you may want to see an optometrist. That guy's name is Scott Pearse, and no one's ever called him Scottie."

"Damn," I said, trying to sound deflated as fireworks exploded through my body, electrified it.

Scott Pearse.

Got you, Scott. Goddamn got you.

You wanted to play? Well, hide-and-seek is over. Let the real games begin, motherfucker.

29

I spent the week sitting on Scott Pearse—following him to work every morning, following him home every night. Angie covered his days while I slept, so I'd leave him when he picked up his truck at a garage on A Street, be watching again when he left the General Mail Facility along the Fort Point Channel after his final mail collection of the day. His routine, that week anyway, was maddeningly innocuous.

In the morning, he'd leave A Street, his truck fully loaded with large parcels. These he'd deliver to the green boxes throughout Back Bay, where they'd be picked up by the mail carriers on foot and brought to people's doorsteps. After a mid-afternoon lunch, according to Angie, he'd head out again, this time with an empty truck, that he'd gradually fill with the contents of the blue mailboxes. Once that was done, he'd drop the mail at the sorting facility and clock out.

He'd have a single-malt scotch every night with his fellow postmen at the Celtic Arms on Otis Street. He always left after one drink, no matter how many men tried to pull him back down to his seat, always dropped ten bucks on the table to cover the Laphroaig and the tip.

Then he'd walk down Summer Street and follow Atlantic north until he reached Congress, where he'd turn right. Five minutes later, he'd be up in his Sleeper Street loft, and he'd stay there until lights-out at eleven-thirty.

I had to work at it to begin thinking of him as Scott and not Wesley. The name Wesley had fit him—patrician and haughty and cold. Scott seemed too bland and middle class. Wesley was the name of the guy you knew in college who was captain of the golf team and didn't like blacks at his parties. Scott was the guy who wore tank tops and loud baggy shorts, organized pickup games, and puked in the back of your car.

But after some time spent watching him in which he acted far more like a Scott than a Wesley—watching TV alone, reading in a slim leather recliner under a gooseneck lamp in the center of his loft, pulling Fit-N-Easy meals from his freezer and nuking them in his microwave, eating them at the bar that curled around the edge of his kitchen—I eventually came around to the idea of Scott. Scott the Sinister. Scott the Asshole. Scott the Marked Man.

The first night I followed him, I found a fire escape with roof access behind the building across the street from his. His loft was four stories off the ground and two below my rooftop perch, and Scott Pearse hadn't bothered with curtains over his floor-to-ceiling dormers except in the bedroom and bathroom. So I had an unobstructed, well-lit view

of his spacious living room, kitchen, and dining
area, the framed black-and-white photographs
that hung from his walls. They were chilly photos
of stripped trees and frozen rivers that snaked
under mills, a massive garbage dump in the fore-
ground with the Eiffel Tower miles off in the
backround, Venice in December, Prague on a black
night awash in rain.

As I moved my binoculars from one to the next, I
became certain that Scott Pearse, himself, had taken
them. They were all exquisitely composed, all had a
detached, clinical beauty, and all were as cold as
death.

In all the nights I watched him, he never did anything out of the ordinary, and that in itself began to
seem bizarre. Maybe in his bedroom, he made the
calls to Diane Bourne or other confederates, picked
his next victim, or planned for the next stage of his
assault on Vanessa Moore or someone else I cared
about. Maybe he had someone chained to the bed-
post in there. Maybe after I thought he'd gone to
bed, he sat up reading private psychiatric files and
stolen mail. Maybe. But not while I was watching.

Angie reported the same thing regarding his
days. Pearse never dawdled long enough in his truck
to have the opportunity to look through any of the
mail he picked up during the second half of his
shift.

"He's strictly by-the-numbers," Angie reported.

Fortunately, we weren't, and in the only joyful
irony of that week, Angie obtained Pearse's phone
number by breaking into *his* mailbox on Sleeper
Street and peeking at his phone bill.

But otherwise, nothing. His facade began to seem impenetrable.

Access to the loft was out of the question. There was no way to bug the place. Each night when he entered, Scott Pearse disengaged an alarm inside the front door. Video cameras were positioned in the upper corners of the loft and triggered, I suspected, by motion detectors. Even if we could get past all that, Scott Pearse, I was pretty sure, had defenses I couldn't see, backup plans to his backup plans.

I was beginning to wonder, as I sat up on the roof every night and fought off sleep while I watched him do nothing upon nothing, if maybe he was on to us. Knew we'd discovered who he was. It seemed unlikely, but still, all it would have taken was a casual anecdote from the postman I'd run into on the street. *Hey, Scott, some guy thought you were his old college roommate, but I set him straight.*

One night, Scott Pearse walked to his window. He sipped some scotch. He stared down at the street. He raised his head and looked directly at me. But it wasn't me he was looking at. In a room bathed in track lighting, with the dark night outside his window forming a slate wall before him, all he'd be able to see would be his own reflection.

He must have been fascinated with it, though, because he stared in my direction for a long time. Then he raised his glass, as if in a toast. And smiled.

We moved Vanessa at night, took her out via the service elevator and along a maintenance corridor, out through a back door into the alley behind her building, and drove her away in Bubba's van. Vanessa, unlike most women if they'd just climbed into a van and found Bubba in back with them, didn't blink several times or gasp or move as far away as possible. She sat on the bench that ran from behind the driver's seat to the rear doors and lit a cigarette.

"Ruprecht Rogowski," she said. "Right?"

Bubba stifled a yawn with his fist. "No one calls me Ruprecht."

She held up a hand as Angie pulled the van out of the alley. "My mistake. It's Bubba, then?"

Bubba nodded.

"What's your stake in all this, Bubba?"

"Guy killed a dog. I like dogs." He leaned forward, elbows on his knees. "Let me ask you—you got a problem spending time with a mental defective who's got what they call 'antisocial tendencies'?"

She smiled. "You are aware what it is I do for a living?"

"Sure," Bubba said. "You got my buddy Nelson Ferrare off."

"How is Mr. Ferrare?"

"Same old," Bubba said.

Nelson, as they spoke, was in fact taking my place on the rooftop across from Scott Pearse's place. He'd just returned from Atlantic City, where he'd fallen in love with a cocktail waitress who'd loved him back until he ran out of money. Now he was back in town, willing to do anything for a little cash and a chance to go back to his cocktail waitress and run out of money again.

"Does he still fall in love with every woman he sees?" Vanessa asked.

"Pretty much." Bubba rubbed his chin. "So we're

clear, sister, here's the deal: I'm going to stick to you like crabs."

"Like crabs," Vanessa said. "How appealing."

"You'll sleep at my place," Bubba said, "eat with me, drink with me, and I'll be with you in court. Till the mailman goes down, you're never out of my sight. Get used to it."

"Can't wait," Vanessa said, then shifted on the bench. "Patrick?"

I turned fully in the captain's chair, looked over at her. "Yeah?"

"You've decided not to guard my body?"

"We have a past relationship. That means I'm compromised emotionally. Makes me the worst choice for the job."

She looked at the back of Angie's head as Angie turned onto Storrow Drive. "Compromised," she said. "Sure."

"Scott Pearse," Devin said the next night at Nash's Pub on Dorchester Avenue, "was born in the Philippines to military parents stationed in Subic Bay. Grew up all over the globe." He opened his notebook, leafed through it until he found the correct page. "West Germany, Saudi Arabia, North Korea, Cuba, Alaska, Georgia, and finally, Kansas."

"Kansas?" Angie said. "Not Missouri."

"Kansas," Devin repeated.

Devin's partner, Oscar Lee, said, "Surrender, Dorothy. Surrender."

Angie narrowed her eyes at him, shook her head.

Oscar shrugged, picked his dead cigar out of the ashtray and relit it.

"Father was a colonel," Devin said. "Colonel Ryan Pearse of Army Intelligence, designation classified." He looked at Oscar. "But we got friends."

Oscar looked at me and jerked his cigar back at his partner. "Notice White Boy always says 'we' when he talks about me and my sources?"

"It's a race thing," Devin assured us.

Oscar tapped some ash off his cigar. "Colonel Pearse was Psych Ops."

"Which?" Angie said.

"Psychological Operations," Oscar said. "Kind of guy gets paid to think up new ways to torture the enemy, spread disinformation, generally fuck with your head."

"Was Scott his only son?"

"You betcha," Devin said. "Mother divorced the father when the son was eight, moved to some shitty subsidized housing in Lawrence. Restraining orders against the father follow. She drags his ass into court a few times, and here's where it gets fun. She claims the father is using psych ops against *her*, fucking with her mind, trying to make everyone think she was crazy. But she's got no proof. Father gets the restraining orders dropped eventually, gains bimonthly visitation rights with the kid, and one day the kid comes home when he's, like, eleven to find Mommy sitting on the living room couch with her wrists cut open."

"Suicide," Angie said.

"Yup," Oscar said. "Kid goes to live with the father on base, joins Special Forces when he turns eighteen, gets an HD after—"

"A what?"

"An honorable discharge," Oscar said, "after serving in Panama during that five-minute conflict over there in late '89. And this made me curious."

"Why?"

"Well," Oscar said, "these Special Forces guys, they're career soldiers. They don't just do a couple of years and muster out like regular grunts. They're after Langley or the Pentagon. Plus, Pearse should have come back from Panama in the catbird seat: He had honest-to-God battle time now. He should have been *it*, you know?"

"But?" Angie said.

"But he wasn't," Oscar said. "So I called another of *my* buddies"—he shot a look at Devin—"and he did some digging and essentially your boy, Pearse, got shitcanned."

"For what?"

"Lieutenant Pearse's unit, under his immediate command, hit the wrong target. He was almost court-martialed because he gave the orders. In the end, he knew some brass with pull because he and his unit escaped with the military equivalent of a severance package. They walked with HD's, but no Pentagon, no Langley for those boys."

"What target?" Angie said.

"They were supposed to hit a building allegedly housing members of Noriega's secret police. Instead they went two doors down."

"And?"

"Wasted a whorehouse at six in the morning. Sprayed everyone inside. Two Johns, both Panamanian, and five prostitutes. Your boy then allegedly walked through the room and bayonetted all the female corpses before they torched the place. That's just rumor, mind you, but that's what my source remembers hearing."

"And the army," Angie said, "never prosecuted."

Oscar looked at her like she was drunk. "It was Panama. Remember? Killed nine times as many civilians as military personnel? All to capture a drug dealer with former ties to the CIA during the administration of a president who used to *run* the CIA. This shit was fishy enough without calling attention to your mistakes. The rule of combat's simple—if there are photographs or members of the press in attendance? You broke it, you buy it. But if not, and you cap the wrong guy or guys or village?" He shrugged. "Shit happens. Set the torches and march double-time."

"Five women," Angie said.

"Oh, he didn't kill 'em all," Oscar said. "The whole squad went in there and unloaded. Nine guys firing ten rounds a second."

"No, he didn't kill them all," Angie said. "He just made sure they were all dead."

"With a bayonet," I said.

"Yeah, well," Devin said, and lit a cigarette, "if there were only nice people in the world, we'd lose our jobs. Anyway, Scott Pearse musters out, comes back to the States, lives with his dad, who's retired, a couple years, and then his dad dies of a heart attack and a few months later, Scott wins the lottery."

"What do you mean?"

"I mean, he won the Kansas State Lottery."

"Bullshit."

He shook his head, held up a hand. "On my

mother. I swear. Good news was he picked the winning six numbers, and the jackpot was for a million-two. Bad news was, eight other people picked the same numbers. So he collects his payout, which is like eighty-eight grand after the IRS gets through, and he buys a black '68 Shelby GT-500 from a classic car dealer, and then shows up in Boston, summer of '92, and takes the postal exam. And from there on in, far as we know, he's been a model citizen."

Oscar looked at his empty mug and empty shot glass, said to Devin, "We staying for another?"

Devin nodded vigorously. "They're buying."

"Oh, yeah!" Oscar waved at the bartender, circled his finger over the table to indicate another round.

The bartender nodded happily. Of course he was happy. When the tab was on me, Oscar and Devin drank only top shelf. And they threw it back like water. And ordered more. And more.

By the time I got the tab, I wondered who'd gotten the better of the deal. And whether the bill would max out my Visa. And why I couldn't just have normal friends who drank tea.

"You want to know how the United States Postal Service deals with several pieces of mail that don't reach their destination?" Vanessa Moore asked us.

"Pray tell," Angie said.

We were on the second floor of Bubba's warehouse, which serves as his living quarters. The front third of the floor is mined with explosives because . . . well, because Bubba's fucking nuts, but he'd somehow managed to deactivate them for the length of Vanessa's stay.

Vanessa sipped coffee at the bar that begins at the pinball machine and ends at the basketball hoop. She'd just come from the shower, and her hair was still damp. She wore a black silk shirt over ripped jeans and her feet were bare and she kneaded a sterling silver necklace between her fingers as she swiveled slowly from side to side on the bar stool.

"The post office deals with complaints first by telling you mail occasionally gets lost. As if we didn't know. When I mentioned that eleven letters were sent to eleven different destinations and none arrived, they recommended I contact the Postal Inspector's office, though they doubted it would do much good. The Postal Inspector's office said they'd send an investigator by to interview my *neighbors*, see if they had something to do with it. I said, 'I put the mail in the box myself.' To which they responded that if I provided them with a list of the destinations, they'd send someone to interview people on the *receiving* end."

"You've got to be joking," Angie said.

Her eyes widened and she shook her head. "It was pure Kafka. When I said, 'Why don't you investigate the carrier or pickup driver on that route?' they said, 'Once we've ascertained that no one else was involved . . .' I go, 'So what you're telling me is that when mail gets lost the presumption of guilt is laid on everyone *but* the person entrusted with delivering it.'"

"Tell 'em what they said to that," Bubba said as he came into the kitchen and bar area from somewhere in the back.

She smiled at him, then looked back at us. "They said, 'So will you be giving us a list of your neighbors, ma'am?'"

Bubba went to the fridge, opened the freezer, and pulled out a bottle of vodka. As he did, I noticed that the hair above the nape of his neck was damp.

"Fucking post office," Vanessa said as she finished her coffee. "And they wonder why everyone's switching to e-mail, Federal Express, and paying bills by computer."

"Only thirty-three cents for a stamp, though," Angie said.

Vanessa turned on the bar stool as Bubba approached with the bottle of vodka.

"Should be glasses by your knee," he said to her.

Vanessa dropped her eyes and rummaged under the bar.

Bubba watched the way her damp hair fell across her neck as she did so, the vodka bottle motionless and aloft in his hand. Then he looked over at me. Then he looked at the bar. He placed the bottle on top as Vanessa placed four shot glasses on the wood.

I looked at Angie. She was watching them with her lips slightly parted and a growing confusion in her eyes.

"I'm thinking I'm just going to cap this asshole," Bubba said as Vanessa poured the chilled liquor into the glasses.

"What?" I said.

"No," Vanessa said. "We talked about that."

"We did?" Bubba threw back a shot and placed the glass on the bar again, and Vanessa refilled it.

"Yes," Vanessa said slowly. "If I have knowledge that a crime is to be committed, I have a sworn duty to notify the police."

"Oh, yeah." Bubba threw back a second shot. "Forgot that."

"Be a good boy," Vanessa said.

"Uh, okay."

Angie narrowed her eyes at me. I resisted the urge to jump off my bar stool and run screaming from the room.

"You guys want to stay for dinner?" Vanessa asked.

Angie stood up awkwardly and knocked her bag to the floor. "No, no. We're . . . We already ate. So . . ."

I stood. "So, yeah, we'll be, ah . . ."

"Going?" Vanessa said.

"Right." Angie picked up her bag. "Going. That's us."

"You didn't touch your drinks," Bubba said.

"You have 'em," I said as Angie crossed the floor in five or six steps, reached the door.

"Cool." Bubba threw back another shot.

"You have any limes?" Vanessa asked him. "I'm in a tequila mood."

"I could scare some up."

I reached the door, looked back over my shoulder at the two of them. Bubba's huge frame was tilted as he leaned his shoulder into the fridge, and Vanessa's lithe body seemed to curl toward him like smoke from the top of the bar stool.

"See ya," she called, her eyes on Bubba.

"Uh, yeah," I said. "See ya." And then I got the hell out of there.

* * *

Angie started laughing as soon as we left Bubba's building. It was a helpless giggle, a stoner's laugh almost, that bent her body and led her out through the hole in the fence and into the playground beyond.

She got control of it as she lay against the jungle gym, looked up at the thick lead glass of Bubba's windows. She wiped her eyes and sighed through a few remaining chuckles.

"Dear, oh, dear. *Your* attorney and Bubba. My God. I've seen it all."

I leaned back on the metal rungs beside her. "She's not *my* anything."

"Not anymore," she said, "that's for sure. After him, she'll be ruined for normal men."

"He's borderline monosyllabic, Ange."

"True. But the man's hung, Patrick." She grinned at me. "I mean, hung."

"Firsthand info?"

She laughed. "You wish."

"So, how do you know?"

"Men can tell a woman's cup size if she's wearing three sweaters and an overcoat. You think we're any different?"

"Ah," I said, still back at the bar area, Vanessa doing those slow swivels on the stool, Bubba watching the way the hair fell across her neck.

"Bubba and Vanessa," Angie said, "sitting in a tree."

"Jesus. Quit it, will ya?"

She leaned her head back on the jungle gym, turned it my way. "Jealous?"

"No."

"Not a little bit?"

"Not even a smidgen."

"Liar."

I turned my head fully to the right and our noses almost touched. We didn't say anything for a while, just lay back on the jungle gym with our cheeks pressed to the rungs, the night softening against our skin, eyes locked. Far off behind Angie, a harvest moon rose in the dark sky.

"Do you hate my hair?" Angie whispered.

"No. It's just . . ."

"Short?" She smiled.

"Yeah. I don't love you because of your hair, though."

She shifted slightly, turned her shoulder into the holes between rungs.

"Why do you love me?"

I chuckled. "You want me to count the ways?"

She didn't say anything, just watched me.

"I love you, Ange, because . . . I don't know. Because I always have. Because you make me laugh. A lot. Because . . ."

"What?"

I turned my shoulder in between the rungs as she had, placed my palm on her hip. "Because since you left I have these dreams that you're sleeping beside me. And I wake up and I can still smell you, and I'm still half dreaming, but I don't know it, so I reach for you. I reach across to your pillow, and you're not there. And I gotta lie there at five in the morning, with the birds waking up outside and you not there and your smell just fading away. It fades and there's—" I cleared my throat. "There's nothing but me left there. And white sheets. White sheets and those fucking birds and it hurts, and all I can do is close my eyes and lie there and wish I didn't feel like dying."

Her face was very still, but her eyes had picked up a sheen like a thin film of glass. "That's not fair." She dabbed her eyes with the heels of her hands.

"Nothing's fair," I said. "You say we don't *work*?" She held up a hand.

I said, "What does work, Ange?"

Her chin dropped to her chest and she stayed that way a long time before she whispered, "Nothing."

"I know," I said, and my voice was hoarse.

Her chuckle was wet, and she wiped her face again. "I hate five in the morning, too, Patrick." She raised her head and smiled through trembling lips. "I hate it so, so much."

"Yeah?"

"Yeah. That guy I was sleeping with?"

"Trey," I said.

"You make it sound like a dirty word."

"What about him?"

"I could have sex with him, but I didn't want him holding me afterward. You know? The way I used to turn my back and you'd slide one arm under my neck and the other over my chest—I couldn't stand anyone else doing that."

I couldn't think of anything else to say but "Good."

"I've missed you," she whispered.

"I've missed you."

"I'm high maintenance," she said. "I'm moody. Got the bad temper. Hate to do laundry. Don't like to cook."

"Yeah," I said. "You are."

"Hey," she said. "You're no walk in the park, pal."

"But I cook," I said.

She reached out, ran her palm over the permanent scruff—thicker than shadow, thinner than beard—that I've kept on my face for three years to hide the scars Gerry Glynn gave me with a straight razor.

She ran her thumb lazily back and forth through the bristles, gently fingered the ruined, rubbery flesh underneath. Not the biggest scars, necessarily, but they're on my face, and I'm vain.

"Can I shave this off tonight?" she said.

"You once said it made me look hot."

She smiled. "It does, but it's just not you."

I considered it. Three years with protective facial hair. Three years hiding the damage delivered on the worst night of my life. Three years keeping my flaws and shame from the world.

"You want to give me a shave?" I said eventually.

She leaned in and kissed me. "Among other things."

30

Angie woke me at five in the morning, warm palms on my newly shaven cheeks, her tongue opening my mouth as she kicked the tangle of sheets off us and covered as much of my body as possible with her own.

"You hear the birds?" she said.

"No," I managed.

"Me, either."

After, we lay with the dawn gradually lighting the room, my body spooned behind hers, and I said, "He knows we're watching."

"Scott Pearse," she said. "Yeah, I got that feeling, too. A week straight of tailing him, he never so much as stops the truck for a coffee break. If he's going through anyone's mail, he isn't doing it there." She turned in my arms, a smooth slithering of her flesh that felt like lightning in my blood. "He's smart. He'll wait us out."

I lifted a stray hair off her eyelash.

"Yours?" she asked.

"Mine." I flicked it off the bed. "He said time

was an issue. That's why he met me on the roof and tried to either buy me off or back me off—because he's pressed for time."

"Right," Angie said. "But we can assume that was when he thought he had a deal with the Dawes. And now that the deal's off, why—"

"Who says it's off?"

"Christopher Dawe. Christ, he destroyed their daughter. They're not going to pay him after that. He's got no more leverage."

"But even Christopher Dawe figured he'd come back at them. Go after Carrie, try to destroy her like he did Karen."

"But where's the profit in that?"

"It's not entirely about profit," I said. "I think Christopher Dawe was right about that. I think it's a matter of principle to Pearse. That money he was extorting? He thinks of it as his already. He's not going to let it go."

Angie ran the backs of her fingers over my abdomen and chest. "But how would he get to Carrie Dawe? I doubt that if she were in therapy, she was using the same therapist as her daughter. So Pearse can't go the Diane Bourne route. The Dawes don't live in the city, so he can't fuck with their mail."

I propped myself up on my elbow. "Pearse's standard MO is to infiltrate through one psychiatrist and one postal area. Okay. But that's just what's on hand, the buttons he can press easily. His father was a professional mind fucker. The son was Special Forces."

"So?"

"So I think he's always prepared. And more than that, I think he's always ready to improvise. And he always, always works off private information. That's the foundation of everything he is and everything he does. He knew enough to pay the right people to get information on us. He found out I cared about Bubba and used that. He found out you were untouchable because of your grandfather, and when he couldn't get to me through Bubba, he went after Vanessa. He's limited, but he's seriously smart."

"Right. And what he knows about the Dawes, he learned from Wesley."

"Sure, but that's old info. Even if Wesley is still around, bankrolling Pearse, who knows—*his* information is ten years dated."

"True."

"Pearse would need somebody who knew the Dawes well and knew them now. A close associate of the doctor's. The wife's best friend. Or a—"

I looked down at her and she raised herself up on both elbows and we said it together:

"A housekeeper."

Siobhan Mulrooney walked into the parking lot of the commuter rail in Weston at six that night, an overnight bag slung over her shoulder, head down, steps quick. As she passed Angie's Honda, she saw me sitting on the hood and picked up her pace.

"Hey, Siobhan." I rubbed my chin between my thumb and forefinger. "What do you think about the new look?"

She looked back over her shoulder at me, paused. "Didn't recognize ya, Mr. Kenzie." She pointed at the light pink scars along the jawline. "You've scars."

"I do." I slid off the hood. "Guy gave them to me a couple of years ago."

"Whatever for?" Her shoulders jerked slightly as I approached, as if each side of her body wanted to run in the opposite direction.

"I had figured out he wasn't who he appeared to be. It made him angry."

"He tried to kill you, yeah?"

"Yeah. Tried to kill her, too." I pointed behind Siobhan at Angie standing by the stairwell that led up to the station.

Siobhan looked back at her, then at me. "Nasty man, then, I'd say."

"Where you from, Siobhan?"

"Ireland, of course."

"North, right?"

She nodded.

"Home of the Troubles," I said, throwing a brogue around the last word.

She dropped her head as I reached her. "You don't make light of it, Mr. Kenzie."

"Lost some family, did you?"

She looked up at me and her small eyes were smaller still and dark with anger. "I did, yeah. Generations of them."

I smiled. "Me, too. Great-great-great-grandfather, I think it was, on my father's side was executed in Donegal in 1798, when the French left us holding the bag. Now my maternal grandfather—me Ma's Da," I said with a wink, "they found him kneecapped in his barn with his throat cut and his tongue cut in half."

"He was a traitor, then, was he?" Siobhan's small face was clenched into a defiant fist.

"A stoolie," I said. "Yeah. Either that or the Orange did him, wanted it to look that way. You know how it is in a war like that, sometimes people die, you can never be sure why until you meet them on the other side. Other times, people die for no real reason, because the blood's up, because the more chaos, the easier it is to get away with it. I hear that since the cease-fire, it's really nuts over there. Everyone running around, taking off heads in revenge hits. Do you know, Siobhan, that more people were killed in South Africa in the two years *after* apartheid than died during it? Same thing with Yugoslavia after the Communists. I mean, fascism sucks, but it keeps people in line. The moment it's over, all that bad blood people have been holding in? Forget about it. People get whacked for things they forgot they did."

"Trying to tell me something, Mr. Kenzie?"

I shook my head. "Just running off at the mouth, Siobhan. So, tell me, why'd you leave the Old Sod?"

She cocked her head. "You like poverty, Mr. Kenzie? You like losing well over half your earnings to the government? You like dreary weather and endless cold?"

"Can't say I do." I shrugged. "It's just a lot of times, people leave the North and can't ever go back because there are too many people waiting to fuck them up when they step off the boat. You?"

"Have anyone waiting back there to hurt me?"

"Yeah."

"No," she said, her eyes on the ground, shaking her head as if by doing so that would make it come true. "No. Not me."

"Siobhan, could you tell me when Pearse is going

to move against the Dawes? And maybe how he plans to go about doing it?"

She stepped back from me slowly, a weird half smile playing on her tiny face. "Ah, no, Mr. Kenzie. Have yourself a nice day, won't ya?"

"You didn't say, 'Who's Pearse?'" I said.

"Who's Pearse?" she said. "There now—ya happy?" She turned and walked toward the stairs, her overnight bag swinging on her shoulder.

Angie stepped aside as Siobhan reached the dark stairwell and began climbing it.

I waited until she reached the landing midway up.

"How's your green card status, Siobhan?"

She stopped, froze there with her back to us.

"Did you somehow manage an extended work visa? Because I hear INS is really cracking down on the Irish. Particularly in this city. Kinda sucks, too, because who's going to paint the houses once they ship them back home?"

She cleared her throat, back still to us. "You wouldn't."

"We would," Angie said.

"You can't."

"We can," I said. "Help us out here, Siobhan."

She half turned, looked down the staircase at me. "Or what?"

"Or I'll call a friend of mine in INS, Siobhan, and you'll celebrate Labor Day in fucking Belfast."

31

"He keeps files on everyone," Siobhan said. "He has a file on me, one on you, Mr. Kenzie, and one on you as well, Miss Gennaro."

"What are in the files?" Angie asked.

"Your daily routines. Your weaknesses. Oh," she waved her hand at the smoke from her cigarette, "there's plenty else. Whatever biographical information he can find." She pointed the cigarette at Angie. "He was so happy when he found out about the death of your husband. He thought he had you."

"Had me?"

"The means to break you, Miss Gennaro. The means to break you. Everyone has something they can't face, don't they. Then he discovered you have some powerful relatives, yeah?"

Angie nodded.

"That was not a day you'd have wanted to be around Scott Pearse, you can be certain."

"My heart bleeds for him," I said. "Let me ask you—why'd you speak to me that first time I came to the Dawes' house?"

"To throw you off the scent, Mr. Kenzie."

"You sent me after Cody Falk."

She nodded

"What, did Pearse think I'd kill him and be done with the case?"

"It seemed a reasonable possibility, don't you think?" She looked down at her coffee cup.

"Is Diane Bourne his only source for psych files?" I asked.

Siobhan shook her head. "He's got a man in the records department at McLean Hospital in Belmont. Can you guess how many patients McLean services in a year, Mr. Kenzie?"

McLean was one of the largest psychiatric hospitals in the state. It handled both voluntary and involuntary committals, had locked and unlocked wards, treated everything from narcotics and alcohol dependency to chronic fatigue syndrome to paranoid disassociative schizophrenia with violent tendencies. McLean had over three hundred beds and an average of three thousand admissions a year.

Siobhan leaned back in the booth and ran a weary hand through her close-cropped hair. We'd left the commuter station in Weston and driven straight into rush hour, pulled out of it in Waltham and stopped at an IHOP on Main Street. At five-thirty in the evening, the IHOP sported only a few patrons, and after we ordered a pot of regular coffee and a pot of decaf, the surly waitress was happy to ignore us and leave us to our privacy.

"How does Pearse enlist people?" Angie asked.

Siobhan gave us an acrid smile. "He's very magnetic, isn't he?"

Angie shrugged. "Never met the man up close."

"Take it on faith, then," Siobhan said. "The man looks straight through to your soul."

I tried not to roll my eyes.

"He befriends you," Siobhan said. "Then he beds you. He learns your weaknesses—whatever those things are you can't face. Then he owns you. And you do what he asks, or he destroys you."

"Why Karen?" I said. "I mean, I know he was trying to teach the Dawes a lesson, but even for Pearse that strikes me as severe."

Siobhan lifted her coffee cup, but didn't drink from it. "You don't see it yet?"

We shook our heads.

"I'm beginning to lose respect for the both of you, I am."

"Gee," I said. "That hurts."

"Access, Mr. Kenzie. It's all about access."

"We know, Siobhan. How do you think we came around to you?"

She shook her head. "I'm limited—a snatch of conversation here, a glimpse of a bank statement there. Scott despises limits."

"So," Angie said and lit a cigarette, "Scott's after half the Dawes' fortune . . ." She saw something in Siobhan's face that halted her in midsentence. "No. That wouldn't be good enough, would it, Siobhan? He wants it all."

Siobhan's nod was barely perceptible.

"So he destroys Karen because she's the heir."

Another tiny nod.

Angie took a drag off her cigarette, considered it. "But, wait, impersonating Wesley Dawe would only get him so far. Even if the Dawes die and the circumstances don't seem suspicious, they're not leaving their fortune to a son they haven't seen in ten years. And even if—even *if*—they did, Pearse's impersonation of Wesley is limited. It's not going to pass muster with estate lawyers."

Siobhan watched her carefully.

"But," Angie said, going really slowly now, "if he destroys Christopher Dawe, he'll still gain nothing."

Siobhan used Angie's matches to light her own cigarette.

"Unless," Angie said, "he's gained access to . . . Carrie Dawe."

The name fell from her mouth and seemed to drop on the table between us as heavily as a plate.

"That's it," Angie said. "Isn't it? He and Carrie are in on it together."

Siobhan flicked her ash into the ashtray. "No. You were so close there for a moment, Miss Gennaro."

"Then . . . ?"

"She knows him as Timothy McGoldrick," Siobhan said. "They've been lovers for eighteen months. She has no idea he's the same man who destroyed Karen and wants to destroy her husband."

"Shit," I said. "We had the picture of him and she wasn't home."

Angie kicked the floorboard of the booth with her heel. "We should have gone to the damn country club with it."

Siobhan's tiny eyes had grown large. "You have a picture of him?"

I nodded. "Several."

"Oh, he won't like that. He won't like that at all."

I shivered and wagged my fingers at her. "Oooh."

She frowned. "You have no idea what his rage is like, Mr. Kenzie."

I leaned into the table. "Let me tell you something, Siobhan. I don't give a shit about his rage. I don't give a shit how magnetic he is. I don't give a shit if he can look into your soul and my soul and has God's phone number on speed dial. He's a psycho? Yes. He's a Special Forces bad-ass who can do spin kicks that can rip your head off your neck? Good for him. He destroyed a woman who never wanted more out of life than to be happy and drive a fucking Camry. He turned a guy into a vegetable just for fun. He cut off another guy's hands and tongue. And he poisoned a dog who I happened to have liked. A lot. You want to see rage?"

Siobhan had pressed her shoulders and head as far back as possible into the red imitation leather behind her. She glanced nervously at Angie.

Angie smiled. "It takes a lot, but once he gets revved up, honey?" She shook her head. "Pack up the kids and get out of town, because Main Street's going to explode."

Siobhan glanced back in my direction. "He's smarter than you," she whispered.

I shook my head. "He's had the advantage of access. Now I do, too. I'm in *his* life now," I said. "I'm in it up until the very end."

She shook her head. "You have no idea what you're . . ." She dropped her eyes, continued to shake her head.

"No idea of what?" Angie asked.

She raised her eyes and her head stopped moving.

"What you're truly up against, what you *really* walked into."

"So tell us."

"Ah, thank you, no." She placed her cigarettes in her purse. "I've given you all I care to. I trust you won't call me to the attention of your INS friend. And I wish you both the best, though I don't think it'll help."

She stood, slid the bag strap over her shoulder.

"Why did Pearse have to be so merciless with Karen?" I asked.

She looked down at me. "I just told you. She was the only heir."

"I understand that. But why not just have her meet with an accident? Why destroy her piece by piece?"

"That's his method."

"That's not method," I said. "That's abhorrence. Why did he hate her so bad?"

She held out her arms, seemingly exasperated. "He didn't. He barely knew her until Miles introduced them three months before she died."

"So why do all that to her?"

Her hands clapped her outer thigh. "I told you— it's his way."

"That's not good enough."

"It's all I have for you."

"You're lying," I said. "Big chunks of this don't add up, Siobhan."

She rolled her eyes, exhaled a weary sigh. "Well, that's the thing about us criminal types, yeah, Mr. Kenzie? We tend to be a bit untrustworthy."

She turned toward the door.

"Where are you going?" I asked.

"I've a friend in Canton. I'll stay with her for a bit."

"How do we know you're not going straight to Pearse?"

She gave us a wry grin. "The moment I didn't arrive on the train into Boston, they knew you'd gotten to me. I'm a weak link now, aren't I? And Pearse doesn't like weak links." She bent for her overnight bag, lifted it off the floor. "Not to worry. No one knows about my friend in Canton, except for you two. I'll have at least a week before anyone has the time to go looking for me, and by then, I expect you'll have all killed each other." Her flat eyes twinkled. "Have a nice day now, won't you?"

She walked to the door, and Angie said, "Siobhan."

"Yeah?" She grasped the door handle.

"Where's the real Wesley?" Angie asked.

"I don't know." She wouldn't look at us.

"Guess."

"Dead," she said. She still didn't meet our eyes.

"Why?"

She shrugged. "He outlived his usefulness, yeah? We all do where Scott is concerned, sooner or later."

She opened the door and stepped out into the parking lot. She walked toward the bus stop on Main without a look back, just a steady shake of her small head, as if simultaneously bitter and bemused by the choices that had led her here.

"She said 'they,'" Angie said. "You notice that? 'They knew you'd gotten to me.'"

"I noticed," I said.

* * *

Carrie Dawe's face cracked in on itself as if it had been hit in the center with an ax.

She didn't weep. She didn't cry out or scream or move much at all as she looked down at the photo of Pearse we'd placed on the coffee table in front of her. Her face merely folded inward and her breath turned shallow.

Christopher Dawe was still at the hospital, and the great empty house felt cold and haunted around us.

"You know him as Timothy McGoldrick," Angie said. "Correct?"

Carrie Dawe nodded.

"What does he do for a living?"

"He's a . . ." She swallowed, snapped her eyes away from the photo and curled into herself on the couch. "He said he was an airline pilot for TWA. Hell, we met in an airport. I saw his IDs, a route schedule update or two. He was based out of Chicago. It fit. He has the trace of a mid-western accent."

"You want to kill him," I said.

She looked at me, eyes wide, then dropped her chin.

"Of course you do," I said. "Is there a gun in the house?"

She kept her chin pressed to her chest.

"Is there a gun in the house?" I repeated.

"No," she said quietly.

"But you have access to one," I said.

She nodded. "We have a house in New Hampshire. For ski season. There are two there."

"What kind?"

"Excuse me?"

"What kind, Mrs. Dawe?"

"A handgun and a rifle. Christopher sometimes hunts in the late autumn."

Angie reached out, put a hand over Carrie Dawe's. "If you kill him, he still wins."

Carrie Dawe laughed. "How's that?"

"You're destroyed. Your husband is destroyed. Most of the fortune, I'll bet, will go to your criminal defense."

She laughed again, but this time tears had sprung out along the tops of her cheekbones. "So what?"

"So," Angie said softly, tightening her hand on Carrie's, "he set out years ago to destroy this family. Don't let him succeed. Mrs. Dawe, look at me. Please."

Carrie turned her head, swallowed a pair of tears that reached opposite corners of her mouth at the same time.

"I've lost a husband," Angie said. "Just as you lost your first. Violently. You got a second chance, and yeah, you've fucked it up."

Carrie Dawe's laugh was one of shock.

"But you still have it," Angie said. "You can still make it right. Make a third chance out of your second. Don't let him take that."

For a good two minutes, no one spoke. I watched the two women hold hands and stare hard into each other's faces, heard the clock tick on the mantel above the dark fireplace.

"You're going to hurt him?" Carrie Dawe said.

"Yes," Angie said.

"Really hurt him," she said.

"Bury him," Angie said.

She nodded. She shifted on the couch and leaned forward, placed her free hand over Angie's.

"How can I help?" she asked.

As we drove over toward Sleeper Street to relieve Nelson Ferrare on the roof, I said, "We've tailed his ass for a week. Where's he vulnerable?"

"Women," Angie said. "His hatred sounds so pathological—"

"No," I said. "That's deeper than I'm looking for. What makes him vulnerable right now? Where are the chinks in his armor?"

"The fact that Carrie Dawe knows he and Timothy McGoldrick are one and the same."

I nodded. "Flaw number one."

"What else?" she asked.

"He has no curtains on most of his windows."

"Okay."

"You've been following him during the day. Anything there?"

She thought about it. "Not really. Wait. Yeah."

"What?"

"He leaves the engine running."

"On the truck when he does his stops?"

She nodded, smiled. "And the keys in the ignition."

I looked out the windshield as we approached the end of the Mass Pike, and shifted lanes from the northbound to southbound exit.

"What are you doing?" Angie asked.

"Going to drop by Bubba's first."

She leaned forward, peered through the wash of a yellow light strip in the tunnel above us. "You've got a plan, don't you?"

"I have a plan."

"A good one?"

"A bit crude," I said. "Needs some polish. But effective, I think."

"Crude's okay," she said. "Is it mean?"

I grinned. "Some might call it that."

"Mean's even better," she said.

Bubba met us at the door wearing a towel and a face completely devoid of hospitality.

Bubba's torso, from the waist to the hollow of his throat, is a massive slab of dark and light pink scar tissue in the shapes of lobster tails and smaller red ridges the length and width of children's fingers that litter the pink like slugs. The lobster tails are burns; the slugs are shrapnel scars. Bubba got his chest in Beirut, when he was stationed with the marines the day a suicide bomber drove through the front gates and MPs on duty couldn't shoot him because they'd been given blanks in their rifles. Bubba had spent eight months in a Lebanese hospital before receiving a medal and a discharge. He'd sold the medal and disappeared for another eighteen months, returning to Boston in late 1985 with contacts in the illegal arms trade a lot of other men before him had died trying to establish. He came back with the chest that looked like a mapmaker's representation of the Urals, a refusal to ever discuss the night of the bombing, and a profound lack of fear that made people even more nervous around him than they'd been before he left.

"What?" he said.

"Good to see you, too. Let us in."

"Why?"

"We need stuff."

"What stuff?"

"Illegal stuff."

"No shit."

"Bubba," Angie said, "we already figured out you're doing the nasty with Ms. Moore, so come on. Let us pass."

Bubba frowned and it thrust his lower lip out. He stepped aside and we entered the warehouse to see Vanessa Moore, wearing one of Bubba's hockey jerseys and nothing else, lying on the red couch in the center of the floor, a champagne flute propped on her washboard abdomen, watching *9½ Weeks* on Bubba's fifty-inch TV. She used the remote control to pause it as we came through the door, froze Mickey Rourke and Kim Basinger going at it against an alley wall as blue-lit acid rain dripped on their bodies.

"Hey," she said.

"Hey. Don't let us disturb you."

She scooped some peanuts from a bowl on the coffee table, popped them in her mouth. "No worries."

"'Nessie," Bubba said, "we got to talk a bit of business."

Angie caught my eye and mouthed, "Nessie?"

"Illegal business?"

Bubba looked over his shoulder at me. I nodded vigorously.

"Yeah," he said.

"Okey-doke." She started to rise from the couch.

"No, no," Bubba said. "Stay there. We'll leave. We got to go upstairs anyway."

"Mmm. Better." She slipped back down into the couch and hit the remote and Mickey and Kim started huffing and puffing to bad eighties synth-rock again.

"You know, I've never seen this movie," Angie said as we followed Bubba up the stairs to the third floor.

"Mickey's actually not very greasy in this one," I said.

"And Kim in those white socks," Bubba said.

"And Kim in those white socks," I agreed.

"Two thumbs-up from the pervert twins," Angie said. "What a boon."

"So look," Bubba said as he turned on the lights on the third floor and Angie wandered off to look through the crates for her weapon of choice, "you got any problem with me, ah, how do I say this—boning Vanessa?"

I covered a smile with my hand, looked down at an open crate of grenades. "Ah, no, man. No problem at all."

Bubba said, "Cause I haven't had a, whatta ya call it, a steady—"

"Girlfriend?"

"Yeah, in like a long time."

"Since high school," I said. "Stacie Hamner, right?"

He shook his head. "In Chechnya, '84, there was someone."

"I never knew."

He shrugged. "I never offered, dude."

"There's that, sure."

He put his hand on my shoulder, leaned in close. "So we're cool?"

"Cool beans," I said. "What about Vanessa? She cool?"

He nodded. "She's the one told me you wouldn't care."

"Yeah?"

"Yeah. Said you two never cared about each other. It was just exercise."

"Huh," I said, as we crossed back toward Angie. "Exercise."

Angie pulled a rifle from a wooden crate and rested the stock on her hip. The barrel towered over her. The rifle was so thick and looked so heavy and mean, it was hard to believe she could hold it without tipping over on her side.

"You got a target scope with this baby?"

"I got a scope," Bubba said. "What about bullets?"

"The bigger the better."

Bubba turned his head, shot me a deadpan look. "Funny. That's what Vanessa says."

On the roof across from Scott Pearse's loft, we sat and waited for the phone call. Nelson, intrigued by the rifle, stayed and sat with us.

At ten on the nose, Scott Pearse's phone rang and we watched him cross the living room and lift the receiver of a black phone attached to the brick support column in the center of the room. He smiled when he heard the voice on the other end, leaned lazily back into the support column and cradled the receiver between neck and shoulder.

His grin faded gradually, and then his face turned into a sickened grimace. He held out his hands as if the caller could see him and spoke rapidly into the phone, his body bending with his pleading.

Then Carrie Dawe must have hung up on the other end, because Scott Pearse jerked his ear back from the phone and stared at it for a moment. Then he screamed and smashed the receiver over and over again into the brick column until all he had left were a few shards of black plastic and a dangling metal mouthpiece.

"Gee," Angie said, "I hope he has a second phone."

I pulled the cellular phone I'd gotten at Bubba's from my pocket. "How much you want to bet he breaks that one, too, once I'm done."

I dialed Scott Pearse's number.

Before I hit send, Nelson said, "Hey, Ange," and pointed at the rifle. "You want me to do the honors?"

"Why?"

"Fucking recoil'll knock your shoulder back a few blocks is all." He jerked a thumb at me. "Why can't he do it?"

"He's got shitty aim."

"With that scope?"

"Really shitty aim," she said.

Nelson held out his hands. "It'd be my pleasure."

Angie considered the rifle stock, then glanced at her shoulder. Eventually, she nodded. She handed the rifle to Nelson, then told him what we wanted.

Nelson shrugged. "Okay. Why not just kill him, though?"

"Because," Angie said, "A, we're not killers."

"And B?" Nelson asked.

"Killing him's too nice," I said.

I depressed the send button on the cell phone and Scott Pearse's phone rang on the other end.

He'd been leaning with his head against the brick column, and he raised it slowly, turned his head as if unsure what sound he was hearing. Then he walked over to the bar curled around the edge of his kitchen and lifted a portable off the top.

"Hello."

"Scottie," I said. "What's happening?"

"I was wondering how long it would be before you called, Pat."

"Not surprised?"

"That you learned my identity? I expected no less, Pat. Are you watching me at the moment?"

"Possibly."

He chuckled. "I sensed as much. Nothing I could put my finger on, mind you—I mean, you're not bad—but in the last week or so, I had the feeling eyes were watching."

"You're an intuitive fella, Scott. What can I say?"

"You don't know the half of it."

"Was it your intuition that told you to bayonet five women in Panama?"

He wandered into the living room, head down, index finger scratching the side of his neck, a wry smile curling up one side of his face.

"Well," he exhaled into the phone. "You've done

some extra credit in the homework department, Pat. Very good."

The grin left his face, but the scratching grew a little faster.

"So, Pat, what's your plan, buddy?"

"I'm not your buddy," I said.

"Whoops. My bad. What's your plan, asshole?"

I laughed. "Getting testy, Scott?"

In the loft, he put a palm to his forehead, then brushed the hair back off his head with it. He looked out at his black windows. He toed a shard of black plastic on the floor with his shoe.

"I can wait you out," he said. "You'll tire of watching me do nothing."

"That's what my partner said."

"She's right."

"I gotta beg to differ on that score, Scottie."

"Really?"

"Sure. How long can you wait now that Carrie Dawe knows who Pilot Tim McGoldrick is, knows you're the same guy who ruined her daughter's life?"

Scott said nothing. A strange, low hissing noise came from his end like the sound of a teapot in the minute before it comes to a full boil.

"You tell me that, Scottie?" I asked. "I'm just curious."

Scott Pearse turned suddenly from the brick column and stalked across his shiny blond floors. He reached the oversized windows and stared out at his reflection, raised his eyes and looked up at what could only be, from his side, the barest outline of our roof edge.

"Your sister lives in Seattle, fuck. She and her husband and their—"

"—children, yeah, Scott, just went on vacation," I said. "My treat. I sent them tickets last Monday, shithead. They left this morning."

"She'll come back sometime." He stared directly up at the roof, and from here I could see cords in his neck strain against the skin.

"But by then, Scottie, this'll be over."

"I'm not that easy to shake up, Pat."

"Sure you are, Scottie. A guy who bayonets a roomful of dying women is a guy who snaps. So, get ready Scott, you're about to start snapping."

Scott Pearse stared defiantly at his windowpane. He said, "Listen to—" and I hung up the phone.

He stared at the phone in his hand, shocked beyond reason, I think, that two people had dared hang up on him in the same night.

I nodded at Nelson.

Scott Pearse gripped the phone between his hands and raised it over his head and the window beside him exploded as Nelson fired four rounds into it.

Pearse vaulted backward onto the floor and the phone skittered out of his hand.

Nelson pivoted and fired again, three times, and the window in front of Scott Pearse imploded in a cascade, like ice pouring from the back of a faulty tailgate.

Pearse rolled to his left and up into a crouch.

"Just don't hit his body," I said to Nelson.

Nelson nodded and fired several shots into the floor a few inches behind Scott Pearse's feet as he scampered over the blond wood. He sprang up like a cat and vaulted over the bar into the kitchen.

Nelson looked at me.

Angie glanced up from Bubba's police scanner as Scott Pearse's alarm bells ripped through the still summer night. "We got, maybe, two minutes-thirty."

I backhanded Nelson's shoulder. "How much damage can you do in a minute flat?"

Nelson smiled. "Fucking boatload, dude."

"Go nuts."

Nelson took out the rest of the windows first, then went to work on the lights. The stained-glass Tiffany lamp over the bar looked like a pack of fruity Life Savers stuffed in a cherry bomb by the time he was through with it. The track lights over the kitchen and living room shredded into popping shards of white plastic and pale glass. The video cameras went up in blue and red blurs of electrical spark. Nelson turned the floor to splinters, the couches and slim leather recliners into piles of white moss, and punched so many holes in the refrigerator, most of the food would probably spoil before the cops finished writing their reports.

"One minute," Angie yelled over the roar. "Let's go."

Nelson looked back over his shoulder at the glittering mass of brass shells. "Who loaded the mags?"

"Bubba."

He nodded. "They're clean, then."

We boogied across the roof and down the dark fire escape. Nelson tossed me the rifle and hopped into his Camaro, tore off out of the alley without a word.

We climbed in the Jeep, and I could hear distant sirens ring up Congress from the piers down the other end of the waterfront.

I spun out of the alley and banged a right on Congress, crossed over the harbor and into the city proper. I took a hard right at the yellow light on Atlantic Avenue, slowed as I cut into the left lane, and took the reverse curve, headed south. I felt my heart return to a normal rate as I reached the expressway.

I picked up the cell phone Bubba had given me as I descended the on ramp, pressed redial, then send.

Scott Pearse's "What?" sounded hoarse, and in the background, I could hear sirens bleating into abrupt silence as they reached his building.

"Here's how I see it, Scott. First—this is a clone phone I'm using. Triangulate the signal all you want, it won't mean shit. Second—you finger me for redecorating your loft, I finger you for extortion of the Dawes. Clear so far?"

"I'm going to kill you."

"Terrif. Just so you know, Scott, that was a warm-up. Care to know what we have in store for you tomorrow?"

"Do tell," he said.

"Nah," I said. "You just wait and see. Okay?"

"You can't do this. Not to me. Not to me!" His voice rose over the hard knocking I could hear at his front door. "You can't fucking do this to me!"

"I've already started, Scott. Know what time it is?"

"What?"

"It's look-over-your-shoulder time, Scottie. Have a nice night."

The police were kicking in the door behind him when I hung up.

32

The next morning, as Scott Pearse loaded mail into a box on the corner of Marlboro and Clarendon, Bubba hopped in his truck and drove away with it.

Pearse didn't even realize it until Bubba turned onto Clarendon, and by the time he dropped his bag and gave chase, Bubba was turning onto Commonwealth and stepping on the gas pedal.

Angie pulled her Honda up beside the mailbox and I left the passenger door open as I jumped out, grabbed the canvas mailbag off the sidewalk, and got back in the car.

Pearse was still standing on the corner of Clarendon and Commonwealth, his back to us, as we drove away.

"By the end of this day," Angie said as we turned onto Berklee and headed for Storrow Drive, "what do you think he'll do?"

"I'm kinda hoping for something irrational."

"Irrational can mean bloody."

I turned in the seat and tossed the mailbag in back. "This guy's proven, he has time to think, it ends up bloody anyway. I want to take thinking out of the equation. I want him to react."

"So," Angie said, "his car next?"

"Uh . . ."

"I know, Patrick, it's a classic. I understand."

"It's *the* classic," I said. "Possibly the single coolest car ever manufactured in America."

She put her hand on my leg. "You said we'd be mean."

I sighed, stared through the windshield at the cars on Storrow Drive. Not one of them, even the obscenely expensive ones, could hold a candle to the '68 Shelby.

"Okay," I said, "let's be mean."

He kept it parked in a garage on A Street in Southie, about a quarter mile from his loft. Nelson had seen him take it out one night, not for any particular purpose, just to open it up along the waterfront, take a spin around the harbor, and then return it to its roost. I know a lot of guys like that, ones who visit their cars in the storage garage like they're pets in a boarding kennel, and then illogically feel pity for the lonely beast, strip off the car cover, and drive it around the block a few times.

Actually, I'm one of those guys. Angie used to say I'd grow out of it. More recently, she's said she's given up hope on that score.

We took a ticket at the booth, drove up two levels, and parked beside the Shelby, which, even under a thick car cover, was instantly identifiable. Angie gave me a pat on the back to buck me up and then took the stairs down to ground level to keep the attendant occupied with a city map, a tourist's confusion, and a black mesh T-shirt that didn't completely reach the waistband of her jeans.

I pulled the cover off the car and almost gasped. The 1968 Shelby Mustang GT-500 is to American automobiles what Shakespeare is to literature and the Marx Brothers are to comedy—that is to say, everything that came before was, in retrospect, a teaser, and everything that came after could never live up to the standard of perfection achieved in one brief blink of time.

I rolled under the car before my knees buckled from the wanting, ran my hand up under the chassis between the engine block and the fire wall, and felt around for a good three minutes before I found the alarm receiver. I yanked it free, rolled back out, and used a slim jim to open the driver's door. I reached in and popped the hood, came around the front of the car, and stared in a near-trance at the word COBRA stamped in steel atop the filter cover and again along the oil tank, the sheer sense of compressed but certain power that emanated from the gleaming 428 engine.

It smelled clean under the hood, as if the engine and radiator and drive shaft and manifold had just been lifted off the assembly line. It smelled like a car that had been slaved over. Scott Pearse, whatever his feelings for the human race, had loved this car.

"I'm sorry," I told the engine.

Then I went around to Angie's trunk for the sugar, the chocolate syrup, and the rice.

After we dumped the contents of Pearse's mailbag in a box on our side of the city, we returned to the office. I called Devin and asked for any data he could find on Timothy McGoldrick and he wrangled two tickets to October's Patriots-Jets game out of me as a service fee.

"Come on," I said. "I've been a season-ticket holder for thirteen years while they camped in the basement. Don't take that game from me."

"How do you spell that last name?"

"Dev, it's a Monday night game."

"Is it M-A-C or just M-C?"

"The latter," I said. "You suck."

"Hey, I noticed on the sheets this morning that someone shot the ever-living shit out of some guy's loft on Sleeper Street. The vic's name struck me as familiar. Know anything about that?"

"Pats versus Jets," I said slowly.

"Tuna Bowl," Devin cried. "Tuna Bowl! Seats still on the fifty?"

"Yup."

"Rocking. Talk to you soon." He hung up.

I leaned back in my seat, propped my heels on the belfry window.

Angie smiled at me from her desk. Behind her, an old black-and-white TV on the file cabinet broadcast a game show. A lot of people clapped and a few jumped up and down, but it had no effect on us. The volume on the thing had kicked the bucket years ago, but somehow we both find it comforting to leave it on when we're up in the belfry.

"We're making no money on this case," she said.

"Nope."

"You just destroyed a car you've waited your whole life to touch."

"Uh-huh."

"And then gave away tickets to the biggest football game of the year."

"That's about the size of it." I nodded.

"You going to cry soon?"

"Trying hard not to."

"Because real men don't cry?"

I shook my head. "I'm afraid if I start, I might not
be able to stop."

We had lunch as Angie printed up her case overview thus far, and the silent TV behind her aired a
soap opera in which everyone dressed really well and
seemed to shout a lot. Angie has always had a narra-
tive talent I've never possessed, probably because
she reads in her off-time while I just watch old movies and play a lot of video golf.

She'd charted the case from my notes regarding
my first meeting with Karen Nichols, through Scott
Pearse's charade as Wesley Dawe, the maiming of
Miles Lovell, the disappearance of Diane Bourne,
the baby switch fourteen years ago that had given the
Dawes a child who would fall through ice and ultimately bring Pearse into their lives, all the way up to
the beginnings of our current frontal assault on Scott
Pearse's life, shaded, of course, in vague terminology
such as "commenced exploitation of subject's weaknesses as we perceived them."

"Here's my problem." Angie handed me the last
page.

Under the heading *Prognosis*, she'd written: "Subject seems to have no viable options left to pursue the

Dawes or their money. Subject's leverage was lost when C. Dawe realized his false identity as T. Mc-Goldrick. Exploitation of subject's weaknesses, while emotionally gratifying, seems to yield no finite result."

"Finite," I said.

"You like that?"

"And Bubba accuses me of showing off my college."

"Seriously," she said, placing her turkey sub down on the wax paper beside her desk blotter, "what possible reason could he have for pursuing the Dawes anymore? We blew him out of the water." She looked at the clock behind her head. "By now, he's been suspended or fired for losing both his truck and a lot of mail. His car's fucked. His apartment's blown to shit. He's got nothing."

"He's got a trump card," I said.

"Which is?"

"I don't know. But he's former military. He loves games. He'd have a fallback position, an ace in the hole. I know it."

"I disagree. I think he blew his wad."

"Nice mouth."

She shrugged, took a bite from her sandwich.

"So you want to shut this case down?"

She nodded, swallowed her piece of sandwich and took a sip of Coke. "He's done. I think we've punished him. We didn't bring Karen Nichols back, but we rocked his world a bit. He had a few million within his reach and we snatched it from him. Stick a fork in him. It's over."

I considered it. There wasn't much I could argue with. The Dawes were fully prepared to face exposure on the baby-switching they'd done. Carrie Dawe was no longer vulnerable to the charms of McGoldrick/Pearse. It wasn't like Pearse could hit them over the head and take their money. And, I was reasonably sure, he hadn't been prepared for us and just how hard we can hit back if you make us mad.

I'd been hoping to anger him to the point where he'd do something stupid. But what? Come after me or Angie or Bubba? There was no percentage in it. Angry or not, he'd see that. Kill Angie, and he'd sign his own death warrant. Kill me, and he'd have Bubba and my case notes to deal with. And as for Bubba, Pearse would have to know that it would be like launching an assault on an armored car with a squirt gun. He might pull it off, but he'd suffer a lot of damage, and again, to what end?

So, I had to agree in principle with Angie. Scott Pearse didn't seem to pose much of a threat to anyone anymore.

Which is what worried me. It's the exact moment that you perceive an opponent as defenseless that you, not he, are most vulnerable.

"Twenty-four more hours," I said. "Can you give me that?"

She rolled her eyes. "Oh, okay, Banacek, but not a second more."

I bowed in appreciation and the phone rang.

"Hello."

"Tu-na!" Devin crowed. "Tu-na! Fucking Pah-cells," he said in his best Revere accent, "I think he's, like, God, but smahta."

"Rub it in," I said. "Wound's still good and fresh."

"Timothy McGoldrick," Devin said. "There's a bunch of them. But one stands out—born in 1965, died in 1967. Applied for a driver's license in 1994."

"He's dead, but he drives."

"Neat trick, huh? Lives at One-one-one-six Congress Street."

I shook my head at the sheer size of Pearse's balls. He kept a loft on 25 Sleeper Street and another place on Congress. It might seem like a short walk, but it got even shorter when you realized that his building on Sleeper Street also fronted Congress and both addresses were under the same roof.

"You still there?" Devin asked.

"Yeah."

"No record on this guy. He's clean."

"Except that he's dead."

"That might interest the Census Bureau, sure."

He hung up and I dialed the Dawes.

"Hello?" Carrie Dawe said.

"It's Patrick Kenzie," I said. "Is your husband home?"

"No."

"Good. When you met McGoldrick, where did you meet?"

"Why?"

"Please."

She sighed. "He sublet a place on Congress Street."

"Corner of Congress and Sleeper?"

"Yes. How did you—"

"Never mind. You thought anymore about that gun in New Hampshire?"

"I'm thinking about it now."

"He's ruined," I said. "He can't hurt you."

"He already did, Mr. Kenzie. And he hurt my daughter. What am I supposed to do with that—forgive?"

She hung up, and I looked over at Angie. "I'm not too keen on Carrie Dawe's emotional state at the moment."

"You think she still might go gunning for Pearse?"

"Possibly."

"What do you want to do?"

"Pull Nelson off Pearse, put him on the Dawes for a while."

"What's Nelson charging you?"

"That's irrelevant."

"Come on."

"A buck fifty a day," I said.

Her eyes widened. "You're paying him a thousand-fifty a week?"

I shrugged. "It's his price."

"We're going to go broke."

I held up my index finger. "One more day."

She spread her arms. "Why?"

Behind her, on the TV, they'd interrupted the soap opera for a live update from the banks of the Mystic River.

I pointed behind Angie's head. "That's why."

She turned her head and looked up at the TV as frogmen pulled a small body from the water and several weathered-looking detectives waved off the cameras.

"Oh, shit," Angie said.

I looked at the small gray face as the head came

to rest on wet rocks, then the detectives succeeded in blocking the cameras with their hands.

Siobhan. She'd never have to worry about seeing Ireland again.

33

Last night, as soon as the police had passed him on the waterfront, Nelson was supposed to turn around and go back, park a few blocks down on Congress Street and watch Pearse's building, see if he went anywhere after the police finished up and left.

As long as he did his job, I didn't mind paying Nelson a grand a week. It was a small price for knowledge of Pearse's movements.

But it was way too much to pay for a fuck-up.

"I *did* watch him," Nelson said when I caught up with him. "And I'm watching him now, too. Dude, I'm on this guy like white on rice."

"Tell me what happened last night."

"The cops drove him over to the Meridian Hotel. He got out, went inside. The cops leave. He comes back out and hails a cab, takes it back to the building."

"He went back to his loft?"

"Fuck no. But he went in the building. I couldn't tell exactly where."

"What, no lights went on? No—"

"Fucking place is a city block, man. You got the Sleeper Street side, the Congress side, and two alleys. How'm I supposed to cover all that?"

"But he went in there and stayed."

"Yeah. Until he left for work this morning. Then he comes back around a half hour ago, looking pissed. He goes in the building, been there since."

"He managed to kill someone last night."

"Bullshit."

"Sorry, Nelson, but there must be a way out of there that we don't know about."

"Where'd the vic live?"

"She was staying in Canton. They pulled her out of the Mystic this afternoon."

"Bullshit," he said again, this time twice as hard. "Patrick, the cops finished up with him last night, it was, like, almost four in the morning. He went to work at seven. How's he gonna slip out of the building without me seeing, somehow get all the way down to fucking *Canton*, ace someone, transport the body up to the North fucking Shore, and then, then he's—what?—he's gonna come *back*, slip by me again and get ready for work? Whistle while he's fucking shaving and shit? How's he going to do all that?"

"It's not possible," I said.

"You're fucking A, it ain't. He mighta done a lotta bad shit, Patrick, but in the last ten hours, he ain't done nothing at all."

I hung up, put the heels of my hands over my eyes.

"What?" Angie asked.

I told her.

"And Nelson's sure?" she said when I finished.

I nodded.

"So if Pearse didn't kill her, who did?"

I resisted the urge to bang my swelling head against the desktop. "I don't know."

"Carrie?"

I raised an eyebrow at her. "Carrie. Why?"

"Maybe she figured out that Siobhan was working for Pearse."

"How? We didn't tell her."

"But she's a smart woman. Maybe she . . ." She held up her hands, then dropped them. "Shit. I don't know."

I shook my head. "I can't see it. Carrie goes over to Canton, whacks Siobhan, drives her to the Mystic, and dumps her body in? How's she going to lift the body? The woman weighs less than you do. Hell, why would she even think to drive clear across to the other side of the city and dump the body?"

"Maybe she didn't kill her in Canton. Maybe she drew her out to a meeting place."

"I'll buy that someone drew her out. Carrie just doesn't fit. I'm not saying she couldn't kill—she could. But it's the dumping of the body that bothers me. It's too cool. It's too methodical."

Angie leaned back in her chair, lifted the phone off the cradle, and hit speed dial.

"Hey," she said into the phone, "I don't have Patriots tickets to trade, but can you answer me one question?"

She listened as Devin said something back.

"No, nothing like that. The woman they just pulled out of the Mystic, what was the cause of death?" She nodded. "To the back of the head? Okay. Why'd she come to the surface so fast?" She nodded again, several times. "Thanks. Huh? I'll ask Patrick on that one and get back to you." She smiled, looked at me. "Yes, Dev, we're back together." She put her hand over the phone, said to me, "He wants to know for how long."

"At least till prom," I said.

"At least till prom. Aren't I lucky?" she told him. "Talk to you soon."

She hung up. "Siobhan was found with a rope dangling from her waist. The operating theory is she was tied to something heavy and dropped to the bottom, where something ate through the rope and part of her hip. She wasn't supposed to come up."

I banged my chair back as I stood and went to the window, looked down at the avenue.

"Whatever his move is, he's going to make it soon."

"Yet we're agreed he couldn't have killed her."

"But he's behind it," I said. "Fucker's behind everything."

We left the belfry and went across to my apartment, entered the living room to a ringing phone. Just as I had that early evening on City Hall Plaza, I knew it was him before I picked up the receiver.

"That was pretty funny," he said, "getting me suspended from my job. Ha, Patrick! Ha ha!"

"Doesn't feel good, does it?"

"Getting suspended?"

"Knowing someone's fucking with you and might not let up for a while."

"I can appreciate the irony, just so you know. Someday, I'm sure, I'll look back on this and just laugh and laugh and laugh."

"Or maybe you won't."

"Whatever," he said calmly. "Look, let's say we're square now. Okay? You go your way, I'll go mine."

"Sure, Scott," I said. "Okay."

For a minute he didn't say anything.

"You still there?" I asked.

"Yeah. Honestly, Patrick, I'm surprised. Are you serious, or are you fucking with me?"

"I'm serious," I said. "I'm losing money here, and you can't get to the Dawes' money anymore, so I'd say it's a draw."

"If that was the case, why'd you shoot up my apartment, buddy? Why'd you steal my truck?"

"To make sure I drove the point home."

He chuckled. "You did. You certainly did. Outstanding, sir. Outstanding. Let me ask you—am I going to blow up the next time I start my car?" He laughed.

I laughed with him. "Why would you think that, Scott?"

"Well," he said happily, "you went after my home, then my job, I figure the next logical step would have been my car."

"It won't blow up when you start it, Scott."

"No?"

"No. But, then, I'm pretty sure it'll never start again."

His laugh boomed. "You fucked up my car?"

"Hate to break the news to you, but yeah."

"Oh, Jesus!" His laughter grew louder for about

a minute, then decreased until it was a barely connected string of soft chuckles. "Sugar in the gas tank,
acid in the engine?" he asked. "That sort of thing?"

"Sugar, yeah. Acid, no."

"Then what was it, huh?" I could hear his frozen
smile. "I figure you for the inventive type."

"Chocolate syrup," I said, "and about a pound of
unconverted rice."

He roared with glee. "In the engine?"

"Uh-huh."

"Did you run it for a while, you wacky bastard?"

"It was running when I left it," I said. "Didn't
sound real good, but it was running."

"Whoo!" he shouted. "So, so, Patrick, you're saying you totaled out an engine that took me years to
rebuild. And . . . and . . . you destroyed my gas tank,
the filters, I mean, everything really but the interior."

"Yeah, Scott."

"I could . . ." He giggled. "I could just kill you
about now, buddy. I mean, with my own bare hands."

"I kind of figured. Scott?"

"Yes?"

"You're not done with the Dawes, are you?"

"Fucked up my car," he said softly.

"Are you?"

"I'm going to go now, Patrick."

"What's the fallback plan?" I asked.

"I'm willing to forgive the suspension and even
the destruction to my loft, but the car's going to
take some time. I'll let you know what I decide."

"What do you have on them?" I said.

"What's that?"

"On the Dawes," I said. "What do you have on them, Scott?"

"I thought we agreed to leave each other be, Patrick. That's how I was hoping to end this call—knowing you and I will never see each other again."

"Under the stipulation that you leave the Dawes alone."

"Oh. Right."

"But you can't do that, can you, Scott?"

He let out a light, airy sigh. "You sound like you might be a half-decent chess player, Patrick. Am I right?"

"Nope. I just never got the hang of the game."

"Why not?"

"A friend of mine says I'm good with general tactics, but I suffer from an inability to see the whole board."

"Huh," Scott Pearse said. "That would have been my guess, too."

And he hung up.

I looked at Angie as I put the receiver back in the cradle.

"Patrick," she said with a slow shake of her head.

"Yeah?"

"Maybe you shouldn't answer the phone for a while."

We decided to leave Nelson on watch at Scott Pearse's place, and Angie and I drove over to the Dawes', watched their house from a half block down.

We sat on it into the night, well after their interior lights had gone out and their exterior security lights had gone on.

Back in my apartment, I lay back on the bed to wait for Angie to come out of the shower, and tried to push back the tug of sleep, the ache and muscle-tightening of too many days and nights spent sitting in cars or up on roofs, the niggle of dread in the back of my skull that told me I'd overlooked something, that Pearse was thinking a few moves ahead of me.

My eyelids drooped closed and I snapped them open, heard the shower running, imagined Angie's body under the spray. I decided to get up off the bed. Forget imagining what I could experience instead.

But my body didn't move, and my eyes drooped again, and the bed seemed to gently undulate under me as if I lay on a raft, floated on a glassy lake.

I never heard the shower shut off. I never heard Angie settle into bed beside me and turn off the light.

It's this way," my son says, and takes my hand, tugs at me as we walk out of the city. Clarence trots beside us, chugging, panting softly. It's just before sunrise, and the city is a deep, metallic blue. We step off a curb, my son's hand in mine, and the world turns red and fills with mist.

We are in the cranberry bog, and for a moment— aware that I'm dreaming—I know that it's impossible to step off a curb downtown and end up in Plymouth, but then I think, It's a dream, and these things happen in dreams. You don't have a son, yet he's here, tugging your hand, and Clarence is dead, yet he's not.

So I go with it. The morning fog is dense and white,

and Clarence barks from somewhere ahead of us, lost to the fog as my son and I step off the soft embankment and onto the wooden cross. Our footsteps echo off the planks as we walk through the thick white, and I can see the outline of the equipment shed gradually take on definition as each step leads us toward it.

Clarence barks again, but we've lost him in the fog.

My son says, "It should be loud."

"What?"

"It's big," he says. "Four plus two plus eight equals fourteen."

"It does."

Our steps should be bringing us closer to the equipment shed, but they don't. It sits twenty yards away in the mist, and we walk quickly, yet it remains in the distance.

"Fourteen is heavy," my son says. "It's loud. You'd hear it. Especially out here."

"Yeah."

"You'd hear it. So why didn't you?"

"I don't know."

My son hands me a map book. It's open to this place, a dot of a cranberry bog surrounded by forest on all sides except the one I'd driven up through.

I drop the map into the fog. I understand something, but then I forget immediately what it is.

My son says, "I like dental floss. I like the feel of it when you slide it between your teeth."

"That's good," I tell him as I feel a rumble on the planks ahead of us. It's moving fast through the fog, approaching. "You'll have fine teeth."

"He can't talk with his tongue cut out," he says.

"No," I agree. "That would be hard."

The rumbling grows louder. The shed is swallowed by the white fog. I can't see the planks under my feet. I can't see my feet.

"She said 'they.'"

"Who?"

He shakes his head at me. "Not 'him,' but 'they.'"

"Right. Sure."

"Mom's not in the shed, is she?"

"No. Mom's too smart for that."

I squint at the fog as it engulfs us. I want to see what's rumbling.

"Fourteen," *my son says, and when I look back down at him, Scott Pearse's head sits atop his small body. He leers up at me in the mist.* "Fourteen should be awfully loud, you dumb shit."

The rumble is close now, almost upon me, and I squint into the fog and see a dark shape as it vaults airborne, arms outstretched, streaking through the cotton-candy fog toward me.

"I'm smarter than you," *the Scott Pearse/my son thing says.*

And a snarling face bursts through the fog at a hundred miles an hour—snarling and smiling and gasping, teeth bared.

It's Karen Nichols's face, and then it's Angie's attached to Vanessa Moore's naked body, and then it's Siobhan with dead skin and dead eyes, and finally it's Clarence, and he hits me in the chest with all four paws and knocks me onto my back, and I should land on the planks of wood, but they're gone, and I fall into the fog, start to suffocate in it.

* * *

I sat up in bed.

"Go back to sleep," Angie mumbled, her face pressed into the pillow.

"Pearse didn't drive to the cranberry bog," I said.

"He didn't drive," she said into the pillow. " 'Kay."

"He walked," I said. "From his house."

"Still dreaming," she said.

"No. I'm up now."

She raised her head slightly off the pillow, looked up at me through blurry eyes. "Can it wait till morning?"

"Sure."

She plopped back to the pillow, closed her eyes.

"He has a house," I said softly to the night, "in Plymouth."

34

"We're driving to Plymouth," Angie said as we turned onto Route 3 at the Braintree split, "because your son spoke to you in a dream?"

"Well, he's not my son. I mean, in the dream he is, but in the dream Clarence is alive, and we both know Clarence is dead, and besides, you can't step off a curb downtown and end up in Plymouth, and even if you could—"

"Enough." She held up a hand. "I get it. So this kid who's your son but not your son, he babbled on about four plus two plus eight equaling fourteen and—"

"He didn't *babble*," I said.

"—this told you what again?"

"Four-two-eight," I said. "The Shelby engine."

"Oh, dear Jesus!" she shrieked. "We're back to the friggin' car? It's a *car*, Patrick. Do you get that part? It can't kiss you, cook for you, tuck you in, or hold your hand."

"Yes, Sister Angela the Grounded. I understand that. A four-two-eight engine was the most powerful engine of its time. It could blow anything else off the road, and—"

"I don't see what—"

"—*and* it makes one hell of a lot of noise when you turn it over. You think this Porsche rumbles? The four-two-eight sounds like a bomb by comparison."

She banged the heels of her palms off my dashboard. "So?"

"So," I said, "did you hear anything in the cranberry bog that night that sounded like an engine? A really goddamned big engine? Come on. I looked at the map before we followed Lovell. There was one way in—ours. The nearest access road on Pearse's side was two full miles through woods."

"So he walked it."

"In the dark?"

"Sure."

"Why?" I said. "He couldn't have guessed we'd be tailing Lovell at that point. Why not just be parked in the clearing where we were? And even if he *was* suspicious, there was an access road four hundred feet to the east. So why'd he go north?"

"Because he liked the walk? I don't know."

"Because he lives there."

She propped her bare feet up on the dash, slapped a palm over her forehead and eyes. "This is the dumbest hunch you've ever had."

"Sure," I said. "Bitch. That helps."

"And you've had some monumentally dumb hunches."

"Would you prefer wine or beer with your crow?"

She buried her head between her knees. "If you're wrong, screw the crow, you'll be eating shit till the millennium."

"Thank God it's approaching fast," I said.

A map took up most of the east wall in the Plymouth Tax Assessor's Office. The clerk behind the counter, far from being the dweeby, bespectacled, balding type one would expect to meet in a tax assessor's office, was tall, well built, blond, and judging by Angie's furtive glances at him, something of a male babe.

Himbos, I swear. There ought to be a law that keeps them from ever leaving the beach.

It took me a few minutes to zero in on the bog we'd followed Lovell to. Plymouth is absolutely rotten with cranberry bogs. Bad news if for some reason you don't dig the smell of cranberries. Good news if you cultivate them.

By the time I found the correct bog, I'd counted four separate times I'd caught Himbo the Tax Stud checking out the places where the frays of Angie's cutoff jeans exposed more than merely the backs of her upper thighs.

"Prick," I said under my breath.

"What?" Angie said.

"I said, 'Look.'" I pointed at the map. Due north of the center of the bog, about a quarter of a mile, I estimated, sat something marked PARCEL #865.

Angie turned from the map, spoke to Himbo. "We're interested in purchasing parcel eight-sixty-five. Could you tell us who owns it?"

Himbo gave her a brilliant smile of the whitest teeth I'd seen on a man this side of David Hasselhoff. Caps, I decided. Bet the bastard wears caps.

"Sure." His fingers zipped over his computer keyboard. "That was eight-sixty-five. Correct?"

"You got it," Angie said.

I peered up at the parcel. Nothing around it. No eight-six-six or eight-six-four. Nothing for at least twenty acres, maybe more.

"Spooky Land," Himbo said softly, his eyes on the computer screen.

"What's that?"

He looked up, startled to realize, I think, that he'd spoken aloud. "Oh, well . . ." He gave us an embarrassed smile. "When we were kids, we used to call that area Spooky Land. We'd dare each other to walk through it."

"Why?"

"It's a long story." He looked down at his keyboard. "See, no one's supposed to know . . ."

"But . . . ?" Angie leaned into the counter.

Himbo shrugged. "Hey, it's been over thirty years. Heck, I wasn't even born then."

"Sure," I said. "Thirty years."

He leaned into the counter, lowered his voice, and his eyes glinted like a born gossip about to dish some dirt. "Back in the fifties, the army supposedly kept a kinda research facility there. Nothing big, my parents said, just a few stories tall, but real hush-hush."

"What kind of research?"

"People." He stifled a nervous laugh with his fist. "Supposedly mental patients and the retarded. See, that's what scared us as kids—you know, that the ghosts running around Spooky Land were the ghosts of lunatics." He held up his hands, took one step back. "It could all have been a ghost story used by our parents to keep us away from the bog."

Angie gave him her most lascivious smile. "But you know different, don't you?"

His ivory skin flushed. "Well, I did do some checking once."

"And?"

"And there *was* a structure on that land until 1964, when it was either razed or burned, and the land *was* owned by the government until '95, when it sold at auction."

"To?" I asked.

He looked at the computer screen. "Bourne is the owner of record of parcel eight-sixty-five. Diane Bourne."

The Plymouth Library had an aerial map of the entire town. It was relatively current, too, the photo taken just a year ago on a cloudless day. We spread the map across a large table in the reference room, used a magnifying glass we'd bummed from the librarian, and after about ten minutes, we found the cranberry bog, then moved a tenth of an inch to the right across the map.

"There's nothing there," Angie said.

I moved the glass in micro-increments over the blurry patch of green and brown. I couldn't see anything that looked like a roof.

I raised the magnifying glass slightly, considered the whole area. "We got the right bog?"

Angie's finger appeared under the magnifying

glass. "Yeah. There's the access road. That looks like the equipment shed. There's Myles Standish forest. That's it. So much for your psychic dream."

"Diane Bourne owns this land," I said. "You telling me that means nothing?"

"I'm telling you," she said, "that there's no house in there."

"There's something," I said. "There has to be."

The bugs were angry. It was another hot, humid day, the heat steaming the surface of the bog, the cranberries smelling sharp and spoiled in the heat. The sun beat down like the flat of a razor blade, and the mosquitoes smelled our flesh and went nuts.

Angie slapped the backs of her legs and neck so much that pretty soon I couldn't tell which red welts were from the bloodsuckers and which were from her hands.

For a while I tried the Zen trick of ignoring them, willing my body to seem unattractive. After a few hundred bites or so, though, I thought, fuck Zen. Confucius never lived in ninety-eight percent humidity on a ninety-two-degree day. If he had, he'd have hacked off a few heads and told the emperor he was fresh out of peppy bromides until someone outfitted the palace with AC.

We crouched along the tree line on the eastern side of the bog and peered through binoculars. If Scott Pearse of the Special Forces and Panamanian brothel massacre did hide out back in these woods, I was pretty sure there'd be trip wires, defenses I couldn't see, Bouncing Betties waiting to make any possibility of Viagra in my future a moot point.

But all I could see from here were woods, parched brambles grown brittle with heat, withered birches and knotty pines, crumbling moss the texture of asbestos. It was one ugly plot of land, fetid and irritable in the heat.

I scoped everything within range of the binoculars Bubba had picked up from a navy SEAL, and even with all that power and clarity, I didn't see a house.

Angie slapped another mosquito. "I'm dying here."

"You see anything?"

"Nothing."

"Focus on the ground."

"Why?"

"It could be underground."

She slapped her flesh again. "Fine."

Another five minutes, and we'd lost blood from every pore and still found nothing but forest floor, pine needles, squirrels, and moss.

"It's in there," I said as we walked back across the bogs.

"I'm not staking it out," she said.

"Not asking you to."

We climbed in the Porsche, and I took one long look across the bog at the stand of trees.

"That's where he hides," I said.

"Then I'd say he's hiding pretty well," Angie said.

I started the car, dropped my elbow over the wheel, stared at the trees.

"He knows me."

"What?"

I glanced at the shed in the center of the cross.

"Pearse. He knows me. He's got my number."

"And you have his," Angie said.

"Not as well," I admitted.

The stand of trees seemed to whisper. They seemed to groan.

Stay away, they said. *Stay away.*

"He knew I'd find this place eventually. Maybe not as quickly as I did, but eventually."

"So?"

"So, he's gotta move. He's gotta move fast. Whatever he's planning, it's either about to happen, or it's already in motion."

She reached out and her palm found my lower back.

"Patrick, don't let him in your head. He wants that."

I stared at the trees, then the shed, then the bloody, misting bog.

"Too late," I said.

"This is a shitty Xerox," Bubba said. He looked down at the copy we'd made of the cranberry bog grid from the aerial map.

"It's the best we could do."

He shook his head. "Intel like this, my headstone would be in Beirut."

"How come you don't talk about that?" Vanessa sat on the bar stool behind him.

"Which?" he said absently, his eyes on the Xerox.

"Beirut."

He turned his huge head, smiled at her. "Lights went out, things went boom. I lost my sense of smell for three years. Now I've talked about it."

She backhanded his chest with her fingers. "Bastard."

He chuckled, looked back at the Xerox. "That's wrong."

"What?"

He lifted the magnifying glass we'd brought, held it over the grid. "That."

Angie and I looked over his shoulder through the glass. All I could see was a clump of green, a bush photographed from two thousand feet.

"It's a bush," I said.

"Ah, duh," Bubba said. "Look again."

We looked.

"What?" Angie said.

"It's too oval," he said. "Look at the top. It's smooth. It's like the top of this magnifying glass."

"So?" I offered.

"So bushes don't grow like that, ya fucking slug head. They're bushes, you know? That makes them, ah, bushy."

I looked at Angie. She looked at me. We both shook our heads.

Bubba thumped his index finger down on the bush in question. "See? It's curved perfectly, like the top of my fingernail. That's not nature. That's fucking man, dude." He dropped the magnifying glass. "You want my opinion, it's a satellite dish."

"A satellite dish."

He nodded, walked to the fridge. "Yup."

"For what purpose? To call in air strikes?"

He pulled a bottle of Finlandia from the freezer. "Doubtful. I'm guessing so's they can watch TV."

"Who?"

"The people living under that forest, stupid."

"Oh," I said.

He nudged Vanessa's shoulder with the vodka bottle. "And you thought he was smarter than me."

"Not smarter," Vanessa said. "More articulate."

Bubba took a swig of vodka, then belched. "Articulatedness is overrated."

Vanessa smiled. "You do make that case, baby. Trust me."

"She calls me 'baby.'" Bubba took another shot from the bottle, winked at me.

"You said this used to be some kind of army nuthouse? My guess is there's still a basement under those woods. A big one."

The phone by his fridge rang and he picked it up, cradled it between his ear and shoulder, and said nothing. After about a minute, he hung it back up.

"Nelson lost Pearse."

"What?"

He nodded.

"Where?" I said.

"Rowes Wharf," he said. "That hotel there? Pearse walks in, stands around on the pier. Nelson stays inside, you know, hanging back, being cool. Pearse waits till the last second, jumps on the airport ferry."

"So why didn't Nelson drive out to the airport, meet him on the other side?"

"He tried." Bubba tapped his watch. "It's five o'clock on a Friday, man. You ever try the tunnel then? Nelson gets over to Eastie, it's five-forty-five. The ferry docked at five-twenty. Your man is gone."

Angie buried her face in her hands, shook her head. "You were right, Patrick."

"How?"

"Whatever he's doing, he's doing it now."

Fifteen minutes later, after I'd called Carrie Dawe, we stood by Bubba's door as he carried a black duffel bag across the floor to us and dropped it by our feet.

Vanessa, so tiny in comparison to the mountain that was Bubba, stepped up close to him and put her hands on his chest.

"Is this where I'm supposed to say, 'Be careful'?"

He jerked a thumb back at us. "I dunno. Ask them."

She looked out from under his arm at us.

We both nodded.

"Be careful," she said.

Bubba pulled a .38 from his pocket, handed it to her. "The safety's off. Anyone comes through that door, shoot 'em. Like a bunch of times."

She looked up at the greasepaint on his forehead and under his eyelids, the smatterings on his cheekbones.

"Can I get a kiss?"

"In front of *them*?" Bubba shook his head.

Angie whacked my arm. "We're looking at the door."

We turned to the door, stared at the metal, the four locks, the reinforced steel bar.

Even now, I don't know if they kissed or not.

Christopher Dawe was where his wife had told us he'd be.

He backed his Bentley out of the Brimmer Street garage and we blocked him in from the front with Bubba's van and from the back with my Porsche.

"What the hell are you doing?" he said as he rolled down his window and I approached.

"There's a gym bag in your trunk," I said. "How much is in it?"

"Go to hell." His lower lip quivered.

"Doctor," I said and leaned my arm on the hood, looked down at him, "your wife told us you received a phone call from Pearse. How much is in the bag?"

"Step back from the car."

"Doctor," I said, "he'll kill you. Wherever it is you think you're going, whatever it is you think you're walking into, you won't walk back out."

"I will," he said, and his lower lip quivered even more and a fragmentation found his eyes.

"What does he have on you?" I said. "Doctor? Please. Help me end this."

He stared up at me, trying for defiance, but losing the battle. He clamped his teeth down on his lower lip, and his narrow face seemed to turn concave, and then tears rolled from his eyes and his shoulders shook.

"I can't . . . I can't . . ." His shoulders jerked up and down, up and down, like he was riding whitewater rapids and had lost his oar. He sucked in a high-pitched breath. "I can't take another *second* of this." His mouth formed a plaintive O and his cheeks turned to rubber, formed riverbeds for the tears.

I placed my hand on his shoulder. "You don't have to. Give me the weight, Doctor. I'll carry it."

He closed his eyes tight and shook his head repeatedly and the tears stained his suit like white rain.

I knelt by the door. "Doctor," I said softly, "she's watching."

"Who?" It came out strangled, but loud.

"Karen," I said. "I believe that. Look in my face."

His head turned tightly, as if pushed to its left, and he opened his bleary eyes, looked into my own.

"She's watching. I want to do right by her."

"You barely knew her."

I held his eyes. "I barely know anyone."

His eyes widened, then immediately closed again, and he tightened them to slits, the tears sprouting out hot and barren.

"Wesley," he said.

"What about him? Doctor? What about him?"

He slapped the seat console several times. He slapped the dashboard. He slapped the wheel. He reached into the inside pocket of his suit jacket and removed a plastic bag. It was wrapped up tight so that it was the shape of a cigar when he pulled it out, but then he held it aloft, and the bag unfurled, and I saw what was trapped inside and I felt the hissing of the night's heat on the back of my skull.

A finger.

"It's his," Christopher Dawe said. "Wesley's. He sent it to me this afternoon. He said . . . he said . . . he said unless I delivered the money to a rest stop on Route Three, he'd send me a testicle next."

"Which rest stop?"

"Just before the Marshfield exit, heading south."

I glanced at the bag. "How do you know it's your son's?"

He screamed, "He's my son!"

I lowered my head for a moment, swallowed. "Yes, sir, but how are you sure?"

He shoved the bag in my face. "See? See the scar over the knuckle?"

I looked. It was faint but unmistakable. It perforated the lines over the knuckle like a small asterisk.

"See it?"

"Yes."

"It's the imprint of a Phillips-head screw. Wesley fell in my workshop when he was young. He embedded the screw head into his knuckle, shattered the bone." He hit my face with the bag. "My son's finger, Mr. Kenzie!"

I didn't lean back from the slap of the bag. I held his wild eyes, willed mine to be calm, flat.

After a while, he removed the bag, rolled it back up very carefully, and placed it back inside his suit pocket. He sniffed, wiped at the wetness on his face. He stared out the windshield at Bubba's van.

"I want to die," he said.

"That's what he wants you to feel," I said.

"Then he's succeeded."

"Why not call in the police?" I said, and he began to violently shake his head. "Doctor? Why not? You're willing to come clean on what you did with Naomi when she was a baby. We know who's behind this now. We can nail him."

"My son," he said, still shaking his head.

"Could already be dead," I said.

"He's all I have. If I lose him because I called the

police, I will die, Mr. Kenzie. Nothing will hold me back."

The first drops of rain found my head as I crouched by the car door and looked in at Christopher Dawe. It wasn't a refreshing rain, though. It was warm as sweat and oily with humidity. It felt dirty in my hair.

"Let me stop him," I said. "Give me the bag in the trunk, and I'll bring your son home alive."

He leaned one arm over the driver's wheel, turned his head to me. "Why should I trust you with five hundred thousand dollars?"

"Five hundred thousand?" I said. "That's all he asked for?"

He nodded. "It's all I could lay my hands on with such short notice."

"Doesn't that tell you something?" I asked. "The short notice, his willingness to settle for far less than he originally asked? He's in a rush, Doctor. He's burning his bridges and cutting his losses. You go to that rest stop, you'll never see your house, your office, the inside of this car, again. And Wesley will die, too."

He dropped his head back into the seat, stared up at the ceiling.

The rain fell harder, but not in drops so much as strips, sheer ropes of warm water that bled down the inside of my shirt.

"Trust me," I said.

"Why?" His eyes remained on the ceiling.

"Because . . ." I wiped the rain from my eyes.

He turned his head. "Because why, Mr. Kenzie?"

"Because you've paid for your sins," I said.

"Excuse me?"

I blinked at the rain and nodded. "You've paid, Doctor. You did a terrible thing, but then she fell through the ice, and first your son and now Pearse have tortured you for ten years. I don't know if that's enough justice for God, but it's enough for me. You've done your time. You've had your hell."

He groaned. He ground the back of his head into the seat rest. He watched the rain cascade down his windshield.

"It's never enough. It's never going to end. The pain."

"No," I said. "But he will. Pearse will."

"What?"

"End, Doctor."

He stared at me for a long time.

Then he nodded. He opened his glove box and pressed a button and the trunk popped open.

"Take the bag," he said. "Pay the debt. Do whatever you have to do. But bring my son home, won't you?"

"Sure."

I started to rise and he put a hand on my arm.

I bent back into the window.

"I was wrong."

"About what?"

"Karen," he said.

"In what way?"

"She wasn't weak. She was good."

"Yeah, she was."

"That might be why she died."

I didn't say anything.

"Maybe this is how God punishes the bad," he said.

"How's that, Doctor?"

He leaned his head back and closed his eyes. "He lets us live."

35

Christopher Dawe drove home to his wife with instructions to pack a bag and check into the Four Seasons, where I'd reach him when this was over.

"Whatever you do," I said before he drove off, "don't answer either your cell phone, your pager, or your home phone."

"I don't know if—"

I held out my hand. "Give me them."

"What?"

"Your cell phone and your pager. Now."

"I'm a surgeon. I—"

"I don't care. This is your son's life, not a stranger's. Your phone and pager, Doctor."

He didn't like it, but he handed them over, and we watched him drive away.

"The rest stop's bad," Bubba said once I climbed in his van. "There's no way to guess at his defenses. I like Plymouth."

"But the place in Plymouth's probably a lot more heavily fortified," Angie said.

He nodded. "Predictably, though. I know where I'd put the trip wires if I was in for the long haul.

The rest stop, though?" He shook his head. "I can't deal with him if he's improvising. It's too risky."

"So we go to Plymouth," I said.

"Back to the bog," Angie said.

"Back to the bog."

Christopher Dawe's cell phone rang just as we pulled off the expressway into Plymouth. I held it to my ear as Bubba's taillights flashed red at the stop sign ahead, palmed the shift into neutral.

"You're late, Doctor."

"Scottie!" I said.

Silence.

I cradled the phone between my shoulder and ear, shifted up to first, and turned right behind Bubba.

"Patrick," Scott Pearse said eventually.

"I'm kind of like bronchitis, don't you think, Scott? Every time you're sure you're through with me, I come back."

"That's a good one, Pat. Tell it to the doctor when his son's aorta shows up in the mail. I'm sure he'll have a good laugh."

"I got your money, Scott. You want it?"

"You have my money."

"Yup."

Bubba turned off the main drag onto the access road that cut through the edge of the Myles Standish forest and would eventually lead us to the bog.

"What sort of hoops do I have to jump through for it, Pat?"

"Call me Pat one more time, Scottie, and I'll fucking burn it."

"Okay, Patrick. What do I need to do?"

"Give me your cell phone number."

He gave it to me and I repeated it to Angie, who wrote it down on the pad held by a suction cup to my glove box.

"Nothing will happen tonight, Scott, so go home."

"Wait."

"And if you try to contact the Dawes, you'll never see a dime of this money. We clear?"

"Yeah, but—"

I hung up.

Angie watched Bubba's taillights turn off onto the smaller road.

"How do you know he won't go back to Congress Street?"

"Because if Wesley's stashed anywhere, he's stashed here. Pearse is feeling his control slip. He'll come back here to see his trump card, to feel that control again."

"Wow," she said. "You almost sound like you believe that."

"Ain't got much," I said, "but I got hope."

We drove past the clearing and down another four hundred yards, buried our cars in the trees, and walked back up the access road.

For the first time in at least ten years, Bubba wasn't wearing his trench coat. He wore all black. Black jeans, black combat boots, a black long-sleeved T-shirt, black gloves, and a black knit hat over his head. We had, per his command, stopped at my apartment on the way out to intercept Christopher Dawe and grabbed black clothes as well, and we donned them before we left the cars behind in the trees.

As we walked back up the road, Bubba said, "Once we locate the house, I walk point. Point is very simple. You stay ten paces behind me." He looked back at us and held up a finger. "*Exactly* behind me. Where I step, you step. If I blow up or trip a wire, you run back the same way you came in. You don't fucking think about carrying me out. Clear?"

This was not a Bubba I'd ever seen before. All traces of psychosis seemed to have vanished. Along with the disappearance of the loose-cannon aspect, his voice had changed, deepened slightly, and the aura of otherness and loneliness that usually hovered around him had disappeared, given way to a total confidence and ease with his surroundings.

He was, I realized, home. He was as in his element as he ever could be. He was a warrior, and he'd been called to battle, and he knew he was born to it.

As we followed him up the road, I saw what men in Beirut must have seen—that if it came to battle, no matter who your commanding officer was, it was Bubba you'd follow, Bubba you'd listen to, Bubba you'd depend on to lead you through the fire and back to safety.

He was a born sergeant; next to him, John Wayne was a pussy.

He unslung the duffel bag from his back and brought it around under his arm. He unzipped it as he walked, pulled an M-16 out, and looked back at us.

"You sure you don't want one of these?"

Both of us shook our heads. An M-16. I'd probably fire it once, break my shoulder.

"Pistols are fine," I said.

"You got extra clips?"

I nodded. "Four."

He looked at Angie. "Speed-loaders?"

She nodded. "Three."

Angie looked at me. She swallowed. I knew how she felt. My mouth was getting kind of dry, too.

We crossed the planks and passed the pump shed.

Bubba said, "We find this house, and get inside? Anything moves, shoot it. Don't question. If it's not chained down, it's not a hostage. If it's not a hostage, it ain't friendly. Clear?"

"Uh, yeah," I said.

"Ange?" He looked back at her.

"Yeah. Clear."

Bubba paused and stared at Angie, her pale face and large eyes.

"You up for this?" he asked her softly.

She nodded several times.

"Because—"

"Don't be a sexist, Bubba. This isn't hand-to-hand combat. All I have to do is point and shoot, and I'm a better shot than either of you guys."

Bubba looked at me. "You, on the other hand . . ."

"You're right," I said. "I'll go back home."

He smiled. Angie smiled. I smiled. In the still of the bog and the dark of night, I had the feeling it was the last time any of us would smile for a while.

"All right," Bubba said. "It's all three of us, then. Just remember, the only sin in combat is hesitation. So don't fucking hesitate."

We stopped at the tree line and Bubba unslung the bag from his shoulder and lay it softly on the ground. He opened it and removed three square objects with head straps tied to the back and lenses protruding from the front. He handed two of them to us.

"Put 'em on."

We did, and the world turned green. The dark bushes and trees were the color of mint, the moss was emerald, the air was a light kelly hue.

"Take your time," Bubba said. "Get used to it."

He removed a huge pair of infrared binoculars and raised them to his eyes, panned across the woods in quarter-inch increments.

The green felt assaultive, nauseating. My .45 felt like a hot poker against the small of my back. The drought in my mouth had worked its way down my throat, seemed to be closing off my respiratory passages. And, quite honestly, with the bulky infrared glasses attached to my face, I also felt really silly. I felt like a Power Ranger.

"Got it," Bubba said.

"What?"

"Follow my finger."

He raised his arm and pointed and I sighted down the tip and followed the seaweed world through bushes and brambles and around trees until I saw the windows.

There were two of them. They suddenly stared back at us from the forest floor like oblong periscopes. They were only a foot and a half tall, but seeing them appear out of the green it was nearly impossible to imagine how we'd missed them.

"No way you could have seen them in daylight," Bubba said, "unless you caught a reflection off the panes. Everything but the glass is painted green, even the trim."

"Well, thanks for—"

He silenced me with a raised finger and cocked his head. About thirty seconds later, I heard it, too, a car engine and tires rolling up the access road toward us. The tires squished the soft earth in the clearing to the north, and Bubba whacked our shoulders and picked up his duffel bag, walked in a crouch to our left along the tree line. We followed as the car door opened and closed, and then shoes crunched down the path to the bog embankment.

Bubba disappeared into the trees at the far edge, and we ducked back in there with him.

A green Scott Pearse stepped out onto the cross and his footsteps banged hard off the wood as he half walked, half trotted past the equipment shed and then over to our side. He seemed about to burst into the woods when he stopped on the embankment and went very still.

His head swiveled slowly in our direction, and for one long moment, he seemed to look directly into my eyes. He bent at the waist and squinted. He held out his arms as if to silence the mosquitoes and mist along the bog, the distant slapping of the fruit in the water. He closed his eyes and listened.

After what felt like a month or so, he opened his eyes and shook his head. He parted the branches in front of him and walked into the woods.

I turned my head, but Bubba wasn't beside us anymore, and I'd never heard him move. He was about ten yards ahead, crouched, hands resting on his knees as he watched Scott Pearse make his way through the woods.

I turned my head back toward Pearse, watched him stop about ten yards before the two windows and reach down to the forest floor. He raised his arm and a bulkhead door came up with it. He bent, lowered himself, and closed the door over his head.

Bubba was suddenly back beside us again.

"We don't know if he's got motion detectors or trip wires he turns on from inside, but I figure we got maybe a minute. Follow me. *Exactly.*"

He moved out onto the embankment again like the world's swiftest, bulkiest jungle cat, Angie followed ten steps behind him, and I followed five steps behind her.

Bubba turned sharply into the trees, and we went in behind him. He never showed a stutter-step's worth of hesitation as he raced silently across the same terrain Scott Pearse had trod.

He reached the door in the forest floor and waved quickly at us.

We reached him and I suddenly felt the strongest desire in the world to slow down, to backtrack, to put the brakes on for a moment. This was all happening faster than I would have imagined. Blindingly fast. Too fast to breathe.

"It moves, shoot," Bubba whispered, and flicked the M-16's selector switch forward to full auto. "Keep your goggles on until we know there's light inside. If there is, don't waste time taking them off your head. Drop them down your face, let 'em hang from your neck. Ready?"

I said, "Ah . . ."

"One-two-three," Bubba said.

"Jesus," Angie said.

"No bullshit," Bubba whispered harshly. "We're in or out. Right now. No time."

I took my .45 from the holster at the small of my back, thumbed off the safety. I wiped my palm on my jeans.

"In," Angie said.

"In," I said.

"We get separated," Bubba said, "I'll see you back in the world."

He grinned and reached for the door handle.

"I'm so happy," he whispered.

I gave Angie a quick, bewildered glance, and she tightened her hands on her .38 to quell her shakes, and Bubba threw back the door.

A white stone staircase greeted us, dropping steeply fifteen steps before it ended at a steel door.

Bubba knelt on the top of the staircase, aimed his M-16, and fired several rounds into the upper left and lower left corners of the door. The bullets hammered the steel and erupted into yellow sparks. The noise was deafening.

The windows ahead of us shattered, and I saw muzzles pointing our way. We ducked low, and Bubba jumped to the bottom of the stairs and kicked the door off its shattered hinges.

We dropped in after him as the rifles fired from the windows, and then we were through the door and facing a cement hallway about thirty yards long with several doors opening off on the right and left.

It was bathed in light, and I dropped the infrared

glasses down my face, let them hang around my throat. Angie did the same, and we stood there, tense, terrified, blinking at the harsh white light.

A small woman stepped out of a doorway about ten yards up on our right. I had time to see that she was thin and brunette and pointing a .38 before Bubba depressed the trigger of his M-16 and her chest disappeared in a puff of red.

The .38 flew out of her hand and into the corridor, and she slumped down the doorway, dead before she hit the floor.

"Move," Bubba said.

He kicked in the door closest to him, and we were met with an empty study. Bubba rolled in a canister of tear gas anyway, then shut the door behind him.

We stepped over to the doorway where the woman's corpse sat. It was a bedroom, small and empty as well.

Bubba toed the woman's corpse. "Recognize her?"

I shook my head, but Angie nodded. "She was the woman in the pictures with David Wetterau."

I took another look. Her head was upside down and askew, her eyes rolled back and blank, blood splattering her chin, but Angie was right.

Bubba stepped in front of the door across from us. He kicked it in and was about to fire when I swung up into his rifle with my arm.

A pale, balding man sat in a metal chair. His left wrist was bound tightly to the arm of the chair with thick yellow rope, and a blue racquetball served as a gag in the man's mouth. His right wrist was free, strands of the yellow rope dangling from underneath it as if he'd managed to somehow extricate his wrist before we got there. He was about my age, and his right index finger was missing. A roll of electrical tape lay at his feet, but his legs were untied for some reason.

"Wesley," I said.

He nodded, his eyes wild and confused and terrified.

"Let's get him out of here," I said.

"No," Bubba said. "This is an uncontained situation. We don't move him until it's contained."

I looked back at the stairwell. Just ten yards back. "But—"

"We're exposed," he said. "Don't you question my fucking orders."

Wesley kicked at the floor with his heels, desperate, shaking his head, begging me with his eyes to untie him and pull him out of there.

"Shit," I said.

Bubba turned to look at the next door, up the hall a few feet and on our right.

He said, "Okay. We're going to do this by the numbers. Patrick, I want you to—"

The door at the end of the hall opened and all three of us spun toward it. Diane Bourne seemed to levitate into the hallway with her hands raised and her feet off the ground. Scott Pearse stood behind her, one arm wrapped around her waist and the other cocked behind her, pressing a gun to the back of her head.

"Weapons on the floor," Pearse called, "or she dies."

"So fucking what?" Bubba said, and settled the

stock of his M-16 into his shoulder, sighted down the barrel.

Diane Bourne's body was wracked with tremors. "Please, please, please."

"Put your weapons on the deck!" Pearse shouted.

"Pearse," I said, "give it up. You're boxed in. This is over."

"This is not a negotiation," he yelled.

"You're fucking A, it ain't. This is bullshit," Bubba said. "I'm going to shoot through her now, Pearse. Okay?"

"Wait!" Pearse's voice sounded as shaky as Diane Bourne's body.

"Ah, no," Bubba said.

But then Pearse's gun dropped from the back of Diane Bourne's head, and Bubba paused, and Pearse's arm swung again and was suddenly extended over Diane Bourne's shoulder and the muzzle centered on Angie's forehead.

"Move an inch, Miss Gennaro, and your skull disappears."

Pearse's voice was not even remotely shaky anymore. His gun hand remained steady as he came down the hallway toward us, his arm still wrapped around Diane Bourne's waist, her feet lifted off the ground as he used her as a body shield.

Angie was frozen, her .38 hanging down by her side, her eyes on the hole at the end of Pearse's pistol.

"Anyone doubt I'll do it?"

Bubba said, "Fuck," very softly.

"Weapons on the deck, people. Right now."

Angie dropped hers. I dropped mine. Bubba didn't

even move. He held his bead on Pearse as Pearse closed to within twenty feet of us.

"Rogowski," Pearse said, "relinquish your weapon."

"Fuck no, Pearse."

Sweat darkened the back of Bubba's hair, but the rifle never wavered.

"Oh," Pearse said. "Okay."

And he fired.

I slammed Angie's shoulder with my own, and then a hot spear of dry ice tore through my chest, just below the shoulder, and I bounced into the cement wall and landed on my knees in the middle of the hallway.

Pearse fired again, but his shot banged off the wall behind me.

Bubba's rifle unloaded, and Diane Bourne disappeared in a haze of red, her body jerking like she'd been electrified.

Angie, on her stomach, crawled for her .38, and I felt the corridor swerve, and my back hit the floor.

Bubba spun hard into the doorjamb and dropped his M-16, grabbed his hip.

I tried to get off the floor, but I couldn't.

Bubba's hand shot out and grabbed Angie by the hair and yanked her into the room with Wesley Dawe. I could hear bullets clanging off the cement around me, but I couldn't raise my head to see where they were coming from.

I turned my head to the left, tilted my eyes up.

Bubba stood in the doorway to Wesley's room and his eyes grew as soft and sad as I'd ever seen them as he looked down at me.

And then he slammed the door closed between us.

The firing stopped. The hallway was still except for the sound of footsteps approaching.

Scott Pearse stood over me and smiled. He ejected the clip from his nine-millimeter and it dropped on the floor beside my head. He slammed another home, and racked one into the chamber. His clothes, neck, and face were saturated with Diane Bourne's blood. He waved at me.

"You got a hole in your chest, Pat. Is that funny to you? 'Cause it's funny to me."

I tried to speak, but all that left my mouth was warm liquid.

"Shit," Scott Pearse said, "don't fucking die on me yet. I want you to see me kill your friends."

He squatted down beside me. "They left all their weapons out here. And there's no way out of that room." He patted my cheek. "Man, you are fast. I was hoping you'd see your little love-bitch take a bullet to the head, but you moved so quick."

My eyes rolled away from him, not because I'd intended them to, but because they suddenly seemed to be on ball bearings, sliding through grease, beyond my control.

Scott Pearse turned my chin and slapped my temple, and the ball bearings jerked my eyes back to face him.

"Don't die yet, dude. I need to know where my money is."

I shook my head slightly. I felt a warm, jagged prickling on the left side of my chest, just below the collarbone. It was very hot, actually, and growing hotter. It was starting to burn.

"You like a joke, right, Pat?" He patted my cheek

again. "You'll love this. You're going to die here, and even as you do, I want you to understand something—you never, even now, saw the whole board. That, I find hilarious." He chuckled. "The money's in your car, which I'm sure is parked close by. I'll find it."

"No," I managed, though I'm not sure any sound came out.

"Yes," he said. "You were fun for a while there, Pat, but now I'm bored. Okay. Gotta go kill your bitch and that big freak. Be right back."

He stood and turned toward the door, and I stretched out a numb hand along the floor as the pain blew up in my chest.

Scott Pearse laughed. "The guns are a good five feet past your legs, Pat. But you keep trying."

I gnashed my teeth together and screamed as I raised my head and back off the floor and managed to sit up, and the blood poured out of the hole in my chest and saturated my waist.

Pearse cocked his head at me, turned his gun in my direction. "Way to take it for the team, Pat. Bravo."

I stared at him, willed him to pull the trigger.

"Okay," he said softly, and pulled back on the hammer. "We'll end you now."

The door behind him flung open, and Pearse turned, got off one round that blew a chunk out of Bubba's thigh.

But Bubba never stopped. He covered Pearse's gun hand with his own and clamped his other arm around Pearse's chest from behind.

Pearse let loose a guttural scream and tried to twist his body out of Bubba's grasp, but Bubba squeezed tighter, and Pearse began to gasp, began to make high-pitched keening yelps, as he saw his gun hand move against his will up toward the side of his head.

He tried to twist his head away, but Bubba reared back and butted his massive forehead into the back of Pearse's head so hard it sounded like a pool ball exploding.

Pearse's eyes spun from the shock of impact.

"No," he yelped. "No, no, no, no."

Bubba grunted with the effort, blood pouring down his leg as Angie scrambled out into the hallway on all fours and grabbed her .38.

She rose to one knee, pulled back on the hammer, and pointed it at Pearse's chest.

"Don't you fucking do it, Ange!" Bubba screamed.

Angie froze, finger curled around the trigger.

"You're mine, Scott," Bubba whispered hoarsely in Pearse's ear. "You are all mine, sweetie."

"Please," Pearse begged. "Wait! No! Don't! Wait! Please!"

Bubba grunted again and slammed the muzzle of Pearse's gun into Pearse's temple, shoved his finger over Pearse's and around the trigger.

"No!"

Bubba said, "Feeling depressed, isolated, possibly suicidal?"

"Don't!" Pearse batted at Bubba's head with his free hand.

"Well, call a hot line, but don't call me, Pearse, 'cause I don't fucking care."

Bubba shoved his knee into Pearse's spine, lifted his feet off the floor.

"Please!" Pearse kicked at the air, tears streaming down his cheeks.

"Yeah, yeah, sure, sure," Bubba said.

"Oh, God!"

"Hey, asshole? Say hi to the fucking dog for me, will you?" Bubba said, and then he blew Scott Pearse's brains out the other side of his head.

36

I was in the hospital for five weeks. The bullet had entered my upper left chest just below the collarbone and exited through my back, and I'd lost three and a half pints of blood before the EMTs reached the house. I was comatose for four days, and I woke to tubes in my chest, tubes in my neck, tubes in my arm, and tubes in my nostrils, hooked up to a respirator, so thirsty I would have signed over the contents of my savings account for a single ice cube.

The Dawes apparently had some pull downtown, because a month after we'd rescued their son, the illegal weapons charges against Bubba simply vanished. Sure, the DA's office seemed to say, you walked into the Plymouth bunker with enough illegal firepower to invade a country, but you brought a rich kid out alive. So no harm, no foul. I'm sure the DA would have adopted a different attitude had he known Pearse's original extortion leverage had stemmed from evidence linking the Dawes to a baby switch, but Pearse wasn't around to discuss it, and the rest of us who knew the secret declined to mention it.

Wesley Dawe came to visit. He held my hand and thanked me with tears in his eyes, and he told me the story of how he'd met Pearse through Diane Bourne, who in addition to being his therapist had also been his lover. She, and eventually Pearse, had controlled his fragile mind through manipulation, mental and sexual power games, and erratic withholding and dispensing of his medication. It had been his own idea, he admitted, to blackmail his father, but Diane Bourne and Pearse had taken the idea several steps further, ultimately turning it lethal when they came to thinking of the Dawes' fortune as their own.

In mid-'98, they'd made him their hostage, kept him tied to the chair or his bed, exercised him at gunpoint.

I hadn't regained my voice yet. It had disappeared when the bullet nicked off a microscopic shard of collarbone and sent that shard careening into my left lung, collapsing it. When I did try to speak those first few weeks, all that came out was a high-pitched wheeze, like a kettle, or Donald Duck losing his temper.

But voice or no voice, I doubt I would have said much to Wesley Dawe. He struck me as sad and weak, and I couldn't shake the image of a little petulant boy who'd stirred up all this trouble—whether intentionally or not—simply because he needed to throw a snit. His stepsister was dead, and I couldn't blame him, exactly, but I didn't feel much desire to forgive him either.

When he visited my room a second time, I pretended to be asleep, and he slipped a check from his father under my pillow and said, "Thank you. You saved me," in a whisper before leaving the room.

Since Bubba and I were both stuck in Mass General for a while, we ended up beginning our physical therapy together, my arm withered and his right hip replaced by a metal one.

It's an odd sensation to owe your life to another. It humbles you and makes you feel guilty and weak and your gratitude is sometimes so immense, it feels like an anvil tied to your heart.

"It's like Beirut," Bubba said one afternoon in hydrotherapy. "What's done is done. Talking about it won't do any good."

"Maybe not."

"Shit, dude, you'd have done the same for me."

And sitting there, I felt a calming certainty in my chest when I realized he was probably right, though I'm not sure that with one bullet in my hip and another in my thigh I'd have been capable of what he pulled off against a guy like Scott Pearse.

"You did it for Ange," he said. "You'd do it for me."

He nodded to himself.

I said, "Okay. You're right. I won't thank you anymore."

"You won't talk about it anymore either."

"Cool."

He nodded. "Cool." He looked around the collection of metal tubs. Mine was beside his, and there were six or seven other people in the room, all soaking in hot, bubbling water. "Know what would be really cool?" he asked.

I shook my head.

"Some weed. Right about now?" He raised his eyebrows. "Wouldn't it, though?"

"Sure."

He nudged the middle-aged teacher in the tub beside his. "Know where we can score some pot, sister?"

The woman Bubba had shot when we'd first entered the bunker was identified as Catherine Larve, a onetime model from Kansas City who'd specialized in print ads for midwestern department stores during the late eighties and early nineties. She didn't have a criminal record and very little else was known about her during the years since she'd left Kansas City with the person neighbors had assumed was her boyfriend—a handsome, blond man who drove a '68 Shelby Mustang.

Bubba was released from the hospital ten days before I was. Vanessa picked him up, and even before they went back to his warehouse, they drove over to the animal shelter and got themselves a dog.

Those last ten days in the hospital were the worst. Summer died and autumn encroached outside my window, and all I could do was lie there and listen to the sounds of seasons trading places in the voices of people ten stories below. And I'd be left to wonder how Karen Nichols would have sounded in the newly minted briskness if she'd held on long enough for the heat to end and a leaf to fall.

I took the stairs to my apartment slowly, one arm around Angie, the other squeezing a racquetball in my hand, working the muscles in my ever-so-gradually healing arm.

The entire left side of my body still felt weak, depleted, as if somehow the blood on that side wasn't as thick, and nights sometimes, it felt cold over there.

"We're home," Angie said when we reached the landing.

"Home?" I said. "You mean my home or our home?"

"Ours," she said.

She opened the door before us, and I stared down my hallway, which fairly reeked of recently applied oil soap. I felt the warmth of Angie's flesh on my good palm. I saw my ratty old La-Z-Boy waiting for me in the living room. And I knew that unless Angie had drunk them, there would be two cold Beck's waiting in the fridge.

Living is not bad, I decided. The good lies in the small details. The furniture you've molded to your shape. A cold beer on a hot day. A perfect strawberry. Her lips.

"Home," I said.

It was midautumn before I could reach both hands above my head and stretch, and one afternoon, I went looking for my torn, frayed, had-it-since-high-school, favorite sweatshirt, which I'd tossed with my good hand up onto the top shelf of the bedroom closet, where it hid in the darkness of a shadow thrown by the top of the door frame. I hid it because Angie hated it, said it made me look like a bum, and I was sure she had homicidal designs on it. I've learned with women never to take their threats against your clothing too lightly.

My hand sank into the faded cotton, and I sighed happily as I pulled it out and several objects fell onto my head along with it.

One was a cassette tape I'd thought I'd lost, a bootleg of Muddy Waters playing live with Mick Jagger and the Red Devils. Another was a book Angie had loaned me, which I'd given up on after fifty pages and stuffed back there in hopes she'd forget it. The third item was a roll of electrical tape I'd tossed up there last summer when I slapped some around a fraying cord and was too lazy to walk it back to my toolbox.

I picked up the cassette, tossed the book back into the darkness, and reached for the electrical tape.

But I never touched it. Instead, I sat back on the floor and stared at it.

And, finally, I saw the whole board.

37

"Mr. Kenzie," Wesley said when I found him down by the pond at the back of his father's property, "what a pleasure to see you."

"Did you push her?" I asked.

"What? Who?"

"Naomi," I said.

He jerked his head back, gave me a confused smile. "What are you talking about?"

"She chased a ball out onto this pond," I said. "That was the story, right? But how'd the ball get out there? Did you throw it, Wes?"

He gave me a small, strange smile, pained, I think, lonely. He turned his head and looked out at the pond. His gaze grew distant. He stuck his hands in his pockets and leaned back slightly, his shoulders tightening, thin body rippling with a slow shudder.

"Naomi threw the ball," he said softly. "I don't know why. I'd walked on ahead." He tilted his head to the right. "Up that way. Lost in thought, I suppose, though I can't remember what I was thinking about." He shrugged. "I walked on, and my sister threw the ball and it got ahead of her. Maybe it took an odd bounce off a rock. Maybe she threw it out onto the ice to see what would happen. It doesn't really matter why. The ball went out on the ice, and she followed it. I heard her footsteps on the ice, all of a sudden, as if someone had, on a whim, flicked on a sound track. One moment I was locked in my fucked-up head as usual, the next I could hear a squirrel pawing the frozen grass twenty yards away. I could hear snow melt. I could hear Naomi's feet on the ice. And I turned my head in time to see the ice break under her. It was so *quiet*, that sound." He turned back to me, cocked an eyebrow. "You'd think not, wouldn't you? But it sounded as if you were crumpling tinfoil in your hand. And she," he smiled, "she had this look on her face of utter *joy*. What a new experience this was going to be! She never made a noise. Didn't cry out. She just dropped. And she was gone."

He shrugged again, then picked a rock up off the ground and threw it high above the pond. I watched it plummet through the hard autumn air and then make a tiny splash in the center of the pond.

"So, no," he said, "I didn't kill my sister, Mr. Kenzie. I simply failed to keep adequate watch on her." He placed his hands back in his pockets and leaned back on his heels, gave me another flash of that pained smile.

"But they blamed you," I said, and looked back across the lawn to the porch where Christopher and Carrie Dawe sat with their afternoon tea and sections of the Sunday paper. "Didn't they, Wesley?"

He pursed his lips, nodded at his shoes. "Oh, sure. Sure."

He turned to his right and we began to walk slowly along the pond in the midafternoon glow of a late October Sunday. His steps seemed uncertain, and then I realized it was more an awkwardness in the roll of his right hip. I looked at his shoes, saw that the sole of the right was two inches thicker than that of the left, and I remembered Christopher Dawe telling us Wesley had been born with one leg shorter than the other.

"Bet it didn't feel good," I said.

"What's that?"

"Being blamed for your baby stepsister's death when you hadn't truly been responsible for it."

He kept his head down, but a wry smile curled up his weak lips. "You have an odd gift for understating the obvious, Mr. Kenzie."

"We all need our talents, Wes."

"When I was thirteen," he said, "I vomited up a pint of blood. A pint. Nothing wrong with me. It was simply 'nerves.' At fifteen, I had a peptic ulcer. When I was eighteen, I was diagnosed with manic depression and low-grade schizophrenia. It embarrassed my father. Humiliated him. He was sure if he just toughened me up—tortured me enough with his mental games and constant put-downs—I'd one day wake up made of firmer stuff." He chuckled softly. "Fathers. Did you have a positive relationship with yours?"

"Not by a long shot, Wesley."

"Forced you to live up to his expectations, maybe?

Called you 'useless' so many times you started to believe it?"

"He held me down and burned me with an iron."

Wesley stopped in the trees, looked at me. "You're serious?"

I nodded. "He also hospitalized me twice and re-minded me on a weekly basis that I'd never amount to shit. He was as close to evil as I've ever come, Wesley."

"My God."

"I didn't drive my sister to her death to get back at him, though."

"What?" He threw his head back, chuckled. "Come on now."

"Here's what I think happened." I snapped a twig off the branch in front of me, tapped it against my outer thigh as we walked along the tip of the pond, then started back down the other side. "I think your father blamed you for Naomi's death and you—some poor fucking basket case back then, I'm guessing—you were this close to cracking up when you stum-bled on the medical records, discovered Naomi had been switched for another child. And for the first time in your life, you had a way to play payback with your father."

He nodded. He glanced down at his right hand, at the small nub of flesh that was all that remained of his index finger, and then he dropped the hand by his side. "Guilty as charged. But you've known that for months. I don't see how you—"

"I think ten years ago?" I said. "You were just a sad, fucked-up freak with a medicine cabinet full of pills and a scrambled, genius brain. And you came up with this easy ploy to get a good allowance out of Daddy, and for a while that was good enough. But then Pearse came along."

He gave me that studious nod of his, half contemplative, half contemptous. "Maybe. And I fell under his—"

"Bullshit. He fell under *your* spell, Wes. You were behind this the whole time," I said. "Behind Pearse, behind Diane Bourne, behind Karen's death—"

"Whoa, whoa. Hold up." He held out his hands.

"You killed Siobhan. It had to be you. Pearse was accounted for and neither of the women in that house could have lifted her."

"Siobhan?" He shook his head. "Siobhan who?"

"You knew we'd come into that house sooner or later. That's why you drew us in with the five hundred grand. I always thought it was a small amount. I mean, why should Pearse settle? But he did. Because you told him to. Because sooner or later, when it all got messy and difficult, you realized the only thing better than getting the money you felt you were the proper heir to would be *becoming* the proper heir again. You reinvented yourself, Wes, as the victim."

His confused smile widened and he stopped at the edge of the pond, glanced over at the back porch. "I really don't know where you get your ideas, Mr. Kenzie. They're quite fanciful."

"When we came in that room, the electrical tape was at your feet, Wesley. That means someone had either been about to bind your feet and forgot, which I find unlikely, or you—you, Wesley—heard us come through the door, popped the racquetball in your mouth, *considered* binding your feet, but then figured you might not have time and went for the rope on *one* wrist instead. Only one of your wrists was bound, Wesley. And why? Because a man can't tie both his wrists to opposite arms of a chair."

He studied our reflections in the pond. "Are you done?"

"Pearse said I couldn't see the whole chessboard, and he was right. I'm slow on the uptake sometimes. But I see it all now, Wesley, and it was you pulling strings from the get-go."

He tossed a pebble at my reflection, turned my face into ripples.

"Ah," he said, "you make it sound so Machiavellian. Things are rarely that way."

"What way?"

"Smooth." He tossed another pebble in the pond. "Let me tell you a story. A fairy tale, if you will." He scooped up a handful of small stones and began to throw them, one by one, out into the center of the pond. "A bad king of haunted lineage and barren heart lived in his palace with his trophy queen and imperfect son and imperfect stepdaughter. It was a cold place. But then—oh *then*, Mr. Kenzie—the king and his trophy queen had a third child. And she was a rare creature. A beauty. Stolen, actually, from a peasant family, but otherwise without flaws. The king, the queen, the older princess, even the weak prince—my God, they all loved that child. And for a few brief, spectacular years, that kingdom *glowed*. And love filled every room. Sins were forgotten, weaknesses overlooked, anger buried. It was golden." His voice trailed off and he stared out over the pond and eventually shrugged his narrow shoulders. "Then, on a walk with the prince—who loved her, who *adored* her—the baby princess followed a sprite into a dragon's lair. And she died. And the prince, at first, blamed himself, though it was clear there was truly little he could have done. But that didn't stop the king! Oh, no. He blamed the prince. So did the queen. They tortured the prince with their silences, days of it, followed by sudden malevolent glances. They blamed him. It was plain. And who did the prince have to turn to in *his* grief? Why, his stepsister, of course. But she . . . she . . . rebuffed him. She *blamed* him. Oh, she didn't say so, but in her blissfully ignorant way—neither condemning nor forgiving—she drove a stake far deeper than the king or queen had. The princess, you see, had balls to attend, galas. She wrapped herself in ignorance and fantasy to block out her sister's death, and in doing so, blocked out the prince and left him alone, crippled by his loss, his guilt, by the physical shortcoming that kept him from reaching the dragon's lair quickly enough."

"Gee," I said, "tough story, but I hate costume dramas."

He ignored me. "The prince wandered in exile a long time, at the end of which his secret lover, a shaman in his father's court, introduced him to a band of rebels who wished to topple the king. Their plans were flawed. The prince knew this. But he went along while his fragile psyche began to heal. He made contingency plans. Many, many contingency plans." He threw the last of his stones into the water, looked up at me as he bent for more. "And the prince grew strong, Mr. Kenzie. He grew very strong."

"Strong enough to cut off his own finger?"

Wesley smiled. "It's a fairy tale, Mr. Kenzie. Don't get weighed down with specifics."

"How will the prince feel when someone strong cuts off his head, Wesley?"

"I'm home now," he said. "Back where I belong. I've matured. I'm with my loving father and loving stepmother. I'm happy. Are you happy, Patrick?"

I said nothing.

"I hope so. Hold on to that happiness. It's rare. It can break any time. Were you to run about making wild accusations you couldn't prove, it could affect your happiness. You'd get wiped out in court by a few good attorneys with acute knowledge of slander laws."

"Uh-huh," I said.

He turned to me, gave me his weak smile. "Run home, Patrick. Be a good boy. Protect your vulner-abilities, your loved ones, and gird yourself for trag-edy." He tossed another pebble at my reflection. "It befalls us all."

I glanced back at the porch where Christopher Dawe sat reading the paper and Carrie Dawe sat reading a book.

"They've paid enough," I said. "I won't hurt them to get at you."

"Considerate," he said. "I've heard that about you."

"But, Wesley?"

"Yes, Patrick."

"They won't live forever."

"No."

"Think about that. They're all that shields you from me."

Something caught in his face for just a moment, the tiniest of tics, a glimmer of fear.

And then it vanished.

"Stay away," he whispered. "Stay away, Patrick."

"Sooner or later, you'll be an orphan." I turned away from the pond. "And that's the day the bloodline ends."

I left him there and walked back across the great lawn toward the expansive porch.

It was a gorgeous fall day. The trees erupted. The earth smelled like harvest.

The sun was beginning to fade, though, and the air—slightly chilled as it slid through the trees—carried with it just the barest hint of rain.